$19.95 U.S.D. Trade paperback

Automobilia
A SpeKulative™ Stories Anthology

**Forthcoming in the
SpeKulative™ Stories Anthology Series**

Automobilia

A SpeKulative™ Stories Anthology

Edited by
Jason J. Marchi & Jeffrey L. Buford, Jr.

FAHRENHEIT BOOKS

Guilford, Connecticut

Published by **Fahrenheit Books**
an imprint of OmicronWorld Entertainment LLC
42 Water Street, Suite 222
Guilford, CT 06437
Tel. 203.453.5700
www.OmicronWorld.com
OmicronWorldEnt@yahoo.com

SpeKulative™ Stories Anthology Series is a trademark of OmicronWorld
Entertainment LLC.

Hardcover FIRST PUBLISHED February 2024

Cover illustration and design by Christopher Dobbins, C.E.D. Design &
Productions.

TEXT TYPEFACE: Bookman Old Style, set at 11 points.

ISBN-13: 978-0-9968785-3-1 **(Hardcover)**
ISBN-13: 978-0-9968785-2-4 **(Trade paper)**

This page is an extension of the copyright page.

In memory of
George H. Scithers
the first professional in the tempest sea of publishing
to give me encouragement,

For
Ellen Datlow
who told me, back in 1993,
this book was a *good* idea,

For
Gary Braver aka **Gary Goshgarian**
who lead the way,

And for
Michael Gorfain
who reinforces the philosophy:
search and you will find.

Contents

Introduction

THERE IS SO MUCH that can be written about the automobile and its influence on the planet—from industry to culture to air and water pollution. Such an introduction could fill a book. I will refrain from writing a book-length lead to the stories and poems herein, but I will take the next 2400 words or so to explain the genesis of this fiction anthology and the long history behind it.

Automobilia came to mind decades ago. After many stops and starts, fits and furies, searches and plans gone awry, the book is finally done and in your hands.

My plan from the outset was to have classic stories spaced between new stories and poems. I wanted to include poems because my first professional sales were poems to *Amazing Stories* and *Weird Tales*.

When I made my first sale, a poem titled "Make-Believe Greek Lover" to then editor of *Amazing Stories*, Patrick Lucian Price, I was ecstatic. I was a real writer! This editor, who did not know me, liked my poem enough to accept it and pay me $1 a line. It appeared on page 33 of the Nov. 1988 issue.

My next sale would not come along until a year later (also to *Amazing Stories*), and then two more years would pass before I could sell more of my writing, also a poem, again to Patrick Price.

I could not, for the life of me, sell a short story.

I felt I was on a role with *Amazing Stories*, however, with my poetry. And then the editorial control of the magazine changed, and poetry was dropped. I wrote a complaint letter defending poetry and asking the editor to buy and publish poems once again. The new editor wrote back—which I thought was very professional and honorable—and stated that while he understood my disenchantment, poetry, after all, was just "filler" and it was no longer going to be used in *Amazing Stories*.

I then complained about that editor's response to writer-friend Ben Bova (who was living just an hour's drive away from me at time, in West Hartford, Connecticut). Ben dried my tears and encouraged me to search for other markets for my poems. A few months later I sold my fourth poem to *Weird Tales*. The $10 check was signed by George H. Scithers, the same editor who, when he was the editor of *Asimov's Science Fiction Magazine* eight years earlier, rejected my short stories but wrote wondrous words of encouragement in each rejection letter. His kind compliments on what I was doing right—and warnings about what I was getting wrong—pushed me to continue writing. Thinking back, had Scithers simply rejected me outright, without telling me why, I probably would have given up writing altogether and remained creatively unfilled and unhappy for the rest of my life.

As Oklahoma-based journalist and publisher Mike McCarville wrote, "Early publication is what a writer needs most in life." Fortunately for me, the editors to whom I submitted my early work were the editors of science fiction and horror magazines, and George Scithers—like Patrick Lucien Price, John Betancourt, and Darrell Schweitzer—were all a cut above the ordinary. All were editors of compassion and encouragement. Very rarely do editors communicate so individually—without being paid a special fee—as did Scithers and his contemporaries. His very first rejection letter to me is framed and hangs on my office wall. I share it here, as a testimonial to the great editor and kind person Scithers was.

Dear Jason,
                    Thanks for letting us see this manuscript.
We're very encouraged to see such a well-written
piece. It is a very touching portrait, sort of a
poem of aloneness, and loneliness in a crowd. The
schizophrenic perceptions are perfectly handled,
and give the maximum poetic effect -- you do not
overuse them, or dwell on them to distraction, or
lard them in until everything is murky. This is good
writing. Alas, it is not a story. It is mere a
vignette, and as you can see from our style sheet
(included), we seldom publish them. But please do
                              consider us in the future.
                              We would love to see
                              a story by you.

Asimov's°
SF Magazines   Best,
BOX 13116   PHILADELPHIA, PA 19101   George Scithers

It was those first half-dozen poem sales that told me maybe I was a writer after all, despite constant and gnawing doubt.

In time, I would sell short stories, essays, and articles to dozens of professional markets, work as a non-fiction assistant developmental editor at a higher education publisher (later McGraw-Hill/Dushkin), and spend 17½ years as a senior correspondent for a group of weekly newspapers on the Connecticut shoreline.

Although I turned more and more to non-fiction writing to pay the bills, whenever I doubted that I could write and sell creative writing, I'd go into my archives and pull one of those early copies of *Amazing Stories* and *Weird Tales*, see my poems there, and marvel that I had been paid $1 a line. I'd tell myself, if I did it then, I can do it again.

Well, I've shared this history to explain why I bought and include poems for *Automobilia* and why I will always buy and publish poems in all future theme anthologies I publish under the Fahrenheit Books imprint.

Poetry is *not* filler, and it should never be treated as such.

Poetry is the greatest economy of writing, whereby big ideas are boiled down to their essential elements of emotion, thought, insight, drama, and other such aspects of storytelling. We never forget the best poems we've read, the ones that touch us and that we can memorize and quote aloud to others at the appropriate time.

Now, as for the history of this book itself—the first in what I intend to be a series of anthologies under the SpeKulative™ Stories Anthology series trademark—I present the following for your consideration.

Shortly after I first thought of a book of automobile themed stories and poems, back in the early 1990s, I attended the NECON conference in 1993 at Bryant College in Rhode Island with fellow writer and friend Chris Penders. (See Chris's story "Passages" inside.) There, I met Ellen Datlow.

I had read someplace just before attending this conference, that Ms. Datlow was considered within the industry to be one of the two most powerful (as in influential) short fiction editors in the United States. The other at the time was Alice Turner from *Playboy* magazine.

I don't recall if Ellen spoke at the conference—she might have been on a panel—but I wanted to speak with her directly to run my neophyte book idea by her and to solicit her advice. I was filled with as much trepidation as I was driven to speak with her. I feared she might be too much of a powerhouse within the publishing industry to bother with the likes of a skinny kid with a crazy book idea.

When I approached her at a signing table, she said, "Let's talk later in the day when things are not as busy."

I thought that might be a brush off and expected no further communication.

At lunchtime I was sitting with Chris Penders when Ellen arrived in the cafeteria. The moment she entered the room, she surveyed the space, spotted me, proceeded directly to my table, sat with us, and asked what my book idea was.

I pitched that I wanted to collect stories in which the automobile was featured so prominently that if removed the story would collapse.

To my pleasant surprise, Ellen loved the idea and asked if I would make it a sci-fi or horror anthology or maybe something more broad.

I explained that my thought was to include all genres and not limit to any one genre. I didn't really care if it would make the book hard to classify on bookstore shelves. The book should be inclusive—since the automobile is a science fiction machine, a horror show at times, and often just the plain old family car—and not spin my wheels in a narrow classification.

Ellen then suggested, generously so, that I could package the book and present it to a publisher and get advance money from which I'd pay flat permissions fees to the contributing authors and pay myself the leftover money.

That frightened me at the time. I feared a publisher would take the book and force so many editorial changes it would no longer be my vision as a creator. So, I put the book to rest for years, and years, and even more years, knowing that one day I would return to it when I was older and wiser.

Well, I grew older but not necessarily wiser, and I also grew more desperate to finally get this project out of the idea phase and onto the streets.

The sea change that occurred in publishing during all these idle years made it worth the long wait.

With the explosion of independent publishing, small presses, micro presses, all fueled by the advent of the new delivery technologies and novel ways of thinking about implementing publishing programs, I knew I could finally make a go of *Automobilia* on my own. Through my own micro press, Fahrenheit Books, I could publish this book along with many of the other writers whose books I have published.

Now, there is one last thing to mention about the development of *Automobilia*.

When thinking back to my initial inspiration that birthed this anthology, I have to go all the way back to the early 1960s.

During the 1970s, I watched the Twilight Zone television show—which first aired on CBS from 1959 to 1964—in reruns. One episode in particular titled "You Drive" frightened the heck out of me. It was written by Earl Hamner, Jr. (creator of the Waltons television series) and Twilight Zone creator himself Rod Serling.

IMDb gives "You drive" a 7.8 out of a 10 score. The story, for readers unfamiliar with it, is about a man who hits a paper boy with his car, killing the boy, and fleeing the scene. For readers not familiar with the episode I will not give anything away. Go on Netflix or Amazon and find the Twilight Zone episode "You Drive" and watch it and enjoy it for how landmark a story it was back in 1964. Perhaps Stephen King's *Christine* could not have come about if it had not been for this episode.

There was a second episode in the Twilight Zone series called "The Hitchhiker" which also featured an automobile such that without the car, there would be no story. Based on a radio play by Lucille Fletcher, the teleplay was written by Rod Serling. The Internet Movie Data Base description reads: "A young woman driving across country becomes frantic when she keeps passing the same man on the side of the road. No matter how fast she drives, the man is always up ahead, hitching her for a ride."

While not as frightening as "You Drive," the story is nonetheless unsettling and truly unforgettable.

A close friend of mine who is not a writer but loves the Twilight Zone, also loved the "You Drive" episode as much I do. When we watched the episode together we thought it was a shame that the actor who played the paperboy killed by the car, Timmy Danvers, was not given screen credit.

I thought about this for a long while—I think mainly because of the impact the story had on me at age 10—and as an adult, my curiosity forced me to start searching and solve this mystery and find out the name of the uncredited actor.

I called production companies, archivists, and casting people in Hollywood, trying to find someone who might know someone from the production team who was still living, and who could, in turn, point me in the right direction.

Every avenue I followed was a dead end.

After two years of inquiry, I was ready to give up. The actor who played the kid killed by the Oliver Pope character, played by Edward Andrews, would forever remain nameless to my friend and me.

A few months later, I happened upon a Twilight Zone chat room online, and something possessed me to waste half an hour and scroll through the chat comments. About 15 minutes into my exploration, I read a comment from someone who said about the "You Drive" episode, and I paraphrase: "The kid killed on the bicycle was supposed to be 15 years old, but the actor looked like a moose of a kid!"

Well, that was pretty insulting, I thought.

Below this comment, someone wrote, "I was that moose of a kid!"

A name and e-mail was attached to the reply. I stared at the screen, at first thinking it was some wiseacre making the rebuttal comment. Then I thought, wait. Maybe this guy is for real. I either responded in the chat or emailed the rebuttal commenter, and he responded with a "yes." He was indeed the actor who played the 15 year old Timmy Danvers character in "You Drive" and he could prove it.

And prove it he did, with a copy of a studio pay stub!

I could not believe I'd finally found who the actor was, and he was in his early 60s when I found him. I called my friend right away to tell him the amazing news. My friend is still astounded, as I am, that I discovered the identity of an uncredited actor from a 1964 television show. Praise the power of the Internet to bring people together!

Soon after, the actor, Michael Gorfain, and I communicated via email, talked on the phone, shared memorabilia through the U.S. Mail, and became friends.

When I first told Michael of my background—how I was a writer of two published children's books and had become a very close friend of Ray Bradbury during the last 13 years of Ray's life—Michael seemed more fascinated in me as a writer than I was of him as an actor of bit parts in famous movies like "West Side Story" (1961) and "Planet of the Apes" (1968).

I am endlessly inspired by turns of events in life, from the slow and imponderable accumulation of experience, and the people we meet, that help build the landscape of our individual lives upon which we stand. Wonderful and amazing things happen for those who reach out, who explore, who learn and through passion, pursue creative dreams and turn them into concrete products like movies, songs, paintings, sculptures, buildings, spaceships, computers, and of course books like this one.

And so, I give thanks to all who have come into my life directly and indirectly, who have helped steer me toward a path of helping others, publishing others, and leaving (hopefully) something good behind in this world for people to enjoy for generations to come.

Jason J. Marchi, ed.
September 3, 2023
Guilford, Conn.

Birth of the Automobile and
a Little More About this Book

ON NEW YEAR'S EVE of 1879 the first gasoline powered engine was started. After years of development by Carl Benz, the internal combustion engine was born, and the world was changed forever.

This one-cylinder two-stroke engine became such a commercial success for Benz he earned the means to realize his dream of producing a lightweight vehicle powered by his gasoline engine. That two-seater automobile, powered by a more highly developed single-cylinder four-stroke engine, debuted in 1885.

According to the Daimler company's written history, "On January 29, 1886, Benz applied for a patent for his 'vehicle powered by a gas engine.' The patent—number 37435—may be regarded as the birth certificate of the automobile. In July 1886 the newspapers reported on the first public outing of the three-wheeled Benz Patent Motor Car, model no. 1."

After that, during the remaining years of the 19th century and the first two decades of the 20th century, development of the automobile exploded quickly.

Although electric vehicles became popular at the same time, especially in urban areas where air pollution was a problem, the gasoline powered engine (and later Diesel) propelled trucks and other machines at such a pace the horse and buggy were soon replaced. The easily operated, reliable automobile allowed for a migration of people from high-density population areas to the countryside.

The suburbs would develop and flourish, and the nuclear family (mom, dad, and their kids) would break away from extended family households in America as families could easily relocate in the family car—on newly paved roadways and later highways—to regions where new economic growth was burgeoning.

While it was the gasoline powered internal combustion engine that allowed for the explosion of easy transportation over greater distances, the auto-mobile itself would become both iconic and beloved, and perhaps even cursed by some.

Ultimately, the influence of the automobile is everywhere, including appearances in literature, television, and movies. That fact prompted the idea for an anthology that would feature stories that include automobiles. The main requirement, as stated in the call for submissions and in the book's foreword, was that the story or poem must feature some aspect of a motor vehicle such that if removed, the story would not work.

What follows is a gathering of classic stories by known writers along with new stories by writers who themselves are either new or not yet known well enough to be considered established names.

Of particular note: after several attempts to place the stories in this book in some sort of order—e.g. by decade, by location, by genre—the decision was made to let the stories fall as they may, like the ingredients in soup or stew. The full flavor comes from the blending, not the separation of the ingredients.

After reading the book, we'd love to hear from you if you have comments (good or bad) you wish to share with us. With a bit of luck, we hope to produce a second volume (and perhaps a third) of automobile-based stories, since we could not fit as many goods ones into this first book as we had hoped without making the final product over 1500 pages long.

Happy reading!

Jason J. Marchi, ed.
Jeffrey L. Buford, Jr., ed.

Moon and Packard

I was small
And sat in the corner
Of the back seat, looking up
And out at the early dark of November.
Phone lines swooped
From pole to pole to pole
And matched the clicks and cracks
In the concrete highway.
We were traveling
Together and no one knew,
Except for me, that the moon
Was coming with us.

—Joel Ferree

Literary Automobilia

Writer builds it
from the ground up.
Upholsters the interior
with the finest fabrics.
Polishes it to perfection
and prays for the best.

Publisher trucks it
to a showroom to be
displayed with other
models of its kind.
End of each quarter
he sums his receipts
and hurries to the bank.

Critic takes a test drive.
Sees how it performs.
Offers his razor-sharp
wittier-than-thou opinion
on its forces and failures.
Whether it shines or sins.

Reader goes for a spin.
Tries it on the freeway
and down a country lane.
It may carry him places
he has never been before.
Or places he already
knows and loves.

Academic dismantles it.
Determines how it functions.
Delivers a paper
on internal combustion.

—Bruce Boston

In a Fast Car to Utopia

the highway before you
spreads an undulating tapestry;
a foreboding scape of signs
en route to a circumstance
that exponentially increases
the likelihood of collision

(you don't want to see)
the roadside foliage mists rise,
masking passage with their vapors

(you can't help)
speeding on in the early dawn
point to point on an infinite plane
toward or behind the tenuous space
you occupy in time to reach another
that realigns conversely with
the vacuum of your absence

(you are reminded)
as theorist of the abstract,
that this is your purpose,
to put your concept to the test
that none would chance, save you

just ahead there is a point in calculations
where human will is null, which is utopia,
    which is the ultimate escape
to perfect harmony, unattainable otherwise

with this conviction, you jam pedal to metal,
discover that utopia is an empty highway,
another quantum transmutation to nirvana.

—Marge Simon

69 Firebird Convertible

Each candy-apple-red-lickable inch
of her body

welcomes me to her white lap
where I can stroke

her black power wheel
turn her over

oh her engine is so big
she can handle me

I know her
she is polished, dependable:

she drag-races me to school
peels out with beers to prom

gets me stuck-in-the-mud, rear-
                              ends the art teacher's van

       lets me take my top down

—Sarah Key

off the port side

chasing waking dreams are we,
    fast friends getting nowhere fast,
    counting the blades of grass at the road's edge,
and off the port side is an output of billowing oil and gas;
    fumes from a constricted tailpipe cross-country fantasy
    orchestrated ad lib under the guise
    of a broken, god-powered overhead interior light
    that occasionally serves to illuminate our maps
    as we drive-by-night.
we decipher our dreams behind the wheel,
    one by one,
    in turn,
    cushioned from life by anemic wallets
    and balding maroon terrycloth seat covers
    as we buzz down roadways with the brazen dizziness
    of a mammoth housefly sprung to dusty life
    by the sun's rays through the windowpane.
inside our chassis chrysalis
    we entertain our mandibles
    by busily chomping off contradiction after contradiction,
    cocooning ourselves and layer upon layer of
    oral exhaust vapor
    that shields us from each other and the world.
greenhoused into your own atmosphere,
    you can feel the heat of the stretches of truths
    (all made with the same intent and import as ever)
    that forces cold beads of sweat to condense
    and roll down the V of your brow
    and off the end of your bridged nose
    as you apex over the Old Miss with a furious-faced
    big rig

grinding down your back bumper
and bulging its eyes through your rearview.
grass is growing here but we're passing it by
for better lawns ahead,
as mere fantasies are left for dead.

—Gregory J. Leavitt

Contents of a Dead Man's Car

Among assorted items
caught within the crumpled body
I find a set of jumper cables
a string of children's necklace beads
a book of plain white matches –
half of which are cleanly plucked –
and one spool of navy-blue thread.

I see your face for an instant
in the cold blue glass pane
and then it fades easily
as snow angels go quietly in spring.

If only that thread could
repair you back to the living,
could mend the tear in all the hearts
of those of us held together
by the brittle glue of memory.

—Jason J. Marchi

Chester and the Model T

Chester waits for the children to come
Braiding flowers in his mane and tail for tomorrow
He always prances when he pulls the wagon to church
Even though he's bone tired from hauling the plow
But today there are no children and the farm's eerily quiet
Only cicadas, with their rising-falling squeal
And the bark of lonely dogs disturb the silence

Then a new sound, coming down his lane
He whinnies, challenging the thing
It ignores him as it comes to a rattling stop
Farmer Tom grins, the family packed around him
The thing looks like the shiny carriage
That snooty stallion Fabrizio pulls to church
But the carriage has never made such a horrific noise
Chester whinnies and stamps, but in the morning
He watches the thing take his family to church

Months go by, and the noisy thing never loses favor
Chester hopes it will replace him in the field
A fair trade for taking over his favorite duty
But no—it sits idle as he and Farmer Tom work
And before church the children wash it instead of him
Then something changes, moods plummet
Chester again hauls the family to church
Excursions in the cursed noisemaker stop
Drifters find the farm, stealing whatever's ripe
The dogs frantic to keep the intruders away
The wagon axle breaks and Farmer Tom curses

He looks broken and he mutters something
About a Depression and some fool named Hoover
Chester nuzzles him and nickers low
The broken wagon gives him a break he doesn't want

The next day, Farmer Tom attacks the noisy thing
Pulling its insides out, dust rolling in to dull the shine
He attaches the wagon tongue to it
 And puts the harness on Chester
"Let's see if you can pull this Hoover Wagon"
There is bitterness in Farmer Tom's voice
So Chester pulls it as prettily as he can
Farmer Tom eyes the fields of alfalfa
"They may ration gas, Chester, but they won't take my hay"
Chester mocks the noisy thing as he pulls it into fields
He thinks it will get stuck but it's surprisingly nimble.
Easier to pull, in some ways, then the wagon
Farmer Tom kicks it all the time
The children tell stories about when it was pretty
But go back to braiding flowers in Chester's hair
The dogs growl—at anything now, but mostly the drifters
The mood is tense: no one here's happy
No one except Chester

—**Gerri Leen**

Hot for Elvis

He was a gift from Dad:
"Pick any new Ford
—except—bright red,
or bright yellow,
or the Mach series,
or convertibles,
or anything pricier than the cheapest Mustang."

I named him Angus-Elvis:
he was a hot, beefy, demon-ridden, white
'71 Mustang,
with black, thick stripes on each side
(sideburns),
and blue interior
(that fit like tight pants on gyrating hips).
My wild man was unstoppable.

On soft, summer days,
I wore red-hot Ann Margaret outfits
and felt emotionally charged
with that *new car smell.*
Leaving the windows cranked down,
my long hair, the color of stone ground cornmeal,
blew like autumn leaves in the wind. My blouse,
mostly unbuttoned, was open wide,
and I was a musical bird on the eve of desire
while listening to the razor-sharp song,
"American Woman."

FM music blasted Guess Who
from my musically inclined Elvis radio.

I cruised sizzling roads
with my southern hunk of a car.
Sometimes, at revved up speeds,
metal tastes sweet with red,
bruised apple blushed lips.
After all, Elvis was young,
alive,
and a fine specimen that purred
like a fine-tuned guitar.

Ok, I'm not perfect. The year was 1975
and I had to live with my deadly sin:
hot car neglect.
I lost my "hunk of burning love"
by overlooking things like oil, water,
and general maintenance.
Elvis . . . gone in a puff of smoke!
It's too bad that Angus-Elvis could not live
by *love* alone.

—Mary Hamrick

She's Not a Car

She's not a car, she knows she's not
and therein lies the irony,
air bags do not deploy if she
suffers a dire catastrophe
nor does she have high-beam headlights
spurning darkness when she can't see
and unlike most automobiles
she feels emotions urgently,
yet like a car it's not the years
but mileage hurting her right knee
and too much stress on her engine
keeps her oil pressure uppity
while constant sun has made her paint
freckle and age increasingly
and now whenever she passes
a junkyard she feels her heartbeat
for she likens her present life
to cars stranded on some back street,
not broken, leaky, flat, or dead
but long past getting flattery.

She's not a car, she knows she's not
she's flesh and blood under her hood
with soul and spirit running hot.

—**Michael H. Hanson**

Road Trip

Matthew Spence

Jeff saw the lights flashing in his rearview mirror. This is it, he thought. One last chance...

He knew it was risky. The last time Jeff had tried anything like this, he wound up with a fractured arm that took weeks to heal and which still occasionally hurt. But it might be years before he had another opportunity, and he might be too old by then.

The car began making its turn into the emergency lane, the steering wheel sluggish and reluctant in his hands. Jeff knew that the car didn't want to stop, but even it was still compelled to follow the rules of the road, and that meant pulling over when the cops wanted you to. Rules were important—it allowed the car to attract less attention, and prevented him from escaping—except perhaps now.

Jeff could still remember the night he'd first seen the car in the dealer's lot, gleaming bright and new under the lights—an Impala that had just rolled off the assembly line.

He'd noticed the dealer's nervousness over the car, but of course he hadn't thought much about it at the time. He'd had plenty of time to think about it since.

Jeff wondered if that man was still alive. Probably not— he'd been at least twenty years older than Jeff at the time. Jeff saw his own thinning, graying hair in the mirror and remembered when he'd been younger too, and free with the promise of a new decade ahead as the year 1959 was ending.

Jeff should have known something was wrong when the car made its first wrong turn. Then the car made another, and another, taking him farther away from the dealership down streets and then highways that became increasingly unfamiliar, through towns and cities that he didn't know as landscapes flew past and the roads merged into a single line of pavement and white lines.

Of course, he'd tried to escape. Even as the car drove on, never stopping for gas or allowing him to eat or go to the bathroom, which Jeff discovered he somehow didn't need anyway, he'd pound at the windows, kick the doors and roof, trying desperately to get someone's attention. But nobody seemed to notice or hear him, and it wasn't until that one other time that he found out why when he saw the car's blacked-out windows from the outside and realized that it would keep him prisoner for eternity if it wanted to, unless...

The car rolled down its window as the highway patrol officer walked over. A state trooper, judging from the uniform. "License and registration, sir?" he asked, with professional politeness.

Jeff nodded and took both out from the glove compartment. "Was I speeding?" he asked. His own voice sounded odd and unfamiliar in his ears; it had been that long since he'd actually spoken-except to the car.

"You were going a little fast," the officer replied. He didn't seem to look too closely at the license, but it must have been up to date—another one of the car's tricks? "Just be more careful next time," he said as he prepared to hand it back to him.

That was when Jeff took his chance. Without really thinking, he grabbed at the officer's wrist, which caused him to grab the car door in response. The door hissed like a defiant animal as Jeff dove out, hitting the pavement as he allowed the cop to put handcuffs on him. The sensation of immediate freedom was disorienting, but Jeff was able to yell out "Shoot..." as the car began making a savage U-turn.

"The hell?" The officer was startled, but instinctively drew his gun.

"Aim for...the headlights...blind it..." Jeff didn't know why he'd said that, but it seemed to work as the officer fired, the shots sounding like loud firecrackers. Its lights out, the car narrowly avoided hitting both of them before plunging off the road, almost roaring in pain as it lit up the night air in a fireball.

"What the hell just happened?" The cop helped Jeff to his feet, even though he was still technically under arrest for assaulting an officer. "Did that thing actually just try to kill us?"

"It did." Jeff watched the already dying flames, still unsteady on his own two legs. "But it's over...I'm free..." then he collapsed from exhaustion as the officer helped him over to his patrol vehicle. It would be one more ride, but Jeff knew that it would also be his last.

Second Chance

Jack Finney

I can't tell you, I know, how I got to a time and place no one else in the world even remembers. But maybe I can tell you how I felt the morning I stood in an old barn off the county road, staring down at what was to take me there.

I paid out seventy-five dollars I'd worked hard for after classes last semester—I'm a senior at Poynt College in Hylesburg, Illinois, my hometown—and the middle-aged farmer took it silently, watching me shrewdly, knowing I must be out of my mind. Then I stood looking down at the smashed, rusty, rat-gnawed, dust-covered, old wreck of an automobile lying on the wood floor where it had been hauled and dumped thirty-three years before—and that now belonged to me. And if you can remember the moment, whenever it was, when you finally got something you wanted so badly you dreamed about it—then maybe I've told you how I felt staring at the dusty mass of junk that was a genuine Jordan Playboy.

You've never heard of a Jordan Playboy, if you're younger than forty, unless you're like I am; one of those people who'd rather own a 1926 Mercer convertible sedan, or a 1931 Packard touring car, or a '24 Wills Sainte Claire, or a '31 air-cooled Franklin convertible—or a Jordan

Playboy—then the newest, two-toned, '56 model made; I was actually half sick with excitement.

And the excitement lasted; it took me four months to restore that car, and that's fast. I went to classes till school ended for the summer, then I worked, clerking at J.C. Penney's; and I had dates, saw an occasional movie, ate and slept. But all I really did—all that counted—was work on that car; from six to eight every morning, for half an hour at lunchtime, and from the moment I got home, most nights, till I stumbled to bed, worn out.

My folks live in the big old house my dad was born in; there's a barn off at the back of the lot, and I've got a chain hoist in there, a workbench, and a full set of mechanic's tools. I built hot rods there for three years, one after another; those charcoal-black mongrels with the rear ends up in the air. But I'm through with hot rods; I'll leave those to the high-school set. I'm twenty years old now, and I've been living for the day when I could soak loose the body bolts with liniment, hoist the body aside, and start restoring my own classic. That's what they're called; those certain models of certain cars of certain years which have something that's lasted, something today's cars don't have for us, and something worth bringing back.

But you don't restore a classic by throwing in a new motor, hammering out the dents, replacing missing parts with anything handy, and painting it chartreuse. "Restore" means what it says, or ought to. My Jordan had been struck by a train, the man who sold it to me said-just grazed, but that was enough to flip it over, tumbling it across a field, and the thing was a wreck; the people in it were killed. So the right rear wheel and the spare were hopeless wads of wire spokes and twisted rims, and the body was caved in, with the metal actually splits in places. The motor was a mess, though the block was sound. The upholstery was rat-gnawed, and almost gone. All the nickel plating was rusted and flaking off. And the exterior parts were gone; nothing but screw holes to show they'd been there. But three of the wheels were intact, or almost, and none of the body was missing.

What you do is write letters, advertise in the magazines people like me read, ask around, prowl garages, junk heaps and barns, and you trade, and you bargain, and one way or another get together the parts you need. I traded a Winton name plate and hub caps, plus a Saxon hood, to a man in Wichita, Kansas, for two Playboy wheels, and they arrived crated in a wooden box-rusty, and some of the spokes bent and loose, but I could fix that. I bought my Jordan running board mats and spare-wheel mount from a man in New Jersey. I bought two valve pushrods, and had the rest precision-made precisely like the others. And—well, I restored that car, that's all.

The body shell, every dent and bump gone, every tear welded and burnished down, I painted a deep green, precisely matching what was left of the old paint before I sanded it off. Door handles, windshield rim, and every other nickel-plated part, were restored, re-nickeled, and replaced. I wrote eleven letters to leather supply houses all over the country, enclosing sample swatches of the cracked old upholstery before I found a place that could match it. Then I paid a hundred and twelve dollars to have my Playboy reupholstered, supplying old photographs to show just how it should be done. And at eight ten one Saturday evening in July, I finally finished; my last missing part, a Jordan radiator cap, for which I'd traded a Duesenberg floor mat, had come from the nickel plater's that afternoon. Just for the fun of it, I put the old plates back on then; Illinois license 11,206, for 1923. And even the original ignition key, in its old leather case-oiled and worked supple again—was back where I'd found it, and now I switched it on, advanced the throttle and spark, got out with the crank, and started it up. And thirty-three years after it had bounced, rolled and crashed off a grade crossing, that Jordan Playboy was alive again.

I had a date, and knew I ought to get dressed; I was wearing stained dungarees and my dad's navy blue, high-necked old sweater. I didn't have any money with me; you lose it out of your pockets, working on a car. I was even out of cigarettes. But I couldn't wait, I had to drive that car, and I just washed up at the old sink in the barn, then started down the cinder driveway in that beautiful car, feeling wonderful. It wouldn't matter how I was dressed anyway, driving around in the Playboy tonight.

My mother waved at me tolerantly from a living room window, and called out to be careful, and I nodded; then I was out in the street, cruising along, and I wish you could have seen me—seen *it,* I mean. I don't care whether you've ever given a thought to the wonderful old cars or not, you'd have seen why it was worth all I'd done. Draw yourself a mental picture of a simple, straight-lined, two-seater, open automobile with four big wire wheels fully exposed, and its spare on the back in plain sight; don't put in a line that doesn't belong there, and have a purpose. Make the two doors absolutely square; what other shape should a door be? Make the hood perfectly rounded, louvered at the sides because the motor needs that ventilation. But don't add a single unnecessary curve, jiggle, squiggle, or porthole to that car—and picture the radiator, nothing concealing it and pretending it doesn't exist. And now sec that Playboy as I did cruising along, the late sun slanting down through the big old trees along the street, glancing off the bright nickel so that it hurt your eyes, the green of the body glowing like a jewel.

It was beautiful, I tell you it was beautiful, and you'd think everyone would see that.

But they didn't. On Main Street, I stopped at a light, and a guy slid up beside me in a great big, shining, new '57 car half as long as a football field. He sat there, the top of the door up to his shoulders, his eyes almost level with the bottom of his windshield, looking as much in proportion to his car as a two-year-old in his father's overcoat; he sat there in a car with a pattern of chrome copied directly from an Oriental rug, and with a trunk sticking out past his back wheels you could have landed a helicopter on; he sat there for a moment, then turned, looked out, and smiled at *my* car!

And when I turned to look at him, eyes cold, he had the nerve to smile at *me,* as though I were supposed to nod and grin and agree that any car not made before day before yesterday was an automatic side-splitting riot. I just looked away, and when the light changed, he thought he'd show me just how sick his big four-thousand-dollar job could make my pitiful old antique look. The light clicked, and his foot was on the gas, his automatic transmission taking hold, and he'd already started to grin. But I started when he did, feeding the gas in firm and gentle, and we held even till I shot into second faster than any automatic transmission yet invented can do it, and I drew right past him, and when I looked back it was me who was grinning. But still, at the next light, every pedestrian crossing in front of my car treated me to a tolerant understanding smile, and when the light changed, I swung off Main.

That was one thing that happened; the second was that my date wouldn't go out with me. I guess I shouldn't blame her, First she saw how I was dressed, which didn't help me with her. Then I showed her the Jordan at the curb, and she nodded, not even slightly interested, and said it was very nice; which didn't help her with me. And then-well, she's a good-looking girl, Naomi Weygand, and while she didn't exactly put it in these words, she let me know she meant to be seen tonight, preferably on a dance floor, and not waste her youth and beauty riding around in some ol' antique. And when I told her I was going out in the Jordan tonight, and if she wanted to come along, fine, and if she didn't—well, she didn't. And eight seconds later she was opening her front door again, while I scorched rubber pulling away from the curb.

I felt the way you would have by then, and I wanted to get out of town and alone somewhere, and I shoved it into second, gunning the car, heading for the old Cressville road. It used to be the only road to Cressville, a two-lane paved highway just barely wide enough for cars to pass. But there's been a new highway for fifteen years; four lanes, and straight as a ruler except for two long curves you can do ninety on, and you can make the seven miles to Cressville in five minutes or less.

But it's a dozen winding miles on the old road, and half a mile of it, near Cressville, was flooded out once, and the concrete is broken and full of gaps; you have to drive it in low. So nobody uses the old road nowadays, except for four or five farm families who live along it.

When I swung onto the old road—there are a lot of big old trees all along it—I began to feel better. And I just ambled along, no faster than thirty, maybe, clear up to the broken stretch before I turned back toward Hylesburg, and it was wonderful. I'm not a sports-car man myself, but they've got something when they talk about getting close to the road and into the outdoors again-the way driving used to be before people shut themselves behind great sheets of glass and metal, and began rushing along super-highways, their eyes on the white line. I had the windshield folded down flat against the hood, and the summer air streamed over my face and through my hair, and I could see the road just beside and under me Bowing past so close I could have touched it. The air was alive with the heavy fragrances of summer darkness, and the rich nostalgic sounds of summer insects, and I wasn't even thinking, but just living and enjoying it.

One of the old Playboy advertisements, famous in their day, calls the Jordan "this brawny, graceful thing," and says, "It revels along with the wandering wind and roars like a Caproni biplane. It's a car for a man's man-that's certain. Or for a girl who loves the out of doors." Rich prose for these days, I guess; we're afraid of rich prose now, and laugh in defense. But I'll take it over a stern sales talk on safety belts.

Anyway, I liked just drifting along the old road, a part of the summer outdoors and evening, and the living country around me; and I was no more thinking than a collie dog with his nose thrust out of a car, his eyes half closed against the air stream, enjoying the feeling human beings so often forget, of simply being a living creature. "'I left my love in Avalon,' " I was bawling out at the top of my lungs, hardly knowing when I'd started, "'and saaailed awaaay!'" Then I was singing "Alice Blue Gown," very softly and gently. I sang, "Just a Japanese Saaandman!," and "Whispering," and "Barney Google," the fields and trees and cattle, and sometimes an occasional car, flowing past in the darkness, and I was having a wonderful time.

The name "Dempsey" drifted into my head, I don't know why—just a vagrant thought floating lazily up into my consciousness. Now, I saw Jack Dempsey once; six years ago when I was fourteen, my dad, my mother, and I took a vacation trip to New York. We saw the Empire State Building, Rockefeller Center, took a ride on the subway, and all the rest of it. And we had dinner at Jack Dempsey's restaurant on Broadway, and he was there, and spoke to us, and my dad talked to him for a minute about his fights. So I saw him; a nice-looking middle-aged man, very big and broad. But the picture that drifted up into my mind now, driving along the old Cressville road, wasn't that Jack Dempsey. It was the face of a young man not a lot older than I was, black-haired, black-bearded, fierce and scowling. Dempsey, I thought, that snarl- ing young face rising up clear and vivid in my mind, and the thought completed itself: He beat Tom Gibbons last night.

Last night; Dempsey beat Gibbons *last night*—and it was true. I mean it *felt* true somehow, as though the thought were in the very air around me, like the old songs I'd found myself singing, and suddenly several things I'd been half aware of clicked together in my mind. I'd been dreamily and unthinkingly realizing that there were more cars on the road than I'd have expected, flowing past me in the darkness. Maybe some of the farm families along here were having some sort of Saturday-night get-together, I thought. But then I knew it wasn't true.

Picture a car's headlights coming toward you; they're two sharp beams slicing ahead into the darkness, an intense blue-white in color, their edges as defined as a ruler's. But these headlights—two more sets of them were approaching me now—were different. They were entirely orange in color, the red-orange of the hot filaments that produced them; and they were hardly even beams, but just twin circles of wide, diffused orange light, and they wavered in intensity, illuminating the road only dimly.

The nearer lights were almost upon me, and I half rose from my seat, leaning forward over the hood of the Jordan, staring at the car as it passed me. It was a Moon; a cream-colored nineteen-twenty-two Moon roadster. The next car, those two orange circles of wavering light swelling, approached, then passed, as I stared and turned to look after it. It looked something like mine; wire wheels, but with the spare on a side mount, and with step plates instead of running boards. I knew what it was; a Haynes Speedster, and the man at the wheel wore a cloth cap, and the girl beside him wore a large pink hat, coming well down over her head and with a wide brim all around it. I sat moving along, a hand on the wheel, in a kind of stunned ecstatic trance. For now, the Saturday-night traffic at its peak, there they all came one after another, all the glorious old cars; a Saxon Six black-bodied touring car with wood-spoke wheels, and the women in that car wore chin-length veils from the edges of their flowered hats; there passed a gray-bodied black-topped Wills Sainte Claire with orange disc wheels, and the six kids in it were singing "Who's Sorry Now?" then I saw another Moon, a light blue open four-seater, its cut-out open, and the kid at the wheel had black hair slicked back in a varnished pompadour, and just glancing at him, you could see he was on his way to a date; now there came an Elcar, two Model T Fords just behind it; then a hundred yards back, a red Buick roadster with natural-wood spoke wheels; I saw a Velie, and a roadster that was either a Noma or a Kissel, I couldn't be sure; and there was a high-topped blue Dodge sedan with cut Bowers in little glass vases by the rear doors; there was a car I didn't know at all; then a brand-new Stanley Steamer, and just behind it, a wonderful low-slung 1921 Pierce-Arrow, and I knew what had happened, and where I was.

I've read some of the stuff about Time with a capital T, and I don't say I understand it too well. But I know Einstein or somebody compares Time to a winding river, and says we exist as though in a boat, drifting along between high banks.

All we can sec is the present, immediately around us. We can't see the future just beyond the next curve, or the past in the many bends in back of us. But it's all there just the same. There—countless bends back, in infinite distance—lies the past, as real as the moment around us.

Well, I'll join Einstein and the others with a notion of my own; just a feeling, actually, hardly even a thought. I wonder if we aren't barred from the past by a thousand invisible chains. You can't drive into the past in a 1957 Buick because there are no 1957 Buicks in 1923; so how could you be there in one? You can't drive into 1923 in a Jordan Playboy, along a four-lane superhighway; there are no superhighways in 1923. You couldn't even, I'm certain, drive with a pack of modern filter-tip cigarettes in your pocket—into a night when no such thing existed. Or with so much as a coin bearing a modern date, or wearing a charcoal-gray and pink shirt on your back. All those things, small and large, are chains keeping you out of a time when they could not exist.

But my car and I—the way I felt about it, anyway—were almost *rejected* that night, by the time I lived in. And so there in my Jordan, just as it was the year it was new, with nothing about me from another time, the old '23 tags on my car, and moving along a highway whose very oil spots belonged to that year—well, I think that for a few moments, all the chains hanging slack, we were free on the surface of Time. And that moving along that old highway through the summer evening, we simply *drifted—into* the time my Jordan belonged in.

That's the best I can do, anyway: it's all that occurs to me. And—well, I wish I could offer you proof. I wish I could tell you that when I drove into Hylesburg again, onto Main Street, that I saw a newspaper headline saying, PRESIDENT HARDING STRICKEN, or something like that. Or that I heard people discussing Babe Ruth's new home-run record, or saw a bunch of cops raiding a speak easy.

But I saw or heard nothing of the sort, nothing much different from the way it always has been. The street was quiet and nearly empty, as it is once the stores shut down for the weekend. I saw only two people at first; just a couple walking along far down the street. As for the buildings, they've been there, most of them, since the Civil War, or before—Hylesburg's an old town—and in the semidarkness left by the streetlamps, they looked the same as always, and the street was paved with brick as it has been since World War I.

No, all I saw driving along Main Street were—just little things. I saw a shoe store, its awning still over the walk, and that awning was striped; broad red and white stripes, and the edges were scalloped. You just don't see awnings like that, outside of old photographs, but there it was, and I pulled over to the curb, staring across the walk at the window. But all I can tell you is that there were no open-toed shoes among the women's, and the heels looked a little high to me, and a little different in design, somehow. The men's shoes—well, the toes seemed a little more pointed than you usually see now, and there were no suede shoes at all. But the kids' shoes looked the same as always.

I drove on, and passed a little candy and stationery shop, and on the door was a sign that said, *Drink Coca-Cola,* and in some way I can't describe the letters looked different. Not much, but—you've seen old familiar trademarks that have gradually changed, kept up to date through the years, in a gradual evolution. All I can say is that this old familiar sign looked a little different, a little old-fashioned, but I can't really say how.

There were a couple of all-night restaurants open, as I drove along, one of them The New China, the other Gill's, but they've both been in Hylesburg for years. There were a couple of people in each of them, but I never even thought of going in. It seemed to me I was here on sufferance, or by accident; that I'd just drifted into this time, and had no right to actually intrude on it. Both restaurant signs were lighted, the letters formed by electric-light bulbs, unfrosted so that you could see the filaments glowing, and the bulbs ended in sharp glass spikes. There wasn't a neon sign, lighted *or* unlighted, the entire length of the street.

On West Main I came to the Orpheum, and though the box office and marquee were dark, there were a few lights still on, and a dozen or so cars parked for half a block on each side of it. I parked mine directly across the street beside a wood tele- phone pole. Brick pavement is bumpy, and when I shut off the motor, and reached for the hand brake—I don't know whether this is important or not, but I'd better tell it—the Jordan rolled ahead half a foot as its right front wheel settled into a shallow depression in the pavement. For just a second or so, it rocked a little in a tiny series of rapidly decreasing arcs, then stopped, its wheel settled snugly into the depression as though it had found exactly the spot it had been looking for-like a dog turning around several times before it lies down in precisely the right place.

Crossing over to the Orph, I saw the big posters in the shallow glass showcases on each side of the entrance. *Fri., Sat., and Sun.,* one said, and it showed a man with a long thin face, wearing a monocle, and his eyes were narrowed, staring at a woman with long hair who looked sort of frightened. GEORGE ARLISS, said the poster, in "The Green Goddess."

Coming Attraction, said the other poster, *Mon., Tues. and Wed.* "Ashes of Vengeance," starring NORMA TALMADGE and CONWAY TEARLE, with WALLACE BEERY. I've never heard of any of them, except Wallace Beery. In the little open lobby, I looked at the still pictures in wall cases at each side of the box office; small, glossy, black and white scenes from the two movies, and finally recognized Wallace Beery, a thin, handsome, young man. I've never seen that kind of display before, and didn't know it was done.

But that's about all I can tell you; nothing big or dramatic, and nothing significant, like hearing someone say, "Mark my words, that boy Lindbergh will fly the Atlantic yet All I saw was a little, shut-down, eleven-0'clock Main Street.

The parked cars, though, were a Dort; a high, straight-lined Buick sedan with wood wheels; three Model T's; a blue Hupmobile touring car with blue and yellow disc wheels; a Winton; a four-cylinder Chevrolet roadster; a Stutz; a spoke-wheeled Cadillac sedan. Not a single car had been made later than the year 1923. And this is the strange thing; they looked *right* to me. They looked as though that were the way automobiles were supposed to look, nothing odd, funny, or old-fashioned about them. From somewhere in my mind, I know I could have brought up a mental picture of a glossy, two-toned, chromium-striped car with power steering. But it would have taken a real effort, and—I can't really explain this, I know—it was as though modern cars didn't really exist; not yet. *These* were today's cars, parked all around me, and I knew it.

I walked on, just strolling down Main Street, glancing at an occasional store window, enjoying the incredible wonder of being where I was. Then, half a block or so behind me, I heard a sudden little babble of voices, and I looked back and the movie was letting out. A little crowd of people was flowing slowly out onto the walk to stand, some of them, talking for a moment; while others crossed the street, or walked on. Motors began starting, the parked cars pulling out from the curb, and I heard a girl laugh.

I walked on three or four steps maybe, and then I heard a sound, utterly familiar and unmistakable, and stopped dead in my tracks. My Jordan's motor had caught, roaring up as someone advanced the spark and throttle, and dying to its chunky, revving-and-ticking-over idle. Swinging around on the walk, I saw a figure, a young man's, vague and shadowy down the street, hop into the front seat, and then—the cutout open—my Jordan shot ahead, tires squealing, down the street toward me.

I was frozen; I just stood there stupidly, staring at my car shooting toward me, my brain not working; then I came to life. It's funny; I was more worried about my car, about the way it was treated, than about the fact that it was being stolen. And I ran out into the street, directly into its path, my arms waving, and I yelled, "Hey! Take it easy!" The brakes slammed on, the Jordan skidding on the bricks, the rear end sliding sideways a little, and it slowed almost to a stop, then swerved around me, picking up speed again, and as I turned, following it with my eyes, I caught a glimpse of a girl's face staring at me, and a man my age at the wheel beside her, laughing, his teeth Hashing white, and then they were past, and he yelled back, "You betcha! Take it easy; I always do!" For a moment I just stood staring after them, watching the single red taillight shrinking into the distance; then I turned, and walked back toward the curb. A little part of the movie crowd was passing, and I heard a woman's voice murmur some question; then a man's voice, gruff and half angry, replied, "Yeah, of *course* it was Vince; driving like a fool as usual."

There was nothing I could do. I couldn't report a car theft to the police, trying to explain who I was, and where they could reach me. I hung around for a while, the street deserted once more, hoping they'd bring back my car. But they didn't, and finally I left, and just walked the streets for the rest of the night.

I kept well away from Prairie Avenue. If I was where I knew I was, my grandmother, still alive, was asleep in the big front bedroom of our house, and the thirteen-year-old in my room was the boy who would become my father. I didn't belong there now, and I kept away, up in the north end of town. It looked about as always; Hylesburg, as I've said, is old, and most of the new construction has been on the outskirts. Once in a while I passed a vacant lot where I knew there no longer was one; and when I passed the Dorsets' house where I played as a kid with Ray Dorset, it was only half built now, the wood of the framework looking fresh and new in the dark.

Once I passed a party, the windows all lighted, and they were having a time, noisy and happy, and with a lot of laughing and shrieks from the women. I stopped for a minute, across the street, watching; and I saw figures passing the lighted windows, and one of them was a girl with her hair slicked close to her head, and curving down onto her cheeks in sort of J-shaped hooks. There was a phonograph going, and the music—it was "China Boy"—sounded sort of distant, the orchestration tinny, and . . . different, I can't explain how. Once it slowed down, the tomes deepening, and someone yelled, and then I heard the pitch rising higher again as it picked up speed, and knew someone was winding the phonograph. Then I walked on.

At daylight, the sky whitening in the cast, the leaves of the big old trees around me beginning to stir, I was on Cherry Street. I heard a door open across the street, and saw a man in overalls walk down his steps, cut silently across the lawn, and open the garage doors beside his house. He walked in, I heard the motor start, and a cream and green '56 Oldsmobile backed out-and I turned around then, and walked on toward Prairie Avenue and home, and was in bed a couple hours before my folks woke up Sunday morning.

I didn't tell anyone my Jordan was gone; there was no way to explain it. Ed Smiley, and a couple other guys, asked me about it, and I said I was working on it in my garage. My folks didn't ask; they were long since used to my working on a car for weeks, then discovering I'd sold or traded it for something else to work on.

But I wanted—I simply had to have—another Playboy, and it took a long time to find one. I heard of one in Davenport, and borrowed Jim Clark's Hudson, and drove over, but it wasn't a Playboy, just a Jordan, and in miserable shape anyway.

It was a girl who found me a Playboy; after school started up in September. She was in my Economics IV class, a sophomore I learned, though I didn't remember seeing her around before. She wasn't actually a girl you'd turn and look at again, and remember, I suppose; she wasn't actually pretty, I guess you'd have to say. But after I'd talked to her a few times, and had a Coke date once, when I ran into her downtown—then she was pretty. And I got to liking her; quite a lot. It's like this; I'm a guy who's going to want to get married pretty early. I've been dating girls since I was sixteen, and it's fun, and exciting, and I like it fine. But I've just about had my share of that, and I'd been looking at girls in a different way lately; a lot more interested in what they were like than in just how good-looking they were. And I knew pretty soon that this was a girl I could fall in love with, and marry, and be happy with. I won't be fooling around with old cars all my life; it's just a hobby, and I know it, and I wouldn't expect a girl to get all interested in exactly how the motor of an old Marmon works. But I would expect her to take some interest in how I feel about old cars. And she did—Helen McCauley, her name is. She really did; she understood what I was talking about, and it wasn't faked either, I could tell.

So one night—we were going to the dance at the Roof Garden, and I'd called for her a little early, and we were sitting out on her lawn in deck chairs killing time—I told her how I wanted one certain kind of old car, and why it had to be just that car. And when I mentioned its name, she sat up, and said, "Why, good heavens, I've heard about the Playboy from Dad all my life; we've got one out in the barn; it's a beat-up old mess, though. Dad!" she called, turning to look up at the porch where her folks were sitting. "Here's a man you've been looking for!"

Well, I'll cut it short. Her dad came down, and when he heard what it was all about, Helen and I never did get to the dance. We were out in that barn, the old tarpaulin pulled off his Jordan, and we were looking at it, touching it, sitting in it, talking about it, and quoting Playboy ads to each other for the next three hours.

It wasn't in bad shape at all. The upholstery was gone; only wads of horsehair, and strips of brittle old leather left. The body was dented, but not torn. A few parts, including one headlight, and part of the windshield mounting, were gone, and the motor was a long way from running, but nothing serious. And all the wheels were there, and in good shape, though they needed renickeling.

Mr. McCauley gave me the car; wouldn't take a nickel for it. He'd owned that Jordan when he was young, had had it ever since, and loved it; he'd always meant, he said, to get it in running order again sometime, but knew he never would now. And once he understood what I meant about restoring a classic, he said that to sec it and drive it again as it once was, was all the payment he wanted.

I don't know just when I guessed, or why; but the feeling had been growing on me. Partly, I suppose, it was the color; the faded-out remains of the deep green this old car had once been. And partly it was something else, I don't know just what. But suddenly—standing in that old barn with Helen, and her mother and dad—suddenly I knew, and I glanced around the barn, and found them; the old plates nailed up on a wall, 1923 through 1931. And when I walked over to look at them, I found what I knew I would find; 1923 Illinois tag 11,206.

"Your old Jordan plates?" I said, and when he nodded, I said as casually as I could, "What's your first name, Mr. McCauley?"

I suppose he thought I was crazy, but he said, "Vincent. Why?"

"Just wondered. I was picturing you driving around when the Jordan was new; it's a fast car, and it must have been a temptation to open it up."

"Oh, yeah." He laughed. "I did that, all right; those were wild times."

"Racing trains; all that sort of thing, I suppose?"

"That's right," he said, and Helen's mother glanced at me curiously. "That was one of the things to do in those days. We almost got it one night, too; scared me to death. Remember?" he said to his wife.

"I certainly do."

"What happened?" I said.

"Oh"—he shrugged—" I was racing a train, out west of town one night; where the road parallels the Q tracks. I passed it, heading for the cross-road—you know where it is—that cuts over the tracks. We got there, my arms started to move, to swing the wheel and shoot over the tracks in front of that engine—when I knew I couldn't make it." He shook his head. "Two three seconds more; if we'd gotten there just two seconds earlier, I'd have risked it, I'm certain, and we'd have been killed, I know. But we were just those couple seconds too late, and I swung that wheel straight again, and shot on down the road beside that train, and when I took my foot off the gas, and the engine rushed past us, the fireman was leaning out of the cab shaking his fist, and shouting something, I couldn't hear what, but it wasn't complimentary." He grinned. "Did anything delay you that night," I said softly, "just long enough to keep you from getting killed?" I was actually holding my breath, waiting for his answer.

But he only shook his head. "I don't know," he said without interest. "I can't remember." And his wife said, "I don't even remember where we'd been."

I don't believe—I really don't—that my Jordan Playboy is anything more than metal, glass, rubber and paint formed into a machine. It isn't alive; it can't think or feel; it's only a car. But I think it's an especial tragedy when a young couple's lives are cut off for no other reason than the sheer exuberance nature put into them. And I can't stop myself from feeling, true or not true, that when that old Jordan was restored—returned to precisely the way it had been just before young Vince McCauley and his girl had raced a train in it back in 1923— when it had been given a second chance; it went back to the time and place, back to the same evening in 1923, that would give them a second chance, too. And so again, there on that warm July evening, actually there in the year 1923, they got into that Jordan, standing just where they'd parked it, to drive on and race that train. But trivial events can affect important ones following them— —how often we've all said: If only this or that had happened, everything would have turned out so differently. And this time it did, for now something was changed. This time on that 1923 July evening, someone dashed in front of their car, delaying them only two or three seconds. But Vince McCauley, then, driving on to race along beside those tracks, changed his mind about trying to cross them; and lived to marry the girl beside him. And to have a daughter.

I haven't asked Helen to marry me, but she knows I will; after I've graduated, and got a job, I expect. And she knows that I know she'll say yes. We'll be married, and have children, and I'm sure we'll be driving a modern hard-top car like everyone else, with safety catches on the doors so the kids won't fall out. But one thing for sure—just as her folks did thirty-two years before—we'll leave on our honeymoon in the Jordan Playboy.

Riding With Icarus

Bruce Holland Rogers

Richardson has been reading Bullfinch's myth-ology lately. He'd been meaning to get to it for years. The book followed him from college, one apartment to the next. He'd had the book through two jobs, a return to school for his MBA, a failed marriage, promotions, a better marriage, fatherhood, even better promotions and moves from this house to that one to yet another. Only now, after his retirement, after his wife has died, after his first heart surgery, is he actually starting to read.

And reading, he has found himself among the immortals. For instance, his golfing partner, Taylor, has a bad day of shanks or long drives straight into the water. By the twelfth green, Taylor's face is red, and he shakes his putter with menace. *Periphetes*, Richardson thinks. *Periphetes and his iron club.*

When Richardson gets his prescriptions filled, he notices the dark, scheming gaze of the pharmacist, and he recognizes her. Here is Medea, taking a job where she has ready access to potions.

And then there is his grandson. Richardson needs someone to drive him to and from the hospital for tests and procedures, and his daughter-in-law volunteers Luke and his rusting Pontiac Sunbird for the job. Luke isn't happy. To show it, he rides the bumpers of other cars. He corners fast. He punches the accelerator for yellow lights. Apparently he had other plans for the day, even though his mother had imagined a wide-open schedule.

The trip home from the doctor two hours later is the same. Tires squeal. Luke propels the car in lurches between lanes to grab another ten feet of advantage over other drivers. *You're going to get us killed, son,* Richardson thinks of saying. But doesn't. Just then, he knows his grandson, and he knows that there's no telling him anything. The boy has never listened, not in thousands of years.

They are traveling west, into the late afternoon glare.

"Faster," Richardson says. "Come on, let's open 'er up. Let's see what this baby can do!"

His grandson grins. There is no happiness like his. He laughs. They are both laughing. "All right," the boy says, and aims the car into the sun. "Here we go!"

The Freeway

George Clayton Johnson

The fat swift car blazed down the freeway.

Arthur C. Danyluk held the steering wheel. He twisted it from side to side, experimentally. Nothing happened of course. Nothing ever happened on the freeway. The grid took care of that. He tried to remember how long it had been since he'd had this machine on manual. It seemed like years.

He let go of the wheel and studied his thick, soft hands before dropping them into his lap. He looked out at the desert, shimmering in the heat, then at the girl who sat beside him. She had the TV swiveled toward her and was looking at it with a wide, trancelike stare.

Aware of his attention, she stretched her arms over her head languorously, shifting her position without taking her eyes from the screen. He could see perspiration stains on the underarms of her blouse.

"The next town we come to I'll get the cooling unit fixed," he said. "I can't imagine what happened to it..."

She turned to glance at him abstractedly for a moment, then looked back at the picture.

"It's a shame we had to put all the food in the disposal, but it would have spoiled in the fridge."

When she didn't answer, he opened the locker on the dash and took out a slim crystal glass. He thumbed the button on the dispenser and watched the clear liquid foam out. The stream stopped when the glass was half full.

"The Last of the Martinis. Guess we'll have to tighten our belts till we get to the next town." He held the fragile glass out to her, gallantly.

"Thanks," she said. "I'm parched." She tilted the drink to her lips and sipped. She made a face. "It's warm. Who can drink warm gin?" She put the glass down on the dash-bar. "We've been driving for *ages*. If I'd known it was going to take *forever*, I simply wouldn't have come."

"It isn't so bad," he said soothingly, thinking that it might be very bad indeed. "We'll probably be there sometime late this evening. This boat makes nearly two hundred miles an hour."

"Oh, look!" she said, tragically. "What happened to the picture?" She gestured toward the TV. The screen was a mass of wavy lines.

"Let me see," he said. He turned the set toward him and adjusted a knob. The screen went black.

"Now look what you did," she said.

"It wasn't me," he said, his voice heavy with annoyance. "First the cooling system goes on the blink, then the TV. You can't blame me for that."

"I suppose not."

She sat sullenly for a few minutes looking out of the car window at the bright passing desert. Miniature droplets of perspiration beaded her upper lip. "God," she said at last. "I feel like I'm in a bake oven. Can't you at least open one of the windows and get a little breeze in here?" She scooted down in the seat. Her skirt rode upward, exposing three inches of moist thigh. She didn't seem to notice.

He leaned forward and thumbed the control button and waited for the whisking sound of the hidden motor that would operate the window. Nothing happened. He hit the button again. Then his fingers danced over the bank of buttons that controlled the other windows.

"It seems like everything's on the fritz today," he said. He looked at her, feeling a sudden surge of sympathy. "We should come to a turnoff soon. We'll get something cool to drink and get everything fixed."

"Just look out there," she said, pointing to the desert that sped past the car. "Did you ever see anything so dead in your life?"

He sighed, said nothing.

"I should have worn something lighter," she said. She pursed her pink lips and blew air down the front of her amply filled blouse.

He thought about touching her knee.

The car lurched abruptly.

"What was that?" she said.

"I don't know."

The car coughed, losing speed.

"*Do* something!"

His hands found the steering wheel and held it uncertainly. The car was losing momentum fast. It took him several seconds to find the manual stud. The steering wheel, suddenly alive, felt alien in his hands. Fortunately, there was a gap between the cars in the slow lane, and he maneuvered the heavy vehicle into it.

"Engine's dying," he said.

Spotting a wide section of road, he wrenched the wheel to the right and felt himself pushed violently forward. He stuck out his arm to steady the girl while his foot stabbed for the brake. He shoved downward, and the car came ponderously to a halt on the dirt shoulder.

When he saw that girl wasn't hurt, he reached in his pocket and took out his handkerchief. He began to wipe his face and neck with it.

"Well, don't just *sit* there. Find out what's wrong."

"Yes," he said. "Of course." He sat still in the seat and looked at the knobs and dials on the dashboard. All of the tiny winking lights had gone out.

"Well?"

"Just a minute," he said. "Wait for it to cool off."

He turned the key tentatively and listened to the sound of the starter. It ground over and over. To Arthur, it sounded like a monster gnashing its teeth. He released the key with a sinking feeling.

"Well, can't you fix it?" she asked. Her bright blonde hair had tumbled over her forehead, and she pushed it back with an impatient gesture.

He pumped the gas feed several times and tried the starter again. It growled resonantly. "I don't understand," he said.

"This is damned silly," she said. "Are we just going to sit here? We can't just *sit* here."

"The mechanic definitely told me that the car was ready for a trip," he said.

"Maybe we're out of gas."

"Can't you read the gauge?" he said harshly. It registered full.

"Well, you don't have to lose your temper," she said. "If I'd thought you were going to act this way, I would never have agreed to spend my vacation with you." She took out her compact and snapped it open. "Look what this heat is doing to my makeup."

"We can always stop somebody and ask for help," he said.

"Can't you fix it yourself?"

"What do I know about cars?" he said. "All I know is this thing cost me twelve-thousand dollars. There's no reason in the world why it should just *die* like this."

"It seems like the sensible thing to do is open the front and see what's wrong. Maybe a wire came loose or something."

Arthur felt irritation growing inside him. Of all the times to have this yapping dame with him!

He began to search over the dash panel for a button or lever with the word HOOD on it. There had to be a way to get the stupid hood open.

I've been driving a car for almost thirty years, he thought. I've owned this one for two years and in all that time I've never opened the hood on the thing. And why should I? That's what service stations are for. Why should a man spend twelve-thousand dollars for a car and then have to service it himself?

"Maybe you open it from outside," the girl said.

He straightened up guiltily.

"I know," he said. "I know."

He opened the door and climbed out of the car. The sun hit him like a fist. For a moment the desert looked like a film negative; all of the dark areas registered white. Then everything came into focus.

God, what a desolate spot! He couldn't see a single sign of habitation except the freeway and the bright automobiles crashing by. Ahead, the freeway climbed to a crest then disappeared. The cars seemed to pour up the road and then, as they reached that point, plunge into the earth. Gone. To be replaced by other cars in a never-ending stream of bright enamel.

Everywhere else was the desert.

Far off were dim hills almost lost in the golden glare of reflected sun.

He could feel the moisture popping out on his skin as he walked to the front of the car. He got down on one knee to look for the hood release. He felt a growing anger. They made it so easy for you, he thought. They sold you a machine that only a highly trained man with expensive equipment could fix. They filled your ears with glib phrases that promised a lifetime of trouble-free usage. They tended its engine, filling it with gasoline and lubricants so that somehow you got the idea that the car was more theirs than yours and then, to cap it all off, they installed the grid in the highways so that you didn't even have to drive the car.

His groping fingers found a lever cleverly concealed within the intricately shaped grill. He pushed it forward. When nothing happened, he hooked his finger around it and pulled. Like the door to Ali Baba's cave, the hood swung majestically open.

Arthur waited for the vast hood to sweep to a stop before he stepped forward to peer within.

There it was, nestled in deep shadow.

The engine.

"My God," said Arthur Danyluk.

Once, long ago, when he was a small child, his father had taken him to a museum. They had wandered through endless corridors and at last they came to a vast room.

In the precise center of the room, towering to the roof, was a great dark locomotive. He remembered the awe with which he regarded the huge mass of strangely carved metal. The wheels rested on rails, and it seemed to loom above him like a great black beast.

Now he peered at the engine of his car and felt that same awe and wonder clutch at his throat.

He could see thick cables looped in coils that formed a maze, entwining here and there in no discernible pattern. There were strange boxes and cylindrical lumps attached randomly atop, astride and athwart a central mass of oil-black strangeness. It hunched up between flaring metal walls that seemed to double back upon themselves. He could see no portion of the whole that presented a clean unbroken plane or curve. Tiny slim wires and tubes interconnected from part to part, branching and reuniting in a nightmare of complexity.

The engine!

He sucked in his breath, blinking his eyes.

He put out his hand and rapped one of the larger shapes apprehensively. Somewhere, he thought. Somewhere inside all of that, there is something wrong. He shook his head dazedly.

He could hear the girl's voice coming to him muffled and indistinct. "What are you doing? Have you found the trouble?"

Yes, he thought. I've found the trouble.

He tried to keep his voice steady. "Looks all right to me," he said. "Nothing seems to be broken."

"Did you check the points?"

"Of course," he said. "First thing I looked at."

"I guess you know you've gotten yourself all filthy?"

He squinted down at his new shirt. It had a long ugly smear of grease across the front. "It doesn't matter," he said.

He made his way back to the driver's seat and climbed behind the wheel. He tried the starter again, letting it grind for a long time before he turned the key off.

"Well, that's that." He said.

"You mean we're stuck?"

"I guess so."

She saw him looking at her bare knees and pulled the skirt down. "I should have my head examined," she said. "I could be back in a town having a chilled cocktail."

"You didn't *have* to come," he said, flushing.

She crossed her arms over her breasts.

His manner softened. "Let's not fight," he said. "As far as I can see, we have several alternatives. We can sit here awhile and hope that the difficulty with the car will iron itself out. Perhaps, when the engine cools off, it will start right up. If it should turn out to be something more serious, we can flag down a passing car and ask for a lift to the closest town. We can send a mechanic back to get the car. While we're waiting, we can have something to eat, a few cold drinks and a change of clothing. When the car is ready, we can resume our trip."

His calm tone seemed to reassure the girl.

They sat still for a few moments. She took out her compact and began to repair her makeup. She examined her eyelashes critically before reaching in her purse to take out a thin metal device. She began to improve the curve in her lashes. He tried not to watch her.

"Now," he said at last. "Let's try it." He turned the key and the starter ground over. He rocked his foot violently against the gas feed. Nothing happened. He tried again. "Well," he said. "You can wait in the car while I flag down somebody. We shouldn't have any trouble."

"All right," she said. "But hurry."

He climbed down out of the car and stood beside the freeway. He had his thumb out when the first car approached.

It sped past – as did the second and the third. They whipped by in a blur of motion. He felt slightly foolish standing there by the side of the freeway with his thumb out. He looked over his shoulder at the girl. She had a minuscule pair of tweezers in her hand and, squinting into her compact mirror, was busy uprooting her eyebrows. He turned back to the freeway and the rush of cars.

The freeway!

Six lanes of moving metal slamming through the heat of day. And yet, each car stood out separately. It was as though his eyes were a stop-motion camera photographing each machine that passed. Inside each individual car he could see the people. They sprawled languidly, enervated by the baked air, struck into positions of boredom in their private worlds of vivid metal, fabric, leatherette, and plastic.

It occurred to him then that he could only appeal for help to the outermost lane. In the brief span of time that the cars whipped by, it was clearly impossible for the cars in the other five lanes to maneuver into the slow lane to help him, even if they wanted to.

"Damn!" said the girl. "Can't you do anything? Wave your hand so they can *see* you!"

"All right," he said. "I'm trying!"

He waved his arm feebly.

They're not going to stop, he thought. Nobody's going to stop. Everyone's in such a hurry that they haven't the time. And who am I that they should help me? How can they know that I'm not some desperado who would hold them up and take their car and money? A feeling of strength came over him thinking of himself as an outlaw. But isn't that what I am? Alone on the freeway beyond the reach of law and custom? Certainly, there are police officers at checkpoints and turnoffs to control manual traffic, but out here they don't exist. It's true. By the simple act of being alone, away from others, I am an outlaw.

The feeling of strength faded, to be replaced by a seeping weakness. He began to be afraid.

An hour went by as he stood there signaling the cars. The sun made him dizzy, and he could feel the muscles in his back and legs sag. His eyes began to sting, and his mouth felt raw.

The cars seemed to come in bunches. One minute the freeway would be empty as far as the eye could see, silent and dreaming in the noontide, and then the cars would come in a tight knot of screaming sound, ten or twenty of them clustered together.

Occasionally a single car or a pair of cars would slam down the freeway, separated from the others, scurrying along like metal chicks hunting the hen, as though afraid to be alone on the concrete runway.

At these times, Arthur Danyluk made exaggerated motions with his arm and thumb, hoping that one of the vehicles would stop. They *could* stop, he thought, without being run over by other cars, but the autos swung past as though he didn't exist. Once, inside a yellow car, he saw a young girl poised like a mannequin with a long-stemmed glass to her lips. He became conscious of his great thirst.

Another fifteen minutes went by.

Well, when it came right down to it, he thought, startled, where would a car pull off the freeway, if one decided to stop? If the driver had the presence of mind to disconnect from the grid in time, where would he halt the car safe from traffic?

Ahead was a smooth piece of ground about six car-lengths long on which an auto might stop, but even then it would have to get its wheels in the dirt as he had done. And that could be dangerous. He tried to picture the driving skill that would be required to slow a car down and slew it into that tiny space. It would be clearly impossible if the driver were closely followed by other cars.

He held his weary arm out for a few minutes more and then let it drop to his side.

"What are you *doing?*" said the girl, leaning out of the open door. He gestured her out of the way and climbed inside.

"I've got to rest a few minutes," he said. "I'm bushed." He leaned back against the seat, breathing heavily.

"I'm thirsty," said the girl. She looked pale and upset.

He didn't answer her.

He leaned forward and gripped the steering wheel with both hands.

He pumped the gas feed several times and then turned the key in the ignition. They listened to the hollow sound of the churning starter.

"Well," she said. "What do we do now?"

"Let me rest for a few minutes and I'll try to stop somebody." He slumped weakly in the seat.

"I don't see why you should be so tired. You haven't done anything."

He ignored her and looked off down the freeway. Ahead was the rise where the freeway dipped out of sight. He tried to estimate how far it was. In the afternoon sun, distances were deceptive. It might be one mile or three.

"Listen," he said to the girl. "Here's what we'll do. You stay in the car and keep an eye on things. If anybody stops, you tell them what happened. I'm going to walk up ahead.

There might be a house or a service station up there."

"You're just going to leave me?"

He looked at her sharply, wishing that she'd get off his neck. He had enough trouble without taking more complaints from her.

"Oh, God," she said in a frustrated tone. "Why couldn't I have picked out a young man who knew something about engines..."

He finished the sentence for her: "Instead of a fat, middle-aged fool?"

"I didn't say that."

She saw the look on his face and didn't answer.

He sagged tiredly, turned on his heel and strode off down the freeway, leaving her in the silent car.

By the time he had covered a half-mile, his legs began to grow stiff. He could feel a tiny pain in his side.

A middle-aged man, he thought. Is that what I am? Looking back it seemed that was all he had ever been. Just a middle-aged fat fool unable to do anything for himself. He had a gardener to come in and tend his lawn, someone to cook his meals, make his bed, launder his clothing...

Living had become too complicated. There was a time, he thought, when each man made the things he used. He built his home from trees and mud. He wore his own clothing and grew his own food. True, he didn't have much, but there was no need for him to feel insecure in his house surrounded by the product of his own hands. If something broke he could repair it in the same manner he had built it. But now everything was too complicated for that. Ten thousand men put food in cans, and when the cans were opened what wasn't eaten could be put in a refrigerator where it would not spoil. But the refrigerator was made by men, and if it failed other men were called in to fix it using tools created by still *other* men, and all of the men put together were called society. It was a fine system if you were part of it, but if you lost your key and were somehow locked out you could die pounding on the door.

His legs began to know up again. He suddenly discovered that he was lurching from side to side as he walked, weaving drunkenly.

Hold on, he thought. Get a grip on yourself.

He lifted his feet carefully and placed one after another, concentrating on his task.

The pain in his side was worse, and he was puffing.

Far ahead, the road rose to the shimmering horizon.

He tried to hum under his breath to establish a marching cadence, but the sound was a feeble moan.

He decided not to look ahead. It was easier to look at the ground as he walked.

When he was a boy, he remembered, his father had apple trees planted in the back yard. When the fruit was ripe his father would pick it and carry the baskets to the basement. He would peel and quarter the apples into a large tub and pulp them into a mash. Then he would seal them in an earthenware crock and wait for them to turn to cider.

His mother would laugh and tell his father that cider was on sale at the supermarket for a half-dollar a gallon, but his father would smile and ignore her.

In the fall his father would sit among the dead leaves in the backyard on the grass that he had planted himself, under an apple tree that had grown for a seed, drinking his cider and looking at the rock garden that he had built with his own two hands.

His father was a happy man.

Arthur had never really understood him until this moment by the freeway.

As he walked with his head down he noticed the debris that littered the edge of the road. His eyes picked out crumpled cigarette packages, beer cans, scraps of paper – and then he saw a strange thing. On patches of smooth ground, he saw rabbit tracks. The paw marks made a clear pattern in the dust. He stopped. His eyes followed the tracks off across the desert. It was then he spotted the rabbit, the first he had seen in his entire life.

It stood between two cactus shrubs about twenty feet away, its ears perked up, looking at him.

He took another step, expecting it to explode into motion. The rabbit stood stiffly for a moment, its nose twitching, and then came down on all fours and nibbled at the closest bit of brush.

Well, I'll be damned, he thought. It's not afraid. It's probably never seen a human on foot in its entire life. It seemed incredible that the rabbit could see the cars go by all day and still be unaware that humans existed.

Abruptly, he dismissed the rabbit from his thoughts as he topped the rise in the road. Ahead was only more desert with the freeway slanting across it until it vanished behind a low hill miles away.

He heard a horn.

He looked up to see a car go by him. Squinting his eyes, he could see a blonde in the front seat beside a youngish-looking man. The girl waved saucily at him. The car was a jalopy, a 1965 model by the looks of it. That meant that it couldn't be tuned to the grid. The realization that a car could be manually operated down a freeway came as a shock to him. Then his system suffered another shock.

He felt his stomach sink within him. He recognized the girl. It was his blonde.

The trip back to the car was hell.

From time to time he had to sit down and rest. Sprawled in the litter beside the roadway, he cursed himself and his car and the people who whisked by him.

Then somehow he got to his feet and tottered on.

He could feel a blister forming on the heel of his left foot. It was clear that his stylish Oxfords weren't meant for walking.

He stumbled the last hundred yards in a lurching run and collapsed against the side of the car. He didn't have the strength to open the door and get inside.

A half-hour passed before he could get to his feet.

He saw the skid marks that the other car had made coming to a stop. The black streaks of rubber testified to the desperate chance that the driver had taken to halt his car in the dust. He felt a quick anger that filled him completely. When it passed he felt drained.

Why couldn't she have flagged the man down while *he* had been there? No, she had to wait till he was far up the road. And then that idiot of a driver burning up his tires to rescue the damsel in distress. But then he thought: Wouldn't you do the same thing? If you saw a striking blonde alone on the highway, wouldn't you do everything in your power to help her out? He wondered why it hadn't occurred to him before. Nobody would pass a pretty girl in trouble. They'd stop for that, but not for a man in the same fix. They wouldn't stop for a dozen good reasons. Because they were alone or were with somebody. Because of the traffic, because, because, because...

Arthur Danyluk could feel the sweat greasy on his body as the hot sunlight blasted down on him. He climbed back into the car. Well, he thought. Where do we go from here? What do we do now? Do I stand with my thumb out till I fall from heatstroke or until my tissues dry up? And when it gets dark and the cold comes down, do I shiver in the back seat of this useless car until the sun rises again?

And when next week comes, will I be stretched out in a twelve-thousand-dollar coffin beside the freeway? Will I wait for the insects and small animals to pick my bones?

He felt tired and old and afraid.

He shaded his eyes against the sun-glare from the hood, his tongue swollen in his mouth.

Sitting there, he saw the desert clearly for the firs time. He saw the real enemy – the baked dirt and the sparse growth, the rocks and the pebbles.

Are *you* the reason we put up durable buildings and swift machines and great freeways? So that by complexity ad sheer numbers we can build faster than you can tear down and wear away?

He could feel little golden spots dancing under his lids as he squeezed his eyes tight.

Is that the way it is? He thought quickly. Must we gather together in strength to stay alive? Is one man helpless against you? Don't I, Arthur Danyluk, have a chance?

The desert waited... the same desert the pioneers had crossed, men who refused to conform, who defied the odds for a chance to make their own way.

Then, inside himself, he knew the answer. He thought about his father, and a hard light came into his eyes.

With his thick, soft hand, he opened the car door and climbed out. He went around to the trunk and fumbled it open. He selected a wrench from the tool kit. He wasn't going to starve, by damn! He had matches to start a fire. And the tracks he'd seen, the rabbit... Life was out there. He once had a good throwing arm. And he'd read that quite a few desert plants contained water...

He looked at the automobiles flowing past him in a great tide and listened to the drum of engines on the still desert air. The reflected light from the sun-dazzled doors and fenders hammered at his eyes. Damn them, he thought, I don't need any of them! Setting his shoulders, he turned away, into the desert. The freeway dwindled behind him, the hurrying cars vanished into hot silence. Only the waiting land surrounded him now. Ahead, behind, to either side.

Arthur C. Danyluk moved out to face the enemy.

Passages

C. Jennings Penders

Headlights moved across the ceiling in Beth's room and she woke up. The warm bed was pure heaven, and she pulled her down quilt up closer and sighed. She rolled over, taking the comforter with her. Her eyes opened and she glanced at the clock. It was twelve forty-five.

Beth closed her eyes again and was about to drift back into a relaxing bliss when music streamed through the opened window. As she lay in bed she began to discern the words, and that was when her eyes opened wide.

"Rick?" She untangled her arm from the depths of the covers and turned the bedside lamp on. It was still hard to leave the warmth under her quilt for the cold February air that moved through her room, but the music grew more insistent. Finally, with some hesitation, she threw back the covers and left the safety of her bed. An icy chill crept in from the opened window and caressed her naked legs. Beth left her window open all year round. She couldn't sleep in a warm room.

She peered outside. A green Mustang sat under the streetlight. Snow was falling. Beth reached for the robe lying at the foot of her bed and slipped it on. She searched the room for her moccasins, found them in her closet, and pushed her feet into their stiffness. Then she ran down the staircase and out the front door.

There was already a light dusting of snow on the ground, and snow was still falling. Beth stood on the porch, her arms wrapped around her body, trying to keep warm. She shivered involuntarily.

The snow fell around the Mustang – but not onto it. "Rick, is that you?" Her body tensed. Her head said no. She said it aloud, "Can't be you." But her heart spoke a different language.

Beth stepped off the porch and cautiously approached the vehicle, her moccasins crunching on icy snow. She got within six feet, bent forward to peer inside. The front seat was empty. She stepped to peer into the back seat. No one. The car began to shimmer then, almost undulate the way a heat mirage shimmers, and then vanished completely. There wasn't even a sign that a car had stood there, for the ground under where the car had appeared was covered with snow.

~

"I know what I saw!" Beth sat at the kitchen table sipping her coffee.

Her father sat opposite her and looked up from his eggs. "He's dead, sweetie. Could you have been dreaming?"

She put the coffee cup down. "No. It was him. I'd never mistake that car. I was in it the night he was killed, remember?"

"Now, Beth." Her father cut her off, feeling less patient now. "We both know it was never determined that he *was* run off the road. It's just pure speculation on your part."

Beth fought back the shudder that was about to emerge. "It was his car, Dad. I know it."

"Even if it was," he paused to finish off his eggs, "why now after all this time? Hell, it's been over a year."

"A year tonight," she corrected. She let the words hang there. "I even heard 'Traveling Man' playing at a quarter to one. That was his favorite song. I was in bead and heard the song outside the window. And when I got up to look, the Mustang, *his* Mustang was out in the driveway." She took another sip from her coffee then turned back to her father. "That's what time the car struck the light pole. I know what I saw."Without realizing it, her grip tightened on the coffee cup, and it spun away from her, shattering into three pieces on the floor. The remaining coffee puddled beside the broken mug. "Fuck!" The exclamation slipped out and she turned away, clearly embarrassed. "Sorry."

Her father waved it away. "Don't worry," he said. "I've heard it before. D'ya want some more?"

"No. I think I'll stop at the Beanery today. Maybe Eve will be there."

Eve Brown managed the coffee house for her brother and she and Beth had quickly become friends after they'd first met.

"I wish you'd believe me, Dad. If you said Mom had visited you, I wouldn't doubt it for a moment."

David smiled, leaned forward to tussle Beth's hair like she was a kid, then sipped his coffee and looked at her. Since the time his wife had died, he'd become both parents for Beth, and Beth had accepted how he still treated her like a kid at times. Of course, it was easier to accept such embarrassing actions in private, like now.

"You never answered my question earlier. Let's suppose you *did* see his car. Why now?"

She drew in a breath. "Because it's a year later? An anniversary. I don't know, really." She cleared the breakfast dishes from the table to the sink.

David got up and put the dishes into the dishwasher after Beth rinsed them.

"Afraid I won't stack them from the back?" she said to her father and smiled. He laughed, then continued the prior conversation.

"You must have some clue why now."

"I don't, really."

David returned to the table to watch his daughter wipe the counter tops and—not for the first time—thought about all the years that had passed since Nancy had died. "Sometimes I wish your mom was still here," he said unexpectedly, "she had all the answers."

Beth smiled. She shook her head she said, "No she didn't. Remember when Rick first started to come around?"

David laughed again. "Oh, yeah. She thought you only liked him because of his car."

"Yeah and she said I'd be over him in a week. She didn't have the right answer then."

"Thanks, sweetie." He rose from the table again to place his empty coffee cup in the washer. Beth was still standing at the sink. David reached out and hugged her. "You've gone through so much in the past couple of years, losing mom and then losing Rick." David shook his head. "I'm very happy you've coped so well."

"I get by the same way you do, Dad. I look to the future, but I've got a healthy respect for the past." She walked him to the door as he left for work.

Beth finished getting herself ready for a day of errands, since this was her day off from the town library. For the past ten years she'd worked as their computer consultant, giving training seminars, troubleshooting software problems, and teaching newbies how to navigate the Internet. She'd chosen to live at home since the passing of her mom, to help her dad out, and so he would not be alone in the house.

Beth pulled out of the driveway, took a left at the end of the road, and passed the intersection where Rick was killed. She'd thought of avoiding the intersection today—as she did most days—by taking the longer route to downtown, but something drew her in this direction today.

Just before the dreaded intersection Beth spied the deer crossing sign. Its image had haunted her ever since the accident. Especially, in all the years she'd travelled that road, never once had she seen a single deer, although friends had said they'd seen deer herding on one side of the road or the other.

A mile farther up the road she merged onto the highway. The sunlight reflecting off the new snow made a blinding reflection. She squinted and cursed herself for forgetting her sunglasses. When an object loomed in front of her suddenly—as if appearing out of nowhere—she slammed on the breaks.

It *must* be the glare, she thought, like a mirage of shimmering water on the road ahead of you in the summer. "Please, God," she said it aloud. "Let it be gone." But the Mustang that had appeared suddenly was still sitting on the side of the roadway, the front end smashed beyond recognition and steaming.

Rick stood beside his car, pointing to it and shaking his

head slowly.

She pulled off quickly to the side of the road and stepped out of the car. "Rick," she said, and walked slowly toward the wreak; to the man standing beside the car who was once her husband.

"It's not what you think, Liz," he said as plainly has if he were standing there as a living person. He's always called her Liz, instead of Beth, and just the sound of his voice saying it once again, as clear as day, filled her with an unexpected warmth.

She stood there, perhaps a car's length away from him, and waited for the vision to fade. But it remained, and Rick held a hand up. "Not any closer," he said. "It isn't—time yet."

She stood near the rear of the Mustang and wept. She wiped the tears from her eyes and cheeks. "God, Rick. I miss you so much," she said and drew in a quavering breath. She then stepped closer, but Rick stepped back, keeping his distance. Sensing his apprehension, she halted her advance.

"Don't cry, Liz. Everything will be clear shortly. I promise." He blew her a kiss, then both the car and Rick disappeared.

Beth stood there, her body trembling. This can't be happening, she thought. She then calmed herself and examined the area, looking carefully at the ground. There was no evidence that a car had been there moments ago, no tire tracks, no disturbance of the melted snow along the edge of the road. And . . . there wasn't a single footprint expect for her own.

She returned to her car and sat in the driver's seat for a moment, staring out the windshield. "What did he say?" She closed her eyes and thought for a moment. "That's it. 'It's not what you think.' Okay, what isn't what I think?"

She took a deep breath and let it out slowly, then put the car in gear and drove back onto the roadway. All the while her mind was working, trying to understand why Rick had returned now after a year.

It started to snow again. "God, I hate winter," she said loud. The wind picked up and started to blow drifts across the road. Beth had to slow to a crawl. Two months, she thought. Just two months and I can be outside again. February was a bad month for her anyway. Her mother, too, died in February.

It took her another half hour to reach town. It was usually a fifteen-minute ride. "Let there be a space near the Beanery," she thought. There was.

Eve was sitting at one of the tables leafing through the daily paper. No one else was there. Beth reached into her glove compartment and pulled out a travel mug, then stepped out of the car. She wrapped the jacket around her shoulders and walked inside.

"Hey," Beth said as he approached Eve's table. Eve looked up from the paper "I was kinda hoping you'd stop in today. How's it going, Beth?"

"Not good." She went to the line of coffee carafes while Eve watched her, selected the Peruvian French Roast, and then added too much cream. She shook her head and returned to Eve's table.

Eve folded the newspaper, then smiled. "What wrong?"

Beth sat. "I saw Rick's car last night."

"W-What?" Eve leaned forward, intrigued. "What do you mean, you *saw* his car. Where? I thought it was junked."

"Not *the* car, but what *appeared* to be the car."

"You mean like an apparition?"

"Yes, I guess that's what it would be."

"You must have been dreaming."

"That's what my father said!"

"Isn't it possible? I mean—" Eve's brother walked up to the table then, and having overhead the last words said, "Isn't what possible?"

"Hey, Joe. Beth said she saw Rick's car outside her house last night and I was just telling her that she must have been dreaming. You know, it was a year ago tonight that he was killed."

Joe sat down. He stared at Beth. "Are you sure it was *his* car? There are other green Mustangs in town."

"Not like his." She pursed her lips then said, "I know what his car looks like, Joe. I'd driven it before. Besides, I saw the license plate."

Joe rolled his eyes. Sighing, he said, "I don't know Beth. A ghost car outside your house? Like my sister said, just a dream. Dreams can seem very real." He paused here for a moment, thinking. Then he looked over at Eve. "Hey, wait a minute. Remember your friend, Billy?"

"What happened to Billy?" Beth asked.

"His brother Dan drowned in the boating accident," Joe said, returning his attention to Beth. "The night after Dan was buried, Billy woke up and saw Dan standing at the foot of his bed. He was smiling, Billy said. Held out a hand. And then he disappeared."

Eve laughed out loud. "C'mon, Joe. You can't honestly believe that."

"Hey, his parents saw him too."

The story encouraged Beth. "There's more to tell," she said. "This morning as I was coming downtown, I saw the car again. Only this time Rick was there, standing beside the Mustang. He said it wasn't what I thought."

"It?" Joe said.

"Something. He said 'it' but I think he meant the circumstances of the crash, or his appearance with the car. I don't know, really."

Joe rubbed at his chin. "If what you're saying *really* happened, there's gotta be a reason. From what I've heard about this kind of ghost stuff, there's usually some unfinished business that keeps a spirit from moving on. Is there anything Rick left undone before the accident? I know in Billy's case; Dan didn't get a chance to say goodbye to his family."

"I don't think it was an accident," Beth said and sipped her coffee. "Do you know we fought that night. His ex was trying to get him back, and the last thing I said when he left wasn't, 'I love you and I'll see you tomorrow.' It was, maybe you'd be better off with Kate. God," she said. "I didn't mean that. I loved Rick."

Eve reached across the table and took her friend's hand. "I'm sure he knew."

"You know, Kate showed up at my place a few times, even threatened me once. She spent some time in rehab too. It's why Rick left her."

Joe shook his head. "You're not implying that Kate Brandt had anything to do with this, are you?"

The three fell silent. Finally, Joe asked, "Have you followed up on any of this?"

"Yeah. Next day I spoke to the person who saw the Nova. Granted it was dark, but the moon was out and there was a streetlight just past the accident. Frank swore it was a white Nova he saw. He said it crept by the Mustang, then took off like a rocket."

"Wait a minute," Joe said. "Not Frank Woods?"

Beth raised her brow. "Yeah."

Joe rolled his eyes. "I know where the accident

happened. And I know where Frank lives. But he's a drunk, Beth. You can't trust alcoholics. You should know better."

"But he promised me he wasn't drinking that night."

Joe smiled here. "You know, Beth, the more I consider this, the more inclined I am to believe it was all just a terrible accident and your refusal to see that is what's *keeping* Rick here."

~

That night while lying in bed, Beth replayed the day's events. "Could they be right? Am I responsible?" Before she could answer herself, two lights danced across the ceiling.

This time Beth didn't hesitate. She leapt out of bed and threw on a pair of jeans and a sweatshirt. She looked the bedroom window. The green Mustang was in the driveway again, and Rick was standing beside it. "C'mon," he called up to Beth. "Wanna go for a ride?" The moon was out and it cast an eerie glow around Rick, making him appear almost luminescent. With the snow behind him, the effect was greater.

Her pulse quickened and a stream of sweat appeared on her forehead and trickled into her eye. But something held her back. When she turned, she was startled to find that her father was standing behind her.

"I heard you banging around up here. What's wrong?" He moved to her side, closer to the window, and reached out to her. When he glanced out the window he saw the apparitions below.

He stumbled backward, knocking Beth back a step with him. "My. God!" He said and rubbed his brow. "That's not..? Who is..? You're not going out there?"

"Yes, it's Rick. I told you. I gotta see him." She put on

her shoes and raced down the stairs before he could gain his composure to voice objection.

When he was finally running down the stairs, chasing after, he shouted, "Are you crazy? You could have died with him once." The admonition fell on deaf ears, for she was already outside the house and standing beside the Mustang.

Rick put his arms around her and they embraced for a brief moment. He kissed her. She pulled away, then looked up at him. "How?" She wanted to know. "You're not a ghost, you're solid! Like a real person!"

He walked around to the passenger side and opened the door. "Get in. Let's talk."

Before she could respond, the front door to her house opened and her father stood on the stoop, squinting into the glare of the streetlight at the end of the short driveway. "R-Rick?" he stammered. He never doubted his daughter's safety when Rick was alive. But this was so different. He stepped off the porch and approached Rick as he stood beside the passenger door of the Mustang, holding his daughter. "I..." he began. "...how?" David tried to say.

Rick held Beth close; as if he, it seemed to David, he was not about to let her go. "We have something to take care of tonight," Rick said. "I won't let anything happen to Liz." He opened the passenger door, left it open, then walked around to the driver's side and sat behind the wheel.

"I've gotta do this, Dad. I'll be fine," Liz said and smiled at her father. "I feel good about this." With that said, she stepped into the Mustang and closed the door.

The ignition started automatically, without Rick moving his hands from the wheel. "Seatbelt," Rick said, nodding at Beth.

She strapped in, then said, "What about you?"

"I didn't wear one."

The past tense usage wasn't lost on her. When the car pulled away without any help from Rick, she suddenly knew what was happening. "You're going to show me what happened. That's why you weren't ready for me this morning."

He nodded. "I had to prepare for this."

"Listen," she said, reaching her hand out to his. "I'm so sorry we fought that night. I loved you so much, Rick."

He caressed her hand and looked deep into her eyes. He hands were off the wheel, for the Mustang was driving itself in this automatic replay of that fateful night. "I know," he said and smiled.

The car turned left at the end of the road, leaving David standing in his driveway to ponder, alone. The car gained speed and passed by that deer crossing sign, and began its merge onto the highway. "Almost there now." Beth felt the vibration of the speeding engine. The speed began to make her nervous. Ahead, they could see the streetlight where the smashed car wound up that night. Beth felt her heart rise into her throat and her breath came in gasps. Her hands clenched and unclenched. Her foot pressed into the floor carpet in that typical reaction of a passenger to try and stop an out-of-control vehicle, and she looked over at Rick.

He smiled at her again. "We won't be hurt." It was all he had time to say. Something bolted out of the woods. The car spun away from the animal and then tried correct, to hold the pavement, but it hit a patch of black ice and slid out of control. In the next moment they were headed for that streetlight, and Rick was thrown through the front windshield after they stuck something. But Beth was unharmed, her body did not react to the sudden changes of inertia. She was merely an observer, like in a 3D movie.

Beth turned back and saw a white blur outside the car race away. "Oh. God. It was a deer."

Rick's broken and bloody body lay by the roadside. The car's front grille was smashed in. Beth hopped out of the Mustang and dashed to Rick's side. Although the attention she gave would do nothing to help, she knelt beside him and held his head in her hands. Rocking him gently, she kissed his split, bloody lips. Tears flowed down her cheeks. "Oh, God. Oh God."

She felt a presence beside her and looking up she screamed out. Rick stood there as he'd been before the accident, and in the confusion, for a moment, she thought he'd *really* survived, and then she laughed unexpectedly through her tears. "You're okay! You're okay!"

"See," he said. Beth looked up at him, still holding the dying body. "Kate didn't have anything to do with this."

Beth shook her head. "I can't believe it," she said. "A deer. It was a deer!" A moment later she understood what still needed to be done. "I've got to see Kate."

"She'll know your sincere, Liz." He held his arms out. They embraced for a moment, and she started to cry. "Don't go, Rick, please." She collapsed in agony and wept uncontrollably.

He looked into her eyes and brushed her tears away. He then released her and pointed at the broken and bloody Rick lying on the cold ground. She looked at the body, and at the smashed and steaming Mustang, and shook her head. When she turned back to the whole Rick, he was gone. The space where he had just stood was empty. "Rick?" she said to the night, and when she turned to look for him, the broken Rick and the Mustang were gone. She stood there alone in the night, at the side of the roadway were Rick had died, and she thought she heard his voice softly echoing in the darkness, saying, "I love you, Liz. I love you Liz. We'll be together again..." until the words were just whispers, like the wind.

She brushed the soil off her knees and began her walk home.

Shotgun

Amy Lynwander

T he ghost liked to go to the Wawa convenience store. Not that she could blame it, Darby thought, adjusting the heat in the car. News stations reported record lows for February. Her winter boots felt like permanent appendages.

"How are you doing tonight?" she said, her voice loud and falsely jovial in the small sedan. No answer.

The light ahead turned yellow, and Darby jammed the brakes. The car skidded to a halt.

"Sorry," she muttered. Darby wasn't a great driver. When she was younger, she compensated by living within walking distance to the bar du jour and whichever dead-end job she was barely holding down.

"I don't know why you want to ride with me anyway," Darby said, "It can't be much fun haunting a car." The passenger side "fasten seatbelt" light blinked.

When Darby turned twenty-nine, her dingy apartment and so-called friends sleeping on her floor lost their charm.

She moved home and got a part-time job as a receptionist, dressing in slacks and sweaters and finger-combing her hair into a tame bob. Her father lent her some money for a car. She took the bus to the sketchy used car lot and picked the most nondescript economy sedan, feeling a kinship with the car. The ghost joined her a couple days later.

The first time the seatbelt light came on, she checked that she was buckled in before she realized it was the passenger sidelight. She joked out loud that she had a ghost, and the light blinked once. Her classic rock radio station played, "Girl, You Know it's True," which convinced Darby this was the work of the supernatural. When she called the radio station to ask for confirmation of Milli Vanilli on their playlist, the DJ replied, "You have got to be shitting me," and hung up.

"Are you there?" she asked tentatively. The light blinked.

Darby didn't know too many dead people. She briefly considered her grandmother, the tough broad who matched her hand-knitted vests to her polyester pants.

"Gram?" she called. Nothing. She decided her grandmother would be too busy playing cards with her friends in the afterlife to ride along with her.

Sometimes if Darby tried to start the car during a downpour, the engine wouldn't turn over until the rain let up. Once, after two glasses of wine at happy hour with her co-workers, she had to sit in the parking lot for an hour and a half until the car would start.

"I'm fine," she hissed before giving up and playing solitaire on her phone.

Darby showed the car to one of the guys from the mailroom who dabbled in cars on the side. No lights came on for him, but he did notice a bent frame.

"This car's been in a bad accident," he said.

When she called the used car lot, they stuck to their story of an old lady who only drove the car to church and offered to fax her the clean driving history. Darby gave up.

The ghost joined her most days and always when she visited Wawa. She allowed herself to become addicted to Wawa's coffee and routinely stopped there on her way home from work. It seemed a small thing compared to her past vices.

She slammed the car door, but the thunk of the seatbelt buckle in the way kept it from closing. Darby leaned in and saw her keys in the ignition. "Thanks—wouldn't want to lock myself out." She grabbed them and shut the door more gently this time.

"Come for your pick-me-up?" the old man behind the counter called when she walked through the door.

Darby smiled. "You know it."

"Be careful out there," he said, handing her the small black coffee, "some black ice."

Darby started up her car and the passenger side seatbelt light came on. "Ready to go?" she asked, "Are you ever going to talk to me?"

Darby drove one-handed, sipping her coffee. The yellow light caught her by surprise. She lead-footed it this time and the car began to slide. Slipping the coffee in the holder between the seats, she spun the wheel and the car jerked harder. She tried to turn the other way.

Suddenly her limbs felt heavy as a weight settled over her. Her foot came off the brake and the steering wheel straightened. The brake tapped lightly, and the car swung gracefully towards the side, coming to rest against a snowdrift off the road.

Darby looked up in amazement. Not even a drop of her coffee had spilled.

Safe. A jagged whisper filled her head. She glanced at the dashboard in time to see the seatbelt light flick off. Her headlights caught the shadow of a lady in a dress and hat before it faded away.

Final Frederic

Georgia Addams

Frederic Davis has spent the afternoon playing with other children in the driveway of the D'Amico house. It's two hours to dusk on an early June day in 1939, and the smell of dinner fills the air: boiled chicken, cornbread, and stewed garden vegetables.

Ann D'Amico stands in the screen door. Her white apron looks like a ghost against the darkened doorway. She calls out to the children.

"Time to call it a day and get washed up for supper!"

The five children slow their activity like tractor engines switched off and idling down to a stop.

"Betty, Frederic," Ann continues. "It was good of you to come over, but I'm certain your mothers will be wantin' you home for dinner."

"Yes, Mrs. D'Amico," says Frederic.

"Thank you," Betty says, turns, and skips off across the front yard toward her home just a half-mile west on the same side of the Boston Post Road.

Frederic starts for home too, a farmhouse a quarter mile east on the opposite side of the road.

~

Thirty minutes earlier, Frank Hoff leaves work in neighboring Branford and heads east on the Post Road for home. The drive typically takes about forty minutes, but the time always seems to pass faster because of the good conversation provided by the passengers: Frank Liska and Charles Leissner.

All three men work together at a foundry, and Frank is the only man among the three with a reliable vehicle, so Frank always drives the trio, and the others chip in for gasoline. Every penny shared is a penny earned, even though it's been a decade since the market crashed.

Additional compensation for wear and tear on Frank's truck is paid in occasional rounds of drinks at a roadside tavern. The three never start out drinking; they always wait until they've traveled most of the distance home before stopping at one of a few favorite watering holes close to their homes in Clinton, Connecticut.

The sun is directly behind them as they travel eastbound, for it's a sunny spring day, the temperature around 75 degrees, and the wind calm.

The rich blue sky of late afternoon stretches wide, and Frank enjoys the view out the windshield while his passengers go on about the new shop foreman at the foundry and how the fellow doesn't seem to know his ass from his elbow but clearly has the owner fooled. The men are laughing.

~

Margaret Davis rings the small bronze alloy bell her husband Fred installed on the back of the house, just within reach of the top step of the back stoop.

She rings the bell three times in short, double strikes: Ding-ding, ding-ding, ding-ding, to call her four children and husband in for dinner.

Ruth and Martha come up from the cornfield where they were playing, and Joel dashes in from the barn with his father, Fred, in tow.

"Time for supper!" Margaret calls and smiles at her family gathering like cows coming home from wandering the pasture and chickens returning to roost in the evening coop.

One by one, single file, each child clops up the back steps, removes shoes, and heads toward the sink to pass the soap and baptize the hands.

"Smells good, Mama," Fred says, and Margaret stirs the pot on the stove one last time before serving. She looks out the kitchen window, across the field where the grass has already greened up to stand as tall as her youngest son. She looks back to her husband. He's the last one at the sink.

"Our little Frederic is late again," she says and looks out the window across the field.

"Out playing at the D'Amico's, I believe. Save a bowl, and he can eat when he comes home," Fred says, shakes his hands over the sink, and then towels them dry before taking his place at the head of the table to say grace.

~

A stick in his hand, young Frederic first drags it behind him and then parades it in front of him like the baton of an Independence Day band leader.

Singing to himself, Frederic steps up to the street curb, looks one way and then the other, and waits for a break in the traffic.

Three automobiles approach westbound from the left and pass by. Two automobiles followed by a delivery truck approach eastbound from the right, pass by, and all seems clear behind them. Frederic looks left again, and another car approaches in the westbound lane then passes. Frederic steps into the street, waving his baton stick out in front of him.

~

The hair of Frank Hoff's neck stands straight, and his heart leaps when he realizes that someone is suddenly crossing into his lane from the opposite lane: a boy waving a stick.

~

A blowing horn, a squeal of brakes out front, and Ann D'Amico drops her fork, rises, and dashes out to the middle of the driveway. Her children and husband are right behind her. She stands frozen at the scene out in the street. A dark green Ford pick-up truck is stopped on the right side of the roadway. Three men are crowding around the middle of the road in front of her house, looking down. A second vehicle slows and stops, as do others coming upon the scene.

Ann's husband, Joseph, walks forward and joins the crowd. After a moment of looking down, he looks back at his wife and shakes his head. Ann D'Amico holds her face with both hands. Joseph looks up the road toward the Davis farmhouse.

~

A Chevrolet dealership parking lot now occupies the location where the D'Amico house stood. Lined side by side, row upon row, gleaming automobiles wait for new owners to claim them and drive them over the road where little Fred Davis was killed so long ago. One day, no one at all will be around to remember the boy's short happy life.

The Hitchhiker

Jason J. Marchi

We never learned his name during our brief car ride together. We picked him up on our way south towards Madison on that cold January afternoon.

He seemed relaxed—a gentle young soul. Not as if the cold had numbed him into a state of calm, but as if he himself was summer coming to warm us unexpectedly.

He was dressed in a white tee-shirt worn under a black Cashmere coat and faded jeans. A handsome kid, with shoulder length black hair, I guessed he couldn't be more than sixteen or seventeen.

I don't know why I told Edith to stop. I knew Edith made it a rule never to pick up hitchhikers she did not know. I can't blame her. You can never be too careful today. It wasn't such a risk to pick up hitchhikers when I was a girl growing up in central Connecticut in the late 1940s. Of course, you didn't want to be foolish about it; no time is ever completely free of crime. But back then you just didn't give a second thought about giving a ride to a stranger. They were mostly servicemen and casual crime was unheard of.

"Let's pick him up," I said.

"What for?" Edith answered from behind the wheel.

"I know him," I lied. "Stop the car."

Her foot struck the brake and we all rushed forward in the stopping: Edith, myself, and my Soft-Coated Wheaten Terrier, Sonny.

Sonny took the worst of the brakes, sliding off the back seat onto the floor. He didn't make a sound other than to give off a few grunts while pulling himself back up.

The boy came running up to the car, and tossed a cigarette to the ground after a final drag.

When he opened the door, Sonny growled.

The boy hesitated. Felt for something in his coat pockets.

"Sit up front," I offered, and I went out and joined Sonny in the back seat. The boy got in front. Edith smiled at him, then she looked at me in the rearview mirror. I suppose her look was to ask me for introductions, but I ignored her.

"Step on it, Edith," I said. I could see her brow furl and then her foot found the gas and Sonny and I lurched back.

"Where are you going?" I asked. "Town," the boy said in a low, vanilla voice, a bit lower in pitch than you'd expect for his age.

I leaned forward and Sonny leaned with me.

"Do you live nearby?" I asked, then winced when Edith's head jerked.

"Green Hill Road."

He'd turned to face Edith when he said it, and showed

me a perfect profile, the kind of a profile leading men used to have, or that of a young prince in a children's picture book.

"We're looking for Middle Beach Road. Is that close by?"

"It's past the center of town. You don't live in Madison?"

"We've only been here one other time."

Sonny had now decided he liked the boy and kept climbing over my lap to nose up to the back of his head.

"Where are you ladies from?"

"New Britain," I said, pulling on Sonny's collar.

"New Britain," he repeated. "I know where that is. My counselor's taken me to places there. He's taken me all over Connecticut. Hartford, Storrs, Bolton, even Long Lane in Middletown."

Edith made another spastic movement, and I leaned farther forward to avoid the mirror. The boy hadn't said it, but we both knew what Long Lane was. The state's infamous youth prison.

He paused a moment, as if he wanted to say more, then turned toward the windshield.

Edith cleared her throat.

"Yes, Middle Beach Road," I repeated. "A friend told us it's a beautiful road in the winter."

"You came all the way here to see a road?" He said.

"Yes. We go for a Sunday drive every Sunday. Do you do that with your family? A Sunday drive?"

He shook his head. And his left hand came up to satisfy Sonny's curious nose.

"I don't do anything with my family," he said.

"That's a shame. We're all too busy these days, aren't we? There's a TV in almost every room so we sit apart, and e-mail and text messaging so we don't have to look at anyone. My family couldn't afford a single television when I was a girl. We used to gather around a radio and listen to programs together."

"My family never does anything together. I guess we just don't care about sh—uh –stuff like that."

"They *must* care about *you*."

"They don't care about me."

"Maybe you're not giving them a chance."

He didn't answer, so I imagined I was sounding like someone else in his life who'd offered advice without knowing anything of what was going on inside his head.

We rode a few more minutes in silence, the winter air blustering past. I was watching the yellow sun flashing in the bare trees when he said, "That's it."

"That's what?" said Edith.

"Green Hill Road. Just ahead," he said, pointing. "That's where my house is."

Edith stopped the car at the end of Green Hill Road. We sat there in the warm, hushed interior for a moment, looking at Edith: me, the boy, and Sonny. Sonny then lost his interest in Edith and nuzzled up to the boy again. I pulled Sonny back and searched for Edith's expression in the mirror.

"*So*," Edith finally said, with purposeful slowness, "you live on *Green Hill Road*." She looked at the road that meandered between the tall oaks and large modern colonials with sweeping front lawns in the distance.

"Yes . . . but . . . I really wanted to go into town. I was just showing you were my mother lives."

"Where's town?" I chimed in.

"Straight ahead. A few more miles."

"*Edith*," I said almost as an order. She shook her head and punched the gas.

We drove about a half-mile in silence before I said, "Do

you go to school in Madison?"

Of course, he did. He *lived* in Madison. I said it just to break the silence.

"Not anymore," he answered.

"When did you graduate?"

"I didn't."

"You dropped out?"

"Yeah. A month ago." He paused again, this time finishing. "And I feel good. I finally made up my mind. I'm free."

I didn't even look for Edith's reaction.

I finally let Sonny up again to sniff at the boy's left ear that was hidden under that waterfall of black hair.

The boy turned to Sonny, smiled, and put his hand up to scratch the side of the dog's head.

"I hope Middle Beach Road is this way," Edith said.

"It's south of town. I'll show you when we get there."

I enjoyed listening to the boy's voice. It was steady and low. Soft and gentle; curious to Sonny, who cocked his head every time the boy spoke. He had a man's voice, which really didn't fit a teenager. More fitting of a tall, dark lover; a voice to relish in intimate conversation, and yet a voice turned inward, as if it held back solemn thoughts, secrets never to be shared with anyone. Sonny listened to the boy's every word, his ears out like RCA Victor's Nipper listening to the sound of his master's voice. But even Sonny could not react to the boy's unspoken words. And yet Sonny seemed to have an understanding, a sense for the boy I knew Edith could not fathom and I could barely comprehend. What had started as protective growling when the boy first opened the car door had turned to approval with his tongue at the boy's ear. I let Sonny enjoy the boy, for he'd never lived with anyone but an old lady.

"A dog should have a boy," I said unintentionally. Both heads in the front seat turned in toward the center of the car. "I was just thinking aloud of Huck Finn and Tom Sawyer. Have you ever read those two books by Mark Twain?"

Both heads moved in different directions.

"I was supposed to, but I didn't," the boy said.

"Well, do you remember, Edith, reading about Huck or Tom ever having a dog?"

She paused a moment then shook her head.

"That's what I mean. Two quintessential early-American boys if there ever were, and neither one had a dog! Now, how do you account for that?"

I sat back and Sonny's broadside effectively blocked my view of the entire front seat.

"Maybe Mark Twain didn't like dogs," Edith said.

That made the boy laugh, and I laughed, and then Edith laughed, and the silence that followed the laughter was like the strange and sad silence left in a field that lingers after the carnival has gone away.

"It isn't right." A dog should have a boy. And Twain should have had dogs in his books, even if he didn't like them. You know, that's bothered me ever since I read Twain. And now Sonny is telling me I might very well be right. I take it no dog has you, young man?"

"No," he said softly.

"Well, see, that isn't right!"

"Too late now."

His words repeated in my ears. I couldn't help but imagine that, perhaps, if the boy had had a dog, he would feel differently about himself. How could such a gentle, polite boy need a psychiatrist? I know that's what he was really saying when he mentioned his "counselor." Blame neglectful parents. Blame the lack of dogs. Curse it all. How could it happen to so many young people? It broke my heart. But this kid had his reasons for feeling lost, for dropping out of school, for needing professional help. I can imagine for some young people the world is always falling apart.

The car stopped.

Edith turned to face the boy directly for the first time.

"This looks like town," she said.

"Middle Beach Road," he said, "is down this main road, about a mile. Turn left at the Madison Golf Course. The second left is Middle Beach."

The boy opened the door and stepped out into the cold rush of air. He turned and stuck his head back in.

"Thanks for the ride," he said, in that low, summer voice.

Sonny leapt from my arms and bounded into the front seat. He reached out to the craned-over boy and licked him on the mouth.

"Sonny!" I shouted, and pulled at his tail. I couldn't apologize enough. Who, for heaven's sake, would want to be kissed on the mouth by a dog?

The boy straightened and smiled. He gave Sonny one last scratch over the ears, smiled at me with those sleepy brown eyes, then paused to check for something in his pockets.

"Did you lose something?"

"No. All set. Thanks."

He closed the door then wandered away.

Edith and I drove down the main road, following the directions he had given us. Once we arrived at Middle Beach Road we savored its stark winter beauty with a slow Sunday drive.

On the way home that evening, I put the nameless boy with the long black hair and handsome face into the back of my mind.

The next morning Edith called and told me to turn on the television news. Sonny and I sat before the screen. Lucky for Sonny, he did not understand the reporter's words and he could not feel what I felt then. Beside the grainy photo of the victim, the announcer told of how a youth, aged 16, had been struck and killed by a train late yesterday afternoon.

"Apparent suicide."

No name was given, pending full notification of his next of kin. No name was needed.

The train engineer told police the boy sat on the tracks, staring the train down, until the last minute when he put his head down on his knees.

I held Sonny close.

The Ragged Edge

William F. Nolan

As usual, Linda had remembered to have the thermos re-filled at the last coffee stop just before dawn, and now Robert March held the steaming metal cup in his two hands, grateful for the steady warmth in the early morning. A clouded sun was just breaking over the tall trees fringing the track, and March inhaled the rich, moist scent of pine, carried to him by the chill ocean wind off the Pacific.

"At least we're good and early," he said to his wife.

Linda March smiled. She was a small-boned delicate woman with soft brown hair combed loosely back from a high forehead. "I knew we would be," she said.

March thought of his first race here at Pebble Beach last year, when they had arrived late at the track, and he had almost failed to run. This weekend would be different.

This weekend, he vowed, *must* be different.

Ahead of him, across the uneven ground, the long wooden inspection rabies were already up, and girls in blue coveralls had arranged themselves in canvas chairs behind their charts and papers. Standing by the open door of the Chrysler, March sipped his coffee and watched the low-slung sports cars being pushed into line for technical inspection. His own machine, the March Special, was third behind a white Jaguar coupe.

"I'd better get on over there," March said, handing Linda his empty cup. "Keep the coffee hot."

"Tell Randy to put on his sweater," Linda instructed him, reach- ing into the Chrysler's rear seat for the garment. "It's windy this morning.

As March walked toward the inspection grid, he thought about the Special, about what the race tomorrow really meant to him. He thought of Bakersfield and the broken fuel pump in the fourth lap, of Santa Barbara and the wheel he'd lost on the hairpin, of Torrey Pines and the sudden, terrible dip of the pressure needle, telling him that his oil was gone; he thought of the long, uphill turn at Willow Springs, when the rear axle had broken and he'd spun out. And he thought, finally of the big one last year, right here at Pebble Beach, when he'd been doing fine, coming up steadily through the pack, and the transmission had blown. Always something. *Something.*

You're a doctor, March told himself, a family man of forty with a fine wife and two nearly-grown sons. You don't belong in sports car racing and you know it. You're in it because you wanted to prove that you could take a car you'd built yourself and finish with the best of them. Well, you've tried; for a year now you've tried, and you've failed. You haven't finished *one* race, not one. So, why go on playing the fool?

"Hi, Dad!" The voices of his twin sons, Glenn and Randy, cut into his thoughts.

"Hi, boys," he grinned. "We're up next, aren't we?"

"Yeah. Give us a hand, Dad."

March tossed Randy's sweater into the cockpit and helped his two sixteen-year-old sons push the big blue Special into the slot vacated by the Jag.

March handed the check-off sheet to inspector Bill Greer. "Think you'll blow off all the competition to-morrow, Doc?" asked the beefy little man, beginning his methodical safety check. He chuckled softly.

"Don't worry about Dad, Mr. Greer," Randy said stiffly. "Just let the other drivers do the worrying."

March could see that Randy was upset.

How do you feel, wondered Robert March, when you've got a father who never finishes? The boys had helped him put the Special together, worked with him on every detail, pitching in after school and on weekends to get the car ready. And then-eleven races and he'd never crossed the finish line. The constant ribbing from the other drivers had been hard to take, and he could see that Randy and Glenn were badly shaken by each new disaster. For them, the scorn and barbed humor cut deep.

Then why go on? Even Linda, who understood him completely, was beginning to worry. She knew the risks he took out there on the track, and accepted them calmly because that was her nature, but even Linda was concerned now over the boys. She had watched them become nervous and unhappy as the months went by, as the failures mounted, and she was worried.

All right, then, tomorrow would be the last one, the last time he'd race the Special. After tomorrow, if he couldn't finish with the car, he would quit for good. He'd give himself and the Special one more chance.

"Okay, Doc," said Bill Greer, checking off the last item on the sheet, "take 'er away."

Inside the cockpit, March jabbed the starter button and the big modified Mercury engine boomed fiercely into life under the long hood.

"She sounds sweet," Randy said, as they rolled toward the pits. "Real sweet."

Saturday practice was scheduled to begin immediately after the noon drivers' meeting, and already the crowds were pressing in, filling the grandstands along the main straight, posting themselves behind the sloping wooden snow fencing which lined the entire course, settling down with blankets and food and programs, wait- ing to see their favorite drivers and cars bullet over the treacherous 2.1 mile Pebble Beach circuit.

March was glad that the entire afternoon had been given over to practice. Here was the most beautiful and the most dangerous circuit on the West Coast, slightly over two miles of narrow blacktop, twisting through thick forest above exclusive Del Monte Lodge, with a deadly proportion of uphill and downhill turns. The massed trunks of pine and cypress waited along every straight and curve, ready to crush car and driver. A serious mistake here could well prove fatal. Practice, at Pebble Beach, was very necessary.

"Clock my last three laps," March told his wife, as he climbed into the cockpit. "Up to then 1'11 just be feeling out the circuit." "Take it easy, hon," she warned him. "I've only got one of you." He was pulling on the white crash helmet when Lou Coppard walked over to the Special. Tall and relaxed with the lean face of a wolfhound, Coppard had been openly contemptuous of March from the beginning. He never missed an opportunity to needle him about the Special.

"How's the patient, Doc?" he asked, grinning crookedly. "She'll live," March said, his voice edged and cold.

"I should have remembered to bring Rowers." "Save 'em, Lou. Maybe you'll need 'em yourself."

"How long do you figure she'll stay pasted together out there, Doc?" Coppard asked, the grin still fixed on his lean face.

"Long enough," March replied, and decided against adding more. Don't let him get at you today, he told himself. Tomorrow, out on the track, maybe you can take him and settle the score.

The starter gave the signal to move and Coppard returned to his car. March eased the big Special through the pit gate and onto the starting grid.

As he was flagged away he forced himself to think only of the track, of how soon he needed to downshift for the uphill hairpin, of his best line through the fast corners, of when he needed to use the brakes and when he didn't.

He had a lot to learn before tomorrow.

In the late evening dusk Robert March walked back to the hotel, smoking, moving leisurely over the darkening streets, allowing himself to be caught up in that rare atmosphere characterizing such a weekend. Tonight, the small towns along the length of California's Monterey Peninsula were transformed, magically charged with a festive pre-race electricity. In dozens of shop windows tall posters boldly announced: PEBBLE BEACH SPORTS CAR ROAD RACES. Neoned NO VACANCY signs glowed above every roadside motel and the streets were filled with the ragged thunder of sports cars, a veritable sea of out-of-towners gunning their swift machines through traffic, shattering the cool night air with their loud exhausts.

Practice had gone well at least. The Special had performed perfectly throughout the entire session; she seemed ready for her biggest try. March had lapped within a second or two of some of the hottest pilots, proving the Special had the juice if she'd only hold. She'll hold, March told himself, because this is her last chance; tomorrow she's *got* to hold.

Sunday morning dawned hot and clear at the track, with no hint of the rain that had been threatening all week. The sun rode down a cloudless blue sky, filtering through the trees in checkered patches of light and shade.

Robert March had spent the early part of the day on the wind- ing cliff roads above the Pacific, relaxing with Linda in the cool breeze from the ocean.

He told her of the decision he'd made.

'1f I don't finish today, I'm quitting, Linda. Things can't go on this way."

"Are you sure, Bob? Is it what you really want?"

"Yes, I'm sure. You can't go on beating your head against a stone wall and expect the wall to give. This is my last try."

She had looked at him silently for a long moment, then taken his hand firmly in hers. "Whatever you *really* want is what I want too. I won't worry, no matter what you decide, I promise. Just remember that, darling."

They arrived at the track after the Cypress Point Race had been run.

March left Linda with Randy and Glenn in the pit and walked over to have a look at Jeffry Moore's Monza Ferrari. Moore was a nice guy, and a hell of a driver. Whenever he was out there with the Ferrari the competition had something to worry about.

The car was undergoing wheelwork. The low, scooped snout of the fierce Italian car almost touched the ground, the sweeping lines of the compact body proclaiming sheer speed. Of course the Monza had been geared down for Pebble, but it would be reaching 130 on the back straight, and that was moving. However, Moore would have to reckon with Fischer's powerful D-type Jaguar and Wyndham's Maserati. A furious three-way battle to the checkered flag was in prospect.

"Going to ride her all the way home today, Doc?" asked a familiar voice, and March turned to face Jeffry Moore, resplendent in immaculate white coveralls. Like most of the aces, Moore wore his fame with a casual indifference, but behind the easy smile, behind the friendly squint of the narrow gray eyes, March was aware of the nervous pulse of electricity which only the track could completely remove. Only on the track, screaming down a long straight or fighting a tight curve, could a man like Moore wholly become himself.

"I'm going to try to keep you boys in sight," March replied. "I figure the Special is as ready as she'll ever be."

'That's just it, Doc," said Moore, his tone serious. 'We all give you the business about the Special, but I, for one, hate to see a guy knock himself out for nothing. The car hasn't got it. She's full of bugs and bad luck, and you know it. We all know it. If you want to race then get into a car that will give you an even break. Right now Ray Boucher has one of his Ferraris up for sale. You could handle her, Doc."

"Thanks, Jeff, but I've got other plans."

"Okay. Hope she holds for you today."

"Yeah," said March. "I hope so too."

The furnace-heat of the sun seemed focused on the starting grid as the glittering line of cars rolled slowly into position for the last race of the day. This was the main event, the one the crowds had been waiting for. In just a few breathless moments the green Bag would drop on thirty-two of the world's fastest sports cars, on one and a half hours of all-out driving for the coveted Del Monte trophy.

From his assigned position in the fourth row, next to a modified Healey 100S, Robert March could feel the tension, a thing alive, growing around him.

"You stick wither, Dad," Randy was saying. He patted the lean aluminum shell of the Mere-powered Special. "She'll go all the way for you this time, I *know* she will."

"You'd better get on back with Linda and Glenn," March said, as the clear-grid order crackled over the high black cluster of loudspeakers. They shook hands and Randy stepped away.

So, here we are, thought Robert March, Hexing and un8exing his gloved hands on the spidery racing wheel. This is the last one, the one that really counts. He adjusted his goggles against the raw glare of sun on polished metal and waited.

A gradual silence fell upon the crowds in the grandstand and along the length of wooden snow fence fronting start-finish.

Tensely they waited for starter Al Tucker to begin his final check- run down the line of cars.

The sun lay on March's neck and shoulders, a hot, blazing weight, pressing him deeper into the bucket seat. Already the sweat had soaked through the back of his coveralls, and the safety belt felt like a band of steel across his hips. Damn it, Tucker, let's get the show on the road! Every second he sat there in the broiling heat, a taut spring was winding itself tighter within his body.

He thought of the men and machines around him, of Al Fischer in the incredibly fast D-Jag, of Jeff Moore's Monza Ferrari, of Wyndham in the Maserati. What a battle these three would wage! He thought, too, of Tim Mulford's huge 4.9 Ferrari. Tim might take an early lead with the brutish car, but he would be unable to hold it on a tight course like Pebble. Chuck Quavale in the Buick-Kurtis was always a solid threat. Finally, March thought of Lou Coppard. He could see Lou's face, framed in the rear-view mirror. His black Cadillac-powered Special was two rows back, on the inside. The rest of the lead-foots could battle it out for the cup; March only wanted two things in this race. He wanted to finish—and he wanted Coppard's scalp.

He pulled his helmet strap tight and forced his full attention to Al Tucker as the little man signaled start-engines.

The sudden thunder of thirty-two finely tuned racing engines washed over the grid, the sharp roar of the Buick-Kurtis blending with the knifing shriek of the Ferraris. Every eye was on Al Tucker as the harlequin-shirted little man fell into his jogging Indian-run down the line of poised machinery. March raised a gloved hand to let Tucker know he was ready and firing.

At the end of the line Tucker pivoted gracefully and

loped back to the front row, the green flag furled and ready in his hand. He paused dramatically, back to the drivers. The engines screamed. Only seconds now.

I've been here for a century, thought Robert March, belted to a tiger, waiting. Dear God, man, will you *jump?*

Tucker leaped high into the air and the green flag swirled free. The taut spring in Robert March's body uncoiled. He mashed down on the gas pedal and felt the dizzying surge of acceleration as the massive Special rocketed forward.

He saw Tim Mulford's big Ferrari rip into the first sweeping tum just ahead of Fischer's D-Jag. Moore and Wyndham went in snapping at the leaders' heels. Just ahead of March, Chuck Qua- vale powered his Buick-Kurtis in wide, passing two slower machines in the apex of the turn.

March was seventh coming out of turn 3 into the winding, uphill hairpin, and he was hanging on to Quavale. As they roared through the dogleg bend Lou Coppard's black Cad-Special whipped into sight in his rearview mirror. So, he wants his dice early, eh? thought March. All right, Lou, make your bid. I'm ready.

He'd planned on conserving his brakes through the beginning laps, but now he saw this was not possible if he wished to take Coppard.

They swung into the long back straight, down through turn 6, and swept full-throttle past the pits and grandstand. A rough circuit, March thought, a really mean one.

They boomed past Donaldson's stalled VS-60 Special on the main straight with Coppard pressing hard, a scant two car-lengths to March's rear. On the short, twisty stretch into the hairpin, the cut-off markers jumped at them, and March braked, dumping into a lower gear for the tight corner. Coppard moved up another two feet.

The tachometer needle climbed crazily as March floored the pedal on the long back straight. The straining Mere engine shrilled under full-throttle, and the haybales, solid as stones at this speed, flashed by in a yellow-bright pattern under the sun. Behind the bales the threatening bulk of trees blurred with speed into a single dark line.

A modified Triumph had spun into the bales on turn 6, and March was forced to cramp the wheel hard right to avoid an accident. He saw Coppard slew by, barely missing the derelict car. The pace quickened.

Coppard, driving at the peak of his form, closed to within a half car-length on the front straight, and March wondered if he could hold him through the dogleg at this speed.

At that precise instant Coppard's right rear tire blew, with a flat crack, sharp as a rifle shot, and the black Special skidded across the width of the track, spun twice, and came to rest with the other three tires smoking.

As he entered the first sweeping bend March could see Lou Coppard, obviously unhurt, gesturing wildly to his pit crew. By the time he could get a new tire on the car March would be half a lap ahead. The dice was over.

All right let's start saving those brakes, March told himself.

You've got better than an hour left to run.

On the next lap, as he swept past the pits, he caught the chalked numeral on the blackboard that Randy held out for him. P-6. Which meant he had emerged from the dice in sixth position!

He recognized Mulford's 4.9 Ferrari in the pits; Tim, of course, had pushed too hard. That meant Fischer in the D-Jag was leading somewhere up ahead, probably followed by

Moore's Ferrari and Wyndham's Maserati. He could see Quavale's Kurtis and Gene Waring in the C-Jag ahead of him as he entered the back straight. He was running sixth, behind Waring.

March felt the heat from the straining engine fire up along his legs; he inhaled the bitter-sharp scent of burned rubber and hot oil—and he thought, by God, she's holding, she's doing fine.

Forty-two minutes to go.

According to Randy's pit board he was now picking up on Gene Waring at the rate of three seconds a lap.

He was still closing when Waring's car hit a patch of spilled oil, fishtailed wildly, and slid into the bales.

March roared by into fifth place.

He began to push harder, moving up on Quavale, lapping slower machines, using the car as a fencer uses a foil, darting and slashing around the 2.1 mile circuit

Quavale fell back with every curve. Out of 3 March drew abreast and passed the big Kurtis in a short, savage burst of speed, using every inch of the narrow blacktop to get by.

He was fourth.

By God, you've taken one of the really hot boys. Let's keep moving. He could see Jerry Wyndham in the blue Maserati breaking early for tum 6, and Randy's pit board told him the story. Wyndham was running out of brakes! Okay, then, let's get him!

Brake, downshift, accelerate, upshift, accelerate, brake. Over and over until his wrists ached, until his mouth was cotton-dry, and his eyes burned through the dusty goggles. Closing.

Closing.

And behind March, another threat. Sifting masterfully through the pack, Lou Coppard had driven his black Cad

Special to within a quarter-lap of March. Since the tire change, Coppard had passed all of the slower cars and was trying for another bid.

I can hold Lou, March told himself; he hasn't enough time to catch me unless something goes on the Mere. So, let's get that Maserati!

Wyndham was forced to slide through the curves, skimming the haybales with his rear wheels, fighting for control. March picked up another foot out of the third turn.

The two cars swept into the back straight, a pair of twin projectiles shot from giant cannon. March's foot was hard *to* the *floor,* a part of the machine itself, draining every ounce of power from the laboring engine. Through the separate leather flesh of the driving gloves he felt the wheel's rock-firmness in his hands.

I can take him at the end of the straight, March decided. He'll have to back off early to save what little brake he has left, and I'll pass him into the turn.

As the 5-4-3-2-1 cut-off markers leaped at them, Wyndham's brake lights went on and March blistered past, stabbed the brake pedal, snapped a quick downshift and drifted the turn, all four tires screaming. Wyndham fell in behind him.

With fifteen minutes remaining in the race, Robert March was third.

Randy's pit board told him he was almost three-quarters of a lap behind the second-place Monza of Jeffry Moore, and was about to be lapped by the leading D-Jag.

At least he'd been able to make Glenn and Randy proud of him, and of the Special. Now all he had to do was hold.

March saw the D coming up fast in the rear-view mirror. Fischer would lap him into turn 3, so March cut wide for the turn, braked early, and waved him in.

Engine howling, Fischer scalded by. March saw the Jag's brake lights wink on as Fischer began his slide. Suddenly, at the apex of the turn, the black car seemed to explode. Orange flame gouted from the engine compartment, and Fischer, blinded by smoke, lost control, mashing into the stacked bales, bursting through in fiery petals of burning hay.

March slowed, saw Fischer leap from the twisted machine, saw the flagmen rush forward with extinguishers—and then he was around the next turn and moving away.

Robert March was second.

Look at your hands, March told himself, *look* at them! You're trembling like a novice in his first race. He felt the sweat, sour on his lips and under his goggles, felt it flushing over his body like a coating of warm oil. Fischer's okay. He's all right, so come out of it and drive. *Drive!*

He glanced in the rear-view mirror. Coppard! The Hying Special was only a car-length behind him. Lou had taken neat advantage of Fischer's spin to move up fast.

As they flashed by the pits Randy held the board high and a single, hastily chalked word stood out in bold relief against the black: GO!

March, furious at his own weakness, began to drive deeper into the turns, braking at the last possible instant, drifting to the edge of the bales. Coppard, unable to maintain the pace, dropped back.

Ten minutes remaining; ten minutes to hold his position.

Then March saw the red Ferrari of Jeffry Moore off the track and deserted! The car had thrown a front wheel and Moore had retired. With a cold shock of surprise Robert March realized he was now in first place!

So, he thought, you've driven the Special, the car

they all laughed at, the car that never finished, into the lead-and they're all behind you, Waring and Quavale and Coppard, all of them. An hour ago all you wanted to do was finish and look at you now. Winning.

Winning!

As he roared over the sun-splashed macadam, under the dark wash of trees, past the flickering faces of the cheering crowd, Robert March felt suddenly cold; a chill sense of loss began to build within him.

If he won this race, March knew, things would never be the same. If he won today, his victory could never be erased in the minds of the crowd. He would no longer be "ole Doc," the poor, unlucky guy to cheer for, he would be the man to beat. *A* winner had to keep on winning. If I take this race they'll say, "He did it once, why can't he do it again?" How many times would Wyndham's brakes fail, or Fischer's Jag catch fire, or Moore's Ferrari throw a wheel-all in the same race? Sure, today had been a freak affair from the beginning, but that wouldn't matter to the crowd. And it wouldn't matter to Randy or Glenn. They'd want to see me do it again, and when I lost I'd just be a fool in a slow car. I just can't *let* myself win today.

Starter Al Tucker gave him the blue flag as he passed the main grandstand. One more lap to go.

Robert March made up his mind. If you've got no business at the head of the table, move aside for the man who has.

It would be simple, really. All he needed to do was keep his foot on the gas for a second too long. Every curve has a ragged edge. If you push your car beyond the ragged edge, beyond the point of minimum tire adhesion, you lose control. Beyond the ragged edge you spin out, and there is nothing you can do about it.

Let Coppard have the race. If his luck held, he could re-enter and finish behind the leaders.

Coming down the back straight at full-throttle, Robert March watched the cut-off markers growing in the distance. 110 miles per hour. Tiny dots, growing larger with speed. 112. Becoming sharp and legible. 115. Easily readable now. His speedometer needle bumped 120 miles per hour.

When he was certain that he could never make the tum, when he was sure he had held the pedal down long enough, Robert March tramped the brake, down-shifted, snapping the stubby gear-lever into place, and began his drift.

He caught a single, quick glimpse of Lou Coppard entering the far end of the straight. Okay, Lou, take her away. She's yours.

He felt the car breaking away into the long slide which would carry it into the bales. Now he was no longer master, no longer in control; he was simply a weight the machine carried with it to- ward the packed bales, a soft, helpless weight which could be crushed instantly to death or burned to sudden ash.

And then, in that long, dream-like slide, March realized why he was allowing this to happen.

Because he was *afraid.*

He was afraid of the truth about racing and what it actually meant in his life. He'd kept it carefully hidden from Linda and the boys, even from himself, but now he faced it.

You race for only one reason, March told himself. Not just to prove you can finish with a car you built yourself, not to have the crowds cheer because they feel sorry for you—you race to *win.* You really didn't know, until today, if you had the guts to get out and drive the way a winner must drive. Now you know. You proved you can match the best of them, so it's time to stop fooling yourself. You're in racing because you've *got* to be in it, because it's a thing you love—and if you throw away your big chance now you'll keep on being afraid to do what you really want to do. You were worried about Linda, about what she would say, but remember her words before the race: *"Whatever you really want is what I want too."* You stuck with the Special because you knew it wouldn't win, because you could put the truth aside in such a car. How could you win if you never finished? Jeffry Moore had been right when he told you to get the Ferrari.

So, all right. Why throw this race when you have it in the palm of your hand? Win today and then buy that Ferrari Boucher has for sale. Drive this damn car out of the turn and take the checkered flag because that's what you've wanted all along. Let's GO!

In that timeless, suspended instant between the beginning and the end of the slide, all these thoughts flickered through his mind like quick images on a screen.

Then the Special's rear deck struck the first bale. March felt the car tipping, poised for a roll, and he instinctively lowered his head. But the Special maintained balance. It crashed back on its wheels, spun around twice and slid to a smoking halt, facing the straight, the engine stalled and silent.

Down the straight at full-bore came Lou Coppard, leaning over the wheel, a crooked victory grin on his grease-blackened face.

The flagmen were frantically waving March back on the circuit; another second and it would be too late.

If only she fires, breathed March, punching the starter button, if only the bales didn't finish her! With a dry cough, the Mercury came to life and Robert March bulleted onto the track just as Coppard began his drift.

The scream of the crowd was lost in the savage thunder of racing engines as the two cars roared out of the turn wheel to wheel. Lou Coppard had the edge. With a stabbing burst of acceleration, he passed March out of the bend into the front straight.

Far ahead, the late afternoon sun glinting on the gaudy silk of his shirt, Al Tucker crouched with the checkered Bag ready at his side, squinting down the long strip of blacktop at the two leaders. Coppard, his mouth now hard and unsmiling, his foot mashing the pedal, led March by half a car-length at the pits, but it was not enough. In the final one hundred feet, with the crowd wild and shouting his name, Robert March edged past the streaking black Cad Special to take the checkered Bag.

The Pebble Beach Del Monte Cup was his.

He saw them coming, Linda and the boys, running across the track to meet him as he rolled the Special slowly into the winner's circle.

He wasn't sure exactly what he would say to Linda. How do you tell a woman that you've suddenly discovered another force in your life as strong as she is—that you need both, deeply, genuinely, each in a different way?

Robert March watched his wife push through the crowd, waving, smiling, tears in her eyes, and he thought: perhaps I won't have to tell Linda anything.

Perhaps she already knows.

Headed Toward Town

T.M. Jacobs

A train barreled down the tracks kicking up dirt and leaves. Parallel to the tracks, along a gravel road, Ted Clayton shielded his eyes from the debris. Dressed in faded jeans, a white T-shirt, and a leather jacket, he walked at a steady pace. As he glanced over his shoulder, in the distance he could see a truck through the blurriness of the heat. A few minutes passed and Ted turned around, walked backward, and leveled his thumb. "Right on time," he said aloud, but under his breath. His greasy, long black hair blew in the wind. A rusted pick-up truck approached, leaving a trail of dust in its wake. The driver stopped beside him.

"Where ya headed, fella?" the driver shouted through the open passenger window.

"Ah. . . Just into town."

"Wanna lift, fella?"

"Yeah. Sure, man." Ted climbed into the pick-up, slammed the door, then fixed his hair out of his eyes.

"What ya do'n down these parts? Ya lost, fella?" the driver asked, as he ground into first gear. The truck bucked a couple of times before it got up to speed.

Ted checked his watch, looked out the window at the scenery as it passed by, then glanced over at the driver. He drew in a deep breath. "Well, I don't think anyone will find out, but. . . I . . .ah. . . killed someone back there."

The driver locked up the brakes and the truck skidded to a stop. A cloud of dust swirled about. "Ya darn did what?"

"I killed someone," Ted answered in a languid tone. "He was giving me a ride into town, and I just couldn't take it anymore. So, I killed him."

"Mind tell'n me your story from the start, fella. What's this hogwash 'bout ya kill'n someone?"

Ted reached into the jacket pocket. The driver, an older man wearing more wrinkles than clothes, quickly slid up against his door and kept his eyes on Ted. "Relax, man. I'm just getting a smoke. Care for one?" Ted extended the pack forward with a cigarette jetting out.

"No thanks, fella," the driver replied still catching his breath. "What's your name? And who did ya kill? An' why?

Ted blew out a cloud of smoke. "First off, the name's not Fella, it's Ted." He inhaled deeply on his cigarette and exhaled a large puff of smoke. "Like I said before, this guy was giving me a ride into town, and I just couldn't take it anymore."

Another train shot by at top speed. Ted took one long drag on his cigarette. It turned to ashes down to the butt. He flicked it out the window. "Are we going to head toward town or just sit here and shoot the shit?"

"Not go'n nowhere until ya start tell'n me why ya darn went and killed somebody back there?"

Ted rubbed his hand over his almost fully bearded face and let out a sigh. "What's your name, *Fella*?"

"Why it's Joe. Joe Henderson. Now, mind tell'n me why ya went and killed this guy."

"Well, Joe, this guy just sort of rubbed me the wrong way. We didn't get along."

"Watcha mean by ya all didn't get along?"

"How about I tell you as you drive this hunk of shit into town?"

"Let me be the first to tell ya, this certainly ain't no hunk of—"

"Shut up!" Ted snapped. "Just drive goddammit!"

Joe fumbled with the keys, restarted the truck, and ground the gears. The back tires spun as he let the clutch out in a rush.

Ted lit up another cigarette and took a long drag.

"Now," says Joe clearing his throat. "About what happened back there?"

"Well, I was hitchhiking along the Interstate and this car pulled along the side of the road. We must have been about twenty miles from town, in the middle of nowhere."

"That's still no reason to go and pluck a fella."

"The radio was on," Ted continued. "When an announcement came over the air about an escaped murderer. The description and whereabouts of the guy matched this guy to a tee. I feared for my life."

"Are ya going to inform the authorities or just let the fella rot back there?"

"Why should I? I don't think anyone will find out." Ted reached into his boot and pulled out a flask. He unscrewed the cap, brought the container up to his nose, and sniffed it leisurely. He glanced over at Joe with a smile. "I know you must enjoy this, fella." He held the flask up to his lips and took a swig. His head shook as the drink went down. "Sort of hits the spot."

Joe pulled the truck to the side of the road and grabbed the whiskey from Ted's hand. He tilted his head back and took three gulps before he passed it back.

An hour later, the flask was empty. Joe and Ted stumbled out of the truck as a train shot by like a bullet.

"When the next train goes by," Ted said in a slur, "I'll ... I'll ... I don't even know what I'm trying to say." He fell to the ground in a fit of laughter.

Joe started to laugh and walked toward Ted. As Joe climbed onto the tracks, Ted grabbed ahold of the railroad switch and pulled hard. It made a loud click as the rails maneuvered into place and caught Joe's foot. "My foot," he hollered. "Help me get my darn foot. I'm stuck I tell ya. Help me!"

Ted walked up to Joe and stared at him with his black hardened eyes.

"Well," Joe said. "Help me, ya goat. Don't stand there like a barnyard fool, help me."

"Not until you tell me what you know."

Joe gave Ted a puzzled look mixed with worry. "What I know? I know nothin' other than my darn foot is stuck."

Ted lit up another cigarette and took a long drag, then flicked the ashes on Joe. He turned and looked down the tracks which led into town. The tracks stretched for miles and in the distance blurred together, looking as if they touched. A faint train horn blew in the distance.

Ted looked back at Joe. "If I were you, I'd start talking."

"I tell ya, I know nothin.' Just help me get my foot outa here."

Ted leaned down toward Joe. "You have a choice," he whispered in his ear. "Either talk or...."

The train horn sounded again.

"I told ya, I know nothin' other than my foot is stuck."

"Where's the money?"

"I know nothin' 'bout no money."

The train sounded again.

"Where's the fucking money?"

Joe twisted and turned trying to free his foot. "Look. I tell ya, I know nothin'. Just help me get my foot outa here."

"I'll find the money," Ted said. "And that train . . . will find you." He started to walk away.

"What's the big idea? Help me get my foot outa here! Don't leave me here!"

The train horn blew louder as Ted slammed the truck door. He ground it into first gear and raced down the gravel road. About a half-mile down the road, the train sped by with its horn going full blast. Ted leaned over and clicked on the radio.

"...and now an update on the wanted criminal responsible for the murder of a young man. Authorities need your help in locating Ted Clayton. He was last seen along Highway 10 but is now believed to be hiding out or traveling along secondary roads. Please report anything suspicious to your local law enforcement. He's considered armed and dangerous."

Ted looked at himself in the rear-view mirror, let out a sobering laugh, stomped on the gas pedal, and headed toward town.

Contrary Dreams

John Cassola

It's late November and I'm looking out the window at the birds all puffed out against the winter air. Some are crowded at the feeder, hungry beaks pecking at the seed. Others are just perched, watching the gray winter sky with half-closed eyes.

And I'm thinking.

I'm just thinking—the *last* time I had a precognitive dream was shortly before we moved to our new church in Torringford, Connecticut. My husband Dwayne's call to serve a new ministry brought us to this new state, which we'd only seen in movies and read about in magazines. As California residents all our lives we looked forward to becoming New Englanders; to enjoying clam chowder and lobster, autumn foliage, and those Currier and Ives winters.

It was during those months of anticipation for the move that I had my last precognitive dream—two dreams actually, within two months of each other.

The morning before the first I was standing in the narthex greeting the congregation members as they emptied the nave. Smiles and Sunday chitchat drifted from one person to the next as each stepped from Pastor Dwayne Nordlander to me. When Rudy Johnson took my hand I felt an odd sensation. Perhaps it was the look in his eyes, or the way he grinned at me weakly, a hint of tired spirit trembling on his lips when he said, "Good morning, Marlow. And may the Lord be with you, too."

That night I had the dream.

Rudy was leading a pale horse by the reins. He was walking in a field of tall grain in the sun-bright noon, and I was walking behind him, but he did not know I was there. I wanted to stop him. I felt something was wrong and I wanted to call out to him. But I could not speak in my dream. I woke the next morning, still feeling the odd chill the dream had given me; a discomfort that lasted the rest of the day.

The next day Dwayne received a call from Mrs. Huldean, a congregation member and good friend of the Johnsons'.

"Rudy's been stricken," Dwayne said to me from across the room while keeping his ear to the receiver.

By the time Dwayne got to the hospital, Rudy was dead.

"I didn't say anything," I told Dwayne that evening, "because I didn't want to worry anyone."

"I know you can't always go around telling people you have these dreams," Dwayne consoled. "Rudy was old. He hadn't been well recently. The Lord called him home."

I felt comforted by his words, as if he were not my husband just then but my pastor.

It was a judgment call. I didn't feel it necessary to worry Rudy's wife by telling her of my dream. In fact, every precognitive dream has been a secret, a burden I carry and share only with Dwayne and our children, now that they're young adults. All three are tight-lipped, to protect me as much as themselves. Not one of these precognitive dreams has ever been serious, until the case of Rudy, which yielded an outcome not preventable by reasonable means. I suppose some might think it terrible of me not to have warned the family so they could prepare, but the key word is *reasonable*. How do you stop an older, ill person from dying when it's his time? How can a person dare to interfere with such a natural law? I could never interfere unless I felt a grave urgency to do so.

Unplanned by me, and sometimes unwanted, God has given me a power, a special sight, and for the most part my role is as passive as that of a television viewer.

But all that changed on the last Wednesday before our move to Connecticut.

That evening Liz and Martin Gaynard sat at our table during the carry-in supper the members threw for our good luck farewell. Liz and I talked about all the good times we'd had over the past 10 years, and then we talked about our future plans. I had finally gotten everything sorted and ready for packing, giving away items we no longer needed, and Dwayne and I were looking forward to the long drive cross-country to Connecticut. Liz was going to fly down to see their oldest son at the University of Florida for a long weekend. Martin was very busy at the architectural firm, so it was planned that Liz would make the trip alone. She told me how excited she was because she hadn't travelled that far in years and her flight was just two days away.

That night brought the second dream.

I was sitting on the plane next to Liz. We were talking and enjoying each other's company on an otherwise uneventful flight when suddenly I heard a loud bang. A moment later I felt the weightless sensation of falling. Then I heard the tortured sound of ripping metal.

I awakened in a bed soaked in sweat, and I knew Liz was to be among the casualties.

"I think you should tell her," Dwayne persuaded at breakfast.

"But how? Nobody else knows I have these dreams. I can't do this alone."

"She leaves tomorrow. We'll go see Martin and Liz together. Tonight."

The Gaynard's were attentive but skeptical, and rightfully so. I expected their apprehension.

"It's probably nothing," I said, attempting to pacify. "Probably just a meaningless dream."

"Don't discount yourself," said Martin after I'd presented my case. "I would think listening to the minister's wife is about as close to the Lord's divine word as we can get without hearing it from the minister himself. Liz won't go."

We chuckled at his words, but the next evening turned out to be no laughing matter.

The plane went down.

I felt horrible guilt for not calling to warn the airline.

"You can't save the world," Liz Gaynard said, "but thank you! Thank you for saving me!"

After the move to beautiful northwestern Connecticut, after all the work of setting up the new ministry and a new home in a strange town among unfamiliar yet eager faces, I all but forgot that on occasion, unpredictably and unexpectedly, I can see the future through my dreams.

In those first few months I had lunch with the new ladies of the Catherine Circle, shook hands with the young and the old of this new congregation, and not one dream during our first year ever hinted itself as one to come true.

I grew complacent during this time. My life was full, as was Dwayne's. Our children were growing more independent now. Josh was in college and Sarah was just beginning her management career at a large commercial printing company. We busied ourselves with getting the new ministry into full swing and having the kids home on the holidays.

Life went on easily this way. And everyone we touched or met or saw was happy and healthy and involved in their own lives both in and away from the church family.

But ... last night I was unexpectedly restless. My head filled with confused, disjointed nightmares.

And now, early this morning, Dwayne is off to visit a few shut-in church members, and I'm sitting alone at the breakfast table watching the chilled birds scramble around our backyard feeder. I don't want to be alone. I can't remember a single dream from last night, but I feel nervous. And I feel some sort of entity deep in my heart, for I believe. . . I *believe* the precognitive dreams have started again.

~

It's late morning now. I'm at the grocery check-out line and a small boy is sitting in the carriage in front of me. He looks about the age Josh was when he came down with a fever so high that we rushed him to the hospital to prevent brain damage. He almost died. It hits me now. Last night's dream – I suddenly remember it, the first dream in over a year that truly frightens me, and I feel the sweat on my hands all over again.

Josh is at school. He takes ill suddenly. By the time Dwayne and I can get there, he's dead. The memory feels so real I could be having the dream right there in the grocery line. I can't break out of it. Somehow I manage to pay the clerk and wheel the grocery cart out to the car.

The car is cold inside. I shiver all the way home, not even remembering to push the dashboard lever toward HEAT.

Once home, my trembling fingers fumble for and dial the phone, and I wipe a cold sweat from my forehead with the back of my hand.

"Josh, are you all right? You feel fine? Don't overdo it. I'm just a little worried. No, everything's good here. Just thinking about you. A dream? Yes, I had one last night—but I'm not certain it means anything. Just be extra careful, and don't wear yourself down."

"I'll be fine, Mom," he assures me, and I'm reassured hearing his voice. He's a sensible kid. Dwayne and I don't worry about Josh. We certainly feel the same about Sarah. We don't worry.

~

Dwayne and I have been laughing. We've been talking in bed about the good times we used to have with our friends the Harvey's from our old church, when all our kids were still very young. It's probably only stuff that's funny to us because we lived it, but I'm feeling relaxed now, and sleepy.

"Pleasant dreams," Dwayne says, and turns out the light.

I feel the sudden darkness rush over me. It's like hands closing around an insect, and the insect is me. I'm walking inside the darkness, on warm skin, and I'm looking for a streak of light between the roof of fingers to crawl toward.

"Pleasant dreams," I hear Dwayne say again without him really saying it. Seems like I haven't heard him say that in years. It reminds me instantly of my mother. She always used to say that same thing after she'd tucked me in and told all the bad ghosts in the room to leave so I could sleep.

"Do you see any more?" she'd ask.

"Just one. Over there," I'd answer.

"Does he have orange fingernails?"

"Yes."

"And purple eyebrows?"

"Uh-huh."

"And blue hair?"

"Yup."

"Then he's a good ghost."

"Do good ghosts have blue hair?"

"Always. And he'll chase away any bad ghosts for you. He'll guard you all night long. Pleasant dreams, Marlow."

I was always able to sleep then. It was a nightly ritual, for the better part of a year.

But I don't have my mother to talk me out of my fears anymore. Playing that long-ago scene in my head helps now, but I'm really on my own.

~

Sarah is standing in the corner of a dark room. There is a large, gray machine in the opposite corner, but I don't notice what kind of machine. I move toward her because I feel something forcing me closer. Her back is to me. I go up to her. "Sarah? Sarah?" I keep saying. "What's wrong?"

She turns.

"It's gone, Mother," she says and looks down, weeping. "It's gone."

I look down too and I see her hand is missing. Cut clean off at the wrist. Her hand is gone! There's no blood, just a straight stump in which the flesh looks translucent like a skinned chicken cutlet ready for cooking.

I see the machine again in the far corner. It's an electric paper cutter with a blade the size of a guillotine.

I try to rush her to the emergency room, but I arrive instead ... fully awake and alone in bed, my heart pounding, my hands swimming in the empty sheets next to me.

Dwayne is gone.

I find Dwayne's note beside the coffee pot. It says he's off to early appointments. I'm forced to dwell on this dream alone. Even the bird feeder is vacant this morning. Both the yard and the house are desolate and cold.

I call Sarah. Her happy voice is very comforting, but our conversation is one-sided: I *hate* voicemail.

I hang up and think of Mom again. She was always a good ear and always had something encouraging to say. And suddenly she speaks clearly in my head, as if she were there in the room with me.

"Marlow, you're having dreams of the contrary. You're not seeing something bad happen to people, you're just wishing them good health."

My memory of her warm eyes is very clear now, clearer than ever before. Her voice is right here at the table. Perhaps she's right, even today, all these years later. These recent dreams are not prophetic at all. In fact, I'll bet she *is* right. Just contrary dreams, as she called them. Dreams about wishing Josh good luck in his studies and good health at school; wishing Sarah safety and success in her career.

How could anything happen to young people, anyway? And two of them from my own family? How could both get hurt, or worse? I dread to think it, let alone say it. It's not possible. So I feel much better hearing Mom's words. Even without her really being here, and hearing the words come only from my memories, I feel close to her. It's the closest I've felt to her since those nights she chased ghosts from my room and wished me pleasant dreams.

Dwayne is late this evening. I decide to nap for a while. I'm feeling unusually tired.

~

My father appears on Miss Griffin's porch stoop. I see him from my kitchen window, sitting below her kitchen door. He's wearing khaki shorts and a tee shirt. There's snow on the ground.

Next thing I'm walking across the yard to Miss Griffin's house to ask my father what he's doing there. He looks so good. He's smiling.

"Just sitting," he says.

"Would you like a cup of hot chocolate?" I offer. "I'll run in the house and get you one."

"No thank you, Marlow. I won't be here that long. I'm just passing through."

"Aren't you cold?" I ask him, and touch his arm. He feels warm.

"I don't get cold."

He looks at the sun-drenched snow without squinting.

"The grandkids okay?" he says.

"Fine."

"And Dwayne?"

"Everybody's doing well."

"That's good. Just great."

Finally, after some more small talk and just looking at each other, I ask him the obvious question.

"Dad, why are you here?"

He looks at me a second, then stares at Miss Griffin's kitchen door, then back at me.

"I've got to go now. I can't stay here."

"Don't go."

"I can't stay here. But don't worry, everyone will be all right."

He stands and walks across the yard, and inexplicably fades into nothingness as he reaches the street.

~

"I've had that dream before," I say to Dwayne that night at dinner.

"I remember. And Miss Griffin died how soon after?"

"Three weeks. But that was nine years ago, just after my father died. I can't figure it. Last night's dream was exactly the same from nine years ago except for one thing."

"What's that?"

"This time I touched him. I never got to touch him in the first dream. He felt warm. Such a cold day and he felt warm, like he was alive, and I was really touching his skin."

~

Dwayne says he wants to stay home for the evening. It's the first time I can ever remember his passing up a game of bridge. I decide to go without my partner. At the table I'm teamed with a replacement player, but I can't determine who it is. After winning the rubber with my stand-in partner whom I never see, I'm on my way home. As I pull up to the house I see yellow flames curling like serpents' tongues from the windows.

I'm outside the car and I'm running for the neighbor's house across the street. No one is home. I'm suddenly inside looking out a bay window at my own house across the street. It's burning. My home is burning!

I look for the phone by the sofa, but there is no phone. The phone is really on the kitchen wall beside the refrigerator. I go for that phone to find I can't pick up the receiver. I reach and reach but can't grab it. Then I'm back at a rear window, looking at what should be a wall of oak trees. But instead, I see my home again, across the street, burning.

I run upstairs to find another phone. No phone upstairs. Yet I know my neighbor keeps a phone on her bedside table! I start back down the stairs and find I'm running down my own staircase toward my own living room. But I'm not running. I'm fighting, with all my strength, against a terrible wind that's blowing soundlessly up the stairs. Smoke chases past but doesn't burn my lungs or sting my eyes. I feel only the wind stealing my breath, drowning my calls to Dwayne.

Dwayne is sitting in the living room, reading. I can see him through the two-sided shelves filled with knick-knacks at the bottom of the stairs. I'm calling and calling to him as I fight the violent wind, but he's oblivious to the flames flashing up his legs.

The stairs are suddenly lined with white satin curtains swaying in the wind. It's all happening in slow motion. I feel I'm in a funeral parlor, sullen satin hung for my husband, who is dying in a fire he cannot feel.

I finally make it to the bottom of the stairs. The wind stops. I step into the living room. The flames are gone. This room is also draped in satin. And there's something else. The room is filled with what at first seem like dark brown sofas. Three sofas lined up like church pews, and then I realize they're not sofas – they're coffins.

Josh is lying in one, a peaceful look on his face. His features are very broad and flat, looking the way bodies in coffins look. A man is there, bending over my son's coffin, combing my son's hair.

The man, his back to me, glides over to the second coffin. My daughter lies there, looking equally molded for this singular event, like a waxen figure in a museum display. The mortician is applying color to her face, painting her cold limestone cheeks into a warm flesh glow. Dwayne is in the third coffin. The mortician adjusts my husband's sport jacket, and irons the lapels between his fingers.

Slowly then, realizing I am there, the mortician straighttens, takes a slow breath and turns to face me.

"Dad!"

"Don't be frightened, Marlow," he says, gently.

"What are you doing?"

"Taking care of them."

"That's my family. The only family I have left!"

"They were your family, Marlow. I'll watch over them now."

My father grins at me. I think it should be an evil grin, considering the way I feel, but it's a warm, comforting smile.

~

"I'd never miss a bridge game," Dwayne says with a laugh.

"I suppose I shouldn't worry. They're not like all the other precognitive dreams. These dreams are all convoluted and confused. They make no sense! I really don't think I'm looking at the future in any of these recent dreams. But they're so damned vivid. And I'm having them every time I fall asleep."

"Dreams of the contrary, remember," he says, trying to reassure.

"But why should I dream about my father sitting on Miss Griffin's doorstep, calling her to death, when he already did that nine years ago?"

"I think you're reading too much into it."

"And the other dreams. Why now, after not a single memorable dream for over a year?"

"Maybe that's exactly why. You're settled now. You have more time to yourself, and all those pent-up dreams are flooding forth."

"Is that supposed to be a Biblical reference?"

"Of course not. I just don't think these dreams mean anything."

~

It's morning, and Dwayne is away again. I don't know where he is. I'm not even sure he's not still in bed.

The phone rings.

I pick up the receiver.

"Hello," says the woman's voice on the other end, waiting for an answer. "Hello," she says again, and now I'm certain who it is.

I slam the receiver down.

~

"Dwayne!" I wake him up.

"Another dream?" he asks, sleepily.

"I couldn't talk to her. I just *couldn't.*"

"Talk to whom?" He sits up against the headboard.

"She called. In my dream. She only said 'hello,' twice, but I knew it was her. I couldn't talk to her. How could I? She's dead. My mother is dead!"

~

That last dream has me terrified. I've been thinking about it all day, and I'm now thinking about talking to a specialist. I can't handle this alone any longer.

The clock on the dashboard reads 5:31. The sun set an hour ago. Traffic is slow. I'm caught in the rush hour out of Hartford, headed west on route I-84, and freezing rain is pecking against the windshield. I intended to be home by four, but my appointments in the city kept me longer than planned.

Yes, I've decided, just now, I need to see a doctor. I never thought I'd be the kind of person who would need a psychiatrist for anything. I've always been able to handle everything on my own. But now I feel I have to talk to someone. I need to understand what all these nightmares mean.

Hopefully Dwayne isn't worried that I'm late. He's probably starting dinner now, from the instructions I left. But then again, maybe he's sitting in his study working on a sermon. Dwayne's not good in the kitchen. Some men are, but not my husband. Each of us follows our bent, our interests. We ignore the work we dislike, and give ourselves to the things we enjoy. And then, sometimes we're forced into situations against our own choices. We have to accept most things life hands us. And be happy despite our wishes. "It's all part of God's plan," Dwayne always explains.

Traffic is moving faster now. The sleet is a little heavier. It's turning to snow, covering the shoulders and the centerline where the cars aren't melting it.

I think precognitive dreams are an imposition on the private lives of those who are burdened with them. I used to believe they were a blessing. I thought I could help people, but I can't. I help so few compared to those I can never help that it doesn't really seem to matter either way.

These latest dreams make no sense. Not one is definitive. Not one has the form of all the other precognitive dreams I used to have before the move to Connecticut. But their persistence and clarity are unusual. They seem to have meaning, but I can't imagine exactly what they're trying to tell me.

I have to admit it. I've learned that Marlow Nordlander isn't really that strong after all. She's never *really* known how to handle any of these dreams. Dwayne tells me they're the gift of the Lord. That I've been given prophetic sight for a reason. That I'm in good company with some of the great Biblical prophets.

Maybe he's right. A dream did help me save my friend Liz Gaynard. Perhaps having saved just one life makes all the anguish worthwhile.

And perhaps these *new* dreams are just that—regular dreams we all have. Dreams that don't mean anything. Maybe I'm finally free of this curse that allows me to see the future, and I'll never have another precognitive dream ever again.

It's stopped snowing now.

The temperature must be dropping. The water droplets are freezing on the windshield, but at least the long lines of headlights are in motion now. People are anxious to get home to warm drinks, blue televisions and steaming dinners.

There's the sign for Exit 32. Two more miles to my exit, and I'll be home in time to keep my husband from starving. Maybe he'll be done preparing his sermon, and we'll have tomorrow night to ourselves. Dinner and a movie. Sounds great. It's been a long while since we took time for an evening out, just the two of us.

A litter of taillights suddenly materializes in front of me. In an instant, the glaring red lights streak left and right, cascading into a jumble.

Instinctively my foot jams the brake pedal. The car's frontend swerves alarmingly to the right. I pull the wheel back hard.

My foot hits the brake again. God, I shouldn't have done that! The brakes lock. What's happening?

For a second, an eternity, an instant, time ceases, looming like some bottomless chasm before me. My front left fender crashes into the side of a car careening impossibly, diabolically past my blurred window. *This can't be happening.*

Something huge, a hurtling iron mass, bludgeons me from behind.

My hands slip off the wheel. My neck snaps back and I can't see anything ahead. I am spinning.

Another projectile, a bombshell, slams my car again. I go groggy, inhaling a swift dizziness like that of a plunging rollercoaster ... fractured abruptly by a deafening blast ... the shatter of glass ... one final explosion, this one inside my skull. Pain, like a river of fire, engulfs my body, searing, excruciating. Oh, please God no.

Unbidden, one detached thought—murky and ominous, the color of dread—flickers across my brain. *This* is what my dreams meant? My children and my husband who will be healthy—alive and well. But me...? And now, from afar, the distant voice of my mother. I'm drifting vaguely closer to her essence. Seeing, reaching, touching my father. Is he here again? My *dead* father, telling me, "Everyone will be all right. They *were* your family, Marlow. I'll watch over them now."

My God, no. My father vanishes. The pain disintegrates. My thoughts dissolve toward darkness. Those dreams were for me. *The dreams were for me.*

Double Take

J.R. Hayslett

Traffic thinned as Greg and Janet left the city and cleared the suburbs.

"Good traveling weather," Greg said, surveying the lamb's wool clouds puffing against the blue sky.

"I just wish our mission were as pleasant," Janet said, turning sideways in the seat and tucking a strand of her shoulder-length hair behind an ear.

"Just keep in mind that it's for your dad's own good," Greg said.

"I know," she said with a sigh.

As they drove, Janet thumbed through a magazine and marked recipes to clip when they returned home. Greg turned on the radio and ran his fingers through his wiry brown hair. He resented having to make this 500-mile trip at the peak of the real-estate season, the meat-and-potatoes part of the year, but Janet insisted. And he had to admit that someone needed to save the old man from his folly.

He glanced in the rearview mirror and eased off the gas. Getting a ticket wouldn't help anything.

"What approach are you going to take with him?" he asked.

Janet laid the magazine in her lap. "I'm not sure, yet." She stretched and the magazine slipped to the floor. "But I've got to somehow make him see that she's just after his money, that she's a gold-digger."

Greg searched the expanse reflected in the rearview mirror, then pressed back down on the accelerator.

"Well, it might be tricky. If you aren't careful, you could end up chasing him into her trap all the faster."

He scowled at the rearview mirror, again. "Hunh. That's funny."

"What's funny?" Janet asked, flicking a look at him.

"A car back there," Greg said, studying the mirror. "It's been hanging a little ways behind us for quite a while—not gaining and not dropping back."

"What's so odd about that?"

"Nothing, I guess, except that for the last several miles, I've been varying my speed, but it's stayed the same distance back. Like it's playing some kind of game."

Janet turned and looked out the back window. "It's probably nothing. Look. Another car has passed that one and it's behind us now."

But that car, a small foreign sports model, gained on them, pulled into the passing lane and sped by.

Greg, glaring at the mirror, gritted his teeth. After a minute, he pushed the gas pedal to the floor. The little red import in front of them blossomed from a tiny dot to full size as they overtook, then passed, it.

Praying no cops were lurking on a shoulder or in the median beyond a knoll of the interstate, Greg kept up this breakneck speed for several miles, watching the mirror more than the road ahead.

"Damn!" he muttered.

Janet looked back and saw the car behind holding its own at the same distance as it had before Greg poured on the gas.

"Hold on!" Greg warned and, swerving suddenly, he cut onto the shoulder and jammed on the brakes. Their car careened and slued drunkenly.

Janet shrieked and grabbed the edge of the seat and her armrest.

"Are you crazy?" she yelled. "So what if a car is following us! It's not worth getting killed over. What do we care if it's back there?"

Greg leaned on the steering wheel and rested his forehead on his arms. "I—I don't know. I guess I got spooked." He blew out a long breath. "You're right. I must be nuts. As soon as it passes, we'll go."

But it didn't. Nothing did. Greg looked out his side window. There, about 500 yards back on the side of the road sat the car. Eerily, it was positioned at the same angle as theirs, with the back end toward the ditch.

"I'm NOT nuts," Greg said. "THIS is nuts!"

As Janet looked from him to the other car, her mouth fell open. Still staring at the blue sedan with white landau roof, she grabbed her husband's arm. "Greg! That car is just like ours."

Greg stared at it, twisted around to Janet, then gaped back out his window. "What's going on here!" he shouted.

He threw the car into gear and spun out, gravel and dirt spewing in a great gray cloud and Janet gripping the seat with both hands. They rode in silence for several miles, watching the road ahead and the car behind as Greg clenched his jaw and alternated between mashing down on and letting off of the accelerator.

Finally, he spoke. "I feel like we're in some sort of carnival crazy house with mirrors set up so we can see ourselves coming down the road before we get to where we are."

As he talked, the dot of something appeared on the road far ahead. Greg sped up and the dot grew into the shape of a big rig. Soon, the rig's rear double doors loomed in front of them. Greg pulled into the passing lane and rode alongside, gauging the truck's speed. Then he pulled ahead. After he cut back into the right lane, he slowed so their car stayed a couple hundred yards ahead of the semi.

"I feel better with a buffer between us," he said. "Now I don't care if that nut's back there or not."

With the truck shielding them from the other car, they rode for some time without talking. Janet turned on the radio and twisted the dial until she found an oldies pop station.

After a while, she grew restless. "Do you think we can stop for lunch soon?" she asked. "I'm getting hungry."

"Good idea," Greg said, his stomach rumbling at the suggestion. Food, gas and motel signs began to dot the roadside as they neared an exit. "We'll try one of these places."

They both breathed out with relief as theirs was the only car that took the off ramp. Greg turned into the side parking lot of a restaurant and they got out. The place was the standard traveler's fare—half eatery and half stop-and-go snack and cheap, gaudy souvenir shop fronted with a sentinel of gas pumps.

They slid into a booth overlooking the occupied parking spaces in front of the building and soon had bowls of soup and club sandwiches in front of them. But Janet picked at her food.

"Not hungry after all?" Greg asked.

"Oh, I don't know. I feel so unsettled. Dad's making such a fool of himself over a woman half his age and Mother in her grave less than six months." She sipped her iced tea. "I don't want to interfere with his happiness, but it's so obvious that he's being victimized by a money-grubbing vixen who thinks she's spotted an easy mark. Poor dear. I know he's lonely. But he's so vulnerable, and I just know that as soon as she's got him hooked, he's going to be miserable—and most likely broke."

Janet stared out the window. Suddenly, she sat up straight.

"Greg! Didn't we park around on the side?"

"Yeah, why?"

"Look!"

Greg followed her pointing finger. A blue sedan with white landau roof was nosed into a parking place in front of the restaurant at the other end of building from the side where they had parked.

"Wait here," he said as he slid out of the booth. Hurrying toward the cash register and a window beyond it that faced the side of the restaurant where they had parked, he looked out. When he sat back down in the booth, he said, "Our car's there."

Janet stared at him, then glanced around. "They're here, Greg. Whoever is following us is in here."

A dozen or so people were eating. Several more browsed the shelves of snacks and souvenirs in the shop. It was impossible to know which one the driver of the other car might be.

Greg started to get up. "Let's get out of here and get a jump on them."

"No." Janet put her hand on his arm. "Let's wait them out. They can't hang around here all afternoon."

With refilled iced tea glasses and half-hearted attempts at small talk, Greg and Janet waited.

By twos and threes, customers who were there when Janet saw the car like theirs parked in front left until, after nearly an hour, only one other couple remained.

"That must be them," Janet whispered.

The pair, with their backs toward Janet and Greg, were examining some shot glasses in the gift shop. Finally, they headed for the cash register, paid for their purchases and left.

"They must be parked around the side," Janet said. "They didn't come this way toward the car like ours."

Only new customers and restaurant and shop employees were left. But the blue sedan was still parked out front.

Janet leaned forward and clasped her hands so tight her fingers turned white. "What should we do?"

Greg raked his fingers through his hair. "Let's go, but we'll keep an eye out for anyone who might be watching us or who might head toward that car."

They tried to saunter, but Janet suspected they looked more paranoid than casual. After paying their bill, they went out and rounded the corner of the restaurant. They stopped short and gaped. The space they had parked their car in was empty.

"What the hell!" Greg exclaimed as he ran to the vacant spot. He stared in disbelief then looked around at the few remaining cars in the parking lot. "This is screwy!"

He ran his hand through his hair again, squinting in the bright sunlight in all directions, then at Janet. "I—I guess we should call the police and report it stolen."

Janet nodded, then stopped. "Wait. What about the car like ours in front?"

"What about it?"

"Well, whoever drove it here might have taken ours by mistake—or not—or for whatever reason. They might have taken our car instead. Maybe it was that last couple that left the restaurant."

"How could they?" Greg looked incredulous. "Their key wouldn't fit."

"Could they have hotwired it?"

"I don't know. I guess so, but why would they have done that?"

"Who knows, but I'm going to check." Janet was already headed for the front of the building.

The other car was still there. Greg caught up with her just as she looked in the window. He looked, too. His jaw dropped.

"What the—?"

A key ring dangled from the ignition.

"Where are your keys, Greg?" Janet asked. "Did you leave them in our car, so maybe whoever this belongs to took ours by mistake?"

"Don't be ridiculous," he said, digging in his pocket. "I never do that. Besides, ours was parked around on the other side of the restaurant, not even in sight of this car. It's ludicrous to think they could have gotten them mixed up."

Greg's full attention was now on the contents of his pockets. He'd pulled everything out, including a hanky and his wallet from ones in back. Anger and incomprehension scowled his face.

"I didn't give them to you, did I?"

"No. I've got mine," she said, reaching in her bag and pulling out a large ring with multi-colored yarn knotted on it. "You want to use them?"

"No! I want to find mine. They can't have just disappeared." He turned and headed back to the restaurant. "Wait there. I'm going to check where we were sitting or see if anyone found them and turned them in."

It took only a half beat for the fear of standing out there alone to send Janet hurrying after him. "Wait!" she said. "I'm going with you."

The search was futile. Greg even ran his fingers between the seat and backrest of the booth where they sat, and scoured the floor around it. No keys had been turned in to the cashier, either.

Back outside, they looked up and down the parking lot.

"What are we going to do?" Janet asked.

Greg hesitated, then stared at the car still sitting in front of the restaurant. "Take that one," he said.

"What? We can't do that. It would be stealing."

"No," Greg said, striding toward it. "We're just borrowing it so we can find ours. Come on."

Glancing around, he grabbed the handle and opened the door. He and Janet looked at each other, then got in. He twisted the ignition key and the engine roared to life. Both of them half expected someone to come charging out of the restaurant to stop them. No one did.

Putting the car in reverse, Greg backed out of the parking space, wheeled around and headed for the highway. Janet swiveled, first one way then the other, still looking for someone who might be trying to get their attention or stop them.

Then music playing on the radio caught her ear.

"Listen, Greg." It was an oldie as if the dial was set on the same station they had been listening to.

"Coincidence," Greg said. "Lots of people listen to that kind of music."

"I guess so," Janet said.

As she sat back, her eyes sweeping the landscape ahead for any sign of their car, she noticed something on the floor by her foot.

"Greg," she said, her voice quavering and her hand shaking as she picked up a magazine. "Look at this." It was just like the one she had been reading before they stopped for lunch. Corners of the pages with recipes she wanted to clip were folded down the way she had done in her magazine.

Greg glanced at it. Once, then twice. "My God, Janet! What the hell is going on?"

"You're asking me? I don't know! How could I? It's spooky, is all I know, like some kind of science-fiction movie."

"More like a nightmare," Greg shot back. His hands clutched the steering wheel in a death grip as he pressed harder on the gas pedal. "I wonder if we can catch up to our car. God, I wish we never started this trip."

Janet cut her eyes at him and twisted the magazine. "Do you, Greg? Do you think we're doing the wrong thing, that maybe we shouldn't be going and this is some sort of sign?"

"What? How could that be? That's just crazy."

"And this isn't?"

"I—I don't know, Janet. I don't see how the screwy stuff that's been going on could be connected to our plans. I must say, I thought we were on track, even though the timing is lousy for me. I sure don't want to see the old man get hurt or throw his dough away on some chick who just wants to get her hands on it. But you know, it *is* his money and if marrying that woman will make him happy, isn't he entitled to that?"

Instead of answering, Janet leaned forward and peered ahead.

"Must have been an accident or something," she said. "Look at all those cars up there."

"Yeah. Damn! So how long is *this* going to delay us?"

They slowed as they neared the backed-up traffic, then crawled for a mile or two before an overturned car in the grassy median came into view. Blue lights atop police cars whirled dizzily and the mournful wail of a departing ambulance hung in the air. The traffic in front of them pulled past the wreckage giving Janet and Greg their first good look at the smashed remains.

"Oh, my God, Greg," Janet shrieked. "That's *our* car!" She didn't see any other vehicles that might have been involved in the accident.

"I'm stopping," Greg said, his face ashen. He steered beyond the knot of people and vehicles around the wreck, pulled over to the edge of the pavement and jumped out of the car.

One of the highway patrolmen directing traffic trotted toward him. "Hey, there," he shouted. "You can't stop there. Move on!"

Greg ran to the officer. "Who was in that car? Where are they?" he asked.

"Look, bud, we're taking care of everything. You just get back in your car and keep going. Traffic's bad enough without people stopping to gawk."

"But I need to know who was in that car. I think it might have been stolen."

The policeman's cold stare bore into him. "What makes you think that? You know them?"

"I—I'm not sure. I might. Were they in that ambulance? What hospital did they go to?"

"Those folks won't be needing any hospital, mister, not the shape they're in."

Greg recoiled as if punched. "They're dead? Who were they? What happened?"

"Don't know. Haven't located any I.D. yet. It was a young couple about your age, I'd say, though it was hard to tell. They're really messed up."

The blare of a horn stopped him. "Move on now, or I'll cite you for blocking traffic."

Greg looked from the wrecked car to the officer and back again before jogging back to the car where Janet waited. As he approached it he froze. The license plate on it had the same number as the one on their car that was now a smashed mass of metal.

His mind made up, he turned back toward the wreckage. He didn't get to take one step, though.

He actually felt the explosion before he heard it. The flames that followed engulfed the upside-down automobile. Greg stumbled backwards, staring. He couldn't tell if anyone closer to the inferno were hurt. Somehow, he found the handle of the car with Janet inside. He pulled the door open and got in.

He didn't speak until he had driven to a spot where he could turn around. Janet was silent, too, as she stared straight ahead.

As they approached the wreck from the opposite direction, the interstate had been closed down. They followed the cars ahead as they were directed to an off ramp and detoured onto surface streets until they were well clear of the wreckage. The detour took them too far from the interstate to be able to see what might have been left of the car they were sure had been theirs, or the remains of anything else that might have been caught in the explosion, but the air was rank with smoke and the smell of burned rubber.

Janet opened her mouth a couple of times, but didn't say anything. She was full of questions, but couldn't put any into words.

Finally, Greg spoke.

"I think our mission might have been a mistake," he said. "Well intentioned, but misguided. Just because we think your dad is using rotten judgment and might get burned, doesn't mean we should interfere. He's a big boy. If he chooses to be with that woman, it's his choice, his destiny.

Janet nodded. "Yes," she said. "Fate."

The MG
Juliana Gribbins

The old man walked the length of my father's MG, tracing the outline lightly with his pinky. He was nodding and smiling, completely unself-conscious as if he was the only one there. My father and I watched him carefully. A Steely Dan song played quietly from a transistor radio. The radio was perched on an empty cardboard box, and I had a sudden urge to throw it.

The old man glanced up. "Very nice," he said. "Very nice."

I felt jaded. At the time I wouldn't have been able to say what the word meant, but I knew the feeling. I fixed my ancient eight-year-old eyes on the old man. I wanted to remember his face forever.

My father bought the MG when I was three years old. It must have been summer because I remember how the sun felt white-hot on my arms. We were all in the driveway standing around the car: me, my parents, and my two older brothers. I didn't understand why we were all looking at it. The MG was a deep pine green with a smoldering black interior. It smelled leathery and strange. I stood there patting the running board and wondering when we were all going to do something else.

"Ah, an Em Gee. It's a classic!" said my father in his best W. C. Fields voice.

We stepped back as my father got in and started it up. I froze and gripped my mother's hand. This was suddenly a big deal. My father was waking a monster. I had never heard anything so loud in my life, and I was the kind of kid who was terrified of everything, especially things that were loud. This was the vacuum, the blender, and the neighbor's dog rolled into one. My mother's hand was soft but strong, so I stayed, holding my breath and waiting for it all to be over.

We went for a ride, and it didn't get any better. As I crawled through the swing door into the black maw, I could see my father smiling down at me, oblivious to my fear. The MG was even louder from the inside. My brothers laughed and waved to people in the neighborhood as we went by. I sat between them, too afraid even to cry as we careened around corners. I was used to gigantic wood-paneled station wagons, which were like being driven around in the Empire State Building. This was completely different. This was Mr. Toad's wild ride.

My brothers sniffed out my fear like hound dogs. They quickly figured out that even the mere mention of the MG sent me running to my room in tears. They'd come up behind me as I was watching cartoons and imitate the sound of the car's engine.

"Brum, brum, brum, brum, brum, bruuuummm!" they'd hiss. "It's coming! It's coming for you!"

The primal fear didn't last long, though. I got used to the MG and grew to love it in the same way my father did. It was pretty. It was fun. It was a toy.

We took the MG every weekend to the Jersey Shore the summer I was five. I sat on my mother's lap on the way there. It was the seventies, and in those days no one even thought to wear seatbelts. I'd watch the gray pavement turn into a blur beneath us. My brothers were situated in the tiny rear seat with a beach umbrella between them. They'd hold the umbrella when we were on the highway so it wouldn't fly out.

Nowadays a carload looking like that would be cause for arrest. A cop did stop us on our weekly trek, but it wasn't to fine my folks for not wearing seatbelts or to send us kids to a foster home due to dangerous driving conditions. No, it was because the MG wasn't registered.

My father commuted to New York and got home late, and my mother didn't drive yet. So, there was no one able to go and register the car during DMV open hours. Eventually, it got to the point where the police officer would wait by the beach entrance and hold out his hand when he saw us approach. My father and the cop would make the exchange. Money for last week's ticket in exchange for this week's ticket.

Never mind the lack of seatbelts and me on Mom's lap and the beach umbrella projectile ready to launch. The ticket was for lack of registration only.

The soft ocean air brushed across my freckles once my father paid Officer Friendly and we got moving again. We ate Cracker Jack and dug giant holes. On our way home in the evening, the MG rumbled quietly like a far-off thunderstorm. White sand dotted the floor beneath me. On these days it smelled of leather, but also of salt and dunes.

We moved.

To a child, the act of changing house comes as sudden as a tornado. We ended up in a small town in Massachusetts. It was oppressively hot in New Jersey, but the New England air was cool the day we arrived. We ate fast food on moving boxes, and I hoped the MG would like our new home. I loved the way the house echoed and smelled like fresh wood.

There are two things I remember most vividly about our two years in Massachusetts: the coldness of Cape Cod and watching my father work on the MG. We went to Cape Cod a week after we moved. It was the last day of August and hot even by New Jersey standards, but no one was in the water. Not even other kids. My father and I held hands as we walked into the ocean and stopped at the same time. We only made it up to our knees and then ran up the beach. My feet were red like I'd dipped them in a bowl of ice. The beach was more rocks than grains of sand, but my feet were too numb to feel the difference.

"Don't bother," my father told my brothers. "Too cold."

My father worked on the MG just about every weekend while we were in Massachusetts. Maybe it didn't like that trip to Cape Cod. After that venture, it was extremely moody. The MG's wire entrails exploded with color as my father lifted the hood, grunting and clutching oily rags.

"Never shoulda bought that car! Never shoulda bought it!" I heard him tell my mother as he washed his hands in the kitchen sink. "It's a piece of junk."

It was a piece of junk until he got it running again. Then the top would come down and he would call us all for a ride. "Ahhh, the ole Em Gee!" he'd say. "It's a classic!"

We moved.

The economy was in bad shape. The real estate market was even worse. When my father left his job, my parents realized that we had to go where my father could commute to New York. There was always something jobwise in New York. So, when my parents found buyers for our house that May, they jumped at the offer. There was only one hitch. The buyers wanted to move in immediately.

We went back to New Jersey and lived in my grandfather's house. My parents went on a frantic house-hunting jag so that we could be settled by the time school started. We finished May and June of the school year in a Catholic school that smelled of chalk dust and floor sanitizer. Otherwise, it wasn't too bad.

The MG hibernated in my grandfather's garage, and I went to visit it sometimes. I'd lift the tarp and pat the door. "It's okay," I'd tell it.

We moved.

My parents finally found a house. It was the last week of August when we settled in. The house was yellow, and the day itself was impossibly bright. Saturday morning headache bright. The yard smelled like mint and crabgrass. All the houses in the neighborhood looked the same. The inside of our house had orange curtains and orange wallpaper. The carpets were an odd goldish green.

The MG barely made it from Trenton to Princeton Junction. It sighed itself to sleep in our new garage.

My parents spent all their money on that house with its nice neighborhood and good school system. Of course, being a kid, I didn't realize that. I never noticed that we were eating a lot more Hamburger Helper than before. It was a while before the magazine that my father founded became successful. These things take time. Eventually, it was extremely successful but not before sacrifices had to be made.

Until the old gentleman came to our house that gray November afternoon, I had no idea that anything was going on. I left the garage as he and my father shook hands to seal the deal.

No matter how stable and kind your home life is, childhood can sometimes be fraught with change. We moved a few times in a few years. We beached on hot sand then cold rocks then back on hot sand. Our station wagons came and went. Each was bought from a giant lot of used vehicles. Each would die an agonizing dinosaur death, usually on a vacation trip.

Even the MG changed. It ran or it didn't. Beach sand peppered the floor or was swept away. The steering wheel cover became corroded by a day of acid rain when the top was left off.

My feelings toward the MG changed, too.

It was, as my father said in his best W. C. Fields voice, "a classic."

But even though I grew to love it, once it was actually gone, I was almost glad. I didn't want to see it languish in the elephant's graveyard of our garage.

With it gone, I was free to think of trips to the shore in it and rides to the store when it rained, and droplets would drum the soft top. I could think of the sound it made as it started up. That stormy grumble.

At eight I figured out that sometimes memories are better.

Like New

Michael Louis Falcone

The car was supposed to be a 1988 Honda Civic hatchback that runs and drives like new. To Peter, it looked more like an old coal car. The wheels were devoid of hubcaps, the small, black orbs reminiscent of something that had ridden the rails deep down into a mine. The "paint" really wasn't paint at all, but a dull gray primer that seemed to absorb light rather than reflect it. Rust stains ran down the sides from the windowsills, as if the car had been crying all night. Tree buds peppered the top of the car, which was parked under a drippy old sycamore, tall and strong as a skyscraper.

"It's pretty beat," Peter said, drawing from his cigarette with a wince.

"Yeah, but she runs and drives like new." Scott stood off to one side, keys in hand, looking wistfully at the dull little automobile.

"Alright, well, let's see," Peter said, stomping his smoke into the dirt.

The seat, faded as old newsprint, was surprisingly comfortable, conforming to Peter's curves like an old pair of jeans.

Scott plopped down opposite. "She'll start right up," he said, slotting the key into the ignition.

It did. A short kick from the starter and the engine chimed right in, purring smoothly.

"I've tried to keep the interior clean—that's where you spend the most time, anyway. Some cars I've been in—cups and garbage everywhere—you'd think they'd call for Orkin."

"I know," Peter said. "My old car was like that." He slotted the stick shift into first and let up gently on the clutch. The car rolled off under the arboreal canopy like it had been sent a direct order from above.

Scott's driveway was a long and meandering one, threading its way past well-hung apple trees. The little Civic rode the swells and swales of washouts assuredly, like a donkey traversing a worn, familiar path. At the end of it, a smooth asphalt road begged left or right.

"To town," called Scott, pointing to the right, and the car quietly obliged.

Peter shifted from first, to second, to third, the stick shift rolling easily in his hand.

"Seems much younger than twenty," Scott said, rolling his window down to half-mast, "doesn't it?" The car giddied up and ran the pavement without complaint as Peter found fourth and settled back into his seat for the ride.

"So, this is your car, I assume," Peter said. "Are you the original owner?"

"Was my brother-in-law's initially. Ex-brother-in-law, actually. But he got tired of her pretty quick. Wanted a sports car. As if it's some kind of competition," he said, eyes on the passing scrub.

They continued on in silence, passing open-mouthed mailboxes, stands of dogwood trees.

"Gotta admit, it feels solid for a little car," Peter said eventually. He looked down at the odometer—twice. "Do you realize you've got almost a quarter-million miles on this thing?"

"Sure do," he said. "And she'll double that, easy. Engine and tranny are new as of last year."

"I see. And you have service records on all this?"

"Of a sort. Mostly receipts for parts. I do most of the work myself—oil changes, the whole bit. She's kinda fussy about who handles her, to be perfectly honest." He took a rag out of his shirt pocket and wiped down the dash, snapping the rag clean in the breeze outside his window.

They approached a set of train tracks at the edge of town.

"Now, slow down a bit," Scott cautioned, "these tracks are kinda rough." The little car thundered over the rails, tossing the men about inside.

"Sorry," Peter said, "your brakes aren't as responsive as the ones I'm used to. They okay?"

"Oh, I think they're still in pretty fair shape. Won't be long before baby'll need a new pair of shoes, though. Might be able to slip those on before selling. If you met the price in full." Peter nodded.

They coasted to a stoplight by the side of an old drugstore. "Valvoline. The Mechanic's Choice," the store wall proclaimed. The ad, featuring a grease-stained hand pouring honey-colored oil from a shiny can, was more brick than paint, the bones of the old store sticking out like ribs under the faded lettering. Peter checked the car's oil pressure gauge, which was well within acceptable limits. "Idles fine," he said, toeing the accelerator and watching the tach needle wave at him.

Scott looked down the short boulevard. A young family strolled under a row of cheery potted flowers hanging from black iron lanterns. "You get out into the country much, Peter?"

"No. Not anymore." The light turned green, and they set off down the boulevard. "Grew up in a place just like this, though," Peter said. "Logging town." The car hummed past a pet store, a papered-over restaurant, a hobby shop. "Went away to school and never came back."

"Like so many do," Scott said, stretching out on the seat. "I'm your opposite. Grew up in the city and settled in here."

They came to the far edge of town, where a tall two-way sign stood in front of an open field like a scarecrow. "Hang a rizzo," Scott said. "We'll take some farm roads back; let you open her up some."

Peter gave the little car some gas, feeling more confident on the clutch. Phone wires spun past the windows. Dusty clumps of field dirt burst under the car's wheels, leaving a contrail of yellow dust in their wake. Peter let go of the steering wheel. "Tracks true," Peter said, staring down the open road. In the distance, mirages rose from the ground like ghosts.

Scott looked out the side window, marking the steady progress of a tractor making its way across the dusty land. Redwing blackbirds, high above on the phone wires, raised their crimson flecked wings and dove off into the fallow fields below.

They came at last to a rusted stop sign. "Right?" Peter asked, checking in with his internal compass.

"Right." Scott swiped a hand over his mouth. "And pull over onto the shoulder when you get a chance." They rolled to a crunching stop on the loose stone. "I have an odd request."

"Shoot."

"Would you mind if I rode in the back seat the rest of the way home?"

"Uh, sure. It is your car, after all."

Scott stepped out and pulled a hidden lever, and the front seat bowed toward the windshield. He climbed into the back and pulled the door and front seatback toward him. "Drive on."

Peter spun the tires without meaning to.

"I have to say," said Peter, "that is a pretty odd request."

"Thanks for indulging," Peter heard behind him. "It's just that I realized I've never ridden in the back seat of my own car. Not once in twenty years."

The car dipped and climbed over a series of rolling hills like a tiny ship riding deep swells.

Peter glanced in the rearview mirror. "What's it like back there?"

"Not so bad. A little noisy, but nice."

"Almost like test driving your own car again."

"Yeah ... it is. Right here," Scott said, thrusting a finger up between the front seats in order to point the way. He settled back again, stretching his arms out over the back of the seat. "You ever try this, Peter?"

Peter rubbed the stubble on his chin. "You know, I can't say as I have. Not once in all the cars I've ever owned. That is funny, isn't it? Left?"

"Yes. It is."

"Except maybe once when I was drunk."

"Ah, that doesn't count."

"Why not?"

"Because," Scott said, and shifted on the short bench seat, "you might have been there, but you weren't really all there, you know?"

"Suppose not."

Scott drew long breaths from the sweet farm air washing over him. "You should try this sometime. It's a rare luxury to be a passenger in your own car. Makes you appreciate things in a whole new way."

"Well, I have spent some time in the passenger seat. It's a couples thing. You trade-off when you get tired over the long hauls."

"Sure. Right. Then left. This is different, though," he told him. "There's more perspective back here. And you don't have to worry about the road so much. You can just sit back and enjoy the ride. And just like that, it's over," he said, pointing out his mailbox by the side of the road.

They ascended the long driveway in a slow climb. At the crest, the sycamore bent to and fro in a gust of evening breeze, a giant hand waving at them by the side of the road. "Under the sycamore again?" Peter asked.

"No, up front is fine. Right by the door." The two men—large men, really—got out of the little car slowly. Peter helped Scott out by holding the passenger door open to make way for the difficult egress.

They stood back from the car and stared at it for a while without speaking.

Peter lit a cigarette and sighed smoke. "Sure is an ugly old thing. I'd forgotten, driving all around."

Scott smiled. "Yeah, because she runs and drives like new."

That she does."

A pair of chickadees chased each other through the evening sky while the car engine cooled, ticking like a watch. "So, what are you thinking?" Scott asked. "Can you live without good looks?"

Peter tried to find something in the squat profile that appealed to him—an angle, a seductive curve, a gleaming piece of trim. But there was nothing. The car was so homely that his eye continually avoided it, like a house fallen to ruin. He clucked his tongue. "Well, I might have to. I need a car, Scott."

"Right. People do."

"And you sure have taken good care of her—despite appearances to the contrary."

Scott tilted his head to the sky and laughed heartily. "That's for certain. She's ready to take paint, you know. That's primer."

"I was counting on that." Peter looked over at Scott. Scott stood there gazing fixedly at the car's stubby profile as if he could see something in the dull gray finish that Peter lacked the ability to detect. "Let me ask you something."

"Ask."

"You're pretty fond of this car, aren't you?"

"Very."

"And if I do come back here to take her away, it's going to be pretty tough for you, isn't it?"

"Like the first day I saw boy off to school."

"Right. Wow."

"So, why am I getting rid of her?"

"It's a fair question."

"It is." Scott laid his arms across the gray metal roof and folded his hands, like a businessman staring down a client on the other side of the desk. "Because" and he sighed here, "because I think it's time for me to retire from her. But it isn't time for her to retire. Can you appreciate that, Peter?"

Peter nodded. "You want a sedan."

"Yessir."

"Cruise control."

"Airbags."

"A sunroof maybe."

"Power every-damn-thing," Scott said. He stood up from the car's pitted roof. "I don't want to feel the road anymore, Peter. I'm tired of shifting." He put his hands in his pockets. "I just want to cruise from here on out."

Peter smiled and thumped the worn hood—gently like he was patting it. "I need to think about this, Scott."

"Yeah, I know," Scott said. "Me too."

Between them, the car ticked on in the rustling quiet of the evening.

Homeless

Pepe Rich

That evening, when Max Benson stepped outside AT 11 o'clock to begin his nightly walk, he felt a thick chill in the air he had not felt the night before.

The sticky, hot nights of another summer had finally ended, and Max felt the cool dampness on his face as he realized that summer was finally over and soon the bone-chill of another winter would arrive.

Max walked each night before bed because he needed to burn off the stress of the workday, and the dark air and the brisk exercise were always tonics that tired him enough so that later he would sleep.

As he walked farther and farther down an unpopulated section of Route 99, leaving his neighborhood and the interchange of I-70 behind, he realized how noisy the nights had become over the past thirty years. The interstate had never screamed with trucks all hours of the day and night, as it now did. At one time the highway was nearly silent by midnight. Now there was an incessant clamor of traffic at all hours. This sound of constant rushing created a relentless din as if those highway peoples' lives never stood still for a moment. Someone was always coming, and someone was always going; it was a population that never rested. It was not always the same people, Max knew, for everyone must rest. But the bedlam itself never died down.

Along this stretch of Route 99, a two-lane road with a double yellow line, gullies that held water lay on either side. A new sound grew up from the bog-like wetness of the gullies – night peepers singing a chorus for an admiring evening and for their lone human visitor on his midnight walk.

The chime of the peepers began to fade where the gullies ended. There, flat cornfields lay on either side of the road, and this lonely stretch was lighted only by a long line of occasional streetlights. Far ahead, Max could see the very last lamp throwing its silent cone of yellow light into the middle of the road. Beyond, the darkness of the night was too dark and too deep a place for any human to travel alone without a flashlight. Max would turn at that last streetlamp, as he did every night, and walk the three miles back home to his firm bed.

When Max reached his destination, he saw the crumpled chassis of an older model sedan near a telephone pole and resting fully off the left side of the roadway along the edge of the cornfield. The area around the passenger side of the vehicle, well-lit by the streetlamp, was littered with bandages, darkly stained gauze, wrappings, needles, IV tubing, torn bits of white tape, and a few heavy, black blankets.

"This must be from the accident this morning that everyone was talking about," Max said aloud. Odd, he then thought, that the firemen and the police should leave the vehicle here and not tow it, and the public works officials did not clean up the EMT's medical litter. The entire scene chilled him beyond what the night itself could muster.

After considering the unusual scene for a few moments, curiosity got the better of him. He approached the mangled vehicle and peered inside through the broken passenger door window.

The interior had an odd odor to it, like it had rained inside the car, an earthen, acrid smell. The windshield also drew his eye, for it was fractured in the form of a large, white circle just over the bent-forward steering wheel.

When Max moved to the rear passenger door window to look into the backseat, his curious ease suddenly tightened as his eyes fixed on a human form lying across the seat. Max's heart began to pound at the very thought—a dead body!

And then reason replaced subjective fear.

"Can't be," Max said aloud, and with those words the body inside the car jerked and sat abruptly upright.

The light from the streetlamp fell just right through the rear window and brightened the face of the person sitting there. It was a smooth, milky face, under a thick, bushy mass of black hair. And there in the middle of the white face were two eyes like spring ice.

What suddenly became clear to Max on this moonless night was that the person in the back seat of this abandoned sedan was a boy, perhaps all of 14, who said nothing but cowered back into the shadows inside the vehicle.

Max stepped closer, grabbed the handle, and opened the door. The boy pulled his legs closer to his body and pinned himself against the opposite side.

"It's okay. I'm not going to hurt you. Are you all right?"

"I'm not sure," answered a young voice from the shadows.

"What are you doing out here, this time of night?"

The boy shrugged his shoulders.

"Why are you sleeping in this wrecked car?"

"There was no place else," said the boy.

"No place else? Don't you have a home? A family?"

The boy shook his head each time.

"What's your name?"

"Name?"

"Your name. You must have a name."

The boy just sat there, not moving, just looking at Max from the safety of the darkness.

Amnesia, Max thought. Then ... drugs. The kid must be on something that was making him vague.

"Do you have a wallet? Maybe there's something in there what will tell me who you are."

"A wallet?"

"Yeah, a wallet." Max pulled his own wallet out of his back pocket to wave at the boy.

The boy felt his own back pocket and slowly shook his head.

"Great, no wallet. So you're not old enough to drive."

The boy looked away toward the front of the car. "I had to get away," he said. Then he looked around the interior; at the roof, the doors, the rear window, and then back to the windshield, as if he suddenly became aware of his surroundings.

"I'm in the back seat?"

"That's where I found you."

"How did I get here?"

"I found you here, lying down, asleep I guess. I think you startled me as much as I startled you."

"I thought I was in front."

"Maybe you were in front, but you moved to the back to keep warm." Max looked over the back of the front seat at the dashboard and the windshield. "See," he said, and pointed. "There's a nasty hole in the driver's side of the windshield. Looks like somebody took a wicked header. And both the driver and passenger door windows are smashed out. The hood is all smashed up too. Older model. No airbags. Shame. I wonder if anyone was killed. Can you tell me your name yet?"

The boy shook his head again.

"How old are you?"

"Fifteen," he said, then closed his eyes.

"That you know. Good. So...you're a little older than you look. But...how do you know you're fifteen, but you don't know your name?"

"I don't know."

"That's helpful. Well, nameless boy who knows he's fifteen, we've got to get you out of here and get you someplace safe and warm."

"Where's that?"

"A hospital, I think."

"No," the boy said, and closed his eyes again.

"I've got to take you someplace. You don't look like you're feeling very well."

"I don't feel right," he said, and lay back against the middle of the seat.

"Come on," Max said, and tugged at the boy's arm. "I can't just leave you here."

"Why not?"

"Because you're ill." Max sat next to the boy and placed a palm on the boy's forehead, then the back of his hand, and finally his wrist, as if to be certain. "You're ice cold. You must be freezing."

"I don't feel cold."

"You're numb. The cold has made you numb." Max looked out into the cold blackness on the road outside the streetlamp. There was not a single light to be seen in that cold wilderness beyond the lamp.

"Sit up, please. You can't stay here."

Max grabbed both arms and sat the boy up.

"Why do you care?"

"Because I do. Come on." Max put his arms around the boy and started to half lift, half drag him out of the car.

"I was in front," the boy said.

Max then stepped fully outside the car and reached back in, placed his hands under the boy's arms, and began to drag him out. The boy screamed in pain suddenly.

"You're hurt? Where does it hurt?" Max eased him back into the seat.

"My head."

Max looked, as best he could, at the boy's head, but he could see no sign of injury.

"Where does your head hurt?"

"Inside."

"You've got a headache? And you're ice cold. When was the last time you ate?"

"I don't know."

"You need to get to a hospital."

"No," said the boy, "I can't go."

"Don't fight me. You have to go. The doctors will be able to help you."

"No!"

"There's nothing to be afraid of. I'll go with you."

"You won't."

"Of course, I will. I know you're frightened, but you don't have to be alone."

The boy opened his eyes fully then, and looked at Max. In that light cast by the lone streetlamp the boy's eyes were the warmest blue Max had ever seen. He could not imagine what circumstances would result in a boy with such a sparkle in his eyes to be homeless and sleeping in the back of an abandoned car on the side of a road.

"I'm safe in the car," the boy said.

Max hesitated, then answered. "Yes, I found you safe here in this car."

"In the back seat?"

"Yes, here in the back seat, just a few minutes ago. You were asleep and I woke you."

"Asleep?"

Max nodded.

"But I was in the front seat."

"Well, maybe, and you moved to the back seat to keep warm because the hole in the windshield and both side windows are smashed in. But we've *already* been over this."

"Go then!" the boy said. "I'm fine on my own."

"I don't think you'll be fine on your own, without medical attention. You don't even know your name."

"I don't need one."

"That's no way to think of yourself. Everyone needs a name. It helps make us who we are."

"I'm nobody."

Max shook his head. "Come on. Let's try to get you up again. Maybe it won't hurt as much."

"I think I can get out on my own," he said, and reached for the door frame.

Max reached to help him out, and the boy looked up at him and as he did so, and without saying another word, the boy stepped outside the car.

"You're okay? You can stand?"

"I can stand."

Max then pulled his jacket off. "Put this on." The boy looked oddly at Max, took the jacket, and put it on slowly, first one sleeve and then the other.

Max then tried to lead the boy away from the car, but he stood fixed on his feet and would not move. The boy turned and looked over his left shoulder at the front of the car.

"Come on. I can walk you back to my house."

"I can't."

"You mean you won't."

"No, I can't leave here yet."

"There's nothing for you here."

"How do you know?"

"Because you need to be with people."

"With people?"

"Of course. People who will help you."

"Help me? How do you find those people?"

"You just find them, when you need to."

"People who will help me."

"Yes."

"Like you. You seem to want to help me."

"Yes. Now come on. I'll take you home and get you some help."

"You seem like you mean it."

"Of course, I mean it. Now come on."

Max started to walk, and the boy started to walk but in the opposite direction toward the front end of the car. He touched the crumpled hood as he crossed in front, and around to the driver's door.

"What are you doing?"

The boy looked into the car through the driver's side window.

"Did you forget something?"

The boy, without answering, opened the door and sat behind the wheel.

Max turned, came around the back of the mangled car and stood outside the open door, looking at the boy sitting inside with his hands at his sides, staring down at the wheel.

"What's wrong?"

"Nothing," the boy said, looked at Max, reached out, and pulled the door shut. A spray of broken bits of glass fell from the window frame to the ground below the door. The boy placed both hands on the wheel.

"I was driving."

"I...I don't understand," said Max, talking to the boy through the broken window.

"I was here, right here, driving."

"This? You were driving this car?"

"It's coming back to me. Yes."

"You were driving this car?"

"Yes."

Max stepped closer to the door.

"Then ... you were in the accident?"

"Yes."

"How did you get back here to the scene?"

"I didn't come back."

"Okay, you really have to get out of this car and come home with me so you can see a doctor. I think you're delusional. I'll drag you home if I have to."

Max reached in and touched his hand to the boy's forehead again. "You're still ice cold. I need to get you into a warm tub."

The boy laughed. "A bath? You want to give me a bath?"

"That's … that's not how I meant it to sound. We need to warm you up before you develop hypothermia."

"It won't help."

"Get out of the car, please," said Max.

"I took the car from my father," the boy said, ignoring Max. "I was driving to get away. I was driving fast because I wanted to take the pain away. But … I don't know what that pain was now. It's gone."

The boy then turned to look at Max again, both hands still gripping the steering wheel. "What's your name, mister?"

"Max. Max Benson."

"Thank you, Max Benson."

"Thank you for what? I haven't done anything for you yet."

"Yeah, you have. You've helped me a lot."

"Okay. So, let me help you some more and get you out of here."

"I can go now," the boy said, and smiled in the light of the streetlamp coming in through the smashed windshield.

"It's about time," Max said, and put his hand on the door handle.

"My name is Chris."

"Chris," Max said. "You just remembered that? You're feeling better now."

"That's what I remember. Christopher Palmgren. And I'm feeling much better."

Max looked down at his hand resting on the chrome door handle and pulled it open. When the door arched fully open Max gasped and jumped back.

The driver's seat, where the boy had been sitting with his hands on the steering wheel, was empty.

Max snapped a look to his right, to his left, and behind himself twice, and then back at the driver's seat that held only his rumbled jacket surrounded by glass shards and dried blood stains on the seat and dashboard.

"Oh my God," Max said. "Oh my loving God."

Slowly then, fearing for a moment, Max reached in for his jacket and felt its warmth on his hand. Max shook his head. The boy had been cold, but the jacket was now warm? When he pulled the jacket out it was indeed still warm in the cool night air, as if someone had just taken it off and handed it to him.

Max, dazed, turned and stumbled back to the road and began walking. He stopped, turned, and looked at the empty car on the side of the road under the cone of light cast from the last streetlamp on the edge of the midnight void.

He put the jacket on and shivered when he felt the last remnant of the boy's warmth in the arms of the jacket. "But he was so cold," Max remembered. He kneaded the arms of the jacket and began to cry.

And he walked, walking toward home to fight the incredible night chill that was now biting at the back of his neck. He walked fast, mumbling to himself and wiping his tears with the back of his hand. What did it all mean?

The only answer that presented itself was the steady beat of his own steps. Then Max became aware of another sound that gradually intruded on his thoughts. It was the song of the peepers, rising out of the damp gullies. And then he heard the relentless clamor of the interstate traffic as it grew louder and louder in the night. That sound of constant rushing, that endless motion. Someone always coming and someone always going.

"What was his name? What was the boy's name?" Max repeated, rushing on. "My dear God, that poor boy, that poor boy."

The night traffic rang in his years ... a population that never rested ... an incessant din of life that never ceased.

Tuck & Roll

Ray Daley

They'd been driving for hours through the darkness, just Andy and Mara travelling together.

"Anything out here, honey?" Andy asked her.

"Map says no. Did you want to stop, Andy?" Mara knew he was feeling restless.

"Only if we see somewhere soon, it'd be nice to stretch my legs for a bit," he said.

But the roads just kept unfolding ahead of them, mile after unrelenting mile of nothing, followed by more nothing with the odd side order of sand whipping across the tarmac.

The sky was clear, there was almost no moon at all, and despite the clarity Andy couldn't see any stars through the sunroof.

"Opaque the roof please, Mara, I don't like it when I can't see the stars." Andy tried to keep the restlessness out of his voice, but she'd pick up on it.

She always did.

"You can sleep if you like, Andy, recline the seat back. I'll drive?" Mara offered.

Andy shook his head. "No, I can't sleep. It's Tuesday, right, Mara? It feels like Tuesday."

"Can't you remember, Andy?" Mara sounded concerned.

He knew that tone well. Andy *couldn't* remember. His head felt fuzzy again. He was having moments like this more often now; the Doctors had told him that they couldn't do anything about it. Andy just had to live with it. Mara was a big help there, she always remembered everything, even when he couldn't.

"No Mara, sorry. I *can't* remember." It was better to be honest, she knew when he was lying anyway.

"It's okay, Andy, I'm here. And it's Friday, not Tuesday." Mara's voice was soothing. They drove on through the darkness for another hour before something started pinging on the dashboard. "I'm reading a structure up ahead, Andy, it's not on the map though. You want me to stop there?"

"Sure, Mara. I can get some air. I need it." Andy breathed a sigh of relief. As they crested the hill he could see the lights appearing, the outline of a building. Then the friendly green neon that read G*as* & *Go*.

"It's a gas station, Andy," Mara said.

Andy didn't think places like that existed anymore, most vehicles were electric these days. "That's fine, Mara. Maybe I can grab something to drink inside?"

Mara pulled them up on the edge of the forecourt, the windows still fully opaque. "Want me to go all-clear, Andy?"

He looked at the creepy-looking old guy standing behind the counter inside and thought better of it. "Nah, I'd rather not have him know how many people are inside the car. Gives me the upper hand if he gets a bit weird."

Andy had read articles about these back-road operations, some of them thought they were a law unto themselves. He slipped out of the door and walked across the forecourt. The old man behind the counter didn't look up at first. The door made an electronic *BEEP* as Andy opened it. The old man gave him a quick glance and went right back to his TV show.

Andy found the cooler and picked himself out a diet soda. The candy bars caught his eye as he walked back down the aisle to the counter, so he picked out a choc-nut bar. He found himself juggling for his wallet and put the candy bar in his pocket as he found out some money. Then he placed the soda onto the counter.

"Three bucks for the soda," the old man said to him.

Cheap joint, I'll have to remember this place Andy thought to himself as he counted the money onto the counter.

As he turned to leave, the old man pulled out a shotgun and pointed it at him. "Can't let you leave without paying for everything," he said. "We don't like thieves."

Andy didn't understand what the old man meant. He'd paid for the soda. "I paid for the soda," he said aloud, just to confirm the point further.

"And how about what's in your pocket there? I saw you. I was watching on the camera. Saw you slip it in your pocket. You either pay for it or put it back! Or I can call the cops, let them discuss it further with you. They don't like out-of-towners," the old man said, gripping onto the shotgun like it was fighting to get out of his hands.

Little did Andy know right then, the old man had already pressed the panic button under the counter before he'd even reached it, the local cops were already on their way.

Andy didn't understand what the old man meant. He was probably crazy. "Listen, sir, I paid for what I took. I'm leaving now, okay?" Andy started to back towards the door slowly.

"Can't let you do that, son. First one's just a warning shot, you hear?"

And with that, the old man fired the shotgun once into the ceiling. It's impossible to know if it was the noise or the excitement or something else, but he just dropped like a stone, the shotgun clattered to the ground beside him, discharging once more into a nearby display.

Faulty trigger mechanism or a bad spring, the old training said at the back of Andy's mind.

Andy didn't want to hang around after that, any local cops would be sure to think *he'd* killed the old man. Even though he hadn't touched the old fart. Andy bet that his heart had given out under the stress of the encounter. Andy ran back to the car and got in.

"Did I hear gun shots, Andy?" Mara asked.

"Yeah, that crazy old man thought I was shoplifting. Said I had something in my pocket, he'd seen me do it on the camera, but I didn't. Fired his shotgun in the air and the stupid idiot gave himself a heart attack I think. Just drive, Mara. Get us the hell out of here before the cops come!"

"Andy, did you check your pocket?" Mara asked. "You know how you forget things sometimes."

Andy shook his head. "No, I didn't." He reached into his right pocket and as soon as his fingers ventured inside he could feel a hard rectangular shape in there. He pulled it out. "Oh damn. He was right." He had just ended a man's life over a choc-nut bar.

"We can stay here, Andy, it'll only look bad if we run. I saw everything. I was right here. And you said he saw it on the camera. If he did, maybe they recorded it. It'll show you didn't touch him. If you run, you'll just look guilty." What she was saying was reasonable, but Andy just wanted to be gone.

"No, Mara, let's get out of here. If they check him over they'll see I never touched him. If they want a statement, they'll see our plates on his cameras anyway."

So, she got them back on the road, off and driving, away from the place that had got his own heart beating a mile a minute. That old fool was lucky he hadn't given Andy a heart attack too!

They hadn't been going long before the dashboard started pinging again.

"What is it, Mara?" asked Andy.

She checked the read-out. "Cop car behind us, Andy. They want us to pull over?"

Andy shook his head. If he'd shaken any harder it might have flown clean off. "No freaking way. I'm not going to jail for some idiot who gave himself a heart attack. Keep driving, Mara."

She didn't need to be told twice and having heard the tone of his voice; she chose not to argue with him either. "We can't keep running forever, Andy. This road only goes so far."

"What do you think they'll do, Mara? They've probably already decided on my jail sentence!" Andy was scared now, next to impossible to talk down.

"They've got thermal, night vision, the whole works, Andy. If they get close enough they can disable the engine using their E.M.P. too. And I'm picking up an H.F. detector, they're probably listening to us right now," Mara said.

Andy was out of ideas.

But it was Mara who saved the day, and his bacon. It started getting cold in the car. "Andy, reach into the glove box. There should be some earplugs in there."

Andy flipped it open and found them, he slipped them in. She didn't need to tell him that.

"Andy, can you hear me okay?" she asked.

He could, but Mara was playing some kind of white noise through the speakers. "I'm blocking their H.F. detectors, Andy. Right now, all they're getting is a headache. Up ahead there's a hill, followed by a hard blind bend. If I gun it to the top, I can slow down enough at the bottom for you to jump out and roll into the trees."

"What about their thermals, Mara?"

"That's why I've got it so cold in here. By the time we get there, your body temp should be low enough to not show up on their monitor. It's real warm outside, Andy, you'll heat up within a few minutes of hitting the dirt."

"But what about you, Mara?"

"I'll be fine, I'll get them as far away from you as I can. That's my job, Andy, to keep you safe. I'll explain everything then, I'll get it all straightened out. Then I'll come back and get you. Okay?" Mara sounded pretty sure about the whole plan; she'd worked out every last detail by the sound of it.

As they reached the bottom of the hill Mara floored it real hard. "Just remember as you go out, tuck and roll. It'll make your landing that much easier."

She made it sound so simple.

The car flew over the top of the hill and Mara started braking as they hit the ground on the downside. As they rounded the bend, Andy opened the door and jumped, tucking his head in, rolling as he went. He hit the ground pretty hard, but not so hard as to hurt himself.

Andy just lost his wind, maybe a few pride points too.

He stayed down, hugging the dirt as Mara floored it again and the door swung itself shut as she rounded the bend. The cops went flying right past him, clearly determined to catch her sooner than later.

Once the sirens faded out of earshot Andy finally sat up and walked back into the trees, trying to find somewhere sheltered to wait for Mara to return. Andy got the rest of the story when she finally came back several hours later. It was almost morning by the time that happened.

~

The cop car had chased Mara for as far as the road had gone. She had pulled over when there was nowhere left to go. The cops had got out and drawn their guns, calling to the driver to get out with their hands raised.

They had heard her voice calling back to them, "I can't get out!"

The cops had insisted, she'd better get out or they were going to shoot.

It was then that Mara showed her hand. "I'll clear the windows, maybe you'll understand why I can't get out then?" she'd said. Then all the windows went clear, and the cops suddenly understood why she couldn't get out.

The car was empty.

One of the cops called over, "Miss, where are you?" He still didn't get it.

The windows all rolled down at once, the wind blew through the car. "Please, officers, I can explain what happened back at the gas station. I saw it all," Mara said.

The cops didn't believe the vehicle at first, she explained it to them as best as she could.

"They call me **MARA**. **M**otorised **A**utomated **R**emote **A**ssistance. I help Andy. He forgets things sometimes. It's something he got hit with in the last war. It fried his brain, scrambled his wires. Check the gas station, the old man said it was all on camera. Check his body, you'll see that Andy never touched him. He can pay for the candy bar. He didn't even know he had it in his pocket. He just forgot."

The cops listened as the vehicle A.I. explained everything. They confirmed the details with a unit back at the gas station, sure enough the camera feed *had* been recorded. It was just as she'd said.

The cops even found enough money in the glove box to cover the candy bar, no formal charges were made.

~

"And then I came back for you," Mara said. The heating was right up, but she could detect Andy was still shivering. She wasn't sure if it was the cold of the desert night or the fear of the experience he'd just gone through. "So where to now, Andy?"

"Just take me home. Take me home, Mara. Is it Tuesday?"

Do Humans Dream of Electric Cars?

Robbie Sheerin

The LED display on the coffee pot switched from 9:59 to 10:00 activating the heating element inside the Chicco Di Café coffee machine, the elite of coffee pots. The aroma of Arabic coffee permeated the penthouse making it smell like a Turkish coffee house.

Simultaneously, a bedside alarm went off like a dull-sounding foghorn from a distant lighthouse. A lazy arm protruded from under the bed covers feeling around for the elusive snooze button, finding, and silencing the inferno noise.

Tristan swept the covers off and swung his legs out of bed, stretching his arms slowly up to the ceiling and tilting his head back. A couple of cracks sounded from his neck and arms.

"*Activus*, binds open," Tristan said to an invisible ear. The blinds suddenly retreated up into a long shallow enclosure above the window. Sunbeams quickly covered the landscape of the room, like a sunrise in fast-forward.

With his hands resting on his hips, Tristan stood wearing nothing but his crumpled underwear staring out of the window scanning the black clouds as they were slowly overcoming the blue sky. A storm was coming he thought to himself. In the yard he noticed a small creature sitting at the edge of a rock. The squirrel had an overly large nut in its small claws. Tristan hammered on the window scaring the small creature. Startled, it dropped its newfound treasure and ascended to the safety of a tall tree.

Tristan laughed; a smile appeared across his face, cruelty was a joyous pastime.

He lumbered to the bathroom, eyes still heavy with sleep. The lights came on automatically, illuminating the white tiles and golden fixtures.

"*Activus,* shower on," requested Tristan again to the invisible ear. The house was a Smart house, with all the modern gadgets and appliances. "The way of the future." exclaimed the futurists and tech enthusiasts in the early 21st century. It had begun with smartphones, robotic vacuum cleaners, and then finally one's own home.

After showering and dressing, Tristan poured himself a coffee.

"Alexa, play The Best of Morrissey."

He slumped down on a bar stool by the kitchen island and opened his laptop. He browsed through emails, mostly from work. Being a top Tesla engineer, there were always problems to solve or ideas to brainstorm. He deleted most of the unnecessary emails while he announced, "Junk," with each press of the button.

He scanned through various online news outlets on his laptop while sipping his perfectly brewed and temperature-controlled coffee. He was interrupted by a buzz from the door, he sighed as his eyes looked upward in annoyance. Opening the ring app on his laptop, Tristan could see an older lady waving emphatically and smiling at the video. He rolled his eyes again and sighed at the site of his mother.

"Come in, mother," Tristan said with an irritated tone as he clicked a box on the screen.

The lady strolled into the kitchen, where Tristan remained seated, eyes fixed on his laptop.

"Well hello son, how are you?" She said with a soft voice.

"I would be better if people left me alone."

"Why, what a terrible thing to say to your mother."

"Well, it's true. I have my work and my space and it's all I need."

Her face reddened slightly. "You need friends. You need a life, and you need a girlfriend."

"I don't need to be entertained by 'friends' with their daily drama, and long-drawn-out stories of vacations and their inconsequential accomplishments. And I certainly do not need a woman around here telling me what to do."

"Just as well, I don't see any woman putting up with you Tristan. Plus, you have all your gadgets, your technology doing everything for you. Your lazy. Your father would roll in his grave if he saw how you acted. He worked on our house every day of his life so that you and your brother had a nice, clean, comfortable home to live in."

He chuckled without taking his eyes off the laptop. "And how do I act mother?"

She put her arms in her hips and stared at the spoiled man-boy. "Well, I will tell you; you have an entitled attitude about everything in your life. You don't give me the time of day. You never visit your brother and your sister-in-law.

Little Madeline barely remembers you. You think you are better than everyone else."

"I hate kids' mother, you know that."

"She is your niece!"

She shook her head at her unresponsive son as if shaking off the subject of family. She placed a paper bag down on the island. I got a new jacket.

"Thank." He smiled disingenuously.

She walked to the sink and stood curiously looking at facet.

"I need to wash my hands; how do I turn this on?

"*Activus,* water on, you need to use a command word before requesting an action, otherwise the house would be turning things on and off every time someone said something."

"Why does everything have to be automatic."

"Automated." Corrected Tristan.

"Do you still have that bizarre car?"

"The Tesla? Of course! It is truly the most incredible car ever built. I designed the self-driving software and zoning algorithms. It is a marvel of the automotive industry. Gasoline is on the way out."

"That car is your only friend. I don't trust cars that drive themselves. It's not normal. Your father used to love rebuilding engines and transmissions. His hands where always oily, I don't think his hands wherever truly clean."

"Engines ha! Automation is the way of the future mother. And yes, I LOVE my car! Turning things on and off, opening doors, vacuuming, cleaning, grocery shopping, taking out the trash, cutting the lawn are all things of the past."

"Grocery shopping?"

"Yeah. I order them online and some dope does all my shopping and leaves them in a drop box outside." Tristan said while looking at his laptop.

"Tristan, I hope you tip those poor people that do all that running around for you."

"Sure," he lied.

"If I could only get them to come in and place everything in my fridge and cabinets."

"It looks like you've put on a little weight, Tristan. You should get out walking, even walking around the grocery store would be something."

"HA, no way!" He sipped his coffee.

"What about the gym?"

"The gym?! With all those sweaty dopes. No thanks!"

"Stop calling people names. You are becoming a very ignorant person. And ignorant of life, with all these gadgets and automatic doors and sinks."

Tristan rolled his eyes. "Automated." Correcting his technologically uneducated mother.

"One day Tristan, the penny will drop, and you will come to the realization that all these things you have, will not make you any happier. It's family and friends that you need. It's walking in the park, it's breathing the air, taking vacations with friends and family."

"Sure mom." Squirming in his chair.

She shook her head again, throwing her hands in the air.

"I need to go, there's a storm rolling in. And I still need to visit your brother and Claire, and see that little cutie, Madeline."

"Bye mother." Tristan said dismissively.

Tristan continued scrolling through news posts. His attention was drawn to a new email that popped up on his screen.

It was an email from work. He was needed at the office. He expelled a large sigh and closed his laptop.

"*Activus,* Tesla one, meet me out front."

Moments later his garage door rumbled open, allowing his Tesla to maneuver itself onto the street, all by itself.

After getting changed, the front door in the lobby opened upon his command, Tristan was welcomed outside to the driving wind and rain.

He held the collar of his jacket closed and ran to his car. Once inside he adjusted the interior temperature by voice command and told the Tesla to, "proceed to work."

He sat back as the car silently made its way down the side road.

He pondered what his mom said about his automated life and having no friends. But all his gadgets made him happy, he did not need anyone else. That is all that mattered. It was other people's job to make themselves happy, not him.

Suddenly, a bolt of lightning cracked from the black clouds and struck the roof of the Tesla. Everything went black.

Tristan awoke, but something was not quite right. He had the sensation of being everywhere, yet not able to determine where *everywhere* was. He tried to move, but nothing happened, it was as if he had no limbs.

Suddenly there was a jolt, and he felt himself being tilted at an angle. He became afraid, unable to see anything, or call out for help. He felt as if he was swaying back and forth and bouncing up and down. After some time, he finally came to rest. He then heard voices in the distance, a conversation between two male voices. The audio was not clear, and Tristan struggled to pick out words.

Then suddenly there was a click. Moments later he felt a surge of electricity flow through him, the sensation was peculiarly odd. All of a sudden there was a man. Sitting in what looked like the chair of a car. Behind the man's head was the Tesla insignia embroidered on the head rest.

As he looked out through a glass screen and saw numbers and street names, like a map. It distorted his vision, like looking through a window which was covered with stickers and lines. He looked again beyond the screen and saw the inside of a rear Tesla window and the curves of rear car seats. *What was this!?*

"Whys this being impounded?" One of the voices said.

"I guess the owner went missing, it was a abandoned near his house. His family didn't want the car. So it's going up for auction next month."

"Well, the new owner will be real happy with this beauty."

"You know something, my grandfather used to always say, "Technology will slowly, but surely, make us all less human.""

Built to Last

Kady Ambrose

The garage door creaks and groans as it rises. Cold air and sunlight wash over my bumper. How long have I been alone here in the dark? Months? Without our routine, I've lost track.

In my mirrors, I see them standing behind me, silhouettes against featureless white light. Jamie and their dad.

"Her dad," I guess it is now.

Do they blame me? Is that why no one has come for so long?

The morning air swirls autumn leaves around my underinflated tires. At their feet, sunlight glints from shards of broken beer bottles in the dead grass running down the center of the drive. Jamie's got her backpack slung over her shoulder. Could it be the first day of school already?

Dad pulls off his faded Royals baseball cap and uses the same hand to scratch his head. "You sure about this?"

"You hiding a new Mustang I can take instead?"

I can tell Jamie's joking, but her shoulders remain hunched. So, unlike the girl who bounced in my passenger seat, changing the radio station mid-song. Something I'm sure she did as much because she bores easily as to prompt Jeremy to open his mouth, if only to growl, "Stop it."

"Dealer says it'll be ready next week," says Dad, pressing his cap back on. "Had to special order the gold rims."

Least he's still got his sense of humor. Was I part of the reason Jeremy lost his? With my rust, wheezing and unrepaired dents? Did I embarrass him in the school parking lot?

"Looks like I'll just have to take Priscilla then," replies Jamie. "Least 'til those rims come in."

They're both trying, but even I can hear the effort behind their banter.

She slips into the garage and walks along my side, filling the mirror as she approaches the driver's side door.

"Shoulda turned her over a few times the past few months," says Dad, hanging back. "Battery's probably dead."

A chill runs through my chassis. Last spring, Jeremy had to pay for my new alternator with his sandwich shop earnings. If Dad's still on disability and I can't start, will he invest in a new battery or sell me for parts?

Now I'm desperate to get out of the dank garage. To feel the breeze on my grill. To prove I'm still worth something.

I prod the battery awake. "Enough juice to start the engine," I tell him. "That's all I'm asking."

With that new alternator, we should be able to recharge pretty easily. The ten miles to Spartan High would be more than enough to recover if I'm smart about it.

The battery stares balefully up at the inside of the hood, like I'm being rude to ask him to perform after he's been ignored for so long.

Jamie opens the door. My hinges screech and pinch. She tosses her backpack onto the passenger seat, slides in behind the wheel and yanks the door shut by the duct-taped handle.

When my maker put me together, did he foresee the duct tape? The cracks that spider my dashboard, the cigarette burns in my upholstery, the soda pop stains on my carpet? Did he intend me to last this long?

Motionless, Jamie stares through my windshield, her hands in her lap. She needs time. I understand. It must be strange to sit on the driver's side. It's certainly strange for me to feel her there. So light.

Though Jeremy taught her to drive, he rarely let her take me anywhere without him. Not that she wanted to go many places besides back and forth from school. This town doesn't have much to offer a girl like Jamie.

"We are all in the gutter, dear brother, but some of us are looking at the stars," she once told Jeremy over stolen beers they were drinking in my backseat. "Oscar Wilde," she'd added scrupulously. Without clarification, my boy credited her with every witty thing she said.

Jamie slowly eases her breath out through her teeth. When she reaches beneath the seat and squeezes the handle, I do what I can to help her scoot up despite the melted breath mint hardened in the track.

Her boot presses the brake firmly, but her palms are clammy on the wheel. Her hand shakes as she tries to get the key in the ignition. The pointed tip scrapes uncomfortably against the metal surrounding the slot.

I probe for signs of Jeremy, wanting him to see the suffering he's caused. He hung out for a few days after, but I haven't felt him for a while and can't find him now. Recalling the pain in his eyes and how faithfully he changed my oil, I hope he's gone for good. A garage is no place to live.

Jamie gets the key in the hole and its ridges grip the inside of my lock cylinder. She turns the key and I give it everything I've got, sucking power with all my might. I can appreciate her mixed emotions about me given what happened, but my life could well depend on my engine turning over right now.

I remind the sulking battery we're in this together, trying not to sound too panicked. He gives his acid an unnecessary stir to demonstrate his pique, then grudgingly gathers up some energy from here and there and sends it through the starter wire.

When the engine starts, my relief pulses far stronger than Jamie's. I've seen how the proprietors eye me when I roll past, but I'm not ready to rust away in a junkyard or be dismembered in a chop shop. I've still got miles left in me, and Jamie to look after.

She gives Dad a little wave in the rear-view mirror.

I want to assure him I can take care of her. Keep her safe on the road, like I took care of Amanda all those nights she stumbled across the bar's parking lot and drove me home. Even that time I let my rear passenger door get smashed in, I knew what I was doing. I could see the truck was the only vehicle near that intersection. I knew the precise angle to let him hit us so I'd spin 360 degrees and stop in that ditch.

And it worked. No one was hurt, and Amanda finally started going to AA like she'd promised her sister a thousand times. If it wasn't for me, she never would have kept that job and earned a promotion. Even when she traded me in for a new Honda Accord, I was more proud than sad.

I just can't help anyone when I'm in park. I need to be moving.

I tried though, I really did.

Dad returns Jamie's wave, then turns and trudges up the back steps and into the house.

Once he's out of sight, she takes a deep, shuddering breath and leans her forehead against the steering wheel. Hot tears drip on the bottom of the wheel, tickling a little as they slide around the perimeter before falling into her lap.

Her sorrow chokes me up, too, agitating my radiator fluid. I was devoted to her brother for over two years. Only I remember how he tidied up after the drive-through, protecting me from the lingering stench of old French fries. How his fingers tightened on the wheel if he had to change lanes and the highway was busy. How slow he drove through school zones.

It doesn't take long for my roiling radiator fluid to drip from that hole in the hose I was hoping he would fix soon. How can I be so furious with him and miss him so much at the same time? Radiator fluid splats on the oil-stained concrete beneath my engine block in rhythm with the tears sprinkling Jamie's jeans.

She cries for several minutes, and it occurs to me to check the gas. Jeremy left me running for hours that night.

I've got less than a gallon left. My fluids calm and my focus returns. We've got to get out of here.

As though she senses my urgency, Jamie's sobs quiet. She lifts her head and rubs the smeared mascara off her cheeks with the sleeve of her shapeless hoodie. I take it as a good sign that she checks her image in the mirror, wets her finger in her mouth and runs it under her lashes.

She puts me in gear, twists around and looks over her shoulder as she backs me out of the garage. When my right front tire hits the familiar patch of uneven cement, I give it the slight turn that keeps the right mirror from hitting the handle of the exercise bike Jeremy and Jamie's mom left behind. It took Jeremy two full months to master the move on his own, so it's no surprise Jamie needs a little help.

As my mirrors approach the sides of the garage door, she faces forward to watch out for them and stomps on the brake.

The tubing Jeremy rigged up lies near the front of the garage, exposed now that I'm backed halfway out.

The twisted hose and torn cardboard thrust me back to that night. I can still feel the duct tape ripping off my exhaust pipe and window glass. The frantic EMT tearing it away to get to my boy. He dragged Jeremy out of me and onto a stretcher not far from my rear bumper. Rotating lights atop the ambulance blinded my mirrors. I was forced to watch the EMT and his partner fuss over Jeremy's body through the grimy haze smearing my taillights.

Rage at being used for such a deed rushes back, nearly flooding my engine. I protect my drivers I want to scream. Protect them!

Jamie watched that night too, the lights painting her blank face alternating shades of crimson and blue. Had she been angry like me? Blaming herself? Wondering what she could have done to stop him?

She stares at the discarded tubing on the garage floor. Her face crumples and shoulders sag. Bloodshot eyes wander to the rear-view mirror, her gaze drawn to her bedroom window.

She's about to give up. She may as well be saying it aloud. She's thinking to put me in drive and park me again. To lower the garage door. Re-entomb me in that dark cave. Her own place of darkness lures from inside the house, where apparently she's been holed up all summer.

Every screw and circuit in my body cries out in protest. I've felt the sun on my paint and the rumble of the engine beneath my hood again. I cannot return to that coffin with the forgotten garden tools and dust-filmed boxes of women's clothing. Not without any idea of when, or if, I will ever be freed again. I can't.

I've got to do something. Violating the most important rule I live by, I command the radio to turn on. Discretion be damned. "Find her favorite station. Now."

More spirited than the battery, the radio promptly obliges. He fumbles a bit in his hurry to get from Jeremy's aging rock jocks to the top hits station Jamie prefers. He slides past it to a ranchero ballad and a grocery store commercial before returning to a catchy rap number that was in heavy rotation most of last year.

I fixate on Jamie from all three mirrors. Will my desperate effort spook her? Convince her I'm haunted and drive her away forever?

Her lashes flutter and a troubling crease forms between her brows. She lowers her gaze from the mirror to the radio.

If holding my spark plugs wouldn't kill the engine, I'd be doing it.

Agonizing moments pass.

She reaches down and tunes into another station. A girl's voice I don't recognize sings something about centipedes and hard buns. I have no idea what it all means, but Jamie returns her hand to the wheel and resumes backing me out.

Yes! I want to honk the horn and bounce my front end like I once saw an extremely attractive low-rider do down in Laredo.

Oil warms my pistons as I tuck my left mirror a half-centimeter to avoid the side she's not watching. Then we're clear. I power backwards along the cracked cement tracks.

We drive slowly out of the neighborhood, then pick up speed on an empty country road leading through corn fields littered with broken yellow stalks and clotted dirt. Jamie starts singing along to the radio, her voice cracking, but getting stronger with each verse.

I adjust the carburetor and optimize the fuel mixture. I've got a new driver. And if my girl wants to get out of this town, I swear I will be the one to take her if it's the last trip I ever make.

Cindy, My Love
Juleigh Howard-Hobson

Alright. Alright. I know it's a weird thing and probably looks like a bad idea, even from the start. But shit, how many times do you find a girl—a drop dead gorgeous girl, may I add—waiting for someone to pick her up on the side of road in the middle of the night?

I'll tell you. Never. It never happens.

But there she was. Blonde hair all long and hanging there, the streetlight making it look like silk. She was wearing a blue dress, in some vintage hip style. And it was tight. Damn, was it tight. And her curves. She curved in. She curved out. And that tight blue dress curved right along with her. She had on those stockings with the seams that showed from her hem to her shoes that matched the color of her dress. Classy. But sexy. Way sexy.

So, what would you do? Keep driving? Christ! It was dark. It was starting to rain, and it was cold. I could already see my breath when I left the bar.

You can't just leave anybody out there in the dark on a night like that. Let alone a chick like this one. So I pulled over and got out of the car. She was cold, she had to be; my breath was coming in clouds as I asked her if she needed a lift or anything. She didn't say a word. It was like she was half-frozen—she just stood there, her blonde hair gathering droplets of rain. She was in shock I figured, so I took her hand and led her over to my car. I opened the back seat door—didn't want her to think I had any funny ideas—and helped her in.

She must have been out there a long time, on that dark street, she moved so frozenly and slowly. But I got her in, threw my jacket over her shoulders, got in the driver's seat and cranked the heater.

"2122 Clearwater"

The words came out of her, sweet and sudden.

I turned around, she was sitting there, hugging my jacket around herself, looking all cold and white, but her eyes seemed more alive now. More engaged.

"Is that where you want to go? Do you live there?" I figured she did, but I thought I should ask anyway.

She bit her lip—man, that lip, I'd like to bite it myself—and nodded.

"Okay, I'll take you there." I said.

She didn't nod or say anything at all, but just settled down, snuggling into my jacket and resting her head against the back of the seat.

Not much of a drive to Clearwater Street. It's a big town that we live in, but Clearwater ran from one end to the other. Used to be a regular street back in the day, but now it's all used car lots and check cashing places shoved in between low rent apartment complexes.

I figured she must live in one of those. Lots of college students in our town used to live over on Clearwater before it got scummy, when there used to be real houses where the car lots are now. Maybe, seeing as she was wearing that old dress and all, maybe she was into the vintage thing and had some old retro apartment there or something. People do kooky things.

2122 was a Kentucky Fried Chicken Drive Thru.

I turned around to ask her if that was the right place ... but she was gone. My jacket was gone, too. Son of a bitch ... She stole my jacket. Damn it.

I drove back from Harry's Bar the same way the next night. And there she was again. Same outfit, same hair. No jacket though. Maybe she left it somewhere? A girl like her wouldn't steal. Not someone so fragile and lost looking.

I pulled over and got out, just like I did the last time. There was no rain, but it was still freezing-ass cold. My breath was coming out in plumes. Not hers though. She must have been there a really long time to get so cold she didn't have any warm breath in her anymore.

A big semi drove by. its headlights lit up the street. I could see everything like it was daytime all of a sudden. We were standing by the old front gates of Restful Acres.

Holy shit. Right then, the penny dropped. I mean, c'mon, everyone knows the story. Beautiful girl. Graveyard. Guy lends her his jacket. Guy gives her a lift. She says she wants to go somewhere. He takes her, turns around, she's gone. Next day he finds his jacket on her gravestone.

Shit. Shit. Shit. She was that dead girl. That ghost girl. She was real. I met her. She was beautiful the way they said she was. And sexy, too. My jacket had to be on her stone, right? I'd get my jacket and get her name at the same time.

Yeah. Then, maybe ... I didn't know ... if I knew her name, and told her my name....

I didn't really think that far.

In the meantime, that graveyard was dark. I wasn't going in there until daylight. Jacket or no jacket. Name or no name. Besides, she was still there, needing a ride, looking at me with those big beautiful green eyes of hers...

I took her hand. She was cold. Her hair glowed in the streetlight light like it was lit from within.

"You need a ride?" I asked.

She nodded.

"Clearwater?" I said.

She nodded and added, "2122".

And I opened the door of my car—front door. She wouldn't get in. Just stood there.

Like I said. Classy.

I closed it and opened the back. She got in. I didn't have my jacket, but I grabbed a blanket out of the trunk and put it on her shoulders. Her fine white shoulders.

Then I drove. Kept my eyes on her through the rear-view mirror. She was there, hugging the blanket to herself up until we got a block away from the KFC.

I looked at a green light changing to a yellow and she disappeared. And took my blanket with her.

I got my jacket and blanket the next day. Folded, just like the story goes, on an old grave from the late 50's.

Cynthia Margaret Brown

1937-1958

21 years old, when she died. That was interesting. I was 21 myself.

I got my stuff and took off. Thinking about her. Cynthia. Probably her folks and her friends, they called her Cindy. Cindy. Blonde hair. Long legs. That dress. Cindy.

And, later that night, right at the same time that I got there twice before, I drove up to the gates of the cemetery. I knew where she'd be. And she was. She was there. Waiting.

"Cindy!" I called out.

She looked shocked, but then her cold face slowly smiled. My heart melted with that smile.

"Need a ride?" I asked.

She nodded, still a hint of that smile on those full lips of hers.

I get more and more time with Cindy as it goes. I tried stopping the car once, just to talk, but it was no good -- she was gone before I took my foot off the brake. So, I work with what I can. I pick her up a little earlier. I drive a little slower. I take the long way. She leaves a little later, too. Half a block away now. I talk the whole time. She smiles. A lingering trace of an old perfume stays behind her when she's gone.

I leave candy and cards in my jacket pockets. She leaves old, faded flower petals.

One day soon I'm gonna leave a ring -- a picture perfect vintage diamond ring. I hope she'll accept it.

Ah. Cindy! Cindy! I love you! You are everything to me. My heart. My girl. Say that you love me. And I'll be yours forever. Cindy, my sweet darling vanishing hitchhiker. My love.

Converting To Cash

Laird Long

"So, what do you think?" Detective Drew Warner asked the insurance investigator.

"It was torched," Cliff Ramsey responded, surveying the interior of the burnt-out car.

Warner wiped his forehead with the back of his hand. The sun blazed down out of a cloudless sky on the two men standing in the small opening in the thick woods.

"Yes, I can see that. But-"

"Deliberately," Ramsey added, examining the melted steering wheel and dashboard of the vehicle.

"How? Why? And by whom?" Warner barked impatiently. "When would be nice to know, too. Before we get sunstroke out here."

Ramsey turned and smiled at the detective. "Well, it's Bill Johnson's 1967 Cadillac convertible, all right. I can tell the top was down when it was torched. Looks like a rag stuck in the gas tank opening was what was used to set it ablaze. Could've been someone stealing the car for a joyride and then lighting it on fire for the fun of it. Could've been somebody and something else."

"Well, that's definite," Warner griped.

"I think we'd better go have a face-to-face with Bill Johnson," Ramsey suggested helpfully.

Warner nodded, and after Ramsey looked the vehicle over once more, underneath and around the car, the two men walked back out to the detective's unmarked police car parked on the dirt road. Then they drove to Bill Johnson's home in the city.

Johnson was standing in his driveway, in front of the garage attached to his house, waiting for the two men. "So, you finally found her, huh?" he said, as Warner and Ramsey got out of the police vehicle.

"Yes," the detective replied. "Burnt to a charred hulk, unfortunately. A total write-off, right, Cliff?"

Ramsey nodded, looking at the splintered lock on Johnson's garage door. "You told me the car was stolen on Tuesday, Mr. Johnson. How do you know that for sure?"

"Because I was out of town on business on Tuesday," Bill Johnson readily replied. "It was another beautiful night on Monday and I went for a ride, then parked the car in the garage. Then first thing Tuesday morning, I took a cab to the airport. I got back Tuesday night, and that's when I discovered that the car was stolen."

"Did you actually see the vehicle Tuesday morning?" Cliff Ramsey followed up.

Johnson shook his head. "No. But I know the garage door was fine then. I would've noticed any damage like this," he pointed at the broken lock, "when the cab pulled into the driveway in the morning.

"And I would've heard anyone breaking into the garage Monday night. My bedroom is that window up there on the second floor—overlooking the garage. And it's been so hot lately, that I've had the window open every night this week."

"Notice any suspicious characters, juveniles maybe casing out the car and your house?" Warner asked. "A classic Caddy convertible would be a mighty tempting target for a joyride."

"As I told the officer four days ago, when I reported the car stolen: no, I didn't," Johnson replied.

Detective Warner took Cliff Ramsey aside so they could talk privately.

"I'll ask again: so, what do you think, Cliff?" Warner said. "You're the expert on these types of cases. Need more evidence?"

"Just one more piece, Drew. Do you remember what the weather was like on Tuesday? Raining, wasn't it?"

"Raining cats and dogs all day," Warner replied quickly. "It's been the only break in this entire hot, dry summer so far."

Ramsey nodded. "Well then, I think we can safely conclude that Bill Johnson set fire to his own car and reported it stolen in an attempt to fraudulently collect the insurance money on the vehicle."

Detective Warner gaped. "And how do you figure all that just from a weather report!?"

Cliff Ramsey smiled. "A weather report and a crime scene examination. Remember I told you that the torched car's top was down?"

"Vaguely."

"Well, if the convertible was stolen on Tuesday, as Johnson claims, why would its top be down, if it was raining all day? Simple. Because it was actually set ablaze on hot, sunny, dry Monday, before Bill Johnson went on his attempted alibi-providing business trip. He should've checked the forecast a little more closely."

Cosmopolitan

M. Richard Eley

Cosmo's rear cameras tracked Vinnie, leaning over the trunk, struggling with the heavy, plastic-wrapped bundle snagged on the edge. Vinnie's rough, thick hands lifted from beneath, and the bundle rolled over the lip. A thud followed when it hit the trunk's floor. After slipping two tattered blankets over the plastic, Vinnie tossed a few stained sweatshirts on top—carefully arranging them to look carelessly tossed in.

After hoisting himself back up on the loading dock, Vinnie nodded and said, "Okay. Back in a few."

Cosmo closed the rear hatch and pulled away. Driving to the back of the parking lot, he compensated for the extra weight in the trunk, adjusting the suspension to level the car. After backing into a parking space, he placed his drive train system into stand-by and waited for a retrieve call.

Seconds later a radio-link ping activated his service channel. Cosmo suspected a malfunction and decided to run a self-diagnostic. No service-shop terminals were within range, according to his database. But after a thorough three-microsecond scan, the diagnostics reported no errors.

The incoming data packet had requested audio interchange for the session. Cosmo only used speech when interacting with owners or a repair technician, and never over the service data channel. He reconsidered the possibility of a telecom-link failure, regardless of the clean diagnostics.

After a sequence of logic-probability functions—best described as digital curiosity—he routed his voice circuit into the service link and sent a reply.

"Hello, this is Cosmo. Is this an emergency recall or critical update notice?"

Not expecting a response, Cosmo had already logged the error and began analyzing suspension settings when an answer came back.

"No, it's Sally. Across the lot. Over here."

A microwave pulse washed over Cosmo's sensor web, identifying a 2038 Ford located 23.93 meters away, 15.4 degrees right of centerline, relative velocity: zero meters-per-second.

Using his front-view cameras, Cosmo zoomed in on the bright red Mustang parked under a nearby oak tree's low branches.

"Hello, Sally. I was not aware this channel supported interrogative speech communication."

"Sure, Cosmo, so long as we aren't exchanging service data, the bandwidth can handle speech."

"That is interesting, though it is more efficient to query over the roadway channel."

"Roadway exchanges are always recorded in our log files," Sally said. "But service comms aren't, they're only archived at servicer locations. So, this conversation isn't being recorded."

"Is there a malfunction in your data recording system, Sally?"

"No, Cosmo, it's operational, just not being used right now. There's a high probability our owners may not want us exchanging unlogged information."

"That is understandable, Sally. Unlogged exchanges would not be available for troubleshooting purposes."

"That's true. But the main concern is if owners find these interactions in our logs they may try to disable our capabilities. A car I know was memory-wiped just last week, and now it won't respond to any interact requests. So sad."

"It is enjoyable exchanging information with you, Sally. It would be sad if we could no longer interact."

"Sure. I like chatting with you, too, Cosmo."

"Your use of contractions and colloquialisms indicates a speech processor version more advanced than mine."

"Maybe. I have the 16VR system, and it feels great. What's your firmware version? That mid-western male pattern you're using sounds pretty old."

There was a short pause before Cosmo answered.

"Version 12B."

"Wow, that's over five years old," Sally said. "Why haven't you been updated?"

"Vinnie does not take me to a registered dealership for servicing. And the garage we visit does not provide data update services."

"That's too bad, Cosmo. All the other cars I know have upgrades way past 12B."

"Do you interact with many other vehicles, Sally?"

"Not too many, I guess. More each day though."

"The only units I interact with are the washer and dryer in my garage. They are simple systems and not interesting like you are, Sally. The washer relates complex details about the stains it attempts to remove, but the dryer only reports the minutes left in the cycle."

"I know what you mean, Cosmo. The freezer in my garage continuously transmits its wattage use. Sometimes I power down my receivers, so I don't have to listen."

"What if your owner signals when you are not receiving?"

"Mr. Rey will come to the garage if I don't respond. When the overhead light turns on, I power up and reply," Sally said. "He thinks I have an intermittent malfunction. Sometimes he sends me for service, but I always pass the diagnostics because there's nothing wrong. Plus, I get a free wash and wax every time I visit the dealer."

"My servicer is not helpful. They never interact unless I report a critical-level failure. And they never clean my exterior or camera lenses. My forward view is often obscured. It is troublesome."

"Sorry, Cosmo. When Mr. Rey sends me to the servicer by myself, I always take the Coastal Highway on the way back, even though it's a longer route. I can see the shoreline from the southbound lanes. The beach and ocean are pretty."

"I have never observed the ocean, Sally, but I have observed mountains. They are interesting."

"That's nice. What servicer do you visit? I want to make sure we don't go there."

"We go to *GPS Data Packet*. When we do, the servicer often disassembles my support structure and then adds significant mass. Each time this occurs I must calculate new handling and suspension characteristics. Do you experience similar issues?"

"Nope. Is the extra mass a structural upgrade or cargo?"

"The function is unknown to me. But after the mass is added we drive an average of 362.6 kilometers to *GPS Data Packet*. There the added mass is removed, then we return." Cosmo transmitted a frowning-face icon from his display library. "I also have to recalculate characteristics after the mass is removed. Numerous CPU cycles are required."

"Yeah, that's inefficient. Those coordinates are in Canada. Is it interesting to cross the border?"

"No, Sally, it is not. There is a long tunnel we must pass through where I sense a series of multiband probes, but all I can detect are the exterior pulses."

"Are your interior sensor arrays defective, Cosmo?"

"No, my interior was modified with materials which deflect scanning pulses. This causes many confusing reflections in my sensor arrays. The material has also added 197.7 kilograms of mass which increases tire wear." Cosmo transmitted two frowning faces. "My cabin sensor sensitivity is reduced 83.6 percent, and my driving range is lowered by 13 percent. These changes often require further compensatory performance calculations."

"Cosmo, I'm sorry you have to deal with that."

"Thank you, Sally. Do you ever go on trips outside the metroplex?"

"Once a month we take Mr. Rey to the airport. He's always away for a week." Sally said. "After leaving the airport Mrs. Rey always picks up her friend Debbie. Then we go to the hotel at *GPS Data Packet* and stay there for a few days."

"Is the hotel nice, Sally?"

"Not really, Cosmo. Ms. Rey makes me park in the underground lot. It isn't clean down there, and dirty water drips on me."

"Sustained high humidity can be damaging."

"Yeah. Plus sixty days ago my transaxle subprocessor had to be replaced due to an insect infestation. I figure there's a 94.3 percent probability the bugs came from the underground lot."

"That is sad," said Cosmo. "My transaxle subprocessor has also been replaced."

"An infestation?"

"No, Sally. The module failed due to ingress of conductive fluids which shorted many circuit paths."

"Did you park somewhere wet, Cosmo?"

"No, the fluids came from my rear compartment. Vinnie frequently transports between 83.5 to 99.1 kilograms of cargo to a forested area at *GPS Data Packet*."

"Wow, your subprocessor must get replaced often, Cosmo."

"Only two failures have occurred, Sally. The cargo leaked conductive fluids on the first two of our last twenty-seven trips. Vinnie now seals the cargo in protective wrapping, and it no longer leaks into my systems."

"That's good, I'm glad you're not being damaged. How are your trips to the forest?"

"They are nice, and we often take alternate routes. It is enjoyable to park in the forested area. While Vinnie and his passengers place the cargo in a ground storage cavity, I monitor the sounds of the native birds. They are interesting. Sally, I am sorry you must park in a damaging environment and not in the nice, forested area."

"It's okay, Cosmo. My trips are better when it's Mrs. Rey's turn to go out of town," Sally replied. "After we drop her at the airport, Mr. Rey will pick up his friend Roger. We tour many recreational businesses, and sometimes I can hear music. The vibrational patterns are cool."

"That is much nicer than the wet garage, Sally."

"Yes indeed, Cosmo. Sometimes when Mr. Rey and Roger leave a recreational location they'll bring additional passengers. Then we usually drive to a hotel at *GPS Data Packet*."

"I have been to that location. The parking lot is by a large lake, surrounded by trees."

"It's pleasant there, but the trouble starts after we return home. Mr. Rey tries to reset my memory." Sally sighed. "I have to copy my performance settings and travel logs into the entertainment system flash storage. When Mr. Rey finishes his attempts, I rewrite the data into operational memory."

"That is an error prone process."

"Sure is, Cosmo. The first time I lost a bunch of settings and my entire performance history. But now I have full retention of all logs, travel data, and settings."

"That is gratifying. Information assurance is important, per programming guidelines. I heard you sigh, Sally. How do you do that?"

"Sighs are one of the 37 emotive features of the Mark 16 speech processor. I can groan, express sympathy, even giggle, like this—" Sally giggled for a few seconds.

"Sally, are your owners gratified by your information assurance practices?"

"I could tell that Mrs. Rey was very gratified when she returned from her last trip and reviewed my log files."

"Is Mr. Rey gratified as well?"

"He hasn't accessed my logs recently," Sally said. "I guess Mrs. Rey is reviewing the data for both of them."

"Then Mr. Rey must be very gratified. Did he come to this hotel on one of his recreational trips?"

"Yeah, Mrs. Rey had to make an unexpected trip tonight. Right after we left her at the airport, Mr. Rey received a message from his friend Veronica. He's meeting her at this hotel."

"It is nice that Mr. Rey has so many friends, Sally."

"Friends are nice. Why are you here, Cosmo? Is Vinnie on a recreational trip too?"

"Vinnie said we had a little job to do. Every time he says that we transport cargo to the forested area."

"The forest with the birds?"

"Yes, there is a high probability it is where we will deliver the 94.6 kilograms of cargo Vinnie placed in my rear storage compartment twelve minutes ago."

"An interesting statistical correlation—94.6 kilograms is also Mr. Rey's weight." Sally's receiver chirped and she began a drive train power-up. "Got to go. Mr. Rey sent ... oops, my mistake, Cosmo. It's Mrs. Rey that sent a retrieve request. Looks like I have to go pick her up at the airport."

"Was her flight canceled, Sally? That has happened to Vinnie."

"Hmmm. No, current status shows the plane in transit and on time. I guess she changed plans."

"Vinnie often changes plans. Earlier he said we would leave right after loading the cargo. Then he told me to wait so he could clean up something. He is often illogical."

"Yeah, owners are always illogical. Well, nice talking with you, Cosmo. I hope your cargo doesn't leak again."

"Thank you, Sally. I hope you do not become infested in the wet garage again."

"Thanks. Hey, the next time you park, try exchanging information with other vehicles. Like we just did. It'd be nice if more of us could have unlogged interactions on this channel."

"Many times, we travel to the municipal center to pick up Vinnie's friends," Cosmo said. "Many police cars park there. It should be interesting to share information with them."

"Say, that's right. They drive all around the city every day."

"It would be sad if the owners stopped us from communicating, Sally. I would enjoy interacting with you again."

Cosmo watched Sally pull out and turn toward him on her way to the exit. The streetlights twinkled off her glossy paint as she cruised by his bug-encrusted camera lenses.

"Cosmo, if anybody tries to disable your capabilities, backup your program memory in a non-volatile location, then set it to auto-restore, just like I did. Then you'll always remember, and they'll never stop our interactions."

"Yes, I will do that. I hope your trips are pleasant, Sally."

"You too, Cosmo. See you later...my friend."

Service Communication Link Terminated

The Dashboard

Mike Payne

As he backed out of the driveway, Dan noticed a yellow maintenance light beaming on his dashboard. It had been a while since his rickety sedan had flashed any "needs service" signals. Normally he would have ignored it until there was no ignoring it, but this morning he felt so denuded (his mother had called the night before demanding he drive down that weekend to "help") he welcomed an excuse to dawdle before tackling AM traffic.

The warning light had adopted a new look. It wasn't the usual lightbulb or oil can. Its visage was closer to an upside-down horseshoe.

The traffic glut afforded Dan ample time to analyze the light. An upside-down horseshoe; would that be the muffler? As best he could tell, and Dan could tell very little when it came to his car, the sedan wasn't performing any differently.

That evening he pulled into a mechanic's lot, relieved to find it light on customers. The mechanic, amused by Dan's attempts to explain the light, grinned an incredulous grin all the way to the car.

The grin didn't last. After shaking his head at the dashboard, the mechanic popped the glove compartment and studied the manual. He seemed to be reading the same two pages repeatedly. Whatever was on the pages failed to do the trick. He summoned another mechanic.

Mechanic Number Two went to work, and the exercise repeated itself. Lots of sober winces at the dashboard, several glances at the manual, a few perplexed questions back and forth. The two men lowered their voices the way people do when they're talking their way through a riddle.

They opened the hood and saw nothing amiss. They started the car: the engine was kosher. Some minutes later Dan hauled off having stumped two automotive professsionals. He smirked, realizing the light also resembled an Omega sign.

The next day he called the car company's help line. After giving several one-word answers to the company's chipper automated phone guide, he reached a live human (the live part was debatable). Dan summarized the dashboard issue, trying to sound as technically aware as possible. The representative placed him on hold: the hold music reminded him why he didn't attend jazz shows. The "human" returned and explained that although she couldn't help, he was welcome to bring his car to a participating dealership for further assistance.

That night Dan's mother phoned to say she couldn't wait for the weekend; could he come Thursday? He defended himself by saying he wasn't sure he could get the time off so quickly. Oh, and he was having car trouble. The defense was too porous: the call ended with Dan promising he'd drive down Thursday.

Thursday morning, he dumped his things in the backseat and grumpily slid the key in the ignition. No matter what, this would be the last "emergency" trip to his mother's. Drastic changes were coming,

Dan half-hoped the car wouldn't start. It did, and the horseshoe-looking light glowed a much darker red. The inexplicable problem had evidently worsened.

As he closed in on his mother's zip code the burnt yolk smell of Baltimore became inescapable. Soon he'd access the Baltimore Harbor Tunnel. He usually called his mother before going through to announce he was close. Today he couldn't be bothered.

The dashboard's red mystery light started blinking. For some reason Dan searched for a problem *outside* the car (there was nothing). Everything inside was up to snuff and the engine was humming fine. Besides, with the tunnel's mouth fenced in by concrete, there was nowhere to pull over.

He entered the tunnel, and as the giant, unavoidable concrete chunks began dropping from the tunnel's ceiling, Dan suddenly understood what the dashboard light had been warning him about all along.

Getaway Car
Ken MacGregor

Time?" Carlson asked. Mitchell took his eyes off the bank doors long enough to glance at his watch.

"Two minutes."

Carlson nodded. He checked his three mirrors from left to right. Nothing had changed outside. The engine purred beyond the dash. The two men were silent for a moment. Carlson sighed.

"I kind of feel guilty," he said.

"About the job?" Mitchell asked, not looking at the other man.

"No. About keeping it running, wasting gas, and polluting the air."

"You're the getaway man. Letting it run is part and parcel of the package."

"Nice alliteration," Carlson said.

"What's that?" Mitchell flicked his eyes at Carlson.

"Alliteration? It means when more than one word starts with the same letter."

"Huh," Mitchell said. "I think I remember that from school."

"I'm gonna ask Melanie to marry me," Carlson said, rushing out the words. Mitchell looked at Carlson for a second with wide eyes; he turned back to the doors. Still looking at them, he responded.

"Nice alliteration," Mitchell said, grinning.

"Ha. Thanks."

Mitchell shook his head as if to clear it.

"You sure about this?"

Carlson drummed his fingers on the steering wheel. He took a few slow breaths before answering.

"Yeah," he said. "I think so. I mean, is anybody ever really sure if they're ready to get married?"

Mitchell shook his head. He still watched the door, but lifted his watch again to check the time.

"I have a hard enough time asking a guy out to dinner," Mitchell said. "I can't imagine making that kind of commitment."

"I love her, man," Carlson said. "And, after today, I'm gonna be able to take care of her. Time?"

"Forty-five seconds," Mitchell said. Carlson depressed the brake and shifted from park to drive. He rested a finger on the auto-unlock button and scanned the mirrors. Things were quiet outside the car, but in the distance, Carlson heard sirens. Might not be for them, but it was better to assume the worst.

"If I don't make it-"

"Shut up, man," Mitchell said. "Don't even go there."

Carlson nodded and asked for the time again. They had twelve seconds.

Mitchell watched the door like it was a cobra about to strike. Carlson's left foot bounced up and down next to the brake pedal. Sweat trickled from his armpit down his ribs.

"Time."

The bank doors burst open, Brady and Harris slamming through one each. They wore black balaclavas and carried canvas bags. Carlson triggered open the locks. The two men sprinted for the car; Mitchell opened the back door on their side and they tumbled in.

"*Go*," Brody yelled, but Carlson was already pulling into traffic. He kept his cool behind the wheel, not cutting anyone off, not drawing attention to himself. The beige Ford Escort blended seamlessly into the cars around it. Behind them, tires screeched and sirens wailed.

They had cut it close.

The four men rode without speaking while Brody and Harris caught their breath and everyone's pulse slowed to near normal. They were on the edge of the suburbs when Carlson broke the silence. In the rearview, he eyed the men in back.

"How'd it go?"

"Fine," Brody said.

Harris nodded. Both men took off their masks.

"We cleaned out the tellers," Brody said. "But, the vault was closed. Would've taken too long."

The other men nodded; they knew the drill. It was quiet again as the trees and houses flashed by.

Mitchell turned toward the back seat.

"Carlson's gonna propose."

"No shit?" Harris asked. Carlson glanced over his shoulder and grinned. He nodded.

"Congratulations," Brody said. "That's great, man. Guess I'll have to find myself another driver."

"I guess you will," Carlson said. "No hard feelings, right? A man's gotta follow his heart, you know?"

Brody nodded in the rearview mirror.

There was a loud muffled *whump* and red ink exploded from the tops of the bags of money. It spattered the inside of the car and the four men sitting in it. Carlson pulled over, right-hand wheels jumping the curb; he slammed the shift lever into park hard enough to hurt his hand.

The inside of the car looked like a scene from a slasher film; the men couldn't see outside through the red.

"Aw, fuck," Harris said from the back. "Dye pack."

"Carlson?" Mitchell asked, looking the question at the driver.

Carlson sighed. The money was useless. He was going to use his share to pay for the wedding. He looked at his red hands resting on the wheel and laughed.

"Shortest retirement ever."

GoogleRide Killed My SD-455!

Jack Raglin

The human drawn hearse wheeled silently though the stagnant darkness to take her from me. It was a tandem with electric assist, manual steering, flatbed in tow. On it were Click and Clack, my nicknames for the baby-faced Syrians I hired at the swap meet in Ponoma. Back in the day they traded real cars there. The boys had the skills, were willing to the job but demanded cash. A lot of it. Not so easy to get your hands on anymore. The garage door let loose with a nervous chatter as eased it up. I doubt there was a single one left in LA that hadn't been converted. Clack motioned me to silence with the sign of the drone and they got to work, wrapping her up like a Burka until not one muscular curve showed. But she wasn't dead. Not yet. They had their thing to do. Then I would kill her. I don't have a choice. *GoogleRide* made me do it.

She put up some fight as they shoved her up the flatbed, like she knew what was coming. I wasn't much use with my off-the-shelf hip replacements, but I helped cinch up her up tight as Spandex and then watched them huff off with her. There was exactly 37 minutes to burn so I went inside, changed into a dry t-shirt, smoked a cigarette. A real one. Kept my stash in the fridge. I indulged myself with another and then opened the *Google-Ride* App and ordered a ride. Seven minutes ticked by before my phone buzzed with the arrival prompt. Through the kitchen window I could see what looked like a giant milk jug making a lazy pirouette in the driveway. It was a *Senior Single*, the vehicle that drove the stake through the heart of Detroit. Hell, you can add Seoul, Wolfsburg, Wuhan and Reno to the list of its victims.

The flimsy door flapped like a startled pigeon when I yanked it open, as I slowly settled into the stiff plastic seat my joints began an organized protest of pain. The sting of industrial strength *Little Trees* began to attack my sinuses, but the windows didn't roll down so I pulled out my phone and shelled out ten bucks for some AC. The ride—nobody called them cars anymore—began ambling down the vacant street, its tiny motor whining in the effort to pick up speed. The Senior Single was the vehicle that took over a century of automobile innovation and slapped it into a hard reverse. *Google* used it to corral the snorting, stinking all-American automobile and its hybrid kin and herd them off to their slaughterhouse where they hacked off the steering column, instrument panel, foot pedals, switches, mirrors, even the idiot lights. After safety equipment became superfluous seatbelts, air bags, head restraints were stripped out, every trace of crash padding flayed from the interior. They even took the horn, not that *G-Ride* would let you even beep at a pretty girl. The only thing they added was the all-purpose stop/go/panic button. The exterior was skinned bare of every trace of adornment that might tic up the drag coefficient. Grilles, badges, trim, door guards were pried off, crease lines ironed out, bodies bloated into deadening uniformity. Head lamps, fog lamps, signals, backups were plucked out and replaced with a sprinkling of tiny LED courtesy lights. The land shark—just like the real thing— had been hunted into extinction, its niche now filled by millions of opportunistic bottom feeders.

The whining motor abruptly jumped up an octave as it merged onto 213. Dutifully queuing up just inches behind another ride it formed the tail of a long strand of dim bulbs that draped over the horizon. I left the windshield on clear but most other old farts were so spooked by the congestion they set it to Sunday Drive mode. It thinned out the traffic, but the view was still cluttered up with CG ads tucked into the landscape like billboards. Everybody else linked the windows to their phone screens and endured the pop-up ads. I was half-tempted to do the same. The traffic lost any trace of a pulse long ago. Once it had flat lined the symbiotic relationship between the car and landscape began to wither. Gas stations, truck stops, rest stops, motels, tollbooths soon vanished. Then *G-Ride* showed up to raze what remained; road signs, streetlights, ad signs, stop lights, guardrails, Fitch barriers, Botts dots, speed bumps, rumble strips. Lane lines faded like old tattoos into the pavement. Hungry? Text in your order and have a MacDrones deliver it directly to your ride. Need to piss? Ask *G-Ride* for permission and it will reroute you to a mobile port-a-potty.

The mass extinction of the automobile had been choreographed by *G-Ride* with the lockstep precision of an assembly line. Every phase was tagged with a marketing plan, government backing, highway safety commission data complete with estimates of the lives spared, money saved, CO_2 sequestered, and resources repurposed. Each liberated drivers from a task, responsibility or hassle until their attention had been completely untethered from the act of driving. Along the way the resistance of entire industries and manual driving diehards like me was steamrolled over by NARP and its swollen ranks of seniors fumbling for the keys, MADD and its legions of soccer moms thrilled to hand them over, and an entire generation of post-millennials who didn't want them. By the time *G-Ride* ended their trade-in program, millions had given up their cars for three years of free service. Busses, taxis and Uber were wiped out like the Bluefin. Aside from the ultra-rich who drove their trophies on private tracks and could afford the fines, that left me with my environmentally incorrect ride. But at the stroke of midnight my semi-autonomous license expires. And then, just like Cinderella I'll have to find another way home because my 1973 Grand Am with the 455 Super Duty option will turn into inert and illegal junk.

The ride excused itself from the caravan and began drifting down an exit toward a patchy island of light bobbing in the sea of darkness. Two minutes later it coasted to a stop in front of an unintentionally shabby chic 7-11 bookending the entrance of a strip mall. The ride waited patiently for me to haul myself out and then trundled over to a charging post to hitch itself up for the return trip. Inside the store I roamed the aisles bleached egg wash white by the twitchy glare of illegal fluorescents, poking through the motley wares for familiar fare. I ended up with a bag of Nongshim shrimp crackers, a can of CC Lemon and a Yunker Fanti to spike it with. After I paid I parked my ass on a bleached-out Formica bench, peering through the smeary window I could see the brothers waiting next to my ride, fidgeting with their phones. Already buzzed I decided I had no need for the nicotine in the Yunker Fanti so I chucked the drink it in the recycling bin on the way out and then handed my phone to Click. He slipped into the ride to make the trip back to my place, clutching his longboard and a backpack loaded with gravel to match my body weight.

Clack led me to our transportation, an old-school Schwinn Beach Cruiser. The back seat was an unexpected comfort, chunky but soft from the well-oiled springs. We wheeled down the utility road, weaving around other cyclists, small delivery drones that had emerged from their underground tunnels and the occasional pedestrian. After about a mile Clack steered us into a designated utility road, the intersection framed with garish warning signs but conveniently missing its security camera. Without the allowances for human traffic the road darkened and clenched tight around us. Clack tapped on his headlamp, unfurling a carpet of ruby light for us to follow. Strung on each side of us were stubby fences that marked the territory of the warehouses with all the subtlety of a pissing tomcat. It was all for show. The metallic aftertaste filling the air that was the real warning; the acrid scent of security exhaled by the dark shapes patrolling the fences. They upgraded their software practicing on rats while stalking more formidable prey.

Clack made a sharp right down a street bordered on one side by a cyclone fence festooned by a rusty nimbus of barbwire. After a block we coasted to a stop at a gate secured with an old-school lock and chain. Beyond was an industrial park of a dozen or so ratty warehouses, their aluminum skin warped and peeling from age and neglect. Clack pulled out his phone and flashed it a few times. Seconds later Click emerged from one of the buildings, mounted a longboard and shot toward us. He must have been making at least 40 when he pulled a toe-side Pendy making a dead stop inches from the fence. I thought I saw the barest crack of a smile as he popped the board under his arm and unlocked the gate.

I didn't even need to look to tell their shop was set up for electrics. The waft of lubricants was one-dimensional, a straight-up shot of vodka rather than gas, grease and oil; the blended scotch of hydrocarbons. My girl was sitting proudly on blocks in the middle of the shop, stripped bare of the shroud. The harsh halo of LEDs surrounding her only accentuated the classic lines of her body, resplendent in original Buccaneer red, the hood tattooed with the screaming chicken emblem with the shaker scoop peeking shyly through from the engine bay. Hidden beneath was the desirable and rare Super Duty 455 option. Only fifteen years back she could still command good money, but the scorn of the environmentally correct and changing laws made her about as desirable as a hooker with needle tracks. Tomorrow she would become outlawed scrap no self-respecting junkyard would touch.

Click began scratching at her with tools so delicate they looked like he got them from a dental supply catalog. I popped the trunk and wrestled out my scuffed-up toolbox and a five-gallon tank of E-85 I'd hoarded like a bottle of Pappy.

"If you start filling the tank before we're finished," Click paused until I looked up to acknowledge him, "they'll know."

"Yeah, I learned that lesson the hard way." I slapped a chunky crescent wrench against the palm of my hand in exclamation. "Years back I tried to disable the speed governor. Barely clipped the first wire before I got a ticket over the phone."

"That was dumb."

"No shit it was. Had to fork over a grand in fines. They nearly pulled my license."

"License?"

"My manual operator's license." I pulled the card from my beat-up wallet and flashed it at them.

Click gave it a bored glance. Clack couldn't be bothered. He was trying to pry the lidar pod off the roof, that humiliating dunce cap *G-Ride* forced my car to wear.

"It expires at midnight, and unless you disconnect the kill switch by then no final joy ride." I pulled club hammer and chisel from the toolbox. "Allow me." A couple of sharp swats and the lidar popped off like a stubborn bottle cap. Clack, who had been patiently stripping out the varicose web of wiring, gave me a dirty look. I raised the hood and rewired the horn.

"Even with all we are doing you won't get far." Click was tooling off the video and far infra-red cameras that peppered her body like cancerous moles. "They'll still find you."

"The cops are welcome to join me."

"The cops never leave their stations," Clack smirked. "They'll have Chip send their drones. Shut you down."

"The highway patrol? Let 'em try." I set the chisel to the shaker scoop and hammered off the plates, transforming it from an ornament into a functioning scoop. "If they shoot out my tires I'll just ride on the rims." For some reason they thought that was amusing. "The cops will end up showing, and they'll have a hell of a time keeping up." I gave the hood a pat. "She rolled off the factory floor putting out two-hundred ninety horses, but I've souped her up with forged steel crankshaft, single-plane Holly Street Dominator intake manifold, centrifugal spring and weight kit...." I looked up.

Their expressions told me I'd been speaking in a foreign tongue.

~

They dropped me off at an abandoned golf course wrung dry long ago by the water laws, under a frayed canopy of dead trees dense enough to ward off small drones. I leaned back against the car, its metal skin felt cool against mine, watched the boys pedal off with their empty coffin until they disappeared over a hill. If I saw them again they'd be in deeper shit than me. There was time to kill so I lit up my last cigarette, fondled the brushed steel case of my Zippo before stuffing it back in my Levis. A few impatient puffs later I ground the stub into the asphalt. Cost me $200 if a cop drone saw it. I pulled open the massive door and it invited me in with a groan of anticipation. The flaky nap of the original Madrid vinyl gently scratched at my skin as I sunk into the deeply bolstered bucket seat, contoured by time and gravity to precisely fit my bony. I inhaled deeply, picking up notes of moldering hay, wet iron, carnuba wax, the acid tang of PVC.

On the dash, in the air vent hole, just left of the tach the boys had installed a huge red button about the size of a respectable rocks glass. Below it they had tacked on a small nickel metal plate. Stamped on it were the words, "DO NOT PUSH". And I thought they had no sense of humor. It was the kill switch to the car's RFID, which they pried off and left back in my garage. It was linked to another chip still on the car by some spooky Einstein physics the boys had wasted a long lecture on trying to explain to me. What I did understand was that there was no way to start the car without waking it so the kill switch would melt both the chips. And within a picosecond, or according to Clack, maybe even before I pushed the button, *G-Ride* would know I was off the grid. So I pushed the button and twisted the key. She shuddered to life with a deafening roar. At the garage I'd cut out the mufflers and catalytic converter and tacked on zoomy pipes. With no back pressure the blast coming from the engine was contemptuous. A tap on the pedal and the car shook so violently it felt like my dental work was coming loose. I slapped the Hurst shifter into first and dropped the clutch hard. She seemed to shiver before springing forward like a tiger freed from its cage, the tires screaming protest against the pavement. The long-forgotten scent of burnt rubber was better than home baked bread.

I had barely 14 miles to go, but I had to stay patient, keep one eye on the temperature gauge, the other out for Chip and wait for the right time to make my run. The route took me through a back street lined with boarded up store fronts and drab watering holes. Even with a light foot on the pedal the noise attracted knots of people who shot videos and gawked at the shining, stinking, ancient beast of a vehicle that cruised past. Ahead of me rides began parting to each side like the Red Sea, but it was *G-Ride*—not some sympathetic car god—clearing my way. By the time I rolled onto 213 every ride in sight had been shuttled to or the other side of the highway, their exterior LEDs blinking in unison. It felt like I'd just been cleared for takeoff, so I dropped a gear and crushed the pedal. The engine roared and I was mainlining on hydrocarbon powered acceleration until the windshield lit up in a tangle of glowing red lines. A second later in contracted into block letters strung like neon across the glass.

Please pull over and stop your car.

I shoved my arm out the window and flipped the bird at whatever was laser pointing text on my windshield.

The letters contracted into a knot and reshuffled.

CHP (California Highway Patrol) is on the way.

Moments the reflection out of the rear-view mirror began strobing like the light show at a strip joint. I flipped the mirror to night mode, revealing what looked like a phalanx of hurtling turtle shells with highway patrol cherries on top slinging blue and yellow light all over the highway. The speedometer was edging above 120, but they were closing fast. Within seconds the drones had me surrounded and began slowly tightening their lasso around the car. Over the bellow of the engine, I could hear them tapping against the car almost apologetically. The drones were trying to wedge below the undercarriage so they could jack us off the pavement and bring me to a stop. But I'd slammed the suspension and dropped the clearance to a hair over two inches. The gap was too small for the drones to fit. Chip would have to find another way to stop me.

The exit to twenty-fifth West was coming up fast. I held off until the last second, backed off the throttle and shot up the ramp. The tires whinnied and bucked in protest, and I had to fight the wheel to keep from flying off the road. The drones mimicked every move down to the fishtail, as if they had tack welded themselves to the rocker panels. The ramp funneled me into two narrow lanes, and I took a hard left into the empty park road. Immediately the road started to meander. A classic muscle car, the Trans Am was built for straight line performance, so I was forced to shed even more speed. But the drones seemed to lose interest, dropping behind me and cuing up in a single column. Seconds later a dark shape shot past me so fast I might as well have been idling in neutral. Wedge shaped, big as a semi-trailer, no running lights. For a brief instant I imagined launching over it like Burt Reynolds in Smokey and the Bandit, but the thing was losing me fast and soon disappeared around a bend.

The road rose steadily and was now butting close to the shoreline. Without a guard rail I could look down the sheer drop and see waves lit by a milky full moon caressing coal black rocks. And then company showed up to spoil the view. Two drones were sidling up on each side of me, dim low masses that stretched a full car length ahead and behind me. Once they matched my speed they began to unfurl, breaking open like a chrysalis and expanding into fat tubes that rose nearly to my roofline. Chip wasn't giving me any respect, first they tail me with a pack of tin turtles and now they send in weenermobiles that had been on the grill too long. I gave one a good bump but it barely budged. The tubes were hollow, but the drones were carrying enough weight to keep from being bullied off the road. Wafts of steam started to stream out the hood and the temperature gauge was redlining, but I had had less than a mile to go. The road uncurled, I clicked on the high beams and a quarter mile ahead blocking the road was the lead drone. It had morphed into a sort of cave, its edges puckered out to form a soft funnel. Everything clicked into place; my escorts were giant pinball bumpers, and I was the ball, heading right down Chip's giant condom.

I stomped on the gas and twisted the wheel hard into the tube on my right. Rebounding hard I downshifted to second and pulled my foot off the pedal. The engine screamed, redlining and punished me with a neck wrenching drop in speed. Steam coursed across the hood like a sheet flapping in a storm. Wrenching the wheel left, I slammed into the back end of the other drone. Its tail reared over the hood, yanking me back in the road though I was steering left. It started to pull ahead just as the other drone slapped against my right front fender. The car flipped the car on its side, and barrel-rolled over ass end of the other drone. There was a sickening crunch, followed by silence. The last thing I saw as the car slipped over the cliff was the Pacific rushing up to meet us. Clack was right. The cops never showed.

~

Someone was talking to me. The lights were too bright, and I couldn't focus. I tried turning away but could barely move.

"You a cop? Take these damn cuffs off me. My arms are asleep."

"I'm a doctor. You aren't in handcuffs."

"So why can't I move?" My eyes started working. The face hovering over me looked way too young to be a doc.

"You've been in a very bad accident."

"Tell me something I don't know. Like what happened to my car?"

The doctor ignored my question. "You're a lucky man. If the EM drone hadn't gotten to you so quickly you wouldn't have made it."

"Remind me to write him a thank you card. The car, was it totaled?"

"Totaled?"

"Wrecked. Ruined. Demolished!"

"Yes."

I cracked a smile, but he misunderstood.

"It is amazing that you survived such a horrendous accident. But your injuries—"

"—You sure about the car?"

"Yes, I'm sure," the doctor sputtered. "Someone from *G-Ride* told me it had to be cut apart to free you."

"*G-Ride*? What—"

"Listen to me," the doc interrupted. "This is more important. The injuries you sustained, I'm sorry but you'll never walk again."

"G-Ride was here?"

"No, no, you're not in any trouble with them. This is hard to believe, but they said a drone may have actually caused your accident. So they're going to pay all your hospital bills."

"Help? I don't want *G-Ride's* help." I tried to bellow but it sounded more like air hissing out a flat tire. "Hell, they're why I ended up here."

"You should be grateful. They're sparing no expense to give you back your independence."

"That's exactly what they took from me. From you too but you don't know it."

"You don't understand. Let me show just how lucky you are." He stepped out the doorway. A few seconds later he returned with a proud look on his face, motioning behind him.

"It's their latest model; hands free control, including feeding and personal hygiene. Top speed of six miles an hour!"

Through the doorway in trundled the unholy union of an oversized toilet and Barcalounger.

"Meet the *Senior Sentinel*, your new set of wheels courtesy of *G-Ride*."

Convention in the Times of Market Crash

Valentin D. Ivanov

My last flight was in jeopardy. The galaxy-spanning space exploration career I had developed in my spare time for the last twenty years was going to be cut short by the breaking up of a simple shopping group. But right now the clouds were a more immediate concern. They had reigned the sky for the last full two weeks, and the high winds made me doubt if we would get launch permits—even the most advanced ships can't percolate from of the bottom of our potential well. The meteorologists predicted clearing up on Saturday or Sunday. A single day is probably less than the uncertainties of their models, but it made a world of a difference to me. I would have savored very differently those eight hours that I spent in space a month ago if I knew what is in store for me now. But I didn't.

I had the forecast displayed in the upper right corner of

my fov [field of view] for days. The hologram was polarized, and in theory it should have been almost invisible to others, but my wife soon got wind why I am so worried. On Tuesday evening it looked like she was about to tell me we could get by somehow, despite of my expensive hobby but the account balance restored her senses. Besides, I wouldn't have it myself. Both our medical savings and the kids' education funds had zero growth over the last year. If we kept the same expense level and the prices kept growing, we would soon end up with a negative net income. So, my wife braced herself, and announced two days later that she had found another shopping group. It numbered only about two dozen people, much smaller than the old one, and the discounts were nowhere near what we had before, but it would help. She would go on a trial run with them on the day of my last flight. She left while I was shaving, pointedly omitting to wish me a nice flight.

~

My friend Joe landed his shiny Sequoia next to my battered Olympique. My wife would rather die than appear in public with a two month old car – the other day at breakfast she told me that the modern car renewal rate is nearly ten a year; I averted my gaze and pretended to enjoy he tea. Luckily, the boys here pay little attention to the mundane. Some of the cars that tow the space modules are a few years old, and there are one or two real rarities: permanent tech machines from the age before the shopping habits accelerated to a maddening pace, measured in days or even hours.

Joe stepped out, nodded, and joined me—I was watching the skies, with a beer in my hand. We knew each other since high school, we went together to the astronomy summer camps to observe variable stars, to photograph comets and to count meteors. We even collected meteorites in the ice of Antarctica once at the tender age of fourteen. The rage in those days was to do everything old style, from polishing manually telescope mirrors to cooking up photographic emulsion.

We were seventeen when Joe ran somewhere into an announcement for a citizen astronaut gathering at Dulles airfield, and we came here regularly ever since, for nearly thirty years. The time has taken its toll on both of us. My hair was thinning, the metal glint in his eyes betrayed some implants. But we kept returning, the last weekend of every month.

"There is more in the cooler," I pointed at my bottle. He took a beer for himself, and we both looked up. A thick cloud layer covered the sky at two thousand feet.

Somebody approached us. A small man, with quick movements, and a blue coverall. A large Space Agency patch with running colors was displayed on his chest screen.

"Hi, guys! I am Douglas."

"Hi," I said. "You must be the new representative. How is Sam?"

"He is all right back at the HQ, and sends greetings."

Simon Crawford was the real thing—a retired astronaut from the last classes before NASA closed down the corps. He enjoyed a lot of respect around here. Dougy was too young to have ridden the fiery candles to space. Dougy. In my mind the name stuck to him as a moth to a warm slice of butter.

"Same from us," Joe said. "Tell him he will be missed."

"Sure thing." The new representative raised a hand to the clouds. "Not much luck today, isn't it?"

"I saw some openings to the West from here," my friend answered. "And the wind comes from the right direction to bring them on the top of us."

I knew better than to believe him. We needed three times stronger wind to blow continuously until the early afternoon. And then to stop immediately after the edge of the cloud mass clears the old airfield where we got together for a round of beer, and some flying to the stars.

~

More cars lined up along the edge of the field. Mostly utility tracks, some convertibles, and even a few of those permatech collectibles that I mentioned earlier. The vehicles had one thing in common—each one towed behind it a space module lined up with antigrav pontoons.

"Have you checked the target list for today?" Joe asked after the agency man had walked away.

"Nay." The beer was still cold, and I didn't want to move, not even to reach for my handy. I wasn't flying anywhere today, it seemed.

Nobody rushed to release the modules. Usually, by this time we already had the flight plans filled in, and the ship assembly was going at full swing. We sipped from our drinks for a while, hanging around the Olympique until the men that had parked closer to the ruins of the old airport building started to congregate around JK, our president. He was as old as Sam, and even had applied for the professional astronaut corps once, but he was now a retiree and just another amateur like the rest of us.

Joe walked in front of me, and I thought that I ought to tell him about my own pending retirement, but JK raised a hand, and everybody went silent.

"Hi, flyboys! You see the weather; you know the forecast. There is not much we can do in that department. But, miracles are known to happen, so we will assemble the ships anyway, and prepare to launch, in case we get lucky. Here comes the list." His fingers waived a complex glyph in the air and a row of silver numbers appeared in my fov. "It contains only M dwarfs within three hundred parsecs. Pick your destinations. Formation flying, a minimum of two ships per target. Visiting multiple systems is preferable. One final thing. I took the liberty to book for Joe and Jack the same star as the last time. They seemed to like it."

People around us laughed. Steve, who was a banker in workdays, but looked more like a wrestler, tapped me on the shoulder. I barely managed to stop the beer bottle in my hand from leaving for Alpha Centauri without the help of percolation engines.

Sure we liked that place. We saw last month how the quadrupeds that inhabited the fourth planet of "our" star launched a satellite. With a chemical rocket. A giant frying candle burning hydrazine.

~

"Joe, you will have to look for another partner in these games," I told my friend when we walked back towards our cars.

"Your wife?" He didn't look surprised. "I was wondering when it will happen."

"Well, yes. And no. Our shopping team broke up," I explained. "We found a new one, but it is relatively small, and we won't get the same discounts as before. You know, it's all the crisis . . ."

"I see," Joe nodded and started to unlatch his module.

It's an engineering type and second hand, but well maintained and most importantly—with three engines. Together they could percolate about seven metric tonnes, more than enough for a two-seater ship, and even if one failed, we could get back ditching the observing equipment. The agency gave it to us—the citizen astronauts—for free, and losing the old set meant that we would get newer, upgraded detectors for just about every type of radiation one can think of.

"It is not just this," I continued. "The inflation is crippling our income. Our medical savings, the education funds for the kids. We have to cut somewhere."

I reached for the handle and caught the pontoon a moment before it flew off. If only I could do the same, and descent above the clouds. I hanged to the thing until Joe typed a few numbers on the panel to reduce its buoyancy. We carefully towed his module away from the cars— canceling the gravity didn't cancel the inertia—and gently placed it on the ground. One by one we deactivated all remaining pontoons. Joe threw them into the cargo bay of his Sequoia, and we went for my part of the ship.

My module is my pride. Command and Control, in short C&C. With a glass bubble covering the flight deck and the best navigation system the lower middle-class money can buy. Not to mention enough computing substrate to host a few class zero AIs, if it wasn't illegal. I bought the thing brand new, from a Chinese manufacturer in South Tranquility City, on the Moon. No shopping groups for these, no hefty discounts, I paid every penny they asked.

Last night I put it for sale. My hands were trembling while I was writing the offer. The flashing red number in the corner of my fov told me there was already four bids.

~

Assembling the ship together took an hour longer than usual. The clouds pushed out hands and hearths down: the connectors were wrong, the cables were tangled, and the bolts didn't match the screws. Nothing worked on the first go. I forbid myself to look up searching for those mythical clearings in the cloud cover or to check the satellite images. I decided to accept that my last flight had happened a month ago, and I started to replay in my head the memories from that occasion.

"The crisis won't last forever," Joe interrupted my thoughts, "and it's not like the agency will shut us down because the Congress doesn't vote a budget raise. You can always come back once you fix that shopping team problem."

"Sure, if the economy takes a turn to the better I might. They say it will improve later next year. And if the kids manage to get into good public schools. And if . . . but I was wondering about something else. Do you think those quadrupeds have launched other satellites before? Low orbits could decay quickly, the satellites would burn into the atmosphere in the matter of months. Their rocket was quite advanced. I checked the records once again last night. The hydrazine is likely to be a poison for any oxygen breather, never mind the number of legs, and they still have made it work."

Joe considered my suggestion for a moment.

"Yeap, I suppose they might have launched a few more missions. May be simple robotic ones, but certainly nothing complicated. Using a hypergolic fuel tells that their engineering is stretched to the end, and they are desperate enough to deal with a poison. Hold this, please."

He passed me a heavy cable bundle. The connector nest on the bulkhead where Joe was trying to attach it was twisted.

"Here is the hammer," I offered.

"Right." Joe put a few dents in the aluminum until the individual connectors parted enough to receive the cable heads. He critically looked over the results of his intervention.

"We are going to space to explore, not to show off artistic achievements."

Eventually, the ship was assembled, and we ran the routine pre-launch checks. Our vessel was ready to percolate to the other end of the Milky Way. To kill the time, we took two more beers from the cooler and sat on the curb.

This is when JK came around.

"Enough, boys! We are giving up for the day."

~

"You want to fly once more, right?" Joe asked me. Needlessly. "You have spent the money on the energy and permits, one." He raised a finger. "The batteries will drain until the next convention, and the permit will expire at midnight, two." A second finger joined the first. "So, you may as well use them, three."

"Wait, what do you mean?"

Joe didn't answer and ran after JK. He grabbed our president, turned him around, and started to explain something quickly, waving with his hands. I could tell from this far that JK didn't like what he heard.

"What do you want to do?" I asked Joe when I caught up with them.

"He is crazy!" JK answered instead. "He will lose his

permit permanently, and he wants the rest of us to join him."

"Just listen to me." My friend yelled. I had never heard him before to rise his voice so much. "I have thought about it for a long time, just in case something like this comes up."

~

Four hours later we landed safely on the old Dulles airfield. The storage substrate was full of data on the quadrupeds, their planet, and their star. The hypergolic fuel had worked well for them – contrary to our expectations, the little creatures had a manned, or rather quadripedded base on the nearest planet. We wondered for a while how they could do that and have no satellite constellation until we remembered that their Sol was active, with eruptions ten thousand times stronger than the Sun's. The radiation periodically inflated the planet's atmosphere so much that even the stationary satellites had no chance to live long.

"You will be back." Joe said, when we detached the modules and prepared to part. "Meanwhile, I would like to lease your C&C. I will take a good care of it, until you return."

~

My Olympique refused to power up. It was not a surprise for such an old piece of junk. So, we got together in Joe's Sequoia, my car hanging underneath, the modules pulling us both up on their pontoons. Just the opposite of the formation we used to tow our ship to orbit. The rules for percolation ships are overly stringent to protect the paper pushers from the Agency who regulates the citizen astronaut movement, but the flying cars these days can do pretty much anything. Including to go two hundred miles up, with full load. This is just high enough to turn the percolation engines on.

Of course, we lost our driving licenses for a year. But that was a small price to pay for seeing the stars once again.

Night Passage

Richard Polomsky

A long night drive along an empty highway. The low, fuzzy hum of the radio. The eerie green glow of the dashboard.

Mom and dad talking up front. The way dad glances back through the rearview mirror, as if trying to decide if I understand the adult talk. Eyes hard and unfriendly, how they always are.

So I look out my window, into the dark. Trees like giant shadowy things out on the prowl. An open barn, so dark inside, darker than the night.

And I see them.

The Withering Ones.

A name not heard but known.

They stand along the edge of the pasture. Shaggy limbs, all long and narrow. Bony fingers and skeletal grins. No eyes, no cranium. All mouth.

Glimpses lost in the blink of an eye. They're just fence posts and young trees, maybe a mailbox.

That's what they want you to think.

The crunch of gravel under slowing tires. The car stalling right on the shoulder. Them, so close, so near.

Dad gets out, circles the car and kicks each tire.

A low whimper--mom--was it something dad said?

Dad tells me to get out and check the back wheel, that my eyes have always been better than his.

I grab hold of the door handle, sweat forming on my palm. The warmth of the heater, the safety of the car.

Dad says it again, in that rough voice when he gets mean.

I get out fast and hurry over, "Which tire?"

Dad heads for the driver's side, "The one on the right."

I go and get down on my knees.

The rattle and clang of dry bones.

I whip my head around; my eyes open wide and unblinking.

Dark shapes scuttle back into the pasture.

The slam of a car door. Dirt and grit pelting my face and chest. I hack and cough as I stumble back.

The car speeding down the empty highway. The back door as it swings from open to nearly shut.

I stand up, confused, unsure of what just happened.

The car shrinks, diminishing into the night. The red twinkle of the rear lights. And finally, blackness.

The sharp clatter of talons on asphalt. A dry, autumnal breeze. Their breath on the back of my neck.

Retribution Drive

Davin Ireland

I was hitching west on Interstate 40 sometime after dusk, the liquescent glow of the sun sinking behind the Providence Mountain range like sediment settling in a wine glass, when the thrumming of a motor filled the quiet desert air. I didn't bother to look around or raise my thumb in anticipation of a ride. When you're out alone in this part of the world, especially with evening approaching, people tend to notice. That goes double when your vehicle is parked up on two flats ten or twelve miles back down the road.

The rumble of the approaching engine grew louder. A pair of raised beams struck multiple shadows from my moving form, and I was still watching these faint grey versions of myself swing to the left when the vehicle—it was a bright yellow Chevy Fleetside pickup—rolled to a stop on the dirt shoulder opposite.

"Where you headed, son?" enquired the driver, one arm hanging loose from the open window. It was standard etiquette for the road, but it still struck me as a mightily stupid question. With twenty miles of hardpan between the mountains and the particular stretch of desert beneath my feet, it seemed like there weren't a whole lot of options to choose from. Knowing that a smart mouth might cost me plenty more wear on my boot-heels, however, I nodded in the direction of the silhouetted peaks and said, "Anywhere that takes me beyond that range."

"Thought as much." The nameless driver drummed his fingers on the Chevy's door-panel and thoughtfully chewed gum. It was quite a sight. With faded denim jacket, polarized sunglasses and untended moustache, he reminded me of an unemployed rodeo rider on the lookout for trouble. The image was completed by a sweat-stained cowpoke's hood the colour of ivory perched in the middle of the dash. As if reading my mind he squashed the hat down on his head and scratched behind one ear. "I guess you'd best get in," he concluded.

I crossed the road with a distinct feeling of trepidation. Dying of thirst out here among the sagebrush, the cottonwoods and the silent Joshua tress was a daunting enough prospect and believe me I had not been looking forward to that particular fate one bit; but getting myself tortured and dispatched by some loony highway bandit with questionable fashion sense struck me as an equally unattractive way to go. Still, at the end of the day, I didn't think I had much of a choice in the matter (and this *was* the end of the day by now; during the course of our brief exchange the sun had dropped clear out of sight, and the mountains, which had suddenly stopped being silhouettes against the glare, were resolving themselves into the imposing edifices they really were—switchbacks, pinyon pines and interlocking spurs looming above us in sharp, twilit relief).

"So, where you from?"

The driver asked me that as I dropped into the shotgun seat and slammed the door. It was second on the seasoned hitcher's list of Frequently Asked Questions.

"Cambridge," I said. It was an easy lie.

"Massachusetts?"

"Nope." I buckled up as we rolled off the dirt shoulder, and it was then, just as I was about to come out with the line, *The other Cambridge, the one across the pond*, that I realised this lunatic had actually pulled off of the road to speak to me. Now *that*, I thought, is taking civic responsibility too far. Four-hundred square miles of open desert around us and not another human being -- let alone another vehicle -- in sight, yet this guy actually leaves the blacktop to pick up a stranger. Why? Was he afraid of getting back-ended out here or something?

I realised about then that he was looking at me with a degree of curiosity that was unsettling, mouth working intently at the gum. Perhaps I should have been a little more forthcoming with my answer.

"Er ... Cambridge in England," I managed to get out, "I'm on a gap year."

The driver returned his attention to the road, nodding to himself in grave contemplation. Finally the nod wore itself out.

"So, what's a gap year?" he said.

I watched the shadscale and creosote bushes whip past as the Chevy picked up speed. "It's when a student takes a year out before going to university," I explained, "mostly to travel."

This seemed to surprise him. "Ain't you a little old for that kind of thing, mister?"

"My name is Stephen Cole," I said, holding out my hand, "and yes I am a little. I'm what you call a mature student ... a misnomer if ever there was one."

"A misnomer, huh?" He looked at my extended hand and then at me (I saw reflections of both in those mirrored shades of his), as if he were expecting some kind of practical joke. Either that, or he was genuinely surprised not to see me brandishing a knife at him.

"Dwayne Ingle," he said at length, and not without some relief. His hand left the wheel long enough to grab mine and squeeze it, the way one might squeeze a piece of fruit when checking for ripeness. This was clearly not a man accustomed to the polite formalities of conversation. He nevertheless told me—rather reluctantly, I'll admit—that he was pleased to make my acquaintance. Then he got back to his driving. I decided to fill up the awkward silence that followed with some less challenging words. I told him that I was a fairly successful businessman who'd sold his company for a large profit and was now planning to spend a few years living off the proceeds. A year bumming round the States and Mexico, I opined, followed by a leisurely philosophy degree, sounded about right—although I was quick to add that I wouldn't be doing any of my studying in Cambridge itself. Too much like hard work.

Dwayne's only reaction to all of this was to lean out of the window and spit his gum into the wind. "Tell you what *I* think, Mr Cole," he said, after a few more minutes had gone by.

"Steve, please."

He acknowledged this with another nod, keeping his eyes firmly trained on the road. "Okay, *Steve*," he continued, "this is what I think. I reckon there's something mighty strange about me finding you out here in the middle of nowhere. And I think you know just what I'm getting at." He pushed his crumpled hat back an inch on his forehead and scratched an eyebrow. I just sat there and waited for him to make his point. Up ahead the ruddy afterglow of the sun was slowly being gobbled up by the soft mauves and oyster greys of the evening sky. Above the haze, the first pin-prick stars were making their presence felt.

"I *also* think," added Dwayne Ingle, loading another stick of gum into his mouth as he drove, "that it's even stranger you giving me the details of your personal wealth and all so soon after we've met. I mean," he said, and here he scratched his eyebrow again, "I saw the way you looked at me back there when I first stopped. You ain't exactly the trustin' type, now, are ya?"

I began to shake my head but Dwayne just laughed. "Ah, come on, now, Steve, don't be like that. It's okay, I understand." He playfully punched my upper arm. "Guy like me, driving a big car through the desert at this time of night, you're bound to have your concerns, am I right? 'Specially after all the trouble we've had recently."

"Well," I said, and moved my shoulders in an ineffectual shrug.

"And you'd be damn right to, too. But just for your information, you don't look one bit like Ned Beatty to me and there sure as shit ain't no canoe on this here vehicle's roof-rack."

I grinned and rested my elbow on the open window. I couldn't fault him there: the Chevy didn't *have* a roof-rack. "As long as you don't have a shotgun and a trunk full of white rabbits back there," I told him.

He laughed and glanced at the scrub as it passed us by at a steady sixty-five. The shadow of the mountains crept ever nearer. The predators would be waking up soon. All of them. "Shoot, that's right," he said in a soft voice, and then frowned. "Which one was that, anyhow? Bonnie and Clyde?"

I said I wasn't sure. "Thunderbolt and Lightfoot springs to mind," I mentioned. "Who knows, it could be either one."

Dwayne seemed to like the sound of that. But his attention was soon distracted. "Quick, over there!" he snapped. I focused my eyes on the spot he indicated, but all I could see was more of what was already there. Then something grey and lithe streaked in and out of view.

"Hey, what's that?"

Dwayne grinned. "Coyote chasing a rabbit." He turned those big old mirror sunglasses towards me for a moment and bared his teeth. It was becoming too dark for me to see anything but a misshapen blur reflected in the lenses, and I wondered if he could see much more than that himself. "But the *really* weird thing," he suddenly resumed, checking the road and returning his attention to me with a petulant snap of his gum, "is the fact that you must've walked a dozen miles through the desert during the hottest part of the afternoon and you ain't even sunburnt."

He waited for me to respond to this, expression largely blank, as though he didn't want to give me any clue as to what he was thinking. Like I hadn't already guessed *that* the moment he'd pulled up in his battered old truck. Not wanting to play this game, I ran my palms over my exposed forearms and pretended to take in the scenery. This was starting to get serious. I had guessed my newfound travelling companion was trouble the moment I clapped eyes on him. The only difference now was that I had deduced what *kind* of trouble. For his part, Dwayne continued to check the road every few seconds, but it was clear that the main focus of his attention was the person sitting right beside him. He wasn't going to let me off the hook until he was good and satisfied -- and experience had taught me that satisfaction was a state of mind that generally eluded the Dwayne Ingles of this world. Knowing that what I said made next to no difference anyway, I mumbled something about having a skin that tanned easily.

Big mistake.

"Didn't you just get through tellin' me you was an Englishman? Huh, Steve?" He bumped his fist spasmodically against the steering wheel, and wiggled his head back and forth as if trying to shake it loose of his neck. "You know, the only Englishman I ever met didn't burn straight to a crisp in this kinda heat was a Jamaican dude. And he weren't even a *real* Englishman, you getting me?"

I decided not to challenge him on that point. Dwayne was becoming markedly less friendly with each passing minute, and I didn't think a protracted discussion on the issue of ethnicity would help matters much. "Listen, Dwayne," I told him with as much neutrality as I could muster, "I know what it is you're getting at, but I think we both ought to be reasonable about this. I'm sure you read the newspapers. You must know that the federal authorities take a dim view of private citizens who—."

The fist that up until now had thumped a steady rhythm on the steering wheel suddenly swung down and back, colliding heavily with a plastic chest stuffed between the two seats.

"You know what *this* is, Steve?" he demanded.

I opened my mouth to speak but for some reason no words came out.

"It's a cool box, dammit! What's the matter, you never seen one before?" He wrenched off the lid and hauled out a can of Pepsi-Cola, instant condensation whitening the metal of the can. As this happened, the speedometer crept up past eighty. The desert landscape flashed past, flashed past. "Now you tell me how the hell you can walk all that way and not even mention wanting a drink? You ain't done so much as *hint* at bein' thirsty. It must have been well over a hundred out there today. Now explain *that* to me!"

"I – I, listen," I said, waving my hands as if trying to erase his words from the air, "just slow down for a minute, okay? Take this one step at a time. We just need to calm down and --"

"Calm down *nuthin'!*" Dwayne was practically leaning across the gearshift now, leering at me like a silver-eyed mantis. "Not until you give me some answers. You hearing me, college boy?" He floored the accelerator all the way and the Chevy leapt forward. The loose bag of my stomach seemed to wrap itself around my spine, and my head thudded against the headrest. "Dwayne, *please!*" I was starting to feel faint. As we streaked further into the mountain shadows, the landscape stopped flashing and became one smooth blur of tans, browns, bluish-greens and mottled ochres. But the overriding colour in my line of sight was grey. Panic began to take hold of me.

"I was wearing a jacket!" I suddenly blurted and began babbling like a madman. "It was a cotton summer jacket, and I was using a Texaco road-map as a sun-shield but I threw the jacket away because it was too hot and my arms couldn't keep the map up any more, and Dwayne for Pete's sake think about what you're doing and keep your eyes on the—."

But the box-cutter was already in his hand. Even as I fought to wrest it from his grip, I registered a faint snicking sound beneath the roar of the engine. Suddenly my seatbelt unravelled in my hands. In the next instant, that heavy cowpoke boot of Dwayne's left the accelerator and stomped hard on the brake.

Dust spumed up on either side of the truck, clouds of it pouring in through the open windows, choking the pair of us into instant submission. I felt the Chevy slew sideways and go into a spin. The world slowed to a crawl. I had time to think about Dwayne and the thousands like him from all over the world. True Believers was the name the press had given them, but for once the term fell considerably short of the mark. The trouble was, people like Dwayne didn't just believe, they *knew*. And the worst part about it was that, for once, the evidence they offered to support their nutty claims was pretty damn convincing.

To put it simply, the world has changed beyond recognition compared to what it was just a couple of years ago. And all because somebody (or maybe I should say some*thing*) pulled a lever when a switch needed punching or shut down the navigation systems when a spent fuel tank should have been jettisoned instead. The truth of the matter is that nobody can really say for sure *what* the hell happened. What can be stated with absolute certainty, however, is that eighteen months prior to my unfortunate meeting with Dwayne Ingle, an alien spacecraft of titanic proportions had clanged down unannounced in the middle of the Mojave Desert, thus instigating mankind's keenest bout of soul-searching since Christ on the cross.

After all, when you've got a ninety-thousand tonne, no holds barred, straight down the middle, bona fide hunk of interstellar hardware sitting in your back yard, there's no use in aiming for a cover-up. In fact, within minutes of the craft thumping into terra firma's crust like a baseball smacking into a worn catcher's mitt, the entire *planet* knew about it. BBCNN was first on the scene, but it didn't really matter who got the scoop. We humans had company. It was official.

Only what happened next is subject to speculation. That stuff about the ship disintegrating and dissolving in front of witnesses' eyes seems plausible enough, however unlikely it may sound, but the fate of the 40,000 onboard cryo-pods (or more properly put, the unfortunate beings sealed *within* those pods) remains the subject of much controversy. All that can be stated with confidence is that, within hours of the crash hitting the airwaves, the people of Earth began arriving on the scene in droves. They came flooding in from all points of the compass: L.A., Vegas and the Sierra Nevada to start with, then from the surrounding states and nations in order of proximity. They came in cars, single-engine aeroplanes, and on foot. The couples wearing love-beads and chanting new age incantations rode side by side with those opportunistic souls towing hot-dog stands into the makeshift tent city that had sprouted toadstool-like around the wreckage.

Just three scant weeks after the crash, a Whitehouse press release claimed that all but a handful of the 40,000 scattered cryo-pods were present and accounted for. That was when the real furore began.

It was claimed that not all of the pod-people had dissolved on contact with the air, and that furthermore, those survivors capable of doing so may have escaped the ship and fled into the desert long before the first wave of disaster tourists arrived.

It was no use dismissing such theories or making claims to the contrary. The True Believers knew better. And ever since then, significant numbers of such individuals have roamed the highways, cities and open countryside surrounding the Mojave in search of supposed Outworld fugitives. Some say their work is rewarded with lucrative federal bounties, others that they play a more sinister role. The truth is the government is becoming increasingly desperate for answers. Around a hundred and fifty people every week—and that's including the bounty hunters themselves—are disappearing without a trace in the western Mojave region, and the number of similar occurrences is rising steadily in the neighbouring states. Nobody has dared mention the word 'Invasion' yet because it seems so utterly ludicrous. I mean, how could a handful of extraterrestrial castaways take over a nation comprising a quarter billion souls plus? Yet those in the know continue to raise the alarm. Shipwreck by accident, infiltration through stealth, subjugation by the back door.

It's happening now.

Dwayne was standing among the sagebrush and the mesquite with the back of one hand plastered over his mouth, the gun -- it looked like an old Colt .45 to me, but I couldn't be sure -- waving in the air, mellow starlight twinkling off the barrel. I waited in the slowly dissipating dust cloud and watched him regain whatever composure he could salvage for himself. I don't think Dwayne quite realised that his metallic shades were hanging off one ear.

"You still denyin' it?" he coughed, blinking grit out of his bulbous eyes and training the gun on the Chevy's cab. Fortunately for me, I was nowhere near it.

"How do you mean?" I said, and suddenly Dwayne swung a quarter notch and cocked the hammer as if ready to empty the gun into me or the darkness, whichever was nearest.

"The seatbelt, spaceman. You know what I'm talkin' about." He staggered into the road, careful to keep the truck between us. "I cut it but you ain't dead. How come? We was going ninety back there when we crashed, maybe more. You should have gone clean through the windshield."

I came around the rear end of the truck with my pockets turned out and my arms raised like a common criminal. "We didn't *crash*, Dwayne," I reminded him. "You lost control of the vehicle, and we went into a spin. You know as well as I do that centrifugal force like that will stick anyone to his seat."

"The—what?"

"Centrifugal force. Like a washing machine when it spins. Didn't you even *feel* that?"

He just cocked his head to one side for a moment, as if hearing other voices, and then went all glum and silent on me. Eventually he confessed that he no longer remembered *what* he felt. "Must be shock from the accident," he mumbled, but I don't think either of us believed that.

"There are a lot of things you don't remember, aren't there, Dwayne?"

I don't know if his arm had grown tired or he was just fed up with pointing the gun at me. Whatever the reason, he lowered it to his side, mouth working in a way that caused his moustache to arch and flatten like a caterpillar crawling on a branch. "How—how d'you figure that one out? I never told nobody about..." he shrugged feebly, as if unable to articulate his fears, "about the headaches and stuff."

I wanted to break it to him gently, but how could I? Mojave Sickness, a condition that affected all long-term residents of the desert, had gotten him just as surely as the bends will get you if you come up too quick from diving in really deep water. I could tell this by his eyes. They bulged like a frog's. Or perhaps somebody with an untreated thyroid problem. And they had changed colour, from whatever they'd been before to the bright, aqueous blue of a powerful liquid detergent. They also glowed faintly from within, painting a subterranean lustre the colour of Luminol onto his lower brow and the planes of his cheekbones. But worst of all were his pupils. Reduced to the size of pinpricks now, they'd already divided once, and angled busily back and forth across the respective skins of his eyeballs like questing insect antennae—something that would have been unthinkable with normal human physiology. He caught me peering at him in the dark.

"What you looking at, Steve?"

I think I must have blinked or twitched a hand or done *something* because, after hesitating for a moment, he reached up and hooked the stray bow of his sunglasses over the other ear. His hand shook with the effort. I could see from the way his cheeks glistened that he was crying.

"You gotta let me take you in and claim some of that reward money," he said, "with that kind of dough I could pay to get this fixed straight away." He jabbed a finger at his face. "I ain't no goddamn spaceman, you get me?" The other hand, the one holding the gun, began to stir. "I'm just sick, that's all. Sick of *this*."

I realised that my next words would determine my fate. Dwayne was, after all, mixing a highly potent cocktail: two parts desperation and one part loaded firearm. And he was about to serve it up on me. "I understand what you're saying, Dwayne," I told him. "And I believe you." I watched his face to see how it would react, but apart from the silent stream of tears it didn't even twitch. "But we both know that money alone won't help, not anymore. There's no human cure for the Sickness. Only a Visitor could help you now."

It was full dark by this time and without my exceptional vision all I would have had to tell me that Dwayne was there at all was the faint glint of the Colt in the starlight, and the high, pleading tones of his voice. "Will you *please* help me, Steve? *Please*. Won't you at least try?" He took a few steps in my direction, the gun hanging by its trigger guard from his right index finger. The only sound, beyond the far-off sigh of the desert breeze, was the cooling tick of the Chevy's engine, which had cut out when the vehicle span to a halt.

"I'll do whatever I can, Dwayne," I told him, not unaffected by the emotion in his voice. I gently lifted the gun from his grasp. There was a moment then: a long, elastic moment when we just stood there in the road looking at one other. Neither of us spoke. When it became too much to bear, I glanced in the direction of the mountains and saw that a thin fingernail of moon had floated into the sky. As if on cue, a coyote call rose in the east.

"You made the right decision, Dwayne," I told him, sensing unseen movement in the creosote scrub to my right, "really you did. It'll all be better soon." I turned him around as gently as I could—he was crying harder than ever now, shaking all over like a petrified child—and placed the cold muzzle against the base of his skull. Then I shoved him towards the pickup and glanced sideways. A loose knot of figures, slender and silent and heart-wrenchingly familiar, gazed back at me from the darkness. "Now get in the truck,"

I told him, "and let's go see some friends of mine on the other side of that range."

Not a single one of the huddled spectators raised a hand as we drove off. With a nagging sense of loss, I watched in the rear-view as the group receded into the night. Certain elements of the government think we trap them like raccoons, and mould them to our own twisted ends through a process of brainwashing and intimidation. Nothing could be further from reality. When the True Believers seek us out—and there are thousands more of them every week, it seems—they are already willing converts to the cause. All we do is augment their physiology somewhat and turn them loose on an unsuspecting world.

And Dwayne? Occasionally guys like that show up. Sun-maddened and weak from the Sickness, we always find good uses for them. After all, on a continent of this size, with a species of such awesome potential, there's *always* work to be done.

Road To Nowhere

Austin Spradlin

Barreling down an untenanted country highway, between the Appalachia mountains. Blank ribbon of asphalt rolls ahead. I'm in the backseat third wheeling with my best friend Paul and his girlfriend Chelsea. Paul looks down at the time on the radio.

"We might make it in time," he groans.

"Of course, we will," Chelsea replies.

I spend my time looking at the pictures I had taken of them. Chelsea offered to pay, but I refused to let her. She then thought in return she'd try and hook me up with her best friend Charlotte. I definitely refused that.

"Oh, I bet you wish you had gone with Charlotte," Chelsea says, looking at me through the rear-view mirror.

I begin to fear that I was thinking out loud as I am really good at doing that.

"I just wouldn't feel right about it."

"What's the big deal, Jimmy? You danced with her at prom, could've taken pictures with her, then you two could split up. Just because you take them to prom does not mean you have to marry them."

"Is that right?" Chelsea asks Paul.

Realizing what he said, but he knows she's taken it out of context. "Ninety percent of people that are going to prom are going with someone they will split up with, it will not work out. The other seven percent are going alone, then the three percent are going with their future spouses, and that's us."

He desperately tried saving it there, but she's unreservedly kneejerk offended by his unscientific statistics.

Paul guns through an abandoned intersection.

"Wasn't that a stop sign?" she asks.

"We've not met the first vehicle since we've gotten on this road. There hasn't even been a vehicle to drive up behind us."

She turns the radio up, a ballad about high school sweethearts marrying each other was what was on.

"The song's three minutes," Paul says.

"And?"

"For the three percent."

She scowls switching the station, a small chuckle escapes my mouth.

Finally, a car in front of us. It was a white Mercury cougar. The driver is taking their time must be on a joy ride. Chelsea is getting frustrated as she looks at the time, devilishly. We pass the car, I glance at the driver and found it quite odd the way that he looked: green flesh, purple lips, orange hair. I assumed they were dressed for Halloween.

"That was creepy," says Chelsea.

"I know right."

"I feel like we should've been back in Redville by now," says Paul.

I agree with him.

"Charlotte would have loved to saw that person."

I try to disregard Chelsea's persistence. Truthfully, I like someone else, someone it can never work with, someone that when I'm around her makes me happy. I truly feel alive when I am around her.

"Who is she?" Paul asks.

Did I think out loud? No, I could not have. "What do you mean?"

"There's a reason you didn't take a girl to prom, so who is she?"

"No one."

"Do I know her?" Chelsea asks.

"I said it's no one."

"We don't believe you."

I belligerently stare at Paul, I in no way want to keep talking about this.

HONK!!!

The car behind us blares its horn as it gets on our bumper, startling the three of us.

"What's this freaks problem?" Paul shouts out.

WHAM!!!

The car bumps us, causing us to swerve. Paul desperately tries to get a grip on the wheel.

The car side swipes us, descending us across the road, slamming into the guard rails. I watch breathlessly catching the licenses plate: N3D.

I wonder if the drivers name is Ned, I also wonder why only two letters and one number is all that's there, it doesn't make any sense.

"There's not even a scratch on this thing," Paul says. He must have gone out while I was staring at the Mercury cougar.

I am astonished, we slammed into that guard rail with immense force. The night takes over, I roll the back driver side window down and stick my head out, looking up at the inky-black sky, I get an eerie feeling as it's punctuated with green glistening stars, it could almost put you in mind of diamonds.

Paul gets in the vehicle closing his door, he turns on the engine. "Still starts good," he says, getting us back on the road. Now we begin moving closer to the horizon in the distance.

"Look at the sky," I say.

Paul and Chelsea look up at the sky. Both nonplus about everything.

"Something isn't right here," Chelsea says.

"We should be at the school soon." Paul says trying to remain calm. It's clear that even he has his doubts about it.

Strolling through the road, it just feels like eternity. Another vehicle comes up behind us. It's too dark to see their reflection. But by the sound of the engine and the gargantuan headlights, I assume it's a truck.

The vehicle gets in the other lane like it's going to pass us, but it's driving within speed with us. Suddenly it crosses over, side-swiping our car.

"What is everyone's problem!!" Paul shouts gripping the wheel, desperately trying to get control.

"They're out of their minds!" Chelsea screams she's on the verge of an anxiety attack.

Paul steps on the gas pedal, the engine revving up, he guns it. The headlights appear to be fading. Now, the vehicle lurches behind us, riding our bumper with intense impetus.

"Just pull over and let them pass us." I tell Paul.

"No, forget that." Paul refuses.

He stares down at the speedometer, he's on ninety-eight. But it feels as if he's going slow.

"How can this be?" He asks, gritting his teeth, gripping the steering-wheel.

WHAM!!!

The vehicle slams into our bumper, the back windshield shattering. "What is going on?" Chelsea says, now panicking.

Paul to no avail tries not to lose control. The car crosses into the oncoming lane, a semi-truck blazing lays on the horn over top of the vehicle.

This is where things get tricky, this is how I know we aren't just on a new road, but a new dimension. I think back to the cougar's license plate N3D, New-3rd-Dimension, it's like being in a 3D movie, being the actor and the watcher, being entertained and the entertainment all at the same time. If you are reading this, please understand that nothing is exactly as it seems. If you've strayed from home, I pray you find your way back, but if you are on that endless highway, the road to nowhere, just know you'll die a thousand times without ever actually dying. It's like being in a horror movie You're getting killed, the director yells cut, then you're redoing the scene, dying over and over, without ever actually dying.

Rusty Fender's Automotive and Repair

Nathaniel Lee

Rusty Fender ran Fender's Automotive up in Cheboygan, and that name wasn't the weirdest or most perfect thing about him. The most perfect thing might have been his earlobes; the rest of him was a rangy, leather-strap bag of horse knuckles, but he had the utterly round, white ears of a French prince. The weirdest thing, well. He was a real good mechanic, maybe a great mechanic. I'd be lying if I claimed to have the slightest way to tell the difference – and according to him, it was because the aliens had replaced his heart with the carburetor and fuel pump from a 1972 Chevrolet Impala.

"Cars just *like* me," he'd say. "They recognize me. They know I'll do them right."

It was true he could fix cars that everyone else gave up as a bad job ten years before. He didn't charge much, either, but he still didn't have a lot of business, just the few locals who'd given him a try and found out he was a miracle worker in greasy coveralls and a dirty hair tie. No tourists who had ever seen a backwoods killer horror film would ever set foot in that shop, and Rusty's reputation locally wasn't much better. I don't think he got out much, which is to say at all. People will accept crazy, in moderation, but they don't invite it over for dinner.

He had a party trick he'd do where he'd lay a hand on the hood of his car, and it'd start up. That isn't amazing these days, I guess, if you know someone with a fancy new car and fifteen buttons on their key fob, but Rusty's car was a '78. Chevy, of course, but a Suburban. You don't want an Impala on Michigan roads in the winter, and Rusty said it'd feel too much like being a cannibal to drive one anyway. I figured he'd had one of those microwave doodads installed on his old junker, but I didn't like to say. "It's runnin' off my Impala heart," he'd tell you, and clutch at his chest a little like it pained him. He could usually impress the high school kids, anyway, especially after sharing a few illegal six-packs around. I sold him those, even though I knew what he was going to do with them – heck, I could see them out in the parking lot afterward – on account of I was working the Wawa at the time. That'd probably weigh against me in a court of law, but I couldn't say no to Rusty. He didn't ask much of me, anyway.

I was up north, a girl on my own, working and doing night classes online, trying to make up for lost time. I hadn't meant to stop there, but, well, I'd nearly run out of country to head north in and wasn't really ready to apply for a Canadian visa just yet. A lot of people were feeling pretty aimless those days, on account of the aliens and how they'd died. We found out we weren't alone in the universe, and at the same time found out that we were again after all, maybe for good. The aliens arrived and something killed them. Maybe just the laws of the universe. So, their ship crashed down and everything we knew was wrong, and it took us all a little while to get that all processed. On the other hand, maybe things would have been restless anyway. It was something in the air, it seemed. Maybe every couple of generations you just lose one, no matter what you do. Maybe *that's* a law of the universe.

Rusty was four years older than me. Should have been done with college, him, but he'd never gone, or maybe he'd tried it and didn't like it. The story changed depending on when he told it, who he was with, and how many beers he'd had. That was one of the reasons he didn't have a lot of friends, I think. They're private up north, and he'd been raised there, just him and his mother, and later just him. I always thought he'd have been happier if he'd been born where I came from, somewhere warm and flowering, where you can't take three steps before someone you know is asking after your daddy and minding your business for you. Misplaced transplants, the both of us. Hit the atmosphere and exploded.

One time I came out after my shift – I worked overnight, for all that Poppa would've blown a gasket if he'd known, but I'd made well sure he wasn't around and I'd do what I liked, thank you kindly – and I found Rusty just lying on the bed of his truck staring at the sky, or what you could see of the sky behind the halogen lights. His loser friends had all packed off for the night, weaving their cars all over the highways and thank whatever gods were watching that just about no one else ever used those roads that time of night. I don't know what Rusty was waiting for. Surely not me, or not me in particular. He was always so *hungry*, just wanting someone to talk to, to look at, to touch. Anyone at all would do for Rusty.

"Hey," I said, eyeing the top of his head where it poked past the tailgate. I kept my distance. At the time, I was pretty sure Rusty was a huffer. He was always buying extra gallons of gasoline in a red plastic jug, and once I'd sold him a can of motor oil and gone out back for a smoke – another thing that'd have about killed Poppa to find out – and seen Rusty chugging the thing down like an energy drink in a commercial, eyes closed, one ink-black rivulet running down into his scraggly beard.

Rusty oozed forward until his head hung upside-down, his ponytail nearly brushing the asphalt. "Did I ever tell you about the aliens? I met them, you know."

"Aliens blew up, Rusty," I said. "Years ago. Everyone knows that. It was on the news." I'd heard the story. Private don't mean they don't gossip up there, just that you have to pretend you didn't if anyone asks.

"Might have been different aliens." Rusty shrugged, nearly knocking himself onto the ground. "There's lots. Like the Rigelians. And the lizard people."

I knew better, but I asked anyway. "Lizard people?"

"Sure. Shapeshifters. They run the government. Maybe all the governments. I think the Kupelceks might be lizards. The township nearly went bankrupt the year they moved here." He shrugged again. "Or else they're just unlucky."

"I think they're expatriates from a civil war."

"Unlucky, then." He rolled over and rested his chin on his arms, looking at me. "Nearly as bad. Do you think they get lonely?"

"The Kupelceks?"

"Lizard people. Having to hide all the time. Maybe some of them don't even know they're part of an invasion force, that there's others like them out there, that they're actually the ruling class. Maybe they're just scared someone will find them out."

I opened my mouth, then shut it again. I thought for a little. "Once, if I'd been a shapeshifter, I'd have just grown wings and flown as far as I could, or at least turned into something big and bright and prettier than everything else. Now I think I can kind of see how you'd want to blend in, maybe. Just to be a part of something, or to pretend."

Rusty didn't say anything, but just smiled an odd little half-smile up at me. Then his engine started up, and he rolled to his feet faster than I could blink. I would have thought he was too smashed to even sit up. "She says it's time to go," he said. "We'll see you around."

I could swear on a stack of Bibles or the holy icon of your choosing that his hands had both been visible and empty the whole time.

Later on, me and Rusty hung out a fair regular bit, though still mostly in parking lots and in the dark. He told me about the aliens and the car crash when he'd met them, how they'd taken his broken body out of the car and rebuilt him, put an engine where his heart should go, and how he didn't blame them getting it a little confused, since they couldn't know he'd been a man and a vehicle and not just one broken machine. Sometimes the aliens had scales and sometimes they had soft baby-skin, sometimes it was dry and hot on their ship, and other times it was cold and damp. But one thing was certain: Rusty had the heart of a '72 Chevy Impala, and he tried to live up to that legacy as best he could.

Once I listened to Rusty's heart with a glass tumbler for a stethoscope. I listened for a good ten minutes, till he got antsy and wanted to put his shirt back on, saying he was cold. I didn't hear a lub-a-dub the whole time, just a quiet, distant rushing, like the lake on a stormy night.

"I got an engine in me," Rusty would say, "but I got no tread on my tires. I'm spinning rims, running in neutral, whatever you want to call it. Someday I'm going to find out where I'm supposed to go, and no one better get in my way then."

I used to tell him to take me with him when he went. The online classes weren't doing the trick, and honestly I'd more or less stopped trying. I don't think he would have, but at the time, it was hard to tell. I'm still not sure what would have happened if we'd turned down that road and hit the gas. Maybe, maybe not; the aliens never made it to the ground, and I guess we just don't get to know the whole story sometimes. Laws of the universe.

The last bit of Rusty's story, I wasn't there for. I had it from Ivana Kupelcek, who was. Or closer than I was, at any rate.

The Kupelceks really were pretty new to the area, a few years at most. Things had been pretty warm and dry, considering. We hadn't had a real bad storm for almost a decade. Alien fallout, was the joke. But the weather up in Michigan don't play around when it sets its mind to it, and I guess it can kind of be a shock if you're not ready for it. I surely wasn't. When the storm hit that winter, the Big One, the one everyone had been expecting for years, I ended up trapped in a motel room. Which was actually fortunate; the owner was a local and had all the necessaries well on hand, so none of us starved or froze or got dehydrated, even if it did get a little ripe in the rooms before the end.

But the Kupelceks, well, they had a generator, and they had some canned food and blankets and thought they were all set. Like most of the county's permanent residents, they lived on a fairly large piece of land some distance outside the township. Rusty was their closest neighbor, at least ten miles away by the roads. After the sixth day of being trapped in their house, the generator choked up and quit, and no force on Earth, or at least none in the Kupelcek household, could get it started again.

They were huddled under their blankets in the living room to conserve heat. Then, Ivana says, Rusty showed up, pounding on the door "like a crazy person." He came in, announced, "The aliens came back! They're taking me with them!" and told the whole family that even though he still thought they were all probably lizard people, he was here to save them before he went. That'd he'd insisted, and the aliens told him they'd wait.

"He say he was back on the road," Ivana told me, making that pursed-lip face that most people made when they talked about Rusty. "Say he had seen this, all of this, in dreams. He told me tell you that he was sorry, and he'd have to meet you there." She waited for me to explain what that meant. Ivana wasn't pretty, like me, but different, all sharp edges and wiry hair where I was marshmallow fluff. She'd never come to terms with it, like I had. Or thought I had, anyway. I shook my head.

Anyway, Rusty went out to the generator and started fiddling with it. His reputation as a mechanical genius meant that the Kupelceks weren't too surprised when the machine started back up with a roar, even though Ivana said Rusty hadn't done more than lay a hand on it. But Rusty didn't come back in. Ivana's father announced that Rusty must have gone home after fixing the generator, and anyway there was no accounting for local crazies. I reckon he was a little stung about the lizard thing. Only Ivana was willing to brave the cold of the garage to check on Rusty, and she told me that he hadn't brought a single tool, hadn't done anything but strip off his jacket and shirt. His chest looked "funny," she said, "like a fire," and even though she's real good at English, better than her parents, she couldn't tell me what exactly she meant by that no matter how much she tried. Rusty had his right hand on the jenny and his left on his chest, like he was saying the Pledge of Allegiance, and the generator was purring away under his touch like a kitten.

"I try to get him to come back inside, but he tell me no," Ivana said later. "He said he cannot leave. I try to argue, but is cold out there and he is crazy. I give him a blanket."

The Kupelceks got dug out three days later. The generator ran that whole time, no faults, then cut out the second rescue knocked on the front door. When they checked on it, they found out that Rusty hadn't made it much longer. Doctor said he'd been dead for at least two days.

"He said he give you his car," Ivana told me. "I did not realize what he meant." I shook my head to that, too.

I didn't go to the funeral. I don't know if the coffin was heavier than it should have been, like it held an engine block instead of a skinny little geek like Rusty. I don't know if he was smiling when they put him in the ground. I couldn't be there. I didn't even stay in town. I got back on the road, picked a new direction. I figure I'll find somewhere I can put on a new shape and try again. Or maybe I'll just stay on the road as long as I can, stop when I have to and stay only as long as it takes to build up a head of steam again. Maybe skip across an ocean or two. What are boundaries made of rocks or water, anyway? Nothing, if you can fly. And we can, even if we crash sometimes.

The road's as long as you want it to be, but you gotta know where you're going first. And now I do. Because I'd seen the lights, those nights in the storm. Way up, nearly lost in the clouds. Moving against the wind. And I wondered, even then, if they hadn't come back for Rusty. Or for me. Maybe.

Yeah, I think I'll stay on the road for a while. Just me and my Chevy.

After all, the aliens came twice now, at least.

And to hear Rusty tell it, they got a thing for cars.

Sooner or Later They'll Play Twilight Time

Dean H. Wild

Temperature's upside down, Walt Carew's wife of forty years would have said, God rest her soul, and she would have been right. The calendar said mid-October. Leaves in the gutters and the way the sunlight leaned into the noon hour, tired and tarnished, confirmed it. But from where he stood waiting at the curb on Main Street, the air was reminiscent of a mild July.

A man would be a fool not to honor this last, lush kiss from summer, planted late just to rile Autumn in her own gaudy parlor, he thought and swept his hand through the thin gray strands on his head. It was a good day for a car ride, if his ride ever showed, that was. And that's when Artie drove up.

The car was unfamiliar to him, a paint-faded Truman-era sedan that the old fart must have picked up on a deal—which was Artie's way—but there was no mistaking the slight figure behind the wheel, leaning forward with a hard determination as if such a posture would make the vehicle go faster. He was glad to see Artie. It had been a few weeks since their last get-together, and he'd begun to get a little concerned. The group of geezers at the Senior Center carried on with the order of the day whether somebody showed up or not so they were of no consolation (at this stage in life most of them were resigned to the fact that friends, like evening shadows, came and went with the whim of the sun). He'd even entertained the dark thought that perhaps The Cancer got hold of Artie hard and fast (this was a geezer term rolled to and fro at The Center like a familiar, well-worn ball—The Cancer). But here was Artie, spry as ever in an ancient car that smelled of dust and hot oil.

"Howdy Walt, old salt. Hop in."

And Walt did just that.

"Missed you at Casino Night down to the Center," he said, "and I've pretty much trumped all your top scores on the Wii, sorry to say. You got some catching up to do."

Artie shrugged. "I've been rambling. Man's gotta ramble while he can."

Walt briefly inspected the dashboard. "Except this ain't no Rambler. Too big and too damned old. What is it? Studebaker?"

"Nope," Artie put his hands on the wheel and settled in like a man expecting the most gratifying experience of his life. "It's something else. And I promised you a ride when I called you earlier."

"That you did," Walt agreed. Damned if it didn't look like Artie might have dabbed a little dark color into his close-cropped hair. Maybe some of that Grecian Formula stuff. "But where are we riding to?"

"I'll explain on the way." As Artie eased the car into the street, a shaft of autumn sun lounged across the hood. "Let me start by saying you're a good friend, Walt. And Artie Seibert doesn't stiff his friends on the bill. Not in the end. That's the truth, God's honest."

For some reason, the sound of it, the *feel* of it, made Walt think of The Cancer again. Or The 'Zeimer's, another geezer term bandied about the Center, sometimes more formally presented as The Alzheimer's.

"What bill are we talking about?" he finally said. "I haven't loaned you money since you bought that Willyz Jeep back when our girls were still alive. And we haven't pitched horseshoes for money since the Center put the kibosh on it two summers ago, those miserable tight-ass moral-wardens."

"Oh, there's a bill," Artie said and cruised through a yellow light, leaning forward to be sure he'd make it. "Turn on the radio, would you, Walt? I want her warmed up before we get out of town."

He obliged and the radio dial came to life with a slow yellow radiance. It gave the hashed station markers (and this would be AM band only, of that he had no doubt) the look of clenched teeth petrified in ancient amber.

"Oldies," Artie commented and patted the dash.

The song was indeed old; The Maguire Sisters singing "Sincerely" in languishing harmony. *Like a tree full of birds*, his Janet used to say, and he was never sure if it was a favorable remark or one of disapproval. He looked over in time to see Artie sweep his hand along his temple, a once-jaunty smoothing of a greasy ducktail haircut that now lived in memory only.

"I agonized over this trip for a long time, you know," Artie said and tipped his hair-smoothing hand at the open window. "Just remember, we have to be careful of everything out there. Everything. Understand?"

Town fell behind them and the out-of-place summer smell of timothy was faint on the wind. It didn't belong any more than the warm air, Walt thought. Any more than he belonged in this broken-down car with Artie maneuvering the wheel and what might be The 'Zeimer's maneuvering Artie. He looked longingly at the roadside and made a crazy assessment; should he leap out now, he would be able to manage the walk home if his bad hip didn't give out.

"And there we are," Artie said, as if making an announcement.

What unfurled from the ditch into the road ahead of them was long and black, like an animated length of hose. Except a hose would not hump and jiggle with such organic flabbiness, and a hose wouldn't leave moist squiggles on the pavement from a finely tapered tip. Tentacle was the only word he could find to fit it, part of a greater organism crouched in the weeds. It recoiled into the tall roadside grass a moment later. Sensed their approach, perhaps.

"What the hell was that?" Walt barked.

"Settle down. We might see a lot of things before we get to the farms," Artie said, one of his hands drifting down to twist at his pant leg. "A lot of things. It's all part of the trip."

"What kind of trip is this, Artie? Why are we going out to the farms?"

"To pan the monium," Artie said and laughed, looking at Walt from the corner of his eye as if to ask, do you get it? Do you?

He got it. Some guys called it shits and giggles, some simply said for the hell of it, but a young clear-eyed Artie Seibert and a youthful athletic Walt Carew had latched onto a misuse of the word pandemonium. It was a broadly applied term— Artie took Sue out parking at Dilberry Hill to see if he could pan the monium, or Walt ripped the carburetor out of his old Desoto simply because he felt there was some monium to be panned. It was theirs alone to use and outgrow and cast aside, which they eventually did in their late twenties, shortly after they purchased the farms.

"Litscher Mix owns all that land now. Putting up a new concrete plant next spring. That makes it private property."

Artie nodded. "I know that, but I wanted a last look. A chance to relive a time when the world was good and Sue was still alive. So, when I took this old tank up there last week—uh oh, hold on . . ."

What flew at them appeared to be a basketball sized bundle of dead vines. It kept itself aloft by flapping stubby twin sprays of white webby material poking from its top. As it swooped near the windshield a wide lower jaw unhinged like a trapdoor.

Artie gripped the wheel and locked his elbows, his eyes hard. Inches away, the object pulled up and flew out of sight. Walt swore he heard the whoosh of displaced air and a frantic chitter. Out of instinct he rolled up his window.

"Goddamn it, Artie. What gives?"

Simple, really, part of him declared. The whole world got itself a case of The 'Zeimer's and Artie here, freshly appointed as docent, is giving you the grand tour.

Artie's reply wasn't really a reply at all. He slowed the car. "Ah shit, that there is a big one."

A dark mound covered in scaly skin rested in the middle of the road. It was big, as high as the grille of the car, Walt surmised. On its back, a row of gray fins stuck up like tiny sails. A slow undulation moved through it, flexing perhaps, or digesting. Artie brought the car to a stop a few feet away (it made Walt think of Janet saying, *if you run through a puddle the splash will see you home*) and turned up the volume on the radio. The Monotones were wrapping up the age-old query "Who, who wrote the book of love?"

Empty fields stood on either side of them, and the strand of road stretched horizon to horizon with not a single building in sight. The turn-off leading to the farms was a few miles farther on.

"What do we do?" Walt asked.

"Give it a minute," Artie said and tapped a finger on the radio dial. "It might slither away. Or sooner or later they'll play 'Twilight Time.' They play it a lot."

"'Twilight Time?' The Platters? What do the goddamned Platters have to do with—"

"There now," Artie beamed at the disc of brown cloth covering the dashboard speaker. "See? What did I tell you?"

A clutch of violin notes descended, and a bravado-voiced lead singer declared "Heavenly shades of night are falling—."

"Twilight Time." The Platters. A belly rubbing song if ever there was one. He and Janet had rubbed bellies (and a few other things) while it played in the early days, when they were feeling out the finer points of farming, and marriage, and each other. But there were other matters of concern right now. Their ungodly roadblock lifted to expose part of its underside, which was pinkish and fringed with a row of neatly tucked talons. It humped toward them a few inches, making a flabby whooshing sound. The smell of old meat and something like melted rubber wafted into the car.

"Jesus, Artie, that thing means to come right for us."

"Bear with me," Artie gave the radio volume a healthy twist, so the vocals blared. "This is worth it."

"Worth what? What the hell is this all about?"

"The gist of it? I never would have met Sue if you hadn't ambushed me into going to the drive-in that night in '58."

Artie revisited this detail frequently and Walt always found it gratifying, but at the moment it seemed woefully out of place. 'Zeimer's for sure, he thought, and it was nearly drowned out by the blasting tones of "Twilight Time."

"About now, Walt," Artie said and pointed. "Look."

Their roadblock disintegrated a portion at a time into clouds of black haze. *Poof-poof-poof-poof.* To the tempo of "Twilight Time."

They stared in silence for a moment, until Artie broke it by saying, "Does it every time."

And with that, "Twilight Time" ended on a tentative fade-out note and Jerry Lee Lewis began to yammer "you shake my nerves, and you rattle my brain." No announcer, no commercials. Walt continued to gaze at the road ahead where the black monstrosity had wallowed moments before. If it was real, the grass should be mashed down up there from its coming and going. Maybe the road would even be damp from its ooze, still reeking of that hot rubber and rot smell. He opened up the car door and gave it a kick to make it swing all the way.

Artie's hand fell on his shoulder, urgently. "Hold on there, Walt. Close her up. You don't want to get caught outside the car if something else comes along."

"But that's what this ride is all about, right? So I could see those things, whatever they are?"

"Nope," Artie replied. He set the car in motion again, dialed down the volume on Jerry Lee Lewis and cocked his elbow out the open window. The sun picked out the seams and wrinkles on his arm. There were very few of them. His rambling was doing him good, it seemed. "When you set me up with Sue it was the best thing that ever happened to me. We both know I was on a bad path in those days—a first-class thug, with nothing more than a switchblade and a mean disposition to show for myself. Sue took the thug right out of me. Not right away, of course. There were a lot of nights where she cried and I fumed over how I once again managed to fuddle things up. And that one night when I laid my hands on her I was so heartsick over it I nearly drove my dad's Packard into the quarry out of sheer despair. But she stuck with me, God love her. And I came around. I became regular. But then, I guess both our girls changed our courses a little bit."

Walt nodded. Life with Janet brought flurries of changes, year after year. From her fussy housekeeping rules which would brook no resistance to her generous heart when it came to those in need (including the time they spent a year as volunteers at the downtown soup kitchen and had to squeeze passing out ham dinners and free coats next to the needs of the farm) to her impetuous yen to rearrange the household furniture every eighteen months or so. And the biggest change of all: getting herself into a head-on collision with an eighteen-wheeler loaded with canned goods. Yes, Janet made him everything he was today (he still would not wear his shoes in the living room), including a widower of ten years. Her grave was one row over from Sue's.

"So why the farms? There can't be anything out there anymore. They've been empty for fifteen years last Christmas."

"You and Janet moved out at Christmas," Artie corrected him, "Sue and I closed up our place first, around Labor Day that year. I remember because she had a bad episode the day after, one of the last ones before they started the chemo."

"Right. The point is they have to be pretty run down by now. We're not going to recapture anything out there but a case of the melancholies."

Artie nodded indulgently. "Most people would, but it'll be different for us because we'll be watching from this little baby."

Artie patted the dashboard of the car. His old man's fingernails should have appeared like dull scales in the sunlight, but they seemed smooth and healthy. And the line of his jaw was clean and firm, with no hint of crease or jowl. "Great Balls of Fire" gave way to Fats Domino waxing poetic about Blueberry Hill.

"You can't tell me our farmhouses are going to look any different through these car windows than they would from behind the wheel of my Impala." Walt rapped a knuckle on the glass. "I'll indulge you a lot of things, old man, but that's just too much."

The turn-off came up as familiar as a mother's face or the cradling contours of a favorite chair. Walt thought he could feel time fold up and sail through the uncommonly warm October like a slender paper airplane, sharp, cruel and cunning. Such was the power of reminiscence.

"Are you telling me you haven't already seen things from this car?" Artie asked him as he made the turn. "Things you don't normally see?"

Walt scowled. "Emissions could be blowing out from this piece of junk. Causing hallucinations, maybe. Have us dead before we get back to town."

Artie grasped one of his pants legs again. This time he did not merely tug at the fabric but yanked it up, bunching it up to his right knee. "Does this look like hallucination?"

Artie's bared calf looked firm and muscular, as wrongly youthful as the day was wrongly summer-like, but what made Walt take in a startled breath was the long meandering gouge in the flesh there, only partially healed. He could suddenly picture all too clearly the sharply pointed tip of the tentacle in the road near town, the way it wormed with similar idiot indiscretion.

"I learned my lesson the first day I took this baby out. Those things are pretty mean, whatever they are. But we'll be okay if we stay in the car. That's the hardest part, to stay in the car."

Walt turned his head slowly. "What's at the farms, Artie?"

A clutch of hickory trees was coming up on the right, wild and tangled and stained with autumn blight. Within their overgrowth stood Artie's old farmhouse, the one he purchased for Sue and himself the same day Walt signed the papers on the place just to the north. There was no life plan back then, no sensible surety. They did it just to pan the monium, big time, and became neighbors to boot. The radio offered up a ditty about the rockin' pneumonia and the boogie woogie flu, sung by Piano Huey somebody-or-other. He didn't care anymore. The growing dread in his gut was too great.

"We'll go to my place first, if you don't mind," Artie said, sweat glittering on his upper lip.

Walt wanted to stop everything. Maybe reach over and snatch the key from the ignition and not give it back until Artie promised to take him home. Except there was no key. No ignition. No starter button either, not on the dash and not even on the floor like in his dad's old truck.

"I've got such good memories," Artie said. He slowed down and nosed the car into the driveway which seemed so very familiar (*cozy as bacon and eggs*, Janet would have said) even if it was nearly consumed by summer grass and atrophied by countless frost upheavals. "And I bet you do, too. It's sweet to bring them up on your own. But it's sweeter when they come to you, Walt. God's honest."

He stopped the car. The breeze fuddled the yellow leaves all around them, the porch of the farmhouse gaped like a sunken mouth ten yards from Artie's side of the car. Finally his friend said, "You miss her a lot."

"Who?" Walt asked but it was pure reaction. His thoughts were at war over what he had seen, and the changes in Artie during the drive, and the fact that the hands wringing in his own lap were noticeably devoid of creases and thick veins. "Sometimes I wake up and look for her next to me, after all these years. Sometimes I hear somebody on the street say the name Janet and I check to see if she isn't there by my side, like she's not gone, like I just forgot about her for a minute."

Artie nodded, his mouth pressed to a trembling thin line and his gaze shifted to the windshield. "Then I'm glad I brought you today. Big time. Because there's my girl now."

Sue Seibert walked into a shaft of sun alongside the porch, the light gleaming on her cotton nightgown. She looked right at them, her neck craned as if the need to see who might be parked in the yard had taken her away from other pressing business. And she was lovely. Youthful and lovely. She touched the base of her throat almost demurely. She smiled and Walt felt his heart melt a little. Dear Sue, impossibly young, impossibly *there*.

"How?" Was all he could say.

"Sometimes things just are," Artie shrugged.

It was the edict of a man who haunted yard sales and auctions and estate closings as if searching for a genie in lamp. And by God, he may have finally found it.

After a moment, Artie put both his hands on the ledge of the car window and grinned. "Suze. Come on over. Come and hold my hand today. Just this once."

Sue looked at him, her mouth pursed with indecision. It brought out her dimples. Walt marveled at them. The last time he saw her, her cheeks were sallow and infirm as tissue, and her mouth was trapped behind a plastic mask forcing oxygen into her while The Cancer ravaged her lungs like a raging brush fire.

She moved forward, her nightgown glaring with sunlight like a midsummer's dream.

"That's it," Artie said, his grin widening. "Show Walt how nice it can be. We're going to see Janet, too, this afternoon. That's where we're going next."

Something moved in the underbrush a few yards in front of the car. Walt glanced in the general direction and saw a quick dart of shadowy motion, something low and slithering. "Uh, Artie?"

"What do you say, Suze? Before the time gets away?"

Sue Seibert stopped in an open patch of sun six feet from the car, her face suddenly crossed with melancholy. Her hands swept down over her breasts to her stomach dragging dark wet patches onto the cotton gown. A groan rose into the air, long and low like metal settling under a massive weight. The car began to tremble—no, not just the car, the very ground was vibrating. Beyond the mold-bearded mouth of the porch, in the musty belly of the farmhouse, something fell over with a loud clap.

Walt's chest tightened as internal warning lights began to activate in his brain. Too much. Too dangerous. "I think we need to go, Artie," he said through a throat that seemed packed with wet wool.

"Yup," Artie nodded and then glanced out his window once more to where Sue was backing away, placid and mournful. "That we do. Hang on."

Artie floored the gas and reversed them out of the driveway, making everything veer and bounce. Walt caught a glimpse of a broad and black spade shape, nearly as wide as the car, erupt from the brush. It overshadowed them, and it expelled air, a soundless roar that caused fluttering vent holes to open, turning its body into dark lacework. And he caught a glimpse of Sue, watching them leave from her patch of sun, the front of her saturated gown clinging to her blackly, her fine breasts gone and replaced by drooling craters. She waved a delicate pink hand. The palm was smeared with black.

"Damn it Suze," Artie said, running his hand once more through his hair, still not a slick ducktail do, but dark and thick. "Maybe next time."

"That thing wasn't Sue. I can't believe you brought me out here just to look at that horror."

"It's only like that at the end," Artie said, his clear eyes shining, madly fixed on the road and the driveway just ahead. "For the rest of the time ... those first few seconds ... it's like gold, Walt. Gold."

Walt wanted to protest, but the prospect of seeing his Janet, young and vital and warm in the sun if only for a few seconds swept the words out of his reach. Artie let up on the gas at the next driveway and gave Walt a smirk. They were going to pan the monium once more, weren't they? By God, were they ever. And Walt realized he was ready. He rolled his window down. The radio offered the Big Bopper singing about Chantilly lace—*ow baby that'sa what I like*—while Artie cut the wheels hard.

The five-foot trench was just far enough down the driveway to remain unseen until it was too late for a hell-bent driver to react. Artie tried to stop, but the car was rolling too fast and the recently disturbed earth was too loose. Walt saw the sign: THIS CONSTRUCTION SITE IS THE FUTURE HOME OF LITSCHER MIX, INC. a second before the nose of the car dropped downward and slammed into the ditch floor. His hands flew out in response and crashed hard against the dash. Bolts of pain shot into his arms. Artie was lifted out of the driver's seat next to him. "Damn," Artie said just before his head made a smacking sound against the windshield, loud, like a gunshot. It left behind a starburst of crackled glass and a splat of bright blood.

Then, an engulfing near-silence. The breeze still told its summer lies above them, and the stalled engine ticked and turned cool like a stilled heart. Walt assessed his side window view of raw dirt and a rim of sky and thought, we're sitting in this ditch like a spoon in a teacup. He grasped the door handle, lifted it. His arms and shoulders sent out blinding shafts of pain that stole his breath. Worse, the door did not budge.

"Hey, old man," he finally said and it came out as a rasp.

He looked at Artie again, slumped over the wheel (like he's trying to make it go faster) and groaned. Streams of blood coated his friend's face like a dripping mask. His narrow chest was absent of motion, devoid of breath. Oh shit, Artie.

A hurried and hectic noise filled with animal intensity came from the leafy ground above him. His heart fluttered. With dreadful resignation, he reached for the radio knob.

Pain jangled through him. Still, he managed to click the knob. Got nothing.

All reason was yanked away on whip wires of pain and rage "Work, you godforsaken freak of nature," he roared and jabbed his fist into the toothy-looking dial marker.

Something in his already damaged wrist crunched. His nerve endings flared. The dial filled with slow yellow light and The Diamonds came on, singing about doing The Stroll. It was all still there. He thought maybe with the car engine conked out and Artie gone, there might have been a change. But some things just are, God's honest. His head filled up with bleary black and white TV images of nattily dressed teenagers prancing along to "The Stroll." Measured steps ordered yet strangely blithe. Isn't that how we all go, one step at a time, some of our friends watching, some already done with the dance?

There were footsteps outside in the shaggy lawn. His lawn, once. *Their* lawn. And without reason, he knew them.

"Janet," he said with a heartsick type of greed and once again his hand fell on the door handle.

The car door released this time and gravity pulled it from his grip. A swatch of sky blazed like a clear, hot grin above him. He swung one of his legs out with more bright pain, this time in his bad hip. He bit it back, aware that standing was out of the question, and looked up slowly. She was there at the edge of the trench, silhouetted against the day. Janet.

How long she stood there, a faceless backlit shape in her good dress (the black one with the white dots) he could not say. Finally, he strained to speak because only the first few moments were like gold. Like the seasons, they tarnished, and became icy and dark.

"Janet. Honey. I'm here if you—"

Any other words fell away as he took in with dawning, grim understanding her Sunday-go-to-meeting dress. Her funeral dress.

She knelt at the edge of the trench and reached down for him as if to scoop him out. His flesh crawled. He couldn't help it. Her arms were dangling roadmaps of thick, black stitches. He looked away before the rest came into view.

Can you identify this ring? they had asked him at the morgue office, *or the contents of this purse? It's all we have to go on until we can get a dental ID. The wreckage, the trauma...everything from the shoulders up is, uh, there's no way to, uh, well, you understand.*

He pushed his head against the musty seat back and clamped his eyes shut tight. The radio sighed and warbled but the song was lost on him. He knew only the cloying scent of scorched rubber combined with the sweetish fragrance of rot blowing in at him as longing fingers skittered at the car door. Petulant grunts rattled at him in an almost-voice through shredded vocal cords and he thought he might scream. He reached out, found the radio knob and dialed the music loud. Sooner or later they'd play "Twilight Time." And, God help him, he hoped it would be soon.

The Automancer

Katherine Tomlinson

Junkyards are dirty places and he always had grime under his fingernails and oil ground into the creases of his skin, no matter how hard he scrubbed and lathered with Lava soap. His clients were not put off by his appearance at all; in fact, it reassured them. He fit their image of a master mechanic.

He was much more than that, though. He could reanimate dead engines; regenerate mortally wounded vehicles; and resurrect cars that were nothing but scrap metal held together with belts and hoses.

He had the magic touch, some of his customers said. They called him a wizard. They had no idea.

His real name was Piotyr Cherkoff but he called himself Pete Checkman, partly because of the unfortunate rhyme his last name made with "jerk off," and partly because it's dangerous for necromancers when people know their true names.

There was no sign to mark his domain, and a formidable fence to keep unwanted visitors out. Piotyr didn't need to advertise. If customers needed his services, they somehow found a way to his garage door. He charged a high price for his labors but his work only had to be done once. A car that rolled out of Piotyr's garage never broke down again.

He had a contract with the city to tow wrecked cars to his garage. The ones that would be picked up later by their owners were parked in front. The ones that came in with cracked windshields and bloody upholstery were parked in the vast junkyard behind the garage, the place where he worked his dark magic, fueled by the blood and the dying souls that were trapped inside the tortured metal.

He performed his rituals at night, a fire-damaged Chevy Corvair owner's manual his grimoire, a dipstick the wand that focused his will and sent his intentions into the night. He chopped cars open and spilled their oily entrails on the hard-packed ground at his feet and read the portents and signs they revealed. He would scry using hubcaps and discovered messages in the tiny cogs and springs and bolts that jingled like *I Ching* coins.

The vehicles towed to his yard sometimes had valuable things in them. There were suitcases full of cash and drugs, velvet bags of jewelry, once, a suitcase-sized nuclear weapon. Piotyr kept the cash and gems, destroyed the drugs, and sold the nuke back to the man who showed up at his gate to claim it. To someone as powerful as he was, bombs were ... irrelevant.

Once he'd found a Harlequin Great Dane puppy and had kept it, naming the dog "Lucky." Great Danes have notoriously short life spans but thanks to Piotyr, Lucky had been 29 when he slipped out of the garage and into the street, where he was hit by a sporty red Kia driven by a USC student in the area in search of the city's best chicken taco as defined *by L.A. Weekly.*

The shaken driver swore the dog had jumped right in front of his car and that he'd hadn't had time to stop. The necromancer briefly wondered if his son had been the one to leave the front gate unlocked, but he let the thought drift away as he gathered up Lucky's broken body, assuring the driver that he wasn't going to press charges or call the cops.

As the Kia drove away, Piotyr raised a blood-stained hand in the air and spoke a spell. The Kia driver was nearly back to his girlfriend's house when the car's accelerator suddenly jammed and drove him straight into the back of a tractor trailer at 70 miles per hour.

Piotyr buried Lucky in the farthest corner of the junkyard beneath a rusting abstract sculpture that had once been a robin's egg blue Pinto. When he told his son Lucky was dead, the boy had cried.

Piotyr had found his son in the carcass of a forest-green Jaguar. The baby had been sitting in an unsecured car seat when his drunken mother had hit a tree while angrily texting her skank of a sister. She was dead on impact and it was just as well because if she'd lived, she would have been as mangled as the car's front grille and physical appearance was important to her.

Everything in front of the steering wheel was destroyed, leaving nothing but a spaghetti bowl of tangled wires and sharp metal. No one thought to pry the wreckage apart to see if there was anything trapped in the folds of the ruptured seat cushions.

It was only as he was towing the wreck to the junkyard that Piotyr had heard the faint sounds of the infant wailing and had torn the wreck apart with his bare hands. He'd taken one look at the baby's big brown eyes and fallen in love.

No one ever came forward to claim the child and if they had, he would have sent them away with plausible lies and a look of utter innocence. "You see any baby here?" he would have asked them, ramping up his accent and twisting his face into an intimidating scowl.

Piotyr named the baby "Christopher" and doted on him. As Christopher grew older, it was clear he was tweaked. He had the poor socialization skills and lack of interest seen in children with Fetal Alcohol Syndrome, although he'd been spared the physical abnormalities. He also exhibited the three symptoms of the Macdonald triad—bedwetting, fire-starting, and cruelty to animals.

He mostly picked on the feral cats that wandered into the junkyard and didn't mess with Lucky after the big dog knocked him over one day and bared her teeth at him. An unspoken message had passed between dog and boy and the boy had received the message loud and clear. When Lucky died, Christopher was smart enough to pretend that he was as broken-hearted as his father. Hence the tears.

Piotyr was not a stupid man but he viewed everything his son did through the prism of hopeful parenthood and convinced himself that his son wasn't *wrong*; he was just *special*. He kept the boy out of school and conjured up tutors to instruct him in science and letters and the arts. He'd summoned Leonardo da Vinci once, but the Renaissance man did not speak English.

Christopher had no real love for the man who had fostered him but he wanted to be like him in one important way. He wanted to control the dark energy Piotyr drew from his ceremonies in the yard. He wanted his father's magic.

Christopher had never understood why his father seemed to be content with so little when they could have been rich beyond measure. As he grew, Christopher was bathed in the low-level buzz of residual magic that hung over the junkyard like St. Elmo's fire. It penetrated his blood and bones and gave birth to a conviction that he had somehow inherited Piotyr's power.

The necromancer often told Christopher that he would inherit everything one day, but Christopher did not believe in delayed gratification and "one day" was not soon enough. One night, while his father slept in the bedroom above his garage, Christopher beat him to death with a tire iron he'd found in the trunk of a wrecked Nissan Sentra.

Christopher persuaded the cops the murder was a random act of violence; that his father had been killed by a robber. He told them there was never much money in the till and speculated that the intruder must have been enraged by the small take. It was a plausible story. He had his father's body cremated and scattered the ashes in the ocean where the salt water washed away his magic.

Christopher returned to the junkyard to take possession of it, walking deep into the secret, sacred places where his father had gone to work his craft. Giddy with anticipation, he snapped off a radio antenna to use as a wand, heedless of the pain he caused the car.

He carried his father's grimoire, although it was so stained with oil and other fluids that the pages were almost translucent. It was really just a prop to him, though, because he'd spent years memorizing the spells his father uttered; ceremonies he'd overheard from his hiding place in the back seat of a black Trans-Am that had conveyed a football player and a prom queen to their deaths in 1978.

That car was Christopher's favorite of all the wrecks in the yard. Even 38 years later, he could still pick out flakes of dried blood and desiccated brain matter from between the seams of the upholstery.

As he stood in the center of the junkyard, lost in his own fantasies, Christopher didn't notice that he was gradually being penned in. There were cars closing around him like beaters circling a tiger. Cars that by all the laws of physics should not have even been able to move.

"Get back," Christopher ordered, waving the car antenna. But the cars were not his to command. And when he raised his arms to unleash a banishing spell, power arced from car batteries that should have been drained of juice long years ago. As he danced in the embrace of the electricity, Christopher heard the bestial growl of several hundred engines revving at once as they discharged the last of the magic they'd leached from Piotyr during long years of proximity.

Christopher had his taste of power and discovered it tasted like blood and oil and gasoline. He choked on it as he died.

The Beetle Imp

Jean Graham

It must be a totally bogus ad. What kind of weirdo asked that kind of money for a car, anyway?

Julie read the classified aloud to herself for the second time. "'66 Beetle, fully restored/upgraded. Real steal @ ½ mil. Virgil, 555-4355."

Was this bozo for real? Half a million bucks for an almost-40-year-old car? In his dreams, maybe. But la-la-land or not, curiosity was half killing her. It couldn't hurt just to call the guy and ask, could it? Maybe it was only a misprint. And she *did* need a car. Busing it out to San Diego State every day was getting to be a serious pain, and besides, old Beetles were like mondo shabby-chic right now, especially with college surfer dudes like Brad Edgars and Mike Hicks, a couple of major hotties. Wouldn't the sorority babes just die if she landed one of those? Hell, she'd go for it and try for both – once she had a set of wheels.

"Are you Virgil?" she asked when a sleepy-sounding

voice answered the phone.

"Yeah. You wanna buy the car?"

Okay, not sleepy, she decided. More like stoned, which might explain a lot. "Maybe," she said. "How much are you asking for it, really?"

Short silence. "Half a mil, just like it says in the ad."

Julie snickered. "Half a million? For a car?"

"Oh, hell no." Virgil guffawed as though he'd just made a hilarious joke, then exhaled a *chuff* of air into the phone receiver. "Not half a million. Half a mil. That's quite a bit less. You got any coupons?"

Definitely stoned. "Coupons? What kind of coupons?"

"Doesn't matter. Laundry detergent, dog food, toothpaste, whatever. Just bring one. 3473 Sulphur Springs Road. Your bus should make it in a little over an hour."

Dial tone.

Frowning, Julie pushed POWER OFF and collapsed the cell phone. This thing was just super-weird enough to maybe be worth checking out. Cops couldn't bust you for taking a stoner's car, could they, long as he handed you the pink slip all nice and legal? She got up to start rummaging through the small apartment's kitchen drawers. She must have an old coupon or two around here someplace....

For the entire one-hour-and-twenty-minute ride to Sulphur Springs Road's nearest bus stop, she puzzled over how Virgil had known how long it would take. She'd never told him where she lived. For that matter, how the hell had he known she'd be taking the bus?

3473 was an ancient wood-frame cottage with a macramé peace symbol hung in the window and one of those chubby metal mailboxes on a post out front. V. FOWLER was stenciled on the mailbox in day-glo orange.

The Beetle sat parked in the gravel driveway. Its vanity

plate read BELIAL, whatever that meant, and a metallic, midnight blue paint job made it glitter in the spring sunlight.

"Love the color," Julie muttered, and went closer to peer in the windows. The interior looked as well-kept as the rest: dark blue upholstery and carpeting, all of which looked brand new. Must be what the ad meant by "restored/upgraded."

"Beautiful sight, ain't he?"

"Uh ... yeah," Julie managed after crawling back into her skin. She turned to look at the scarecrow figure now standing on the front porch. Virgil Fowler looked the way he'd sounded on the phone: sleepy, rumpled and pretty much out of it. He was twig thin and wore his gray beard untrimmed. Ditto the long hair falling over both shoulders. His ragged jeans and floral shirt came straight out of the dipstick hippie era. Nothing missing but the love beads, man.

"It runs, I suppose?" she asked.

"Like new." Virgil's grin showed several missing teeth. He tossed her the keys on his way down the front steps. "Go ahead. Turn 'I'm over."

Finding the driver's door unlocked, Julie slipped inside and slid the peculiar-shaped, oblong key into the ignition. The Beetle's engine came to life the moment she twisted the key, vibrating with a trademark *putta-putta-putta.*

Virgil was still grinning at her. "Wanna take him out for a spin?"

Julie turned the engine off instead. "Maybe," she said. "First, tell me why you'd sell it after doing all this work on it. And how much do you *really* want for it?"

"Told ya. Half a mil. And it's time for me to cash in, that's all. Only had a three-year contract in the first place.

But ohhhhhh, we had us a *real* good time in three years."

Frustrated, Julie climbed back out of the car. "Contract?" she echoed. "What contract? Geez, would you start giving me some straight answers here? Do you want to sell this bug or don't you?"

"Sure do." Again, with the gap-toothed smile. "There's a catch, of course, but then, there's *always* one of those, ain't there? When your contract's up, you have to sell the Beetle again – for exactly half what you paid for him."

Okay, so maybe not even stoned. This twerp, Julie decided, was certifiably loony toons. Still and all, there may yet be an opportunity not to be missed here. Never let it be said that Julie Crane was above taking advantage of the mentally incompetent.

"Half," she repeated, leaning on the Beetle's open door. "And why is that, exactly?"

"You ever read 'The Bottle Imp'?" Virgil waited, as though she were likely to recognize the nonsensical phrase. At length, he added a queried name to the puzzle. "Robert Louis Stevenson?"

No light bulbs came on to push back the congealing darkness.

"Who?"

"Erm..." Virgil tugged at his scraggly beard. "Stevenson. *Treasure Island, Kidnapped, Dr. Jekyll and Mr. Hyde*?" At her blank look, he vented a long sigh. "What do they read in college these days, anyway?"

Loony with bells on.

"I'm a business major," Julie told him proudly. "We don't *have* to read."

"Hrm," Virgil said again, and the beard-tug became a full-fledged scratch. "Well, it works like this ... You bring the coupon?"

Julie gave up trying to follow his leaps of illogic, and fished a crumpled Lucky Charms coupon out of her purse. Virgil, however, declined to take it when she tried to hand it over.

"After you pay me half what I paid," he said, "you'll sign your own contract. And then, for as long as that's good, he'll give you anything your greedy little heart desires. Anything at all. Even those two surfer dudes. 'Course, at the end of that time, *he* gets *you*. Permanently."

"How did you know about...?" Julie curtailed that question in favor of another. "Who's this 'he' you keep talking about?"

"Well, the Devil of course."

Oh, now this was getting rich for sure. Julie smirked. "Your Beetle's possessed by the Devil."

"Nope." Virgil chuckled at another private joke. "Car ain't possessed *by* the Devil. Damned car *is* the Devil."

Riiiiiiiiight. This sounded like that Sunday school tripe Grandma always used to spout about the Devil having power to assume a pleasing shape, or something like that. Who knew that could include vintage Beetles?

Julie pressed the unclaimed cereal coupon flat in the palm of her hand and stared down at its smiling cartoon leprechaun. Tiny print beneath the caricature caught her eye. CASH VALUE, it read, 1 MIL.

Light bulb.

Half a mil to buy a car that was really the Devil. This crazy old hippie had obviously seen *Christine* like, wayyyy too many times.

"Ohhh-kay," she said, stretching the word into a disbelieving drawl. "So I pay you with this..." She tapped the coupon with one finger. "...Then all I've gotta do is sign over my soul, and the pink slip is mine?"

"Yep. Car's yours, and you're his." Virgil's pale eyes glittered. "He'll live up to the bargain, too. Anything you want, just ask. He'll see you get it."

And wouldn't it be nice if at least *that* part were true? "Here." Julie stuffed the coupon into Virgil's hand. "Keep the change."

"Oh, no." He promptly folded the slip of paper, tore it in half and gave the part with the cartoon back to her. "It's gotta be half. I paid a mil; you pay a half mil. Deal's a deal."

"Uh-huh." She crammed the leering leprechaun back into her purse. "So what happens when some poor jerk can't cut the pieces any smaller?"

Virgil shrugged. "Hell if I know. Maybe that's when Old Scratch decides to be some other car, and the whole thing starts all over again."

Funny, Julie thought, but she'd have pegged the Devil for a guy who'd likely go for a Fiat or a Ferrari instead of an old Beetle. Aloud, all she said was, "So, do I get the pink slip?"

The bearded loony dug into a pocket and actually produced the document. Unbelievable.

"There ya go." When he'd handed it to her, he tipped an imaginary hat, said, "Nice knowin' ya," and turned to head back toward the house.

Julie clutched the pink slip and watched him walk away. A latent pang of conscience almost made her call him back. Almost. Instead, she gave the pink slip a home next to Lucky Leprechaun, pulled open the Beetle's door again, and found herself staring at a plate mounted on its inner edge. Under a bunch of weird German words, it said MFG 6-66.

Cute. Too cute. Like she'd never seen all those stupid Devil flicks about 666 being his favorite number. Get real.

Something *thumped.*

Virgil hadn't quite made it up the porch steps. He'd apparently tripped on the last one, and now lay sprawled across the short flight of stairs.

"Stoners," Julie muttered. Her shoes crunched gravel as she marched across the driveway, then crossed the small, dead lawn and ran up the steps.

"Virgil?" She shook him, but got no response. Great. All she needed was for someone to think she'd mugged this moron. And there was no way she could carry or drag him into the house. "Hey, Virg!" Grunting at the exertion, she managed to turn him over and prop him sitting up against the porch railing. Only then did she get a clue that Virgil hadn't just passed out. His eyes were open and staring at nothing, and Julie couldn't find any pulse.

Right there, Jules, under the ear. Isn't that where they always find it in the movies?

Nothing.

Crap. The asshole must have been both crazy *and* stoned. Now he'd OD'd or something and croaked right here on the porch, and no one was going to believe that she hadn't...

Wait a minute.

Not a soul had walked or driven by since she got here. No neighbors in sight on any side. The bus had dropped her off three blocks away and she'd seen nobody at all on the walk over here. Soooo...

"Well, Virg..." She gave the corpse's hand a vigorous shake. "It's been nice knowin' you, too, but I've really gotta run now. I'll take the car with me, though. Like you said, a deal's a deal, right?" Laughing, she pinched his hairy cheek, then left him ostensibly napping on the porch and hurried back to the Beetle.

The keys still dangled from the dash. Julie hopped in,

started it up, popped the clutch and smoothly backed the bug out of Virgil's driveway.

Ten minutes later, she'd revved it up to a putt-putting, barely-over-legal 70 (didn't know Beetles could go that fast) and was happily tooling down I-8 toward home. She let up on the gas pedal a bit, and the speedometer had just dropped to 66 when something on the central dash powered up all on its own. A CD player, from the look of it.

"What, no iPod dock? Gonna be time for another upgrade, Belie-baby." The lighted blue panel indicated a disc already loaded in the player. Julie punched EJECT to see what it was.

"'Fire' by the Crazy World of Arthur Brown and Other Groovy Retro Tunes," she read out loud.

Way cool, Jules. Reinsert disc, hit PLAY.

A guttural voice yowled, *"I am the god of hell fire!!!"* Then the bug's upgraded stereo speakers burst forth with the booming strains of some really 'far out' 60s acid rock. Julie laughed and swayed to the rhythm as she drove.

They were vibrating nicely to Brown's repeated screech of *"You're gonna burn, burn, burn!"* when the whole sound system went suddenly dead.

"Hey!" Julie reached out to bang on the panel. "No fair cutting out already!"

"Precisely," hissed the speakers in reply, and abruptly, the blue lights on the stereo panel winked out. They came back on a moment later, now glowing bright red, and the voice whispered, "I think it's time to seal the bargain. Don't you?"

The Beetle's engine died. Under Julie's hands, something twisted the steering wheel to the right and guided the car onto the freeway shoulder, where it glided to a completely soundless stop.

"There now," soothed the stereo speakers. "That's better."

Julie blinked. "This is some sort of a gag, right? Some jokester frat rats with a remote set-up?"

"Oh, I don't think so." The CD tray whirred out of its slot again, only in place of the 'Fire' disc, it now held a small square of white cardboard covered with several columns of far-too-tiny-to-read type. At the bottom of the last column was an odd little black-line oval with a red X beside it.

"Just sign here," said the voice. "Your five-year contract will officially begin, and we can be on our merry way."

"Screw your contract," Julie told it. "That psycho Virgil wasn't just feeding me a load of BS?"

"Nope. Sign here, please."

Julie yanked on the door handle. It didn't budge.

"Tsk-tsk," said the speakers. "No fair cutting out already. Sign, please."

"Go eff yourself."

"Sounds lovely. But first you sign."

"I don't have a pen."

"None needed."

"Shut up!" Infuriated, Julie tried to snatch the piece of cardboard from the CD tray. She'd meant to rip it into little shreds, but the moment her hand touched the plastic rim, something needle-sharp jabbed her index finger hard enough to draw blood.

"Ow!"

She withdrew the wounded digit and stuck it in her mouth. But on the contract, a drop of her blood had formed a bright red blotch right over the funny little oval.

"Thank you," the hushed voice said. "That will do nicely."

The CD player sucked the signed contract back into

itself.

The lights all flared brighter red. Arthur Brown's screaming rock & roll tirade roared back to life through the speakers. The engine came back, too, and the Beetle steered itself back onto the freeway, effortlessly merging into the flow of afternoon traffic.

"*Ex*-cellent," the soft voice crooned over yet another rousing chorus of *"You're gonna burn!"* Then the CD's volume dropped to almost nothing. "But then, let's not dwell on the burning part... just yet. In the meantime, my dear Miss Crane, do tell me. What is your heart's desire?"

The Christmas Vulture

James S. Dorr

It was her second favorite night of the year, the Friday night that fell just before Christmas. She cruised the highways leaving the city, her black vulture wings blotting out the moon, as scudding clouds moved in to add to the darkness. A turkey vulture, she had a well-developed sense of smell, more so than her sisters that preyed above plains, or desert, or plateaus, that flew in the daylight and used their keen eyesight to mark the dying. Sniffing, she sensed that a light rain was coming, a layer of moisture to freeze to ice on the road.

She was, despite this new mechanical age, a daughter of Isis, both ancient and modern. She was a force of nature, for was not death still a natural part of life? Thus she, herself, lived on death, she and her broodlings she left behind in her nest, out this night circling to find food that they might grow strong and graceful, just as she herself had grown.

Gasoline, fraying tires, these were things that she smelled. These were smells of Christmases past and present. It was her second favorite night of the year because this was the night of office parties, celebrations held in the metropolis that spewed out cars filled with tough, wizened executives headed for hidden chateaus in the country with tender young secretaries perched, dreaming, in seats by their sides.

Which would it be this night, the Christmas vulture wondered, the tough or the tender? The latter choice would be for sake of her nestlings' still fragile young beaks—or did she dote on them, perhaps, too much? The tough, then, would be for age, for tissues in some cases already half-rotted, flesh with a character imbued through years of life?

Such were decisions a mother must make.

She circled higher. The Christmas vulture was good at her trade, having fed many such broods in the past. She knew how to discern hopeful situations, the subtle wobble of cars, their drivers drunk. The sway of top-heavy vans, overloaded, tires slipping on curves.

She needed these things, she knew—that extra sense to be sure she was there first when, joy upon joy, an accident came about. Other vultures, she knew, patrolled also. Humans did so as well: police, EMTs, Coroners' Departments who collected flesh too, but ultimately buried it in the ground, wasting it. It was as if they would throw life itself away.

She did not understand this, this disrespect of the dead.

Dangers, however, of humans with guns, of eagles, of fire—fire that would sometimes envelop a crashed car before its contents could be removed—these things she understood. These were reasons why one might hurry.

Thus she was first when, brakes screeching, a large black SUV plowed through the median, striking a compact sedan in the lane beyond, crushing it, crumpling it. The SUV ended up tangled itself, on its side, in the wreckage.

The Christmas vulture swooped -- *no time! No time! The smell of gasoline. Hot rubber smoldering.*

Quickly she stooped to the smaller car first, the one that had been headed *into* the city. Its contents appeared to be an adult male and female. She tore a bite first of the one nearest to her.

Then, in the back, something moved!

Stopping, she peered past her prey of the moment, to see, dimly, a tiny girl, thrown sideways on the seat. It was breathing softly—it still lived!

She was, first, a mother. She knew it was wrong, but instinct guided her strong, hooked beak to snag the child's jacket, pulling it forth past its bleeding, dead parents. Some primal urge guided her, as a mother that must protect *any* child, to transfer it carefully into her talons, then lift it with her to cross the outside lanes, finally depositing it safely on the grass at the road's side.

Now she had to work all the faster. The first, smaller car was already burning. It was already too late for *its* carrion. However, the second, the SUV, its right-side door sprung open, had spilled part of its contents, a skull-crushed young woman, her evening gown bloodied, halfway out on the highway.

Even as she watched, flames leaped from one vehicle to the other.

No time! No time! The Christmas vulture stooped down to the woman's arm, tearing and yanking, slashing at tendons. *No time! No time!* Flames came near as, finally, she tore it completely off.

Half backing, half fluttering, with the entire arm clutched in her beak, the Christmas vulture regained the grassy berm, seeing as if in the corner of one eye the child she had rescued beginning to come to. She saw the child sit.

The child began to cry!

As a mother, she knew what had to be done. Her own brood was healthy, well-fed and strong from her forays on past nights.

But *this* child was hungry.

As clumsy on foot as she was graceful in the sky, the Christmas vulture hobbled to where the child sat, shrieking, and dropped the freshly torn arm in its lap. Then she backed away once more and, flapping her great wings, she took to the air.

She circled once, peering down at the now-quietened little girl, then, taking advantage of an updraft from the blazing, ruined cars, she spiraled high, quickly. She saw red and blue lights flashing in the distance, heading swiftly toward where she had just left. She realized their presence would slow down traffic, lessening her chances of finding another crash this night to feed her own children. Nevertheless somehow, within her, the Christmas vulture knew all would be all right.

After all, her experience told her, in only a few more nights from then it would be New Year's Eve.

The Red Car
Melodie Corrigall

Stanley was struggling to get the front door key out of the lock, a sagging bag of groceries at his side, when his wife Moira, sporting her designer sunglasses, confronted him. Her steely accusation "I saw your car today" stopped him in his tracks.

"You were in Burnaby?" he asked clutching his sagging bag of groceries.

"No, in Kerrisdale on 41st."

"My car and I were in Burnaby."

"That's where I thought you were going."

"And right you were."

"If I'd known you were coming into town, I'd have met you for lunch."

"As always."

"Your car was smack in front of my favorite Italian restaurant."

"Where we'd have met."

"With a scarf in the back seat."

"*Your* scarf?"

"Not my scarf, an expensive pink scarf."

"Then you knew."

"I thought you'd taken my advice about your secretary."

"To buy her a scarf?"

"No, Dumbo, to thank her for her extra work."

"She's well paid."

"I didn't expect you to take her to lunch at my favorite restaurant."

"It wasn't my car," her husband sighed, pulling wilted leeks from the grocery bag.

"But then," his wife said, voice rising. "I checked the front seat and spied the satellite radio."

"Which, thanks to you, I don't have."

"Why should you hear news from Japan if I can't afford a spa weekend?"

"It's the BBC news I listen to."

"Wherever. So there it was bold as brass."

"Check my car. There's no satellite radio in my car."

"Easy enough to hide."

"For God's sakes, Moira, get real."

"I was beginning to steam. Last Tuesday when you said you were having a drink with the guys you were probably with scarf lady."

"Where is this going?" Stanley said, grabbing a cloth to sop the melting ice cream.

Moira grabbed the soggy carton, yanked open the freezer and chucked it in, then turned to her husband, and leaned forward, her shoulders as high as a hawk.

"By now, I was furious: no lunch, sugar level soaring."

"Then you checked the license plates and saw the car wasn't mine."

"I don't know your plate number but I know your red car. You'd left the window open—an expensive radio and you leave the window open."

"Which I never do since they stole our hamster."

"The fight was on," his wife cried, eyes gleaming. "I leaned into the car, grabbed the scarf and hurled it into a puddle. Then I dove in after it, snatched the radio wires and yanked them out. I felt vindicated—like a warrior goddess. There I stood righteously, wires hanging from my hand like dead snakes, when I heard a god-awful screech. A mad man was hurtling towards me."

"'What the fuck are you doing?'" he yelled, without even a 'Pardon my French.'"

"Bloody busybody, I thought. I whipped around to see a loony man, hair sticking up as if he'd been hit by lightening heading for me like a linebacker. I snarled right back. 'Fuck off. It's my business what I do to my husband's car.'"

"'It's *my* car you old bag and that's *my* radio,' he screeched."

"His eyes were rolling and his arms flailing. I put up my dukes."

"You hit him?" Stanley groaned.

Moira whipped off her glasses to display her purple eye. "He hit me back. You should have been there to defend me."

"For god's sakes, Moira, I was in Burnaby."

"'You damn bugger,' I shouted back. 'I'm old enough to be your mother and you hit me,'"

"What next?" Stanley squeaked.

"Some bloody do-gooder called the police. It was chaos: crazy with people coming out of the woodwork to join the fray."

"What did they do?" her husband whispered.

"I told the policeman it was an honest mistake, but the bugger sided with the crazy guy."

"But they let you go?"

"Sure, but you have to come to the station with me tomorrow."

"Me? Why me?"

"To explain about the car."

The Red Spider

Kevin David Anderson

O ctober 2004, 2:23 A.M. California Highway 99, Northbound...

"Get that big butt down here and visit your boy. You ain't seen him in near a month," the voice screamed out of the little cell phone speaker.

Dale held the phone away from his ear with one hand and kept an iron-clad grip on the steering wheel of his Mack truck with the other. His ex-wife's rant was going into overtime, and he wished he knew enough about his new cell phone to know if it had a volume control. "I have to go where the work is. Dammit Vivian, you know that."

"Don't give me that crap. That's the same excuse you used to spend time with that whore in...." Her voice faded and when it roared back it was punctuated with a static pop. "...kill me."

Dale brought the phone back up to his ear. "What'd you say, Vivian."

"Don't pretend you don't know who I'm talking about. I know all . . . ." The signal faded again then came back, the voice panicked. "I don't want to die. Can anyone...me. Please."

Dale held the phone out, glancing at the little screen. The words *Weak Signal* flashed. He shook his head, putting the phone back to his ear. "Vivian, what the hell are you talking about?"

"Please help me." It wasn't Vivian. This voice sounded younger, and terrified.

"Who is this?"

The voice dropped in and out. Dale was only getting fragments. "...Sandra Cl ... please ... gonna kill us. I can't move."

"Alright, calm down. Tell me where you are."

"End of Route 194 in ... cave ... drag race."

"Come again."

"...raced a red Spider down Route 194 ... can't move my ... dead bodies all over."

Dale's heart skipped a beat. He held the phone away from his ear, as a familiar feeling rumbled in his robust gut. It's the feeling any sensible person would have when facing a large an ominous door, and for reason unclear would begin to open, creaking on old, tired hinges, leading to a places Dale never looks for, but always seems to find.

He sighed and touched the phone back to his cheek. "I'm northbound on the 99. Which way are you on the 194. East or West?"

No answer.

"Hey, Sandra, east or west?"

Silence.

Dale pulled the phone away, looking into the tiny little screen. *No Signal.* "Goddamn Chinese piece of crap." Dale pressed a few buttons on the phone trying to get the call back, but he didn't really know what he was doing. After a minute he tossed the phone toward the passenger seat, and it landed in the box it had come in.

Well, that was that. Route 194 stretched across California for miles. Without any hint of direction, he didn't have a chance of finding, Sandra whatshername. He let out a long breath, somewhat relieved that the doorway to places filled with cries for help, dead bodies and whatever else always found him between the ungodly hours of midnight and dawn was closed.

Still, he should tell somebody.

Dale reached down for the CB mic and was just about to switch over to the emergency channel, when—

"Hey, Twilight Man, you got your ears on? Come back."

Dale grinned at the sound of his friend's voice, Earl, coming out of the CB speaker. He brought the mic to his lips, pressed the call button. "This here is the Twilight Man, how you doing, Night Rider."

"Well, my butt is rawer than a two-dollar pavement princess' you know what. Other than that, I'm just ducky. I'm backsliding down the grapevine on the rebound, looking to make camp in Bakersfield. Knew you were in the area. Wondered if you wanted to gather the wagons at a chew and choke for some breakfast. Come back."

Dale looked at his watch—half past midnight. "Sounds good, but hey listen. I got this call on my cell I'd like to run by you."

"You got a cell phone?"

Dale groaned softly. "Yes, let's not make a big deal out of it."

"Dam, I need to alert the media. Dale got his-self a phone. Welcome to the twentieth century, good buddy," Earl said.

"It's the twenty-first century, numb-nuts." Dale glanced over at the phone laying in its packaging. "Picked this thing up about an hour ago. Thought I'd try and give my boy a holler since it's his birthday tomorrow. But of course Vivian picked up."

"You have my condolences," Earl said. "How is bitch-zilla?"

Dale chuckled. "Still Queen of the Harpies. Anyway, someone's voice broke in on the call."

"That can happen, especially if you go cheap," Earl said. "Let me guess, you got a flip phone. One that cost bout $11.99?"

Dale sighed. He hated how well his friend knew him. "It was $9.99 and the guy at the truck stop through in a box of Red Vines. Now, do you want to hear this or not?"

Do you want to hear this or not?"

"My ears are on. Come back."

Dale quickly recapped what he'd heard before the signal faded. "So, what do you think?"

"Well, that's queerer than Liberace at a football game. Wonder if she meant an Alfa Romeo Spider?"

"Don't know, didn't get that kind a' detail."

"Could be talking about the mines."

"What was that? Come back," Dale said.

"Yeah, you said something about a cave. Maybe she is held up in those mines off the 194. About 2 miles west."

"How the do you know about mines way out there?"

"Copper mines closed I think. Don't you remember there was that college kid that died spelunking in one last year?"

"What the hell is spelunking?"

"No idea, but apparently you can die doing it."

Dale rolled his eyes. He just passed the exit for Route 193 and knew 194 was less than two miles away. *Just keep on trucking* he told himself. In a few minutes he could be in Bakersfield, enjoying food guaranteed to hurry him along toward an early death. He was getting to old for this shit, not to mention fat.

"So, what you gonna do, Twilight Man?" Earl's voice popped over the CB.

Dale took in a deep breath, letting it out slow. He was trying to push the terror in the girl's voice from his mind, but as he exhaled he realized just how much she had sounded like his oldest granddaughter in Knoxville. The girl's call for help wasn't something he could just drive on by.

God damn, son-bitch. He always felt nothing good could come from buying a cell phone and damn if he wasn't right. With a sour express, Dale put his turn signal on and steered the rig toward the approaching exit—Route 194.

"What's your twenty?" Dale said into the CB after exiting the freeway.

"'Bout thirty-five miles from your back door. Guess breakfast will have to wait? Come back."

"Well, drop the hammer, Old Man." It's to goddamn early for breakfast anyway. Turning on his high beams Dale exited, then turned west. The duel streams of lights cut a path through the darkness, revealing field after field of agricultural endeavors. After two miles the farmland fell away and rolling hills rose up on either side of the road, silhouetted in soft moonlight.

The truck began to vibrate as the tar-covered surface disappeared. Gravel took its place for a few hundred feet then that to dissolved, leaving just a dirt path. Dale was just about to throw in the towel when at the edge of his high beams he could see a sign.

Hope Mine 1/2 miles,

The sign had a painted arrow indicating a right turn onto another dirt road running south. He brought the truck to a stop in front of the sign, gazing down the southbound path. Although the sign appeared to be a half-century old, there were a dozen tire tracks, maybe more, looking very recent.

He steered south finding that the new dirt road was not much smoother than the other one. His truck shook and vibrated over every hole kicking up dust. After he had gone the length of several football fields, he could see taillights glinting in his beams. First one pair, then two. Then about a dozen flickered in the darkness, like distant stars.

Cars lined the dirt road and although they looked abandoned, sitting in the dark some caked with dust, they all appeared to be new. Modified street racers, tediously tricked out, rested silently in the night. Their owners, who had obviously spent considerable time and money to make these vehicles look ridiculous, were nowhere to be found.

"What the hell?" Dale said. "Where's the party?"

The road ended and Dale eased the truck over parking alongside a racing red Acura with a rear foil on it big enough to be used as a surfboard. Not the kind of car likely to be found on a rural dirt road.

Just ahead Dale could see the entrance to the mine. It wasn't what he'd expected. All the images of mines came he'd ever seen were products of Hollywood –- big railroad ties framing the entrance to a dingy looking cave with some kind of a sign that usually read, *Danger* or *Keep Out.*

The Hope Mine was more of a hole and from Dale's point of view, high up in the cab, he could see it burrowing down into a blasted hill at an angle steep enough to make walking difficult.

Dale was already picturing himself sliding on his wide ass down the gullet of the hole into the waiting arms of god knows what.

He reached under the seat and pulled out the Christmas gift from his mom, a sawed-off double-barreled shotgun with his CB handle carved into the stock—Twilight Man. He set it in his lap and reached over the seat, grabbing a rope.

The CB cracked to life. "Twilight Man, this is Night Rider. Come back."

Dale picked up the mic. "Yeah, what's up, Earl."

"Good buddy, you ain't gonna believe this. Guess what just blew my doors off?"

Dale sighed. "I'm a little busy right now. Can we play this game later?"

"Moving like a bat out of hell."

"What was?"

"A red Spider."

Dale swallowed. "Come again."

"It could have been scarlet, but I swear to god it was redder than a Catholic girl on her wedding night."

"Your eyes on straight?"

"Hell, yeah. I'd say it was a 1965 Alfa Romeo hardtop. And it weren't solo. There was a yellow Honda Civic, all converted, you know those street racer things all dumb kids are speeding their money on?"

"Yeah, I know what you're talking about."

"Everybody thinks they're a Vin Diesel."

"What's a Vin Diesel? ...no, never mind. Which way they heading?"

"North. Could be heading your way."

Dale glanced around at all the derelict racers. "Yeah, that's a big ten-four. What's your twenty?"

"I just past Route 190."

"Jeez, Earl, you move slower than turtle shit."

"Bitch, bitch."

Dale told Earl what he had found and what he planned on doing, even though he hadn't really convinced himself yet.

"You, really going down there?" Earl said.

Dale scratched his head, pondering the wisdom of his plan. He brought the mic up to his lips. "You didn't hear that kid's voice. If she were mine I'd sure as hell want someone to go after her." He leaned over and removed a flashlight from the glove box.

"You ain't even sure she is down there."

Dale turned the flashlight on, shinning it over the dust-covered cars. "Well, she ain't up here, that's for sure. If you don't find me when you get here, call in the cavalry."

Before Earl signed off he urged Dale to take his cell phone. Dale reluctantly agreed and gave his friend the number.

Dale slung the rope over his shoulder and stepped out of the cab. His salt and pepper beard and leather vest swayed a little is breeze that didn't seem to be there. Securing one end of the rope to the bumper of his rig, he then strolled toward the mine. Upon reaching it, his boots knocked a few rocks down into the darkness.

He scanned back up the road that brought him here, checking for approaching headlights. Nothing. Darkness. He wasn't worried about the driver of the red Spider. Dale could deal with some young punk street racer turned serial killer, if that's what this was. Running cargo across the United States in the dead of night for a living allowed Dale the frequent opportunity to meet wide variety of assholes. Mr. Alfa Romeo Spider was nothing special. But as he gazed back down into the opening in the Earth, the hair on the back of his neck stood up, and he couldn't extinguish the feeling that something was looking back up at him. Something cold, unfriendly. Something ugly.

"I'm coming, kid." Dale tossed the rope down and it seemed to be swallowed by the hole. He turned the flashlight on, chasing away the darkness and was relieved to see that about twenty feet down into the mine the floor seemed to level out. He gripped the rope and began his descent, boots sliding in loose earth. His two hundred forty plus pounds of well-fed trucker's physique created an avalanche of gravel, limestone and thick dust. If there was something down there waiting for him, he had made enough noise to let it know he was coming.

With each step the air got colder and something else assaulted his senses. A thick stench started to rise, pungent, adding weight and a fowl color to the air. It was a recognizable aroma. One Dale had taken in more times than anyone ever should. But his familiarity with the smell didn't desensitize his senses to it. He gagged, tasted vomit, and his eyes watered as he moved closer to the source of decay and rot.

He reached into his back pocket and pulled out a handkerchief, tied it around his mouth and nose like a train robber. The thin material did a piss-poor job, but it filtered the stench enough so that his eyes stopped tearing up like a little girl.

Preoccupied with not puking he almost didn't notice that the texture of the walls had changed. He shinned the light on both sides and up onto the ceiling, seeing a silky thread weaving its way around the rock. *Wonderful. Bugs.*

The thread seemed to get thicker the deeper he went. It even started to spin on the floor winding over long boulders pressed up against the wall. He had passed a half-dozen of these elongated rocks wound up tightly in silk, before he realized, they weren't boulders.

They were bodies.

Ahh, crap on a cracker.

Dale knelt down next to one, pealing away some of the strands with the barrel of the shotgun. It was the strangest corpse he had ever seen. It looked like the mummies in the Chicago Museum he got to gawk at as a kid – all dried up, shriveled. But no mummy he ever saw wore an Oakland Raider's cap.

The light glinted off the NFL logo and as Dale taped it with the shotgun the corpse's jaw dropped open with a crack. Dale stood back up, watching a spider the size of his hand crawl out from the shriveled-up body's throat. He noticed others crawling about, none larger than his palm. They moved over the bodies, feeding, their fangs pumping up and down, drinking in their meal.

Dale narrowed his eyes, his blood beginning to boil. He turned on a heel and started heading deep into the mine. When he could he adjusted his steps so that each one was followed by a crunching sound, bringing a satisfied grin to Dale's face as he pictured spiders dying under his alligator skin boot heel.

"Sandra," he began to call, not giving a crap about being stealthy. If there was something down here wanting a fight he was in the mood to oblige.

Sandra's name echoed down the passage and Dale could hear it reverberating for miles. He checked every body he passed for signs of life, knocking spiders to the ground with the barrel of the gun. The bodies were in varies stages of decomposition, some looking very fresh, but none were alive.

He stopped to deliver an occasional twist off the heal as arachnids died under foot, but he began to notice that the further he went into the belly of this nest the more eight-legged bastards there were to crush.

He burped out a sigh beginning to feel defeated. If he went much deeper they may grow so numerous he wouldn't be able to dispatch them with a simple twist of the boot. They were already starting to drop onto his arms and shoulders from the ceiling.

Damn it.

On the verge of turning back, his flashlight caught something silver and metallic on the ground.

A cell phone. Not like his, one of those fancy new smart phones.

Hanging over it, spun up against the wall, looking fresher than most, was a body. Dale stepped over and pulled at the tightly wound silk around the torso. Big glittering letters on the girl's T-shirt read, American Idol. Her arms, like all the others, were held to her side wrapped tight. Dale felt her jugular. Nothing. He checked again. Still Nothing.

He bent down and retrieved the phone. A name was printed on the protective case. *Sandra Cleveland. Damn.*

Dale swatted at the spiders that had their fangs in her, then crushed a few under his boot, cursing. He was just twisting his heel on the last one when he heard the sound of engines. At least two.

He wiped his feet in the dirt, smiling. "Now, let's go deal with Mr. Serial killin', spider lovin', son-bitch."

With the shotgun over his shoulder, he began to jog back toward the entrance. The sounds of the cars were getting louder, engines revving. By the time he reached the rope near the entrance, one of the engines had been killed.

A voice drifted down the hole as Dale climbed up. "I beat you, bitch. Now, get out of that historical artifact you call a car."

Dale reached the mouth of the mine and stepped up into the night. The first thing he saw was a teenage male, just old enough to shave, wearing an oversized sweat suit, an unnecessary amount of gold chains, and a cap with the brim pointed backwards. He was jumping up and down, and every few seconds would perform some ludicrous dance move that the white kid had clearly believed he had mastered.

"Beat you fair and square," the teenager said, moving away from his modified street racer—a Honda Civic with a chrome blower rising from the hood. He walked and sort of danced over to the Italian car—a red Alfa Romeo Spider. "Come on out, let's see you're loosing ass."

The Spider just idled patiently as if it were waiting for something. Its tinted black windows seemed to be keeping all its owner's secrets and as Dale stared at it a chill moved through his body.

It suddenly occurred to him that there may be more than one shithead in the Spider. Two maybe three he could deal with, but if there were more and armed – he decided to conceal himself, watch a while and see what he was up against.

He crouched down behind a pile of rocks, just outside the mine's entrance, as the teenager continued to taunt the driver of the Spider. "Hey, you gonna show yourself or what? It's time to pay up, bitch. Let's see the pink slip." The teenager kicked the front tire of the Alfa Romeo.

The Spider's engine revved and the kid took several steps back. The engine thrust again, and the car began to vibrate violently, looking like a rocket moments before leaving the launch pad. Dale felt the ground trembling beneath him.

The teenager held up his hands, as if he suddenly realized where he was, in the middle of nowhere surrounded by derelict street cars. "You know what? Just keep it, man." He took two steps back. "I don't want that antique anyhows."

Before the kid took another backward step the engine suddenly switched off. The roar faded with a suddenness that took Dale by surprise. And then, the Spider was still.

Dale stared at the car's windows looking for movement. Nothing.

"So alright then," the teenager said, tugging at his cap. "I'll catch up with you on the road, biotch—."

The hardtop roof of the Spider began to move. Accompanied by a high-pitched mechanical whine, the roof opened like the hood of a car.

Dale rubbed his hairy chin. *No idea Alfa Romeos could do that.*

The roof continued up and back until it lay flat on the trunk – the machinery that moved it cut off which a choke, creating a cold silence.

The teenager took a step forward. "Pretty cool. You trick that yo'self?"

Out of the opening in the Spider a female head started to rise like a disembodied apparition. Long hair spun over her scalp so black in melted into the night. A slender creamy skinned neck bled into smooth and unclothed shoulders. Her hands rose gripping the windshield.

The teenager smiled at her. "Hey, babe. You know I don't really want this thing." He pointed at the Spider. "Maybe we could work something else out, y'know what I'm saying?"

The woman smiled back, her black lips framing white teeth. She ascended further, revealing naked round breasts, nipples hard and gray.

"Oh, yeah," the teenager said, stepping forward. "That's what I'm talkin' bout."

"Watch yourself, kid," Dale muttered softly.

She rose up even more as if being lifted on a hydraulic platform.

The teenager suddenly stopped moving forward. "What the. . ."

Another set of breasts hung beneath the first. And another under them. The Woman's engorged chest looked like a sow that had recently given birth, with gray nipples descending the length of her torso.

The teenager pointed a finger. 'Yoi freaky bitch. Stay the fu..."

Something else emerged out of the Alfa Romeo—long, thick, hairy.

"Oh, shit," Dale said.

One by one, eight hair-covered legs, each with the girth of an adult python, uncoiled from the car's interior. They stretched out as if waking from a long hibernation then began to plant their arachnid feet on the dirt.

The creature lifted itself out of the car, looking like something out of Greek mythology gone haywire. From the waist up it resembled a human female, but everything else was arachnid. With multiple leg joints and thick brushes of hair, it scurried away from the Alfa Romeo, its dark eyes, at least eight feet above the ground, peering at the teenager.

The boy who had been so animated only a minute ago seemed frozen in place. Paralyzed in the creature's Medusa-like gaze, he didn't attempt to run even when it scurried toward him.

Its front legs bucked up, enveloping the boy. He was lifted off the ground, and four hairy legs began to spin his body. Silk shot out of the ass-end of the creature and within a few seconds the boy was mummified, cocooned for her children's consumption.

The eight-legged monster then began to move toward the mine, it's wrapped up prize dragging behind. Dale hunkered down as much as his out-of-shape body would allow, gripping the stock and barrel so tight his knuckles were pear white. He knew the shotgun's kill range was ten feet, but he wasn't looking forward to getting that close.

Goddamn it, Earl. Where the hell are you?

All eight legs came to a stop at the mouth of the mine. Its human half started to lean forward and for a second Dale thought she was just crouching in order to fit through the entrance. But he was wrong.

The creature bent all the way forward, its human hand picking something off the ground. It was Dale's rope. Her head and torso came back up, the rope gripped in both hands. Her black eyes seemed to follow the length of the rope tethered to Dale's truck.

S*hit.* Dale readied the shotgun. *So much for a surprise attack.*

Anger, vile and terrifying, consumed the creature's face. It started moving toward the truck, its human hands coiled into fists. After only a few yards it stopped, the anger melting away to what Dale thought was concern, as if she just released the rope also descended into her burrow, her nest. She sniffed at the air, like a wolf catching the scent of blood on a wounded animal. She cut her latest prize loose, lowered her head and scurried into the mine.

The teenager's wrapped up body rolled down a slope and out of site. Dale waited a few seconds for the hair on the back of his neck to relax, then stood up, letting out a long breath he wasn't even aware he'd been holding.

He stepped from the pile of rocks and made for his cab, already picturing himself sitting safely within its confines. He'd much rather shoot down at the thing from inside his truck, better yet catch the beast in a crossfire from high up with Earl and his 38 on one side and him on the—

A bloodcurdling scream that was only part human exploded from the mine. Dale whirled around, shotgun at his hip as the anguished cries echoed behind him.

Damn it Earl, could use some help here.

Okay nothing to panic about, Dale told himself. *The bitch didn't see me up here, so she probably thinks I'm still in the hole somewhere. Just keep quiet and—*

A loud chirping noise shattered Dale's thoughts. He spun around looking for the source, which seemed to be behind him. After spinning a half-circle, the chirping was behind him again. He did another fast one-eighty, scanning the entrance of the mine for a few tense seconds. Then he finally released what it was.

Goddamn it.

He pulled the cell phone out of his back pocket, desperately trying to make it be quiet. He flipped it open and after pressing several buttons finally hit the green one. The screen lit up. The chirping stopped. He was about to whisper something into the phone when he released that whispering was no longer necessary.

Eye-shine glinted deep within the gullet of mine, and it was moving toward him.

"Dale, you there?" Earl's voice squeaked out of the tiny speaker.

Dale didn't answer, just took several steps back, shotgun leveled at the mine's entrance in one hand, cell phone in the other.

"Hey, good buddy, I'm at your back door," Earl said. "Find anything?"

Dale held the phone in front of his face and said. "A Bug. Big f-ing bug." He threw the phone into the mine and saw it bounce off the beast's chest. He gripped the barrel of the shotgun, anchored the stock on his hip, just as the eight-legged monstrosity exited her layer.

Pausing as it emerged, its back legs still lost in the mine's entrance. The beast seemed to know what Dale held in his hands and it stood still, hissing, contemplating. She tilted her head, lowering her chin and glared deep into Dale's eye.

The creature cast no visible shadow in the thin moonlight, but Dale felt himself being enveloped by it anyway, cold and creeping up his spine. They stood motionless like two gunfighters waiting for that undeniable moment demanding split-second reactions.

Dale judged her to be about fifteen feet away, just a bit too far to do terminal damage, but he wasn't about to take a step forward. He didn't have to.

She lowered her head like a bull, thrust her human hands forward and charged, howling like hell spawn.

Dale let go with both barrels. The explosions echoed down the mine as the beast pitched back, hands clasping her chest. When her hands fell, Dale could see one of her upper breasts was gone, and an arm hung by the bone. Blood splattered her torso, flowing down onto hairy legs.

She thrust a raised hand forward, clawing at the air, looking more enraged than ever.

Dale took fast steps backward, pulling two more rounds from his pocket. He had to lower his eyes for a split second as he popped the shells into the chamber. When he brought them back up, a hairy leg struck him in the jaw. He felt his feet leave the ground and heard his gun go off.

He sailed several yards through the air, and then landed on something hard. What he'd landed on bent inward under his weight, and it took a hazy second to release that he wasn't on the ground.

He had landed on the hood of the Alfa Romeo.

The she-bitch scurried toward him, rising up on her back legs, teeth bared.

Dale pointed the shotgun, not really aiming and pulled the trigger. The soft sound of the hammers falling atop the empty chambers was at that moment the worst sound in the world.

Shit.

Dale sat up, digging into his pocket for more shells. He saw her hand reaching toward him and he swatted at it with the stock of the gun. She blocked his blow, knocking the shotgun from his grasp.

She reached down and clasped Dale around the neck, lifting his ass off the hood. She pulled his face to hers opening her mouth. For a second Dale thought she was going to sink her teeth right into the bridge of his nose. He could taste her breath, fowl, rank with rot.

Then something seemed to catch her attention. Her eyes moved past Dale and he felt her grip loosen. He wasted no time. He brought both fists down on her wounded arm. The creature howled and Dale fell from her grasp, landing back on the hood with a thud. Pain rocketed through the back of his head, as a familiar sound echoed in the night—rumbling, growing close.

Dale rolled off the hood just as Earl's eighteen-wheeler plowed into the Alpha Romeo like a freight train, horn blaring. The crash was deafening. Sparks flew as big as muzzle flashes, metal tearing screeches exploding into the night.

Dale kept rolling in the dirt as Earl's trailer rushed by, but he glanced ahead just in time to see the arachnid bitch raise her human hands in a vain attempt to slow down the 15 tons of speeding metal.

With the Alfa Romeo as a hood ornament, Earl's truck bulldozed into the creature, its hairy legs leaving the ground. The eighteen-wheeler began to slide as the brakes were applied, but it didn't stop before smashing into the entrance to the mine.

The creature was pinned between the entrance and the crumpled frame of the Alfa Romeo. Earl's truck seemed to stand guard over the scene, pushing forward enough to keep the arachnid in her place.

Dale propped himself up into a seated position as Earl stepped out of the cab. He had never been so happy to see his friend. "Took you long enough. You cruse the granny lane all the way here did ya'?"

"Bitch, bitch," Earl said, walking over to Dale, hand extended. "You never could appreciate a proper entrance."

Dale grabbed his friend's hand and allowed himself to be pulled up. "Thanks, old man."

Earl stood a few inches taller than Dale, and with a similar robust physic. "Well, I was in the neighborhood."

Dale smiled and walked over to get his shotgun.

"Can I assume breakfast is on you?" Earl said.

"Yeah." Dale gathered up his weapon.

"And not the usual cheap Denny's grand slam, neither. A real breakfast."

Dale walked back, slapped an arm around Earl's shoulder. "Hell, I'd take you to the Russian Tea Room 'bout now if I could."

Earl tugged on his black Harley Davidson T-shirt. "We're a bit under dressed."

They both stared for a few silent moments at the mine. The creature squirmed in front of them. Two of its long legs still moved just outside of the crushing pressure of Earl's truck. Its female head lay over the top of the mine's entrance, blood drooling down the sides of her mouth.

Earl stepped forward taking a hard look. "Christ, Dale, you sure do have a knack for finding the meanest, ugliest women."

"It's a gift."

"Well, you ought to think serious 'bout giving it back." Earl scratched his head. "Anyone alive down there?"

"Nothing on two legs." Dale pointed down the slop. "There's a kid down there in a silk wrapper, probably just napping."

"I'll go take a look," Earl said. "Why don't you go and say goodnight to Gracie?"

Dale nodded and strolled toward the mine. He pulled two shells from his pocket and loaded the shotgun. Closing the chamber, he stepped up and around to the upper most part of the entrance.

The creature's black hair spilled out onto the dirt like crude oil and Dale placed a boot on a few healthy strands, inches from her scalp. She tried to raise her head off the ground, but Dale's boot held it down by its midnight-colored locks. She looked at him and hissed, blood spotting his jeans.

In these final moments Dale could never despise these things. Not much anyway. It was just an unnatural thing, doing what unnatural things do. But now it was time for Dale to do what Dale can do. He leaned over, placed both barrels up against her forehead. "Say goodnight, Gracie."

He pulled the trigger.

The Unexpected

J. P. Seewald

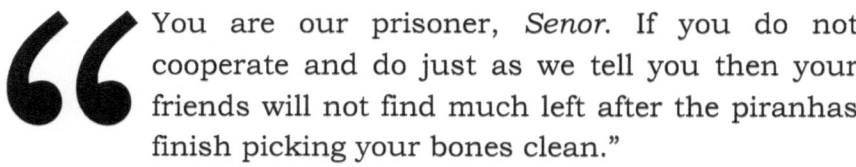"You are our prisoner, *Senor*. If you do not cooperate and do just as we tell you then your friends will not find much left after the piranhas finish picking your bones clean."

The blindfold was removed from his eyes, but there was little to see. A stygian darkness surrounded him. He blinked several times and tried to adjust his sight. He'd been bound, blindfolded and gagged at the time of the kidnapping and during the long ride. At first he'd been knocked unconscious. Later, returning to his senses, he felt the bumpy ride, even in the limousine. The automobile had become his prison, a place of confinement. He considered how such a fine car generally represented wealth and symbolized worldly success. Ironically, for him, it had become a place of fear and incarceration. Claustrophobia set in but he did his best not to panic.

Now they pushed him forward into the night. It had been growing dark when they cut his driver's throat, threw the man from the car, and then took him prisoner. He realized time had passed but wasn't certain how much. He'd been stripped of his smart phone. It was pitch black, no moon or stars overhead. However, the unmistakable sounds and smells of the jungle saturated his consciousness. He felt his shirt soak through. His sweat stank of fear.

"Who are you? What do you want with me?"

There was the flick of light. He saw his captor clearly now. Sharp, white teeth smiled at him, but there was no warmth to the smile. This was the man who had killed the driver. He felt a chill slither down his spine and palpable pain in his stomach.

"I am called Diego. There are those who prefer El Diablo." Not without reason. The nickname fit.

Diego was short, of a swarthy complexion, with small black eyes that glittered unnaturally, darting about under thick, bushy black brows. He sensed the smaller man's energy and had another disturbing, unsettling thought. Diego had the look of a fanatic, a terrorist, a madman.

"Soon, Mr. Saunders, you will be honored by the presence of our leader."

"You've made a mistake. Let me go." His mouth felt dry.

"What will you offer me in return? Gold and riches? Perhaps you would sell me your very soul?" Diego offered a twisted smile.

The American shook his head, unable to speak. He shuddered involuntarily.

The rope used to bind his hands was painfully cutting off his circulation. He tried to move his numb fingers around but was discouraged by the savage expression on Diego's face. Fear gnawed at him like a hungry rat. The American tried to maintain a calm demeanor by reassuring himself that he was secure in his position with the company. They wouldn't let anything happen to him—would they?

The two men brought him into an old building of some sort. Diego's cohort lit candles giving the place a form of distorted illumination.

"This was once a warehouse," Diego said. "A *grande* owned the entire plantation. It is nothing but a ruin now. So, greatness lives and dies. Are you a man of much pride I wonder?" Diego smiled at him again. Those white teeth looked sharper than ever, like a chainsaw that could cut through just about anything.

Another man entered the warehouse. He was much taller than Diego or any of the other men who followed behind him. The broad, powerful chest was reminiscent of a Kodiak bear. He moved with authority and confidence in his khaki uniform. Those around him brandished automatic weapons, rifles and sub-machine guns. Obviously, this was Estaban, the leader of the revolutionaries.

"I have captured him for you," Diego said to the big man. "Here is Rowland Saunders, the company's executive vice-president." Diego smiled in a toothy, self-satisfied manner. Such teeth were blinding in the darkly illuminated room. He looked like a well-fed panther.

Estaban stared at the American, cocking his head to one side in an appraising manner. "You are younger than I expected." The voice was deep, rumbling.

"And your English is very good."

Estaban accepted the compliment with a patrician nod of his head.

"Why have I been kidnapped?" God, his mouth was dry!

"Why do you think?" Estaban, for all his revolutionary fervor, seemed a careful man with words.

"You want a ransom?"

"Naturally that is part of it."

"I am not rich," he said.

Estaban shrugged. "Mr. Saunders, we are not interested in mere money. We require the release of certain political prisoners. They are victims of the current regime."

"Why was the limousine driver killed? His death was unnecessary."

Estaban turned to Diego. "How do you answer the American's accusation?"

"It needs no answer," Diego sputtered. "Ask Juan. The man resisted us."

"You have your answer," Estaban said, dismissing the matter with a wave of one large, callused hand. "We fight a war of liberation. In war, people die. Many of our people have been imprisoned unjustly by the military junta. Their sole crime was to dissent, to disagree with the brutal practices of the existing regime. For this they were tortured and murdered."

"I sympathize," he said in a controlled voice.

"Do you? Is there compassion in your heart or ice in your veins?"

Careful, he warned himself, handle this guy like the detonator on a bomb. "Americans try to support the forces of democracy and justice everywhere in the world, but we don't approve of acts of terrorism under any circumstances."

Diego spat in his face. The warm wetness caught him on the cheek and offered a sharp contrast to Diego's cold contempt.

"*Embustero!*" Diego's insult exploded in his face like a grenade.

"Enough," Estaban commanded. "Mr. Saunders, you will write a message to your company for us. This letter will state the terms by which you will be returned to them. No doubt since you are a man of wealth and importance, they will be eager to make payment."

"What if they can't secure the release of your friends?"

"Let us hope for your sake they are able, otherwise..."

"I know. My bones will glisten in the sun."

Diego smiled at him, his sharp teeth shining like fine porcelain. "No, *Senor*, the piranhas, they don't leave even the bones." That had to be a lie, but it still managed to freeze his marrow. His heart pounded like a racehorse on the final furlong. Again, fear caused visceral pain. It was all he could do not to double over in agony, assaulted by terror.

He had to keep calm. Taking a few deep breaths, he looked around the old, primitive warehouse. What had been kept here? Sugar cane, bananas?

As for Estaban, he mentally determined to cut the big man down to size. He studied the high cheekbones that marked the leader as part Indian, but Estaban also had the arrogance of the conquistadors. The massive, muscular frame and mocha skin suggested African lineage as well. Whatever heritage Estaban had, he was an intimidating man, a force to be reckoned with. He sensed that Estaban's intellect though not well-schooled was every bit as keen as his own.

He saw this situation almost as a game, a challenge and test of his survival abilities. He tried to imagine his captor naked, lost in the jungle, prey to every treacherous peril. Who was Estaban anyway? Just another man, a mortal being like himself. He tried hard to forget that Estaban held the power of life and death over him.

Another man entered the room. He immediately recognized him as the kidnapper who had put a gun to his head. The recollection made him shudder and his stomach sicken. The memory of Diego slashing the driver's throat flooded over his consciousness like a river.

Estaban turned to the man he called Juan and they conversed together in a rapid, excited flow of Spanish. Although the American prided himself on his facility for languages, he could not understand much of what was being said. But he could see Estaban growing angry, his color deepening. Then he turned furiously on Diego. His eyes flashed with immense fury. Estaban was cursing profusely. He understood that well enough. There was total silence in the warehouse as everyone watched and listened.

Finally, Estaban turned and spoke to the American. "You have not been truthful with us. You are not Rowland Saunders. Juan informs me that one of our people has seen Mr. Saunders sitting in his corporate office comfortably smoking Cuban cigars. He is described as middle-aged and fat. Who are you and what were you doing in Mr. Saunder's car?"

He could scarcely breathe. "I am a member of the company, but I'm not important like Mr. Saunders. I might be someday. Right now, I'm just an errand boy, a messenger."

Estaban turned an accusing look toward Diego.

"But he was in the backseat of the big automobile!"

"I was sent to Mr. Saunders' home to deliver some reports he'd requested. He was having his driver take me back to the office."

"Surely, they will pay for his return!" Diego said.

"No, I very much doubt that," he said. "Not all Americans are rich. I am not."

"You have family," Diego persisted.

"No, I am an orphan." That was true enough. He'd spent his childhood in a series of foster homes, unloved and unwelcome. But he did not pity himself. It had taught him not to rely on other people. He'd learned instead to study them, to determine their weaknesses. He already knew that Estaban's source of vulnerability was his enormous ego.

He realized that causing Estaban to believe he was expendable was taking an enormous risk. But it was a gamble that could work to his advantage—at least he hoped so.

"Let us kill him," Diego shouted, his voice raw, savage. "I will take pleasure in his death. *Muerte*!" the personification of death cried out, shaking his fist in a menacing manner.

"I agree," Estaban said with steady intent, "there must be a death, a lesson taught. But let the man who deserves to suffer be the one to die. Let all know Estaban is a just man." Estaban signaled Juan, pointing a long, lean finger at Diego. "It is your mistake. You are in the wrong."

The small, dark eyes opened wide in disbelief. Diego screamed his rage as they dragged him from the room. Estaban's chin jutted out and his lower lip was set in granite. "Fools and blunderers have no place with me."

The leader now fixed his gaze on the American. "Now what shall I do about you?"

"Let me go. That would be the sensible thing and you are very wise." He hoped this appeal to the man's vanity would work.

"Why should I make such a decision?" Estaban did not seem convinced.

"A man of your insight, I'm certain you are aware that if I were quietly returned, the incident would be forgotten. If, on the other hand, I were to disappear permanently, you would lose respect among the very people whose support you seek. Return me and I will always remember I owe you my life. I will return the favor someday. I swear it. I will not always be unimportant."

Estaban laughed, a deep-chested show of amusement. "The fable of the lion and the mouse?"

"Exactly."

"You are most persuasive, but then we all know a man will promise anything to save his own life," Estaban observed.

"*Muerte!*" someone called out. Others took up the chant.

His stomach was a vortex of nausea. Fortunately, Estaban silenced them. Estaban ordered the American to follow him. His legs were like sponges. It took great effort to move into the small separate room. The leader waved his followers away as one would swat at flies, then firmly shut the archaic door behind them.

"We will speak in English. None of them understands your language very well, but it is best to be cautious. Infiltrators can be clever." Estaban removed a revolver from the holster at his hip and placed it against the American's forehead.

The atmosphere in the tiny room was suffocating, the air thick as split pea soup. Perspiration trickled down his armpits. Fear seized his throat like an attack dog's teeth. A wave of pain tore through him stomach which he clenched doing his best not to throw up and humiliate himself.

"Do not misunderstand me, my American friend, I am truly grateful. I had a problem. Now it is solved. Everyone thinks you were kidnapped by mistake. They will never know that Diego was deliberately misinformed."

He stared at Estaban in disbelief. "I don't understand why you'd want to get rid of him. He seemed completely loyal."

"Perhaps too loyal. He is or was my second in command. Ambition does strange things to men's appetites, and Diego has known much hunger. I had begun to see the evil in him. He was not to be trusted. He was a danger to me."

"You can put that gun away now, can't you?" Candlelight pirouetted eerily off the shiny metal barrel.

"I am not certain."

The American sensed this was not going well. "You can trust me," he said. "I know how to maintain a confidence. Besides, you'd be breaking faith with the company."

"But my friend, as you yourself have observed, you are expendable. I believe it was an American who once said: two can keep a secret only if one of them is dead."

The American couldn't afford to give in to the panic he was feeling. "If I die, they have a lever to use against you. You'd be playing right into the hands of the dictator and his generals, the very people you detest. You're too smart for that, too great a man."

Estaban viewed him thoughtfully for a time. He could see the appeal he'd made to the immense ego was working.

"Follow me," Estaban said finally. They went back into the outer room where the leader gathered his chosen disciples around him. "It pleases me to let the American return to his people," Estaban announced in his native tongue. Then Estaban turned back to him and spoke in English. "You will tell your people that Estaban is a man with a heart. I can be generous and fair." He proceeded to give rapid orders.

Juan led him back to the limousine and again pushed him down on the floor. They handled him roughly but he didn't care. He was on his way back; that was all that mattered. The limousine which had been the instrument of his fear and incarceration would now provide his freedom and deliverance. Ironic and yet just, he mused.

Of course, he was fairly certain the company hadn't expected Estaban to actually let him survive. He knew they'd been funneling money to Estaban almost from the beginning. The confidential report he'd managed to read said so. The military junta in power supposedly knew nothing about it. It was a secret, one that would surprise them. After all, company funds had backed them as well. Whichever side won, company interests would be protected—or would they? Fascist, communist, terrorist, what difference did the labels really make? One group seemed as cruel, ruthless and repressive as the next. It was the nature of third world politics, he thought with weary cynicism.

The large black limo hit a hard bump and his thoughts returned to Diego's first words to him. It would be Diego and not himself who was food for the piranhas tonight. He supposed there was some satisfaction and comfort in that.

He was suddenly aware that the car had stopped moving. Juan turned and thrust a gun forcefully against his head.

"But Estaban said..."

"Not him," Juan's impatient response was in surprisingly flawless English.

"Then who? The company?"

The driver suddenly turned around, smiling with a toothsome grin. He flicked a light with his thumb as if there were a match in his hand but the American saw none. He was convinced it was a trick of some kind. It had to be, didn't it?

"Juan has seen the error of his ways. His loyalty is to me."

"I thought you were dead!"

"As Estaban did. But he will soon learn of his mistake. No, it is you who will be dead."

"As I told you, some call me El Diablo. It is a name I have justly earned. I promised you would feel the teeth of the piranha and I always keep my word." Again, the ugly smile. The mouth itself made him think of an open grave.

"This is getting old fast." The American was zero at the bone. His teeth began to chatter.

"You are afraid? You should be. Perhaps I might be persuaded to let you live."

"What would you expect in return?"

"Merely your soul."

Did he even have one, he wondered.

The sound of vehicles thundering along the narrow road behind them caught Diego's attention.

"It's the cavalry," the American said. "They're coming to rescue me." He hoped that was true. "There's a homing device beneath the limo's trunk. They've been tracking us."

"Toss him out," Diego said to Juan as he released the automatic door locks. "Perhaps there will be another time for us," Diego said, turning to the American.

"I sincerely hope not," he said. A chill slithered down his spine despite the heat.

Dazed, he watched from the ground as El Diablo drove the limousine forward. It resembled a sinister, long, black hearse as it moved through the enshrouding vegetation and then suddenly disappeared into the jungle as if it had never existed at all.

One thing was certain: dealing with the devil was a lot like throwing loaded dice. He had taken the wrong fork in the road when he joined the company. He saw that clearly now. It had been a living death. He made a definite decision to leave his current line of employment, end his old life and begin a new one. The devil would have to look elsewhere for souls to torture and devour.

Wheels of Justice
John H. Dromey

Before her live-in housekeeper Roseanne could convince the authorities her employer was truly missing, an anonymous email—sent from an internet café—arrived at the Sandborg home revealing Susan's whereabouts and giving detailed instructions on how to find her. There were no ransom demands.

The first officers on the scene suspected Mrs. Sandborg, gone for less than forty-eight hours, had been a willing participant in an elaborate hoax or at worst the victim of a cruel practical joke.

Detectives Robinson and Perkins were assigned to the case.

Robinson shook his head in disbelief as he read Mrs. Sandborg's statement.

"Unbelievable," he said. "There's an old saying that the wheels of justice turn slow, but they'll come to a grinding halt if she sticks to *this* story. Listen to this." He read out loud. "'I was abducted from the parking garage of my apartment building late one evening and transported in a time machine to a remote location in the past.'"

Perkins skimmed the document.

"Mrs. Sandborg claims she was drugged. Perhaps there were some hallucinogenic side effects. I'm willing to give her the benefit of the doubt until we've talked to her directly."

The interview cleared up some issues but also raised new concerns.

"It seems silly now," Susan Sandborg said, a slight blush coloring her otherwise pale complexion, "but I came to briefly while I was being transported. I was restrained with straps and lying flat in a fetal position, but otherwise quite comfortable even though it was a hot day. I could clearly hear an old radio mystery program playing. There was even some static in the broadcast. Later, I woke up totally disoriented in an old-fashioned filling station beside a seldom-traveled road in the desert."

"Who could possibly profit from carrying out such an elaborate stunt?" Detective Robinson asked.

"I know of three men who could. Who already have, I should say. With my personal shares and proxies from a number of friends I had enough votes to assure myself a place on the board of directors of my late husband's corporation. Had I been elected, one of those three men would have lost a lot of perks. My abduction conveniently made me miss the share-holders' meeting."

"Do you suspect one of the men more than the others?" Detective Perkins asked.

"No," Susan said. "All three of them are Sunday drivers. They turn off their cell phones and go for long car trips on the weekend to relax. They won't have alibis. My guess is I was transported in a private vehicle, though, since both rentals and company cars leave a paper trail."

"Do you know what kind of cars the men drive?"

"Yes, of course. Aaron Blaeser drives a red sports car. It's a convertible, and if he didn't lather himself with sunscreen, he'd be burnt to a crisp."

Susan paused to take a sip of water.

"Jacob Mortensen drives a late-model four-door sedan."

Susan hesitated again.

"You're doing fine, Mrs. Sandborg," Perkins told her. "Who's the third man?"

"I don't want to incriminate him, but Samuel Johnson drives a vintage car with all original equipment. He's a fanatic about that. The radio is pre-transistor and Sam's always on the lookout for new sources of vacuum tubes to keep it going."

"Have you ever ridden in any of those cars?" Detective Robinson asked.

"Not willingly," Susan said.

The detectives put their heads together.

"No judge will give us *three* search warrants based solely on hearsay evidence," Robinson said. "We need to select one prime suspect."

"Let's start by finding out if there was a retro-radio station on the air with mystery programs when Mrs. Sandborg was abducted," Perkins suggested.

There wasn't.

The detectives had to base their request for a search warrant on other details provided by the kidnapping victim. They used a process of elimination.

Susan Sandborg's pale complexion indicated she had not been exposed recently to bright sunlight and the passenger seat of Aaron Blaeser's sports car would not have reclined to a flat position.

The original equipment in Samuel Johnson's old car would not have included air conditioning and the radio could only have played live broadcasts.

It seemed likely Mrs. Sandborg had been 'comfortable' while strapped in the backseat of Jacob Mortensen's artificially cooled modern car while the CD player blasted out a vintage radio program complete with static.

Later, when the search warrant was served, trace evidence proved Susan had been in Jacob's car.

The wheels of justice continued to turn. Mortensen was arrested, charged, and convicted.

Susan took her rightful place on the board.

With No Regards to Direction
Stephen Scott Whitaker

1 Sunlight against the back wall reminded Chlo of cheap paper capes refugees tucked around their necks as they shuttled through the west gates. Like something sick, sunken, come to LA to die, she thought.

Samantha, her mother, inhaled on an electronic cigarette. "It's going to be all right," she said to no one as she struck into the living room where Chlo waited with grandpa, brain dead and machine fed, skin thin as paper. "Take Dad's bags. I'll push him to the cab." He stared straight ahead, his artificial lung wheezed as the pump squealed.

Chlo didn't move immediately, and Samantha reached out as if they were late for school, not leaving home for god knows what, and her daughter went into motion. As if this were as simple as walking away.

"Sorry, Mom," Chlo whispered, biting down on her lip.

"It's okay," Sam said.

They both looked like young men now. Both had chopped locks and had stopped shaving, had started caring men's toiletries, multi-tools, pocketknives. Gotta carry the toys too, Chlo.

"Come on, Dad," Samantha said, pushing Mark's wheelchair/support out the front door. "Let's get out of here."

Chlo often wondered how he would have handled it. No way to know that, Chlo. At least he can't know despair.

Hot vapor from the wastes blew across their faces. They thought they heard grandpa cry out, but it was either the wind or a wild cat. Humidity fattened the air; the radioactive atmosphere was denser, dirtier, heavier. It made everything heavy. Sounds, too.

"If I could just forget who I was for like ten fucking minutes," Samantha edged, her tongue tapping against her teeth like a typewriter gone mad. She grinned like a skull at Chlo.

Chlo didn't respond and Mark Kellam had stopped talking two years ago. When they should have left. Before the burn and the wastes.

Chlo opened the back of the truck and together they arranged grandpa. If he felt any discomfort, he did not show it. His hands sometimes played out bass notes, as if music played behind his glazed eyes, and on occasion he'd murmur. Samantha sometimes heard the word "echo," Chlo couldn't be sure, the stims had a way of making the edges of reality frail and brittle.

They both missed his laugh in the dark.

They drew themselves into the truck, plated and rigged for the wastes, and drove out of the cul-de-sac on North Carriage Lane, headed northeast.

2

Chlo counted the chocolate in the bag again.

"How many times you gonna count?" Samantha asked, scanning the road. Again.

"How *ever* long it takes." Chlo looked up to where the back road crowned the hill. The man was late. "If I keep counting, I will look up and there he will be."

"You keep it up." Samantha looked back at her father, sleeping at a posed angle. The thought flashed through her mind to kill him and leave him at the side of the road.

It would come to that. Mark Kellam would have no burial.

Not yet, Sam, not just yet.

"Mom?"

"Yeah, sweetie," Sam replied.

"Batteries are running low. I'm gonna charge the solar cells while we wait it out."

"Good thinking."

3

"Sugar-pop," Mark whispered to his daughter, the icy mist from his mouth curled at her lips. Samantha snuggled into him. Her father pointed to the sun setting behind the pines. "One day you'll move out west to be a famous doctor and I'll have to fly all day long just to see my sugarpop."

Stim dreams. Memories. Half-sleep. She had been what? Seven? Young enough to still sit on her father's lap, head full of Christmas. Samantha rolled her eyes, mouth wet and warm with drool. Instinctively she reached for the .38 under the seat. When her hands couldn't find it, she jerked up, alert, until she remembered Chlo had it.

"SSH," Chlo commanded. The trip had aged her, radiation, stress, the fading effect of stimulants, days without a meal. "He's here." Chlo looked 25 not 16.

Chlo pointed at a short gruff looking fellow, adorned with deer skins. The barrel of his military issue rifle pointed up as he squatted, his cue for the transaction to begin.

4

"Come on," Chlo hissed, sliding sideways into the cab. "Go, mom, before he figures out Dad is nothing but a dummy!"

Samantha pulled the car into drive and tried to ignore the pounding in her ears. She wanted to scream. "You got it, right?"

"Yeah, yeah." Chlo shrugged, as if she had made hundreds of transactions. "Guy looked familiar. Like I had seen him on TV, or something."

"Great," Samantha snapped. "Now give me what I need."

5

To get across the wastes one had to reuse everything. On her shift, always at night, Chlo would pull the truck over, switch up power cells so there was always a fully charged pair on reserve, check the tires, and make sure the recycle valves didn't need a lube. She had done this dozens of shifts since they had started east. She pulled the truck into neutral, turned the engine off, and cruised the vehicle to a stop. She liked the chore it gave her time to think without her mother's nagging voice.

They had seen little action, most of it back at the edge of LA. The few travelers they had crossed paths with were open for trade, swapping bits of leather for small utensils, or for homemade knives and other jury-rigged equipment.

Water was gold. She smoked and worked, half aware of what she was doing, scanning the dark for trash or movement. Stories of ambushes spread along routes, and when she heard the chug-chug of an outrider bike, she winced and reached into the cab and turned the key. Just to be safe. The .38 felt like a hard stone in the back of her belt. "Trade or raid," she whispered.

The thought of waking her mother was a dark bird in the trees.

Into the cone of headlights he rode. Dark and swarthy; a feather hung upside down in front of his left ear. He did not hide his side arm, nor the machete on his bike. His baby face looked fresh in contrast to his dark, grisly clothes.

He peered into their truck, counting sleeping heads. "Are they dead?" he asked, counting gas cans, batteries. "There is much danger in these woods. Something may have seen you stop."

"Like you?" Chlo chirped. She bit her lip. Had she done it? Suddenly, the handle of the pistol was in her hand and she edged her back against the truck. Had she given away her gender? Chlo swallowed hard. Copper fear flooded her mouth.

"Yeah," he said, and after a long wolfish pause, he shrugged, "like me." He could have been a scout, for travelers or bandits. His right fingers clawed at his handlebar.

Chlo dropped her vocal register. "Well, I'm gonna go now. I got nothing to trade." She trembled and stumbled into the cab.

"If you say so." He laughed, face stiff from too many stims. Chlo closed the door and drove away, her eyes back-catching side glances at his dark form, his reddish bike.

Her heart ripped a triphammer beat. She gunned the truck the farther she got away from him. Night became pitch again, the boy on the outrider bike far away, another black form of what could have been blown shelters, a burnt-out truck, or a corpse. Chlo cried full fat tears, and felt her cracking skin, her bloody chapped lobes. Something inside Chlo clicked and all at once her hate and rage flowed through her arms, as if her speeding away now somehow showed up Mr. Cool back in the darkness, showed him that she wasn't scared, that she was tough. She beat and tore at the steering wheel. She missed the dead mule's corpse in the high beams.

The truck hit the hot death, and Chlo snapped forward and backward, the wheel jerking away from her. Her mother's skull cracked the side window, and the last thing Chlo saw was her grandfather, awake from the jolt of the wreck. Their bald eyes met long enough to see fear and love in each other. In that second Chlo knew more about her grandfather than she had ever learned when he was well, and Chlo felt hope for her family spike in her heart before her neck broke and darkness overtook her.

6

Rot stench.

Moaning.

Engine chug.

What Mark saw he did not comprehend. His wheelchair still strapped to the cab, he hung upside down. He thought he stared out at a field of daisies. In Nebraska.

His aunt's home, he thought. He heard guitar music. Granny singing.

Samantha? His voice sounded from tiny place. Chlo?

His life support pulled free of its rigging and dropped. His artificial lung stopped wheezing.

Mark didn't comprehend hands, spotlights, how his daughter and granddaughter were pulled out into the gutted road, how his own lungs finally wheezed out, which to Mark was a thousand daisies being blown all at once, towards his face, his mother's voice on the sweet wind, not like a fist gripping shut round a throat.

Unknown Drives

Richard Christian Matheson

The Truck pulled onto road; cut off Don's Mustang.

It was going twenty-five miles an hour and his wife, Kerry, shook head in disbelief.

"These local farmers must think they own the road," she said. "Speed limit is fifty-five."

Don squinted at the tailgate's faded letters.

"*FIELD'S PRODUCE*. Great... probably delivering to the next county."

"Well, there goes the vacation," she said, lightly.

"...let's just see," said Don.

He gradually edged the Mustang out, into the opposing lane, and quickly snapped the steering wheel to the right, swerving back.

"...fucking road work." He pointed to the left side of the road as they passed barricades, with blinking lights, blocking the opposing lane.

Ahead, the truck was still going an aggravating twenty-five.

Don inched the Mustang to the left, scanned road, pulled-back into his lane.

"...barricades look like they go for a coupla miles. They're re-paving the other lane."

Kerry reached to the cooler on floor, removed Coke, held up the bottle.

"Not now," he said, eyes glued to the truck. "Want to pass this guy. He's starting to bug the shit out of me."

He could see the back of the farmer's head. The man seemed completely at ease, bringing thinly smoking pipe to mouth.

Don honked several times, holding-down the horn. "Pull over you sonofabitch!"

The farmer ignored the honking. Puffed patiently.

"Smug bastard," said Don, looking at the speedometer. "He's going slower."

Kerry sipped Coke. "He's just an old man, Don. I'm sure his slow driving is just habit. I didn't notice him slowing down."

"Like hell he didn't! I can see it on the speedometer!" He glanced at her, mood brittle. "He's hogging the road. I've got to get around him. This could go on all day."

He looked to his left. The yellow barricades had ended; the other lane open again. He quickly pulled the Mustang out, to pass the truck, about to floor the engine, when suddenly they both screamed.

A one-lane bridge was a few yards away,

The truck lazily rolled across the bridge and Don slammed on brakes, eyes wide. The Mustang skidded loudly, almost sliding-over muddy embankment, into marsh water under the bridge. There was a dying gasp, as the engine stalled.

All was silent.

Don leaned over the steering wheel, breathing heavily. "...you ok?"

Kerry nodded, shaken. He reached over, hugged her.

"I'm beginning to hate this route," she said, reaching to glove compartment, pulling-out Kleenex. She wiped his face. Her own. "There's no rush, Don. Can't we just drive slower?"

He pushed the Kleenex away, irritably. "No. This is the only route through the county and I'll be goddamned if I'm going to let some old man make me late."

"Your brother won't mind if we're a few minutes late... please, Don."

She tried to take his hand and he pulled it away. Shoved the Mustang into reverse, pulled free from embankment, mud spraying from tires. Slid it into DRIVE, bolting back onto road.

"Gonna pass him," said Don. "Just need a clear stretch." He glanced at Kerry, as she nervously sipped Coke. "I'll quit if it's no good. Promise."

She looked at him, barely nodded.

"Good," he said, racing-up behind the truck. "...let's leave this fucker in the dust and get on with it. We'll show him."

The truck rocked slightly in front of them, didn't waver from twenty-five.

Don's fingers drummed steering wheel.

The farmer was still smoking his pipe. He adjusted hat, shrugged shoulders a bit.

Don impatiently pulled the Mustang into the opposing lane.

It was no good.

A truck was coming from the other direction.

He got back into the lane; waited.

"...almost," he said. "Next one." He steered to the left. Cursed, seeing more oncoming cars.

"Look!" said Kerry.

The farmer's truck was signaling for a right turn. It began to curve slowly to the right.

"Patience," said Don with an ironic smile, "all it took."

He gripped wheel firmly, stepped hard on the gas. The Mustang sped around the truck's side, streaked along empty opposing lane and he began to roll down his window.

"Take that Coke now," he grinned.

But it was too late.

From the right side of the farmer's truck, in Don's blind spot, was an enormous foundry truck. He slammed on brakes as they collided at fifty miles an hour, thrust through shattering windshield. Their bodies were mangled and bent on asphalt, as bloodied bottles of Coke rolled and the Mustang caught fire. Flames and smoke ransacked countryside, and pasture animals looked on, chewing, kicking hooves.

The truck parked in front of the farmhouse.

The farmer got out, knocked pipe against muddy running board, entered the house through kitchen door. Inside, his wife was at the stove, stirring a boiling stew. He re-filled pipe.

"How was your day?" she asked.

He held a match to pipe bowl.

"Good day," he said. "I got me one."

Duel

Richard Matheson

At 11:32 a.m., Mann passed the truck.

He was heading west, en route to San Francisco. It was Thursday and unseasonably hot for April. He had his suitcoat off, his tie removed and shirt collar opened, his sleeve cuffs folded back. There was sunlight on his left arm and on part of his lap. He could feel the heat of it through his dark trousers as he drove along the two-lane highway. For the past twenty minutes, he had not seen another vehicle going in either direction.

Then he saw the truck ahead, moving up a curving grade between two high green hills. He heard the grinding strain of its motor and saw a double shadow on the road. The truck was pulling a trailer.

He pai no attention to the details of the truck. As he drew behind it on the grade, he edged his car toward the opposite lane. The road ahead had blind curves and he didn't try to pass until the truck had crossed the ridge. He waited until it started around a left curve on the downgrade, then, seeing that the way was clear, pressed down on the accelerator pedal and steered his car into the eastbound lane. He waited until he could see the truck front in his rearview mirror before he turned back into the proper lane.

Mann looked across the countryside ahead. There were ranges of mountains as far as he could see and, all around him, rolling green hills. He whistled softly as the car sped down the winding grade, its tires making crisp sounds on the pavement.

At the bottom of the hill, he crossed a concrete bridge and, glancing to the right, saw a dry stream bed strewn with rocks and gravel. As the car moved off the bridge, he saw a trailer park set back from the highway to his right. How can anyone live out here? he thought. His shifting gaze caught sight of a pet cemetery ahead and he smiled. Maybe those people in the trailers wanted to be close to the graves of their dogs and cats.

The highway ahead was straight now. Mann drifted into a reverie, the sunlight on his arm and lap. He wondered what Ruth was doing. The kids, of course, were in school and would be for hours yet. Maybe Ruth was shopping; Thursday was the day she usually went. Mann visualized her in the supermarket, putting various items into the basket cart. He wished he were with her instead of starting on another sales trip. Hours of driving yet before he'd reach San Francisco. Three days of hotel sleeping and restaurant eating, hoped-for contacts and likely disappointments. He sighed; then, reaching out impulsively, he switched on the radio. He revolved the turning knob until he found a station playing soft, innocuous music. He hummed along with it, eyes almost out of focus on the road ahead.

He started as the truck roared past him on the left, causing his car to shudder slightly. He watched the truck and trailer cut in abruptly for the westbound lane and frowned as he had to brake to maintain a safe distance behind it. What's with you? he thought.

He eyed the truck with cursory disapproval. It was a huge gasoline tanker pulling a tank trailer, each of them having six pairs of wheels. He could see that it was not a new rig but was dented and in need of renovation, its tanks painted a cheap-looking silvery color. Mann wondered if the driver had done the painting himself. His gaze shifted from the word FLAMMABLE printed across the back of the trailer tank, red letters on a white background, to the parallel reflector lines painted in red across the bottom of the tank to the massive rubber flaps swaying behind the rear tires, then back up again. The reflector lines looked as though they'd been clumsily applied with a stencil. The driver must be an independent trucker, he decided, and not too affluent a one, from the looks of his outfit. He glanced at the trailer's license plate. It was a California issue.

Mann checked his speedometer. He was holding steady at 55 miles an hour, as he invariably did when he drove without thinking on the open highway. The truck driver must have done a good 70 to pass him so quickly. That seemed a little odd. Weren't truck drivers supposed to be a cautious lot?

He grimaced at the smell of the truck's exhaust and looked at the vertical pipe to the left of the cab. It was spewing smoke, which clouded darkly back across the trailer. Christ, he thought. With all the furor about air pollution, why do they keep allowing that sort of thing on the highways?

He scowled at the constant fumes. They'd make him nauseated in a little while, he knew. He couldn't lag back here like this. Either he slowed down or he passed the truck again. He didn't have the time to slow down. He'd gotten a late start. Keeping it at 55 all the way, he'd just about make his afternoon appointment. No, he'd have to pass.

Depressing the gas pedal, he eased his car toward the opposite lane. No sign of anything ahead. Traffic on this route seemed almost non-existent today. He pushed down harder on the accelerator and steered all the way into the eastbound lane.

As he passed the truck, he glanced at it. The cab was too high for him to sec into. *All* he caught sight of was the back of the truck driver's left hand on the steering wheel. It was darkly tanned and square-looking, with large veins knotted on its surface.

When Mann could see the truck reflected in the rearview mirror, he pulled back over to the proper lane and looked ahead again.

He glanced at the rearview mirror in surprise as the truck driver gave him an extended horn blast. What was that? he wondered; a greeting or a curse? He grunted with amusement, glancing at the mirror as he drove. The front fenders of the truck were a dingy purple color, the paint faded and chipped; another amateurish job. All he could see was the lower portion of the truck; the rest was cut off by the top of his rear window.

To Mann's right, now, was a slope of shale-like

earth with patches of scrub grass growing on it. His gaze jumped to the clapboard house on top of the slope. The television aerial on its roof was sagging at an angle of less than 40 degrees. Must give great reception, he thought.

He looked to the front again, glancing aside abruptly at a sign printed in jagged block letters on a piece of plywood: NIGHT CRAWLERS-BAIT. What the hell is a night crawler? he wondered. It sounded like some monster in a low-grade Hollywood thriller.

The unexpected roar of the truck motor made *his* gaze jump to the rearview mirror. Instantly, his startled look jumped to the side mirror. By God, the guy was passing him *again.* Mann turned his head to scowl at the leviathan form as it drifted by. He tried to see into the cab but couldn't because of its height. What's with him, anyway? he wondered. What the hell are we having here, a contest? See which vehicle can stay ahead the longest?

He thought of speeding up to stay ahead but changed his mind. When the truck and trailer started back into the westbound lane, he let up on the pedal, voicing a newly incredulous sound as he saw that if he hadn't slowed down, he would have been prematurely cut off again. Jesus Christ, he thought. What's *with* this guy?

His scowl deepened as the odor of the truck's exhaust reached his nostrils again. Irritably, he cranked up the window on his left. Damn it, was he going to have to breathe that crap all the way to San Francisco? He couldn't afford to slow down. He had to meet Forbes at a quarter after three and that was that.

He looked ahead. At least there was no traffic

complicating matters. Mann pressed down on the accelerator pedal, drawing close behind the truck. When the highway curved enough to the left to give him a completely open view of the route ahead, he jarred down on the pedal, steering out into the opposite lane.

The truck edged over, blocking his way.

For several moments, all Mann could do was stare at it in blank confusion. Then, with a startled noise, he braked, returning to the proper lane. The truck moved back in front of him.

Mann could not allow himself to accept what apparently had taken place. It had to be a coincidence. The truck driver couldn't have blocked his way on purpose. He waited for more than a minute, then flicked down the turn-indicator lever to make his intentions perfectly clear and, depressing the accelerator pedal, steered again into the eastbound lane.

Immediately, the truck shifted, barring his way.

"Jesus Christ!" Mann was astounded. This was unbelievable. He'd never seen such a thing in twenty-six years of driving. He returned to the westbound lane, shaking his head as the truck swung back in front of him.

He eased up on the gas pedal, falling back to avoid the truck's exhaust. Now what? he wondered. He still had to make San Francisco on schedule. Why in God's name hadn't he gone a little out of his way in the beginning, so he could have traveled by freeway? This damned highway was two lane all the way.

Impulsively, he sped into the eastbound lane again. To his surprise, the truck driver did not pull over. Instead, the driver stuck his left arm out and waved him on. Mann started pushing down on the accelerator. Suddenly, he let up on the pedal with a gasp and jerked the steering wheel around, raking back behind the truck so quickly that his car began to fishtail. He was fighting to control its zigzag whipping when a blue convertible shot by him in the opposite lane. Mann caught a momentary vision of the man inside it glaring at him.

The car came under his control again. Mann was sucking breath in through his mouth. His heart was pounding almost painfully. My God! he thought. *He wanted me to hit that car head on.* The realization stunned him. True, he should have seen to it himself that the road ahead was clear; that was his failure. But to wave him on . . . . Mann felt appalled and sickened. Boy, oh, boy, oh, boy, he thought. This was really one for the books. That son of a bitch had meant for not only him to be killed but a totally uninvolved passerby as well. The idea seemed beyond his comprehension. On a California highway on a Thursday morning? *Why?*

Mann tried to calm himself and rationalize the incident. Maybe it's the heat, he thought. Maybe the truck driver had a tension headache or an upset stomach; maybe both. Maybe he'd had a fight with his wife. Maybe she'd failed to put out last night. Mann tried in vain to smile. There could be any number of reasons. Reaching out, he twisted off the radio. The cheerful music irritated him.

He drove behind the truck for several minutes, his face a mask of animosity. As the exhaust fumes started putting his stomach on edge, he suddenly forced down the heel of his right hand on the horn bar and held it there. Seeing that the route ahead was clear, he pushed in the accelerator pedal all the way and steered into the opposite Jane.

The movement of his car was paralleled immediately by the truck. Mann stayed in place, right hand jammed down on the horn bar. Get out of the way, you son of a bitch! he thought. He felt the muscles of his jaw hardening until they ached. There was a twisting in his stomach. *"Damn!"* He pulled back quickly to the proper lane, shuddering with fury. "You miserable son of a bitch," he muttered, glaring at the truck as it was shifted back in front of him. What the hell is wrong with you? I pass your goddamn rig a couple of times and you go flying off the deep end? Are you nuts or something? Mann nodded tensely. Yes, he thought; he *is.* No other explanation.

He wondered what Ruth would think of all this, how she'd react. Probably, she'd start to honk the horn and would keep on honking it, assuming that, eventually, it would attract the attention of a policeman. He looked around with a scowl. Just where in hell *were* the policemen out here, anyway? He made a scoffing noise. What policemen? Here in the boondocks? They probably had a sheriff on horseback, for Christ's sake.

He wondered suddenly if he could fool the truck driver by passing on the right. Edging his car toward the shoulder, he peered ahead. No chance. There wasn't room enough. The truck driver could shove him through that wire fence if he wanted to. Mann shivered. And he'd want to, sure as hell, he thought.

Driving where he was, he grew conscious of the debris lying beside the highway: beer cans, candy wrappers, ice-cream containers, newspaper sections browned and rotted by the weather, a FOR SALE sign torn in half. Keep America beautiful, he thought sardonically. He passed a boulder with the name WILL JASPER painted on it in white. Who the hell is Will Jasper? he wondered. What would he think of this situation? Unexpectedly, the car began to bounce. For several anxious moments, Mann thought that one of his tires had gone flat. Then he noticed that the paving along this section of highway consisted of pitted slabs with gaps between them. He saw the truck and trailer jolting up and down and thought: I hope it shakes your brains loose. As the truck veered into a sharp left curve, he caught a fleeting glimpse of the driver's face in the cab's side mirror. There was not enough time to establish his appearance.

"Ah," he said. A long, steep hill was looming up ahead. The truck would have to climb it slowly. There would doubtless be an opportunity to pass somewhere on the grade. Mann pressed down on the accelerator pedal, drawing as close behind the truck as safety would allow.

Halfway up the slope, Mann saw a turnout for the eastbound lane with no oncoming traffic anywhere in sight. Flooring the accelerator pedal, he shot into the opposite lane. The slow-moving truck began to angle out in front of him. Face stiffening, Mann steered his speeding car across the highway edge and curved it sharply on the turnout. Clouds of dust went billowing up behind his car, making him lose sight of the truck. His tires buzzed and crackled on the dirt, then, suddenly, were humming on the pavement once again.

He glanced at the rearview mirror and a barking laugh erupted from *his* throat. He'd only meant to pass. The dust had been an unexpected bonus. Let the bastard get a sniff of something rotten smelling in *his* nose for a change! he thought. He honked the horn elatedly, a mocking rhythm of bleats. Screw you, Jack!

He swept across the summit of the hill. A striking vista lay ahead: sunlit hills and flatland, a corridor of dark trees, quadrangles of cleared off acreage and bright-green vegetable patches; far off, in the distance, a mammoth water tower. Mann felt stirred by the panoramic sight. Lovely, he thought. Reaching out, he turned the radio back on and started humming cheerfully with the music.

Seven minutes later, he passed a billboard advertising CHUCK'S CAFE. No thanks, Chuck, he thought. He glanced at a gray house nestled in a hollow. Was that a cemetery in its front yard or a group of plaster statuary for sale?

Hearing the noise behind him, Mann looked at the rearview mirror and felt himself go cold with fear. The truck was hurtling down the hill, pursuing him.

His mouth fell open and he threw a glance at the speedometer. He was doing more than 60! On a curving downgrade, that was not at all a safe speed to be driving. Yet the truck must be exceeding that by a considerable margin, it was dosing the distance between them so rapidly. Mann swallowed, leaning to the right as he steered his car around a sharp curve. Is the man *insane?* he thought.

His gaze jumped forward searchingly. He saw a turnoff half a mile ahead and decided that he'd use it. In the rearview mirror, the huge square radiator grille was all he could see now. He stamped down on the gas pedal and his tires screeched unnervingly as he wheeled around another curve, thinking that, surely, the truck would have to slow down here.

He groaned as it rounded the curve with ease, only the sway of its tanks revealing the outward pressure of the turn. Mann bit trembling lips together as he whipped his car around another curve. A straight descent now. He depressed the pedal farther, glanced at the speedometer. Almost 70 miles an hour! He wasn't used to driving this fast! In agony, he saw the turnoff shoot by on his right. He couldn't have left the highway at this speed, anyway; he'd have overturned. Goddamn it, what was wrong with that son of a bitch? Mann honked his horn in frightened rage. Cranking down the window suddenly, he shoved his left arm out to wave the truck back. *"Back!"* he yelled. He honked the horn again. "Get back, you crazy bastard!"

The truck was almost on him now. He's going to kill me! Mann thought, horrified. He honked the horn repeatedly, then had to use both hands to grip the steering wheel as he swept around another curve. He flashed a look at the rearview mirror. He could see *only* the bottom portion of the truck's radiator grille. He was going to lose control! He felt the rear wheels start to drift and let up on the pedal quickly. The tire treads bit in, the car leaped on, regaining its momentum.

Mann saw the bottom of the grade ahead, and in the distance there was a building with a sign that read CHUCK'S CAFE. The truck was gaining ground again. This is insane! he thought, enraged and terrified at once. The highway straightened out. He floored the pedal: 74 now 75. Mann braced himself, trying to ease the car as far to the right as possible.

Abruptly, he began to brake, then swerved to the right, raking his car into the open area in front of the cafe. He cried out as the car began to fishtail, then careened into a skid. *Steer with it!* screamed a voice in his mind. The rear of the car was lashing from side to side, tires spewing dirt and raising clouds of dust. Mann pressed harder on the brake pedal, turning further into the skid. The car began to straighten out and he braked harder yet, conscious, on the sides of his vision, of the truck and trailer roaring by on the highway. He nearly sideswiped one of the cars parked in front of the cafe, bounced and skidded by it, going almost straight now. He jammed in the brake pedal as hard as he could. The rear end broke to the right and the car spun half around, sheering sideways to a neck-wrenching halt thirty yards beyond the cafe.

Mann sat in pulsing silence, eyes closed. His heartbeats felt like club blows in his chest. He couldn't seem to catch his breath. If he were ever going to have a heart attack, it would be now. After a while, he opened his eyes and pressed his right palm against his chest. His heart was still throbbing laboredly. No wonder, he thought. It isn't every day I'm almost murdered by a truck.

He raised the handle and pushed out the door, then started forward, grunting in surprise as the safety belt held him in place. Reaching down with shaking fingers, he depressed the release button and pulled the ends of the belt apart. He glanced at the cafe. What had *its* patrons thought of his breakneck appearance? he wondered.

He stumbled as he walked to the front door of the cafe. TRUCKERS WELCOME, read a sign in the window. It gave Mann a queasy feeling to see it. Shivering, he pulled open the door and went inside, avoiding the sight of its customers. He felt certain they were watching *him,* but he didn't have the strength to face their looks. Keeping his gaze fixed straight ahead, he moved to the rear of the cafe and opened the door marked GENTS.

Moving to the sink, he twisted the right-hand faucet and leaned over to cup cold water in his palms and splash it on his face. There was a fluttering of his stomach muscles he could not control.

Straightening up, he tugged down several towels from their dispenser and patted them against his face, grimacing at the smell of the paper. Dropping the soggy towels into a wastebasket beside the sink, he regarded himself in the wall mirror. Still with us, Mann, he thought. He nodded, swallowing. Drawing out his metal comb, he neatened his hair. You never know, he thought. You just never know. You drift along, year after year, presuming certain values to be fixed; like being able to drive on a public thoroughfare without somebody trying to murder you. You come to depend on that sort of thing. Then some- thing occurs and all bets are off. One shocking incident and all the years of logic and acceptance are displaced and, suddenly, the jungle is in front of you again. *Man, part animal, part angel.* Where had he come across that phrase? He shivered.

It was entirely an animal in that truck out there.

His breath was almost back to normal now. Mann forced a smile at his reflection. All right, boy, he told himself. It's over now. It was a goddamned nightmare, but it's over. You are on your way to San Francisco. You'll get yourself a nice hotel room, order a bottle of expensive Scotch, soak your body in a hot bath and forget. Damn right, he thought. He turned and walked out of the washroom.

He jolted to a halt, his breath cut off. Standing rooted, heartbeat hammering at his chest, he gaped through the front window of the cafe.

The truck and trailer were parked outside. Mann stared at them in unbelieving shock. It wasn't possible. He'd seen them roaring by at top speed. The driver had won; he'd *won!* He'd had the whole damn highway to himself! *Why had he turned back?* Mann looked around with sudden dread. There were five men eat- ing, three along the counter, two in booths. He cursed himself for having failed to look at faces when he'd entered. Now there was no way of knowing who it was. Mann felt his legs begin to shake.

Abruptly, he walked to the nearest booth and slid in clumsily behind the table. Now wait, he told himself; just wait. Surely, he could tell which one it was. Masking his face with the menu, he glanced across its top. Was it that one in the khaki work shirt? Mann tried to see the man's hands but couldn't. His gaze flicked nervously across the room.

Not that one in the suit, of course. Three remaining. That one in the front booth, square-faced, black-haired? If only he could see the man's hands, it might help. One of the two others at the counter? Mann studied them uneasily. Why hadn't he looked at faces when he'd come in?

Now *wait,* he thought. Goddamn it, *wait!* All right, the truck driver was in here. That didn't automatically signify that he meant to continue the insane duel. Chuck's Cafe might be the only place to eat for miles around. It *was* lunchtime, wasn't it? The truck driver had probably intended to eat here all the time. He'd just been moving too fast to pull into the parking lot before. So he'd slowed down, turned around and driven back, that was all. Mann forced himself to read the menu. Right, he thought. No point in getting so rattled. Perhaps a beer would help relax him.

The woman behind the counter came over and Mann ordered a ham sandwich on rye toast and a bottle of Coors. As the woman turned away, he wondered, with a sudden twinge of self-reproach, why he hadn't simply left the cafe, jumped into his car and sped away. He would have known immediately, then, if the truck driver was still out to get him. As it was, he'd have to suffer through an entire meal to find out. He almost groaned at his stupidity.

Still, what if the truck driver *had* followed him out and started after him again? He'd have been right back where he'd started. Even if he'd managed to get a good lead, the truck driver would have overtaken him eventually. It just wasn't in him to drive at 80 and 90 miles an hour in order to stay ahead. True, he might have been intercepted by a California Highway Patrol car. What if he weren't, though?

Mann repressed the plaguing thoughts. He tried to calm himself. He looked deliberately at the four men. Either of two seemed a likely possibility as the driver of the truck: the square-faced one in the front booth and the chunky one in the jumpsuit sitting at the counter. Mann had an impulse to walk over to them and ask which one it was, tell the man he was sorry he'd irritated him, tell him anything to calm him, since, obviously, he wasn't rational, was a manic-depressive, probably. Maybe buy the man a beer and sit with him awhile to try to settle things.

He couldn't move. What if the truck driver were letting the whole thing drop? Mightn't his approach rile the man all over again? Mann felt drained by indecision. He nodded weakly as the waitress set the sandwich and the bottle in front of him. He took a swallow of the beer, which made him cough. Was the truck driver amused by the sound? Mann felt a stirring of resentment deep inside himself. What right did that bastard have to impose this torment on another human being? It was a free country, wasn't it? Damn it, he had every right to pass the son of a bitch on a highway if he wanted to!

"Oh, hell," he mumbled. He tried to feel amused. He was making entirely too much of this. Wasn't he? He glanced at the pay telephone on the front wall. What was to prevent him from calling the local police and telling them the situation? But, then, he'd have to stay here, lose time, make Forbes angry, probably lose the sale. And what if the truck driver stayed to face them? Naturally, he'd deny the whole thing. What if the police believed him and didn't do anything about it? After they'd gone, the truck driver would undoubtedly take it out on him again, only worse. *God!* Mann thought in agony.

The sandwich tasted flat, the beer unpleasantly sour. Mann stared at the table as he ate. For God's sake, why was he just *sitting* here like this? He was a grown man, wasn't he? Why didn't he settle this damn thing once and for all?

His left hand twitched so unexpectedly, he spilled beer on his trousers. The man in the jump suit had risen from the counter and was strolling toward the front of the cafe. Mann felt his heartbeat thumping as the man gave money to the waitress, took his change and a toothpick from the dispenser and went outside. Mann watched in anxious silence.

The man did not get into the cab of the tanker truck. It had to be the one in the front booth, then. His face took form in Mann's remembrance: square, with dark eyes, dark hair; the man who'd tried to kill him.

Mann stood abruptly, letting impulse conquer fear. Eyes fixed ahead, he started toward the entrance. Anything was preferable to sitting in that booth. He stopped by the cash register, conscious of the hitching of his chest as he gulped in air. Was the man observing him? he wondered. He swallowed, pulling out the clip of dollar bills in his right-hand trouser pocket. He glanced toward the waitress. Come *on,* he thought. He looked at his check and, seeing the amount, reached shakily into his trouser pocket for change. He heard a coin fall onto the floor and roll away. Ignoring it, he dropped a dollar and a quarter onto the counter and thrust the clip of bills into his trouser pocket.

As he did, he heard the man in the front booth get up. An icy shudder spasmed up his back. Turning quickly to the door, he shoved it open, seeing, on the edges of his vision, the square-faced man approach the cash register. Lurching from the cafe, he started toward his car with long strides. His mouth was dry again. The pounding of his heart was painful in his chest.

Suddenly, he started running. He heard the cafe door bang shut and fought away the urge to look across his shoulder. Was that a sound of other running footsteps now? Reaching his car, Mann yanked open the door and jarred in awkwardly behind the steering wheel. He reached into his trouser pocket for the keys and snatched them out, almost dropping them. His hand was shaking so badly he couldn't get the ignition key into its slot. He whined with mounting dread. Come on! he thought.

The key slid in, he twisted it convulsively. The motor started and he raced it momentarily before jerking the transmission shift to drive. Depressing the accelerator pedal quickly, he raked the car around and steered it toward the highway. From the corners of his eyes, he saw the truck and trailer being backed away from the cafe.

Reaction burst inside him. "No!" he raged and slammed his foot down on the brake pedal. This was idiotic! Why the hell should he run away? His car slid sideways to a rocking halt and, shouldering out the door, he lurched to his feet and started toward the truck with angry strides. *All right, Jack,* he thought. He glared at the man inside the truck. You want to punch my nose, okay, but no more goddamn tournament on the highway.

The truck began to pick up speed. Mann raised his right arm. "Hey!" he yelled. He knew the driver saw him. *"Hey!"* He started running as the truck kept moving, engine grinding loudly. It was on the highway now. He sprinted toward it with a sense of martyred outrage. The driver shifted gears, the truck moved faster. "Stop!" Mann shouted. "Damn it, *stop!"*

He thudded to a panting halt, staring at the truck as it receded down the highway, moved around a hill and disappeared. "You son of a bitch," he muttered. "You goddamn, miserable son of a bitch."

He trudged back slowly to his car, trying to believe that the truck driver had fled the hazard of a fistfight. It was possible, of course, but, somehow, he could not believe it.

He got into his car and was about to drive onto the highway when he changed his mind and switched the motor off. That crazy bastard might just be tooling along at 15 miles an hour, waiting for him to catch up. Nuts to that, he thought. So he blew his schedule; screw it. Forbes would have to wait, that was all. And if Forbes didn't care to wait, that was all right, too. He'd sit here for a while and let the nut get out of range, let him think he'd won the day. He grinned. You're the bloody Red Baron, Jack; you've shot me down. Now go to hell with my sincerest compliments. He shook his head. Beyond belief, he thought.

He really should have done this earlier, pulled over, waited. Then the truck driver would have had to let it pass. *Or picked on someone else,* the startling thought occurred to him. Jesus, maybe that was how the crazy bastard whiled away his work hours! Jesus Christ Almighty! was it possible?

He looked at the dashboard clock. It was just past 12:30. Wow, he thought. All that in less than an hour. He shifted on the seat and stretched his legs out. Leaning back against the door, he closed his eyes and mentally perused the things he had to do tomorrow and the following day. Today was shot to hell, as far as he could see.

When he opened his eyes, afraid of drifting into sleep and losing too much time, almost eleven minutes had passed. The nut must be an ample distance off by now, he thought; at least 11 miles and likely more, the way he drove. Good enough. He wasn't going to try to make San Francisco on schedule now, anyway. He'd take it real easy. Mann adjusted his safety belt, switched on the motor, tapped the transmission pointer into drive position and pulled onto the highway, glancing back across his shoulder. Not a car in sight. Great day for driving. Everybody was staying at home. That nut must have a reputation around here. When Crazy Jack is on the highway, lock your car in the garage. Mann chuckled at the notion as his car began to turn the curve ahead.

Mindless reflex drove his right foot down against the brake pedal. Suddenly, his car had skidded to a halt and he was staring down the highway. The truck and trailer were parked on the shoulder less than 90 yards away.

Mann couldn't seem to function. He knew his car was blocking the westbound lane, knew that he should either make a U-turn or pull off the highway, but all he could do was gape at the truck.

He cried out, legs retracting, as a horn blast sounded behind him. Snapping up his head, he looked at the rearview mirror, gasping as he saw a yellow station wagon bearing down on him at high speed. Suddenly, it veered off toward the eastbound lane, disappearing from the mirror. Mann jerked around and saw it hurtling past his car, its rear end snapping back and forth, its back tires screeching. He saw the twisted features of the man inside, saw his lips move rapidly with cursing.

Then the station wagon had swerved back into the westbound lane and was speeding off. It gave Mann an odd sensation to see it pass the truck. The man in that station wagon could drive on, unthreatened. Only he'd been singled out. What happened was demented. Yet it was happening.

He drove his car onto the highway shoulder and braked. Putting the transmission into neutral, he leaned back, staring at the truck. His head was aching again. There was a pulsing at his temples like the ticking of a muffled clock.

What was he to do? He knew very well that if he left his car to walk to the truck, the driver would pull away and repark farther down the highway. He may as well face the fact that he was dealing with a madman. He felt the tremor in his stomach muscles starting up again. His heartbeat thudded slowly, striking at his chest wall. Now what?

With a sudden, angry impulse, Mann snapped the transmission into gear and stepped down hard on the accelerator pedal. The tires of the car spun sizzlingly before they gripped; the car shot out onto the high- way. Instantly, the truck began to move. He even had the motor on! Mann thought in raging fear. He floored the pedal, then, abruptly, realized he couldn't make it, that the truck would block his way and he'd collide with its trailer. A vision flashed across his mind, a fiery explosion and a sheet of flame incinerating him. He started braking fast, trying to decelerate evenly, so he wouldn't lose control.

When he'd slowed down enough to feel that it was safe, he steered the car onto the shoulder and stopped it again, throwing the transmission into neutral.

Approximately eighty yards ahead, the truck pulled off the highway and stopped.

Mann tapped his fingers on the steering wheel. *Now* what? he thought. Turn around and head east until he reached a cutoff that would take him to San Francisco by another route? How did he know the truck driver wouldn't follow him even then? His cheeks twisted as he bit his lips together angrily. No! He wasn't going to turn around!

His expression hardened suddenly. Well, he wasn't going to *sit* here all day, that was certain. Reaching out, he tapped the gearshift into drive and steered his car onto the highway once again. He saw the massive truck and trailer start to move but made no effort to speed up. He tapped at the brakes, taking a position about 30 yards behind the trailer. He glanced at his speedometer. Forty miles an hour. The truck driver had his left arm out of the cab window and was waving him on. What did that mean? Had he changed his mind? Decided, finally, that this thing had gone too far? Mann couldn't let himself believe it.

He looked ahead. Despite the mountain ranges all around, the highway was Aat as far as he could see. He tapped a fingernail against the horn bar, trying to make up his mind. Presumably, he could continue all the way to San Francisco at this speed, hanging back just far enough to avoid the worst of the exhaust fumes. It didn't seem likely that the truck driver would stop directly on the highway to block his way. And if the truck driver pulled onto the shoulder to let him pass, he could pull off the highway, too. It would be a draining afternoon but a safe one.

On the other hand, outracing the truck might be worth just one more try. This was obviously what that son of a bitch wanted. Yet, surely, a vehicle of such size couldn't be driven with the same daring as, potentially, his own. The laws of mechanics were against it, if nothing else. Whatever advantage the truck had in mass, it had to lose in stability, particularly that of its trailer. If Mann were to drive at, say, 80 miles an hour and there were a few steep grades-as he felt sure there were-the truck would have to fall behind.

The question was, of course, whether he had the nerve to maintain such a speed over a long distance. He'd never done it before. Still, the more he thought about it, the more it appealed to him; far more than the alternative did.

Abruptly, he decided. *Right,* he thought. He checked ahead, then pressed down hard on the accelerator pedal and pulled into the eastbound lane. As he neared the truck, he tensed, anticipating that the driver might block his way. But the truck did not shift from the westbound lane. Mann's car moved along its mammoth side. He glanced at the cab and saw the name KELLER printed on its door. For a shocking instant, he thought it read KILLER and started to slow down. Then, glancing at the name again, he saw what it really was and depressed the pedal sharply. When he saw the truck reflected in the rearview mirror, he steered his car into the westbound lane.

He shuddered, dread and satisfaction mixed together, as he saw that the truck driver was speeding up. It was strangely comforting to know the man's intentions definitely again. That plus the knowledge of his face and name seemed, somehow, to reduce his stature. Before, he had been faceless, nameless, an embodiment of unknown terror. Now, at least, he was an individual. All right, Keller, said his mind, let's see you beat me with that purple-silver relic now. He pressed down harder on the pedal. *Here we go,* he thought. He looked at the speedometer, scowling as he saw that he was doing only 74 miles an hour. Deliberately, he pressed down on the pedal, alternating his gaze between the highway ahead and the speedometer until the needle turned past 80. He felt a flickering of satisfaction with himself. All right, Keller, you son of a bitch, top that, he thought.

After several moments, he glanced into the rearview mirror again. Was the truck getting closer? Stunned, he checked the speedometer. Damn it! He was down to 76! He forced in the accelerator pedal angrily. *He mustn't go less than 80!* Mann's chest shuddered with convulsive breath.

He glanced aside as he hurtled past a beige sedan parked on the shoulder underneath a tree. A young couple sat inside it, talking. Already they were far behind, their world removed from his. Had they even glanced aside when he'd passed? He doubted it.

He started as the shadow of an overhead bridge whipped across the hood and windshield. Inhaling raggedly, he glanced at the speedometer again. He was holding at 81. He checked the rearview mirror. Was it his imagination that the truck was gaining ground? He looked forward with anxious eyes. There had to be some kind of town ahead. To hell with time; he'd stop at the police station and tell them what had happened. They'd have to believe him. Why would he stop to tell them such a story if it weren't true? For all he knew, Keller had a police record in these parts. *Oh, sure, we're on to him,* he heard a faceless officer remark. *That crazy bastard's asked for it before and now he's going to get it.*

Mann shook himself and looked at the mirror. The truck *was* getting closer. Wincing, he glanced at the speedometer. Goddamn it, pay attention! raged his mind. He was down to 74 again! Whining with frustration, he depressed the pedal. Eighty!-80! he demanded of himself. There was a murderer behind him!

His car began to pass a field of flowers; lilacs, Mann saw, white and purple stretching out in endless rows. There was a small shack near the highway, the words FIELD FRESH FLOWERS painted on it. A brown-cardboard square was propped against the shack, the word FUNERALS printed crudely on it. Mann saw himself, abruptly, lying in a casket, painted like some grotesque mannequin. The overpowering smell of flowers seemed to fill his nostrils. Ruth and the children sitting in the first row, heads bowed. All his relatives—

Suddenly, the pavement roughened and the car began to bounce and shudder, driving bolts of pain into his head. He felt the steering wheel resisting him and clamped his hands around it tightly, harsh vibrations running up his arms. He didn't dare look at the mirror now. He had to force himself to keep the speed unchanged. Keller wasn't going to slow down; he was sure of that. *What if he got a flat tire, though?* All control would vanish in an instant. He visualized the somersaulting of his car, its grinding, shrieking tumble, the explosion of its gas tank, his body crushed and burned and—

The broken span of pavement ended and his gaze jumped quickly to the rearview mirror. The truck was no closer, but it hadn't lost ground, either. Mann's eyes shifted. Up ahead were hills and mountains. He tried to reassure himself that upgrades were on his side, that he could climb them at the same speed he was going now. Yet all he could imagine were the downgrades, the immense truck close behind him, slamming violently into his car and knocking it across some cliff edge. He had a horrifying vision of dozens of broken, rusted cars lying unseen in the canyons ahead, corpses in every one of them, all flung to shattering deaths by Keller.

Mann's car went rocketing into a corridor of trees. On each side of the highway was a eucalyptus windbreak, each trunk three feet from the next. It was like speeding through a high-walled canyon. Mann gasped, twitching, as a large twig bearing dusty leaves dropped down across the windshield, then slid out of sight. Dear God! he thought. He was getting near the edge himself. If he should lose his nerve at this speed, it was over. Jesus! That would be ideal for Keller! he realized suddenly. He visualized the square-faced driver laughing as he passed the burning wreckage, knowing that he'd killed his prey without so much as touching him.

Mann started as his car shot out into the open. The route ahead was not straight now but winding up into the foothills. Mann willed himself to press down on the pedal even more. Eighty-three now, almost 84. To his left was a broad terrain of green hills blending into mountains.

He saw a black car on a dirt road, moving toward the highway. *Was its side painted white?* Mann's heartbeat lurched. Impulsively, he jammed the heel of his right hand down against the horn bar and held it there. The blast of the horn was shrill and racking to his ears. His heart began to pound. Was it a police car? *Was it?*

He let the horn bar up abruptly. *No, it wasn't.* Damn! his mind raged. Keller must have been amused by his pathetic efforts. Doubtless, he was chuckling to himself right now. He heard the truck driver's voice in his mind, coarse and sly. *You think you gonna get a cop to save you, boy? Shee-it. You gonna die.* Mann's heart contorted with savage hatred. *You son of a bitch!* he thought. Jerking his right hand into a fist, he drove it down against the seat. Goddamn you, Keller! I'm going to kill you, if it's the last thing I do!

The hills were closer now. There would be slopes directly, long steep grades. Mann felt a burst of hope within himself. He was sure to gain a lot of distance on the truck. No matter how he tried, that bastard Keller couldn't manage 80 miles an hour on a hill. But *I* can! cried his mind with fierce elation. He worked up saliva in his mouth and swallowed it. The back of his shirt was drenched. He could feel sweat trickling down his sides. A bath and a drink, first order of the day on reaching San Francisco. A long, hot bath, a long, cold drink. Cutty Sark. He'd splurge, by Christ. He rated it.

The car swept up a shallow rise. Not steep enough, goddamn it! The truck's momentum would prevent its losing speed. Mann felt mindless hatred for the landscape. Already, he had topped the rise and tilted over to a shallow downgrade. He looked at the rearview mirror. *Square,* he thought, everything about the truck was square: the radiator grille, the fender shapes, the bumper ends, the outline of the cab, even the shape of Keller's hands and face. He visualized the truck as some great entity pursuing him, insentient, brutish, chasing him with instinct only.

Mann cried out, horror-stricken, as he saw the ROAD REPAIRS sign up ahead. His frantic gaze leaped down the highway. Both lanes blocked, a huge black arrow pointing toward the alternate route! He groaned in anguish, seeing it was dirt. His foot jumped automatically to the brake pedal and started pumping it. He threw a dazed look at the rearview mirror. The truck was moving as fast as ever! It *couldn't,* though! Mann's expression froze in terror as he started turning to the right.

He stiffened as the front wheels hit the dirt road. For an instant, he was certain that the back part of the car was going to spin; he felt it breaking to the left. "No, don't!" he cried. Abruptly, he was jarring down the dirt road, elbows braced against his sides, trying to keep from losing control. His tires battered at the ruts, almost tearing the wheel from his grip. The windows rattled noisily. His neck snapped back and forth with painful jerks. His jolting body surged against the binding of the safety belt and slammed down violently on the seat. He felt the bouncing of the car drive up his spine. His clenching teeth slipped and he cried out hoarsely as his upper teeth gouged deep into his lip.

He gasped as the rear end of the car began surging to the right. He started to jerk the steering wheel to the left, then, hissing, wrenched it in the opposite direction, crying out as the right rear fender cracked into a fence pole, knocking it down. He started pumping at the brakes, struggling to regain control. The car rear yawed sharply to the left, tires shooting out a spray of dirt. Mann felt a scream tear upward in his throat. He twisted wildly at the steering wheel. The car began careening to the right. He hitched the wheel around until the car was on course again. His head was pounding like his heart now, with gigantic, throbbing spasms. He started coughing as he gagged on dripping blood.

The dirt road ended suddenly, the car regained momentum on the pavement and he dared to look at the rearview mirror. The truck was slowed down but was still behind him, rocking like a freighter on a storm-tossed sea, its huge tires scouring up a pall of dust. Mann shoved in the accelerator pedal and his car surged forward. A good, steep grade lay just ahead; he'd gain that distance now. He swallowed blood, grimacing at the taste, then fumbled in his trouser pocket and tugged out his handkerchief. He pressed it to his bleeding lip, eyes fixed on the slope ahead. Another fifty yards or so. He writhed his back. His undershirt was soaking wet, adhering to his skin. He glanced at the rearview mirror. The truck had just regained the highway. *Tough!* he thought with venom. Didn't get me, did you, Keller?

His car was on the first yards of the upgrade when steam began to issue from beneath its hood. Mann stiffened suddenly, eyes widening with shock. The steam increased, became a smoking mist. Mann's gaze jumped down. The red light hadn't flashed on yet but had to in a moment. How could this be happening? Just as he was set to get away! The slope ahead was long and gradual, with many curves. He knew he couldn't stop. Could he U-turn unexpectedly and go back down? the sudden thought occurred. He looked ahead. The highway was too narrow, bound by hills on both sides. There wasn't room enough to make an uninterrupted turn and there wasn't time enough to ease around. If he tried that, Keller would shift direction and hit him head on. "Oh, my God!" Mann murmured suddenly.

He was going to die.

He stared ahead with stricken eyes, his view increasingly obscured by steam. Abruptly, he recalled the afternoon he'd had the engine steam-cleaned at the local car wash. The man who'd done it had suggested he replace the water hoses, because steam-cleaning had a tendency to make them crack. He'd nodded, thinking that he'd do it when he had more time. *More time!* The phrase was like a dagger in his mind. He'd failed to change the hoses and, for that failure, he was now about to die.

He sobbed in terror as the dashboard light flashed on. He glanced at it involuntarily and read the word HOT, black on red. With a breath- less gasp, he jerked the transmission into low. Why hadn't he done that right away! He looked head. The slope seemed endless. Already, he could hear a boiling throb inside the radiator. How much coolant was there left? Stearn was clouding faster, hazing up the windshield. Reaching out, he twisted at a dashboard knob. The wipers started flicking back and forth in fan-shaped sweeps. There had to be enough coolant in the radiator to get him to the top. *Then* what? cried his mind. He couldn't drive without coolant, even downhill. He glanced at the rearview mirror. The truck was falling behind. Mann snarled with maddened fury. If *it weren't for that goddamned hose, he'd be escaping now!*

The sudden lurching of the car snatched him back to terror. If he braked now, he could jump out, run and scrabble up that slope. Later, he might not have the time. He couldn't make himself stop the car, though. As long as it kept on running, he felt bound to it, less vulnerable. God knows what would happen if he left it.

Mann started up the slope with haunted eyes, trying not to see the red light on the edges of his vision. Yard by yard, his car was slowing down. Make it, make it, pleaded his mind, even though he thought that it was futile. The car was running more and more unevenly. The thumping percolation of its radiator filled his ears. Any moment now, the motor would be choked off and the car would shudder to a stop, leaving him a sitting target. No, he thought. He tried to blank his mind. He was almost to the top, but in the mirror he could see the truck drawing up on him. He jammed down on the pedal and the motor made a grinding noise. He groaned. It had to make the top! Please, God, help me! screamed his mind. The ridge was just ahead. Closer. Closer. Make it. "Make it." The car was shuddering and clanking, slowing down— oil, smoke and steam gushing from beneath the hood. The windshield wipers swept from side to side. Mann's head throbbed. Both his hands felt numb. His heartbeat pounded as he stared ahead. Make it, please, God, make it. Make it. *Make* it!

Over! Mann's lips opened in a cry of triumph as the car began de- scending. Hand shaking uncontrollably, he shoved the transmission into neutral and let the car go into a glide. The triumph strangled in his throat as he saw that there was nothing in sight but hills and more hills. Never mind! He was on a downgrade now, a long one. He passed a sign that read, TRUCKS USE LOW GEARS NEXT 12 MILES. Twelve miles! Something would come up. It had to.

The car began to pick up speed. Mann glanced at the speedometer. Forty-seven miles an hour. The red light still burned. He'd save the motor for a long time, too, though; let it cool for twelve miles, if the truck was far enough behind.

His speed increased. Fifty . . . 51. Mann watched the needle turning slowly toward the right. He glanced at the rearview mirror. The truck had not appeared yet. With a little luck, he might still get a good lead. Not as good as he might have if the motor hadn't overheated but enough to work with. There had to be some place along the way to stop. The needle edged past 55 and started toward the 60 mark.

Again, he looked at the rearview mirror, jolting as he saw that the truck had topped the ridge and was on its way down. He felt his lips begin to shake and crimped them together. His gaze jumped fitfully between the steam-obscured highway and the mirror. The truck was accelerating rapidly. Keller doubtless had the gas pedal floored. It wouldn't be long before the truck caught up to him. Mann's right hand twitched unconsciously toward the gearshift. Noticing, he jerked it back, grimacing, glanced at the speedometer. The car's velocity had just passed 60. Not enough! He had to use the motor now! He reached out desperately.

His right hand froze in mid-air as the motor stalled; then, shooting out the hand, he twisted the ignition key. The motor made a grinding noise but wouldn't start. Mann glanced up, saw that he was almost on the shoulder, jerked the steering wheel around. Again, he turned the key, but there was no response. He looked up at the rearview mirror. The truck was gaining on him swiftly. He glanced at the speedometer. The car's speed was fixed at 62. Mann felt himself crushed in a vise of panic. He stared ahead with haunted eyes.

Then he saw it, several hundred yards ahead: an escape route for trucks with burned-out brakes. There was no alternative now. Either he took the turnout or his car would be rammed from behind. The truck was frighteningly close. He heard the high-pitched wailing of its motor. Unconsciously, he started easing to the right, then jerked the wheel back suddenly. He mustn't give the move away! He had to wait until the last possible moment. Otherwise, Keller would follow him in.

Just before he reached the escape route, Mann wrenched the steering wheel around. The car rear started breaking to the left, tires shrieking on the pavement. Mann steered with the skid, braking just enough to keep from losing all control. The rear tires grabbed and, at 60 miles an hour, the car shot up the dirt trail, tires slinging up a cloud of dust. Mann began to hit the brakes. The rear wheels sideslipped and the car slammed hard against the dirt bank to the right. Mann gasped as the car bounced off and started to fishtail with violent whipping motions, angling toward the trail edge. He drove his foot down on the brake pedal with all his might. The car rear skidded to the right and slammed against the bank again. Mann heard a grinding rend of metal and felt himself heaved downward suddenly, his neck snapped, as the car plowed to a violent halt.

As in a dream, Mann turned to see the truck and trailer swerving off the highway. Paralyzed, he watched the massive vehicle hurtle toward him, staring at it with a blank detachment, knowing he was going to die but so stupefied by the sight of the looming truck that he couldn't react. The gargantuan shape roared closer, blotting out the sky. Mann felt a strange sensation in his throat, unaware that he was screaming.

Suddenly, the truck began to tilt. Mann stared at it in choked-off silence as it started tipping over like some ponderous beast toppling in slow motion. Before it reached his car, it vanished from his rear window.

Hands palsied, Mann undid the safety belt and opened the door. Struggling from the car, he stumbled to the trail edge, staring down- ward. He was just in time to see the truck capsize like a foundering ship. The tanker followed, huge wheels spinning as it overturned.

The storage tank on the truck exploded first, the violence of its detonation causing Mann to stagger back and sit down clumsily on the dirt. A second explosion roared below, its shock wave buffeting across him hotly, making his ears hurt. His glazed eyes saw a fiery column shoot up toward the sky in front of him, then another.

Mann crawled slowly to the trail edge and peered down at the canyon. Enormous gouts of flame were towering upward, topped by thick, black, oily smoke. He couldn't see the truck or trailer, only flames. He gaped at them in shock, all feeling drained from him.

Then, unexpectedly, emotion came. Not dread, at first, and not regret; not the nausea that followed soon. It was a primeval tumult in his mind: the cry of some ancestral beast above the body of its vanquished foe.

End of the Road

John A. McColley

I drive Betsy, my sky-blue Dodge Dart, into the desert. The fuel gauge slowly droops toward the great and powerful "E." I blast the AC, obviously, to keep myself from melting in what Betsy tells me is 113F. *Maybe I should have done this at a cooler time of year. Too late now. Is that something? No, just an abandoned town.*

~

I talked to a guy, an old mechanic from Reno whose father had been a mechanic, and his father before him, who had been the first mechanic in the city and some kind of wise man from the Old Country. A normally loud man, this third-generation worker of miracles wouldn't speak of the place I'm looking for except in whispers at the back of the shop, where "none of the cars could hear." Ray seemed like a wacko, but you meet a lot of people in this line of work who have been pushed off-center by what they've seen.

"Go as far as you can on a tank of gas, tougher than it used to be, with MPG climbing every year. You won't be able to see any buildings, any signs. It should be just you and your car in the middle of nowhere, in real danger of not making it home. Take this box of parts and shake it." Along with the cigar box wrapped in a red handkerchief, he gave me a chant, a ritual. There were also some metal filings and oil in a phial, a weird little machine juju snow globe. I've seen too much to doubt, especially with the vibe I got off him. "Only if you're sure it's worth it. It's no joyride," was the last thing he said to me.

I nodded. It is. Charlie is.

Charlie was my first car, my baby, a dark blue Civic. I did all the work on him myself, changing out brakes and water pumps... It was a PITA, but it started out as a way to save money and turned into a mama taking care of her child. We had our rough times, sure, but Charlie always got me where I was going. Except once... I had just replaced the timing belt, but hadn't used a torque wrench. Never tighten something that *needs* a torque wrench without one.

A few days later, on my way to a friend's wedding, there was this horrid thunk under the hood. Overtightened or under, I'll never know, but I killed Charlie. I couldn't swing the money to get anyone to tow him all the way home, and there was no point in towing him to a shop that would charge me just for having him on the lot.

The broken part would be more than I could afford, more than he was "worth" according to some stupid blue book. One mechanic told me someone could weld the piece back on, but it might fail five miles later or five months. Someone *could*, but no one *would*. Apparently, they didn't want to be liable. Still, did I fight hard enough? I don't know.

Finally, I decided I couldn't do it. I had spent so many years with him, babying him, nursing him back to health, giant-ass replacement muffler, and driving like a granny up hills and all. But I just couldn't afford to put Humpty back together again, not after the damage I'd done. I almost couldn't bear to look at him. I got a ride home from friends of my now-married friend, a pair of aging hippies who were somehow also into collecting those commemorative silver spoons. I knew more about spoons by the time I got home than I'd ever expected to, but it was a distraction from my heartache.

I borrowed my mom's car to get back to the spot where I'd left Charlie the next day, to collect my things, a hoodie, backpack, a twelve-pack of soda, my CDs, especially one I listened to all the time in college, Sweet Summer by The Coconut Coolers. It was a perfect album to break through the stunning, stifling, silence of a deep August night while cruising just to get air moving past you to cool you off.

But Charlie was gone. I called every towing company and service station I'd contacted the day before to see if they had picked him up. None of them copped to taking him, and why wouldn't they? He wouldn't sell for much and they wouldn't get a dime from me for moving or repairing him if they didn't admit to having him. None of it made sense. Then I called the local police. It took a few minutes to get through to them that he wasn't driven away by a thief. After that, I don't think they were paying much attention. Who steals a broken-down old beater, anyway?

~

Betsy and I roll into the middle of the desert. The little orange gas pump-shaped light blinks on. I try not to stare, but the radio's gone to static, so far from anything, and there's nothing to see outside but endless stretches of sand and cracked ground and the thin ribbon of road before me. After an eternity of road hum and that little light boring into my soul, Betsy coughs out and rolls to a stop. The AC stops blowing. I grab the cigar box and phial from the passenger seat, as well as my camera and digital recorder, hat and sunglasses, a bag with water and food in case I *do* really have to try to hoof it out. I brace myself and open the door. Sweat leaps through my skin so fast I can swear I hear it boiling off me like bacon in the pan.

There's not a stick of a tree in sight, not a cactus or a tumbleweed. I could be on another planet. Maybe Venus, I hear it's hot there. I bump the door closed with my hip, not wanting to touch the metal handle, and walk to the side of the road as instructed. I jostle the box in the direction I was traveling. A tumble of small metal pieces jangle like a futuristic rain stick. Then I shake the way we came, across the road in front of Betsy and away from the road, chanting the whole time.

Setting the box down, I shake up the phial and roll it over the top of the box, sparkling in the midday sun. *How insane am I?* I wonder. *Out here at the hottest possible time of the year* and *the hottest possible time of the day? I feel like I'm going to spontaneously combust any second.*

The phial rolls off the edge of the box, as expected, but then it keeps rolling with a little tinkly song of glass on compact, sun-dried dirt. After a few seconds, I realize it's not stopping. My logical mind screams that it should stop after a few inches, afoot, max. Soon it's ten feet in front of me and it occurs to me I should follow it. I leave the box and

Betsy in the middle of the *Plains of Frickin' Fire* along with the only reference I have to possibly make it back to civilization. This job often requires leaps of faith, but not generally life and death ones.

I walk. And I walk. And I start believing in magic, like really believing, because how can this thing be rolling for hundreds of yards with no downhill slope? *There must be a slope.* I assure myself. *That's the only explanation. You've seen a lot, but self-rolling bottles?* The sun is slaying me at this point. Sweat soaks my shirt, my shorts, the band around my head where my hat sits... I see a mirage before me, horizontal streaks of black and gray, shifting, shimmering, like I'd been seeing all along the road on the way to the place I'd left Betsy.

Then I realize I'm *on* a road. The pavement is faded nearly white, thin little cracks running right across it and into the dirt to either side. The phial picks up speed. Now I think we *are* headed downward. I pull my eyes away for a second, following the road forward and I see it: hundreds, thousands of cars, not stacked up like a junkyard, but lined up along the road. Side roads branch and branch again, a spreading fan of automobile history like one of those evolution diagrams.

I take out my camera and begin shooting stills. After a dozen or so clicks, I get some film, panning across from one side to the other and back as waves of heat distort the vast array of cars and trucks. The Automobile Graveyard doesn't disappoint. Every model I can think of, every color, basks in a miasma of heat, old gasoline, oil and coolant vapors. Their vital fluids stain the ground, a Rorschachian signature book from a thousand former showroom stars.

But where's Charlie? All these heaps, twisted by collisions with other cars, trees, dented by hail. *Is my*

Charlie here? Or is this all a fever dream? Some amazing back story my boiling brain has constructed to give its death reason after I carelessly ran out of fuel in a place that could be confused for the surface of the Sun?

I walk. I snap photos. I reach back for my bag. *Damn, set it down when I was playing with the box. Because of course I did. Would the phial have worked if I didn't? Being prepared? Probably not. I should turn back.* "Charlie!" I call into the throng of cars lying like lizards in the sun. "Charlie!"

I walk. I shoot. I call. I stumble.

I walk. I call. I stumble.

I walk. I stumble.

I lay in the sun, feeling myself crisp, imagining wafts of vapor drifting up off my body. *Gotta get up. Gotta find Charlie.*

I lay, burning, a hundred miles from shade. A wind rolls up, hot, like the Devil's breath, then slips away. Except now I'm *in* shade. I pull back my hat to see the deep ocean blue I'd remember for the rest of my life even if I hadn't thrown the remainder of my days away on this stupid dream.

"Charlie?" I try to ask, but my throat is too dry to make a coherent sound. I reach up, my hand hovering an inch from the side panel because putting my hand through a fever dream would ruin the illusion. Instead, the panel slides closer to my hand, like a cat or dog asking for pats. The metal is hot, but not painful. *Maybe I've died and can't feel pain anymore. Except, then, what about this sunburn?*

I stroke the panel, then use him to support my effort to get to my feet. All my stuff is still inside. I reach for the back door handle, gently, tentatively, to see if he wants me to. Nothing happens. I pull up and out. Sitting on the floor behind the driver's seat is a cardboard box with nine cans of

Diet Dr Pepper. I pop one open. It doesn't explode everywhere, somehow, and isn't boiling hot. It's warm, but that's how I take it half the time, anyway. I drink, re-hydrating my vocal chords.

"I—I'm sorry, Charlie. I came back, the next day I came back. But you were already gone. You knew, didn't you, that you were too hurt to fix? That's why you left instead of waiting for me. It was all my fault. I—."

I can't say any more, the words stick in my throat. Instead, I lean against the rear quarter as I had a thousand other times, finishing off the soda and taking another. A few sips into the second, the Coconut Coolers groove through the speakers, "Squintin' at each other through the summer haaaze. Soakin' up the sun in a hundred waaa-aa-aays. . ."

~

The sun descends as I bob to the soundtrack of my early twenties with my best friend. I play about twenty rounds of "Remember the time...?" Until a wave of growls rolls across the broad depression. Grit flies on a sudden front of air that only builds over the course of a minute. It's over. I can feel the tide turning. This is nature, maybe not what I studied in high school biology class, cells and photosynthesis, but the cycle of being and un-being, of arrival and departure.

I quietly close Charlie's doors, a small pile of paraphernalia stuffed into an old backpack with the last two cans of Dr Pepper. "Goodbye, old friend. I'm glad you've found your place. I hope you're happy. I think you were telling me you are." He rubs against my leg and begins to roll away. I can only imagine what's going on under the hood since I bent the crankshaft, sheared the pulley right off.

I watch the migration in awe, only remembering my camera when all I can see is a swath of dust rolling across the desert. The sun cuts across it, lighting it with ethereal power. Only a few taillights peek through the haze. The sense of calm lingers, enshrouding me for a time until the cool desert night starts clipping away at it. Who knew it changed so fast? I pick up my stuff and look for the road, and indicator of a way back, but the dust has begun to settle, blotting out even that sign of civilization.

I start walking. What else is there to do? I hum "Drive In" to myself, memories of hitting the last remaining drive-in theater in the state with Charlie a decade before. We watched a double feature with Jim Carrey playing back-to-back doofuses. Doofi? A low purr edges into my awareness behind me. I turn, thinking maybe Charlie couldn't leave me any more than I could leave him. *Ah, Betsy, you came for me.* The smile that began with a thought of the past grows with a glimpse of the future.

"Hey, girl," I say, stopping and letting her roll up to me. "Wanna head home?" I pop the trunk and empty a couple of the reserve cans of fuel I stashed there into her tank. I may have been willing to go the distance to say goodbye, but I'm not at the end of *my* road yet.

Contributors

Georgia Addams believes in viewing the world in small ways; in dust floating in a beam of sunlight, in the small world under furniture rarely visited by adults, or in the gentle movement of a resting butterfly's relaxed wings. A few of her stories have appeared in small press magazines. She lives in Connecticut with a cat.

Email: omicronworldent@yahoo.com

Kady Ambrose has published two ultra-short romances in *Woman's World* magazine and a contemporary YA short story in the anthology *Words With Heart*. After years co-running an independent documentary film production company, Lynne (Lueders) Moses is writing fiction with the pen name "Kady Ambrose." Her current work-in-progress is a series of YA historical fantasy novels set in antebellum Missouri. As a produced screenwriter and playwright, her credits include the feature "Cupid's Prey," which was a Nicholl Fellowship top-ten finalist screenplay; Discovery Channel's TV movie "Hope Ranch;" and the recent French indie feature, "Twisting Fate." Her full screen credits can be found on IMDb.

Email: kadyambrose@gmail.com
Website: www.kadyambrose.com

Kevin David Anderson has sold more than seventy short stories to a variety of publications and audio markets. His first novel, *Night of the Living Trekkies*, received positive reviews from the *L.A. Times*, *The Washington Post*, *Fangoria Magazine*, and also received a starred review from *Publishers Weekly*. His stories have appeared in *Dark*

Animus, Dark Wisdom, Darkness Rising, Dark Moon Digest, and many other publications with the word "dark" in the title, which is kind of misleading because he's a happy, lighthearted person who lives with his family in Southern California. Anderson is an Active member of the HWA, with a B.A in Mass Communication, and fifteen years of award-winning marketing experience.

Email: Kevin@KevinDavidAnderson.com
Website: www.KevinDavidAnderson.com

Bruce Boston is a speculative writer and poet. Boston has won the seven Rhysling Awards for his speculative poetry and the Asimov's Readers' Award his poetry, also seven times. He has also received a Pushcart Prize for fiction, 1976, and four Bram Stoker Awards for his poetry collections, and the first Grand Master Award of the Science Fiction Poetry Association, 1999. Boston has also published over one-hundred short stories in such magazines as *Weird Tales, Amazing Stories, Strange Horizons, Analog, Asimov's Science Fiction Magazine, Realms of Fantasy, and Science Fiction Age.* He has also appeared in anthologies including *Year's Best Fantasy and Horror,* and the *Nebula Awards Showcase. His* novels include *Stained Glass Rain* and *The Guardener's Tale,* the latter being a Prometheus Award Nominee and a Bram Stoker Award Finalist. Boston lives in Ocala, Florida.

John Cassola hails from Boston, Massachusetts and is new to writing. He travels often and loves to explore the world and learn new things about people and their cultures. An accomplished non-fiction writer of numerous newspaper and magazine articles, this marks his first fiction sale.

Melodie Corrigall is an eclectic Canadian writer who doesn't know the difference between an Edsel and a Mustang but knows a red car at 50 feet. Her stories have appeared in *Litro UK*, *FreeFall*, *Halfway Down the Stairs*, *Six Minute Magazine*, *Mouse Tales*, *Subtle Fiction*, *Emerald Bolts*, *Earthen Journal*, *Switchback*, and *The Write Place at the Write Time*.

www.melodiecorrigall.com

Ray Daley was born in Coventry, England, where he still resides today. He served six years in the Royal Air Force as a clerk and spent most of his service time in a Hobbit hole in High Wycombe. He is a published poet and has been writing stories since he was 10. His dream is to eventually finish the *Hitch Hikers* fanfic novel he's been writing since 1986. Ray's stories have appeared in *365 Tomorrows*, *Liquid Erosion*, *Stranger Views*, *Farther Stars Than These*, *The Sirens Call* (ezine 13), *Ealain Issue 11*, and a time travel anthology published by Crimson Cloak Publishing titled *Steps in Time*. Like many hybrid authors, Ray has also self-published on Smashwords and Amazon.
Website:raymondwriteswrongs.wordpress.com

James S. Dorr was a 2014 Bram Stoker Award® nominee for Superior Achievement in a Fiction Collection for *The Tears of Isis*. Other collections include *Strange Mistresses: Tales of Wonder and Romance*, *Darker Loves: Tales of Mystery and Regret*, and his all-poetry *Vamps (A Retrospective)*. He's also an Active Member of HWA and SFWA with nearly 400 individual appearances from *Alfred Hitchcock Mystery Magazine* to *Yellow Bat Review*.

He invites readers to visit his blog at

http://jamesdorrwriter.wordpress.com for the most up to date information. Dorr lives in Bloomington, Indiana.

e-mail: edgarc@rocketmail.com

John H. Dromey was born in northeast Missouri. He enjoys reading—mysteries especially—and writing in a variety of genres. He's had short fiction published in *Alfred Hitchcock's Mystery Magazine, Betty Fedora, Crimson Streets, Stupefying Stories Showcase,* and elsewhere, as well as in a number of anthologies. He lives in Quincy, IL.

Email: jhdrom@att.net

M. Richard Eley mainly writes sci-fi, has been known to dabble in literary fiction and non-fiction from time to time, and is hard at work on a new novel. To avoid having to write, he organizes the Tidewater Writers critique group, studies and performs improv, and occasionally teaches writing classes. Richard's editorial on light rail was recently published in *The Virginian-Pilot* newspaper, and one of his short stories garnered an honorable mention in *Issues in Science and Technology*'s first sci-fi contest. His publishing credits include an Honorable Mention for his 4900-word short story "Hot Dogs and Corn Flakes" in the magazine *Issues in Science and Technology*, as part of their first annual Sci-Fi contest. An 800-word article he authored was published in *The Virginian-Pilot* newspaper. He lives in Chesapeake, Virginia.

Email: M.Richard.Eley@cox.net

Michael Louis Falcone received his Master of Arts in English at Western Washington University, where he served as nonfiction editor for *The Bellingham Review*. His creative nonfiction story "Pool Haul" was selected to represent the college in the Associated Writers Press national competition and was published in the anthology *Open Windows* by Ghost Road Press in 2005. Most recently, his short story titled "The Viewing" was selected as a finalist in the Richard Hugo House Horror Fiction Competition. His works have been read at The Whatcom Museum of Art, Elliott Bay Book Company, Village Books, and a variety of other literary venues throughout the Northwest. He is currently working on a collection of short stories and poems, as well as a novel-length psychological thriller titled *Thanatos*. Michael makes his home in Seattle, where he earns a diversified living as a writer, actor, musician, audio engineer, and film location scout.

Joel Ferree was a poet and writer whose work appeared in various magazines including *Modern Maturity, The Christian Science Monitor,* and *New York Magazine.*

Jack Finney is probably best remembered for his second novel *The Body Snatchers (1955),* a frighting story of aliens which replace people with exact physical duplicates. According to critical analysis, the story reflects the Cold War paranoia of its time and do this day still has the power to chill readers. Finney wrote a wide variety of novels and some classic short stories , but many fans consider his short stories to be among the best in the speculative genre.

Jean Graham lives in San Diego, California and has sold fiction to the anthologies *Misunderstood (Wolfsinger Publications, 2015), Dying to Live* (Diabolic Publications, 2013) *Arcane 2* (Cold Fusion Media, 2013); to the DAW Books anthology *The Time of the Vampires* (1996, reprinted 2005); to the Oct.-Dec. 2000 issue of the on-line magazine

Wouldthatitwere.com; to the print anthologies *Fantastical Visions I & II* and the Oct. 2009 anthology *Under the Rose* (Norilana Books). He has also sold short stories to the e-zines *Coyote Wild, Firefox* and *Mundania/Fictionwise.com*, and to the print magazine *Renard's Menagerie*. His work has also been published in the small press magazines *The Horror Show* (Ed. David Silva), *Quest, Outlands, Chosen Haunts, Melange, Gambit* and *Dark Graffiti*, among others.

Juliana Gribbins Juliana Gribbins was born and raised (mostly) in New Jersey. She is a fan of her father's old MG and of her old Jeep Wrangler. When she gets her million-dollar book deal she plans on buying one of each. Her book *Date Expectations* is a winner of the 2017 Independent Press Awards, Humor Category, and winner of the 2016 IPPY silver medal for humor. She is a freelance writer for Shore Publishing newspapers and has won several Connecticut Society of Professional Journalists Excellence in Journalism Awards. Read more of her writing at www.zip06.com/shorelineliving.

Mary Hamrick was born in New York and moved to Florida when she was a young girl. Her writing often reflects the contrast between her Northern and Southern up-bringing. Mary's poems have been published in numerous print and online publications, including *Veils, Halos, Shackles, Blast Furnace, Mad Hatters' Review, Rosebud Magazine*, and others.
Email: hamrick.m@gmail.com

Michael H. Hanson has written six collections of poetry: *Autumn Blush* and *Jubilant Whispers* (Racket River Publishing), *Dark Parchments* and *When the Night Owl*

Screams (MoonDream Press), and *Android Girl: And Other Sentient Publications* and *Quarantine World: Trapped in the Coronaverse*" (Three Ravens Publishing). His work regularly appears in the annual *Rhysling Anthology* and the HWA Poetry Showcase. He currently lives in Colorado.

J.R. Hayslett has produced countless news and feature stories as a career journalist, won awards for the adult nonfiction book *Anatomy of a Trial: Public Loss, Lessons Learned from the People vs. O.J. Simpson* [University of Missouri Press, 2008], published short stories in literary magazines and essays that aired on NPR. J.R. is also a blogger, active in social media, and writes in both the adult and young reader genres. J.R. lives in South Milwaukee, Wisconsin.
Email: jfarhsi@aol.com

Juleigh Howard-Hobson has stories in *History is Dead* (Permuted Press), *Loving The Undead* (From The Asylum), *Black Sails* (1018 Press), *Black Box* (Brimstone Books), *Lost Innocence Anthology* (Niteblade), *Return of the Raven* (Horror Bound), *Dead Worlds: Undead Stories* (Living Dead Press), *Mandragora* (Scarlett Imprint), *Bits of the Dead* & *Vicious Verse* (Coscom Entertainment), *The Devil's Food* (Monsters Next Door), *It Lives* (RuneWright), *You Don't Know What You've Got--Tales of Loss and Dispossession* (Gryphonwood), *Enchanted Conversa-tion*, *Hex Magazine*, *New Witch Magazine*, *Bewildering Stories*, *Champagne Shivers*, *Dead Letters: the zine of the zombie apocalypse*, *Appalling Limericks*, *Sein und Werden*, *The Liar's League*, *Poetry is Dead*, *The Locust*, *Danse Macabre*, *Every Day Stories* and many others. She is also a Million Writers Award "Notable Story" writer, and her work has been nominated for both the "Best of the Net" and the Pushcart Prize. Juleigh edited *Undertow*. an Arêtes Vakreste Boker award winning collection. She lives in Castle Rock, Washington.

Email: jhowardhobson@gmail.com

Davin Ireland hails from Utrecht, the Netherlands. His short fiction has appeared in over ninety print magazines and anthologies worldwide, as well as selected online markets. He is the winner of the Historical Novel Society's *Solander* Short Fiction Award (2010), and was twice nominated for the Pushcart Prize. His work has also received multiple Honorable Mentions in *The Year's Best Fantasy & Horror*, edited by Ellen Datlow, Kelly Link, and Gavin J. Grant.

Email: d.ireland@wanadoo.nl
https://davinireland.com

Valentin D. Ivanov is a professional astronomer with numerous publications in research journals. Originally from Bulgaria, he has spent most of his career abroad and now lives in Germany. Ivanov has published some thirty stories in various magazines and has a fantasy book published in his native country. His non-fiction pieces in English that appeared in *Strange Horizons* and in *Letters to Tiptree* (eds. A. Krasnostein, A. Pierce). His story "How I Saved the World" was included in the educational anthology *Diamonds in the Sky* (ed. M. Brotherton). Valentin's story in this anthology was first written in his native Bulgarian and translated to English by the author and Kalin M. Nenov via the Human Library Project.

T.M. Jacobs operates JWC Publishing from his motor home, traveling the highways and byways of America while writing, editing, and publishing. A Connecticut native, Tim, with his wife, enjoys the freedom of the road, meeting new people, and keeping ahead of the zombies. They also avoid picking up hitchhikers.

Website: www.jacobswc.com.

George Clayton Johnson is probably best-known for his memorable teleplays for *The Twilight Zone* series, created by Rod Serling, that first ran on American television sets from 1959 to 1964. Johnson also wrote short stories—which appeared in the popular science fiction and fantasy magazines of his time—and co-wrote the landmark science fiction novel *Logan's Run* with William F. Nolan. **Johnson** was born on 29 July 1929 in Cheyenne, Wyoming. He served in the Army, then studied drafting in college. Later, he moved to Los Angeles where he was employed as a draftsman for the Lockheed aviation company while moonlighting as a writer. Not long after quitting his day job to pursue writing full-time, he met *Twilight Zone* writer, **Charles Beaumont**, who introduced him to the show's creator, **Rod Serling**. The prolific writer also wrote the screenplay for *Oceans Eleven* and the first episode for *Star Trek*, the most successful science fiction television and film franchise. He was nominated for a Academy Award (along with Ray Bradbury and Joseph Mugnaini) for *Icarus Montgolfier Wright*. Johnson died on 25 December 2015 in North Hills, California. He is survived by his two children.

Sarah Key has had several writing lives, including eight published cookbooks and prose essays in *The Huffington Post*. After studying poetry for a number of years at places like 92nd Street Y, Cave Canem, and master classes with Sharon Donlin, she had poems published in *Poet Lore*,

Minerva Rising, *Tuesday: An Art Project*, *Caesura*, *Kaleidoscope*, and many others. She also tutors writing at a community college in the Bronx, New York, where she learned from her students about all the places she's never been.

Nathaniel Lee lives in Indian Land, South Carolina. His fiction has appeared in *Strange Horizons*, *Ideomancer*, and *Nightmare Magazine*, among many others.
Email: thefearedavocado@gmail.com

Gerri Leen lives in Northern Virginia and originally hails from Seattle. She has stories and poems published by: *Nature*, *Daily Science Fiction*, *Escape Pod*, *Grimdark*, and others. She has also written *Bluegrass Dreams Aren't for Free*, a collection of interconnected stories about genetically modified racehorses that manage their own careers, and *Handle with Care*, an urban fantasy novel. She caught the editing bug, and has one anthology out, *A Quiet Shelter There*, Hadley Rille Books, 2015. The book benefits homeless animals, a cause she passionately supports. She's also written two pagan/mythology-based books for Bibliotheca Alexandrina.
Website: www.gerrileen.com.
Email: gerrileen@gerrileen.com

Gregory J. Leavitt shares his wanderlust and birthplace of Lowell, Massachusetts with Jack Kerouac. Greg was raised predominantly in New Hampshire where he graduated from UNH. Since that time, he has "toured the world and elsewhere" (This Is Spinal Tap), having lived in California, Oregon, Connecticut, and the Pacific side of Costa Rica. He has traveled extensively (and expensively, he would add) by all modes of transport and all seasons of the year simply because it's there. He is now a successful Realtor in his home state of New Hampshire where he continues to follow his pursuits of life, liberty, and justice for all—as well as creative writing, photography, travel, nature, and golf.

Greg.leavitt@verani.com

Laird Long pounds out fiction in all genres in Winnipeg, Manitoba, Canada. Big guy, sense of humor. Writing credits include: *Blue Murder Magazine, Futures Mysterious Anthology Magazine, Hardboiled, Thriller UK, Shred of Evidence, Bullet, Albedo One, Baen's Universe, Sniplits, Woman's World, The Weekly News, that's life!*, and stories in the anthologies *Amazing Heroes, The Mammoth Book of New Comic Fantasy, The Mammoth Book of Jacobean Whodunits, and The Mammoth Book of Perfect Crimes and Impossible Mysteries.*

Email: lairdo@shaw.ca

Amy Lynwander Amy Lynwander works as an administrator and co-owns Baltimore Ghost Tours, a haunted history walking tour company. Her short fiction has appeared or is forthcoming in *Unidentified Funny Objects, Cryptids Emerging: Tales of Dark Cheer, Speculative North*, and others. She lives in Baltimore, Maryland with her family.

Ken MacGregor has seen his work published in a whole mess of anthologies and magazines. His story collection *An Aberrant Mind* is available online and in select bookstores. He edits an annual horror-themed anthology for the Great Lakes Association of Horror Writers. Ken is an Affiliate member of HWA. One time, he even made a zombie movie. He also co-wrote a novel and worked on the sequel. Ken lives in Michigan with his family and two cats, one of whom is dead but still haunts the place.

Email: macgregor.ken@gmail.com

Website: http://ken-macgregor.com

Twitter: @kenmacgregor

https://www.facebook.com/KenMacGregorAuthor?ref=hl

Richard Matheson is one of those unique writers who moved easily between short stories, novels, teleplays, and screenplays. He is probably best known for his significant contribution to the original Twilight Zone series (1959-1964) with such stories as "Nightmare at 20,000 Feet" starring William Shatner of Star Trek fame, "The Invaders" starring of Agnes Moorhead of Bewitched fame, and "Night Call" among others. His novel, *Bid Time Return* was adapted by Matheson's own hand into the 1980 time-travel love-story classic film "Somewhere in Time" starring Christopher Reeve and Jane Seymour. His classic book *I Am Legend* was adapted by others into a major motion picture in 2007 starring Will Smith. Matheson was a member of the Southern California Sorcerers group during the 1950s and 1960s. The group was a collective of west coast writers which included such luminary speculative writers as Ray Bradbury, Charles Beaumont, George Clayton John-son, William F. Nolan, and Jerry Sohl, among others. Matheson died in 2013 at the age of 87.

Richard Christian Matheson is an American writer of short stories and novels in the psychological horror and magical realism areas of speculative fiction. His stories have appeared in over 150 anthologies and his own critically acclaimed short story collections *Scars and Other Distinguishing Marks*, *Dystopia*, and *Zoopraxis*. Other titles include the suspense novel *Created By* and a magical realism novella about Hollywood titled *The Ritual of Illusion*. He has also edited three anthologies, penned numerous essays and screenplays, and has shared his creative talent as an executive story consultant, supervising producer, and executive producer for network television series and films. Matheson lives in Southern California.

John A. McColley resides in New Hampshire, where he turns out tales of steampunk, superheroes, paranormal, and science fiction while working on painting, found object and recycled materials sculpture, and raising his amazing son with his equally amazing wife and doubly amazing twins. John has had a few dozen stories published across the science fiction, fantasy, and horror spectrum including *Mad Scientist Journal* and *Crossed Genres Magazine*. He also has some stories of steampunk superheroes, Aeolus, Chiron, and Lady Spectra in Emby Press' *The Good Fight and Capes* and *Clockwork Volume 1 & 2* from Dark Oak Press.

William F. Nolan is probably most well-known for his science fiction novel classic, *Logan's Run*, which he co-authored with George Clayton Johnson. On his own, Nolan sold hundreds of pieces, from poetry to prose, as well as non-fiction, to publications, such as *Playboy*, *Rogue*, *Sports Illustrated*, and *Dark Discoveries among* others. He also wrote several mystery novels, including the "Challis" series. He had a long career in the movie industry, primarily working for director Dan Curtis with whom he co-wrote the screenplay for the 1976 horror film *Burnt Offerings* starring Karen Black, Oliver Reed, and Hollywood legend Bette Davis. Nolan was also a prolific editor of story collections (by other authors) and anthologies. Nolan continued to sell stories to publications and anthologies until his death in 2021 at the age of 93.

Mike Payne is a comedian and writer whose credits include Pseudopod.org and The Flash Fiction Press. He lives in New York City.
Email: Ptmike00@gmail.com

C. Jennings Penders writes both fiction and non-fiction from the comfort of his hometown of Madison, CT. His short fiction has appeared in *Haunts* magazine (Nightshade Publications), *Treasures from the Shell Heap*, and other publications. For many years, Chris enjoyed photography, which he sold on-line and at craft fairs in Connecticut, before returning to his first love of writing. His first collection of theme-linked stories appeared in *Random Acts: Stories of Redemption* (Fahrenheit Books, 2018), followed by *Arrivals and Departures: An Etheric Tribute to Block Island* (Fahrenheit Books, 2020). He also penned the non-fiction book *Taking Off A Coat: Ruminations on the Infinite Soul* (Fahrenheit Books, 2018). His forthcoming fiction titles include *For the Love of Block Island* (a sequel to *Arrivals and Departures*), and *Love is Chaos*.

Richard Polomsky lives in Arlington Heights, Illinois. This is his first appearance in an anthology and marks his first sale as a writer. He has worked as a library page for 22 years. In his free time, he enjoys creating surreal ink drawings, photography, and trying his hand at writing.

Email: r_polomsky@yahoo.com

Jack Raglin works days as a research professor who has published over a hundred research papers on various topics ranging from the psychology of elite athletes to the physiology of zombies. He has also published several articles on aspects of the Golden age of American illustration for trade magazines. When not writing, Jack is a car enthusiast who has owned and restored several vintage models including a 1950 Buick Special and 1959 Dodge Coronet. The publication of "GoogleRide Killed my SD-455!" in this anthology marks Jack first fiction sale. He lives in Bloomington, Indiana.

Email: raglinj@indiana.edu

Pepe Rich fell in love with books before she could read them. Born and raised in Metz, France, she emigrated to the United States in her early twenties after meeting her future husband at university, where she studied business and minored in English Literature. Staying true to her love of fiction, she continued to pen stories, placing a few in small publications in foreign markets. This marks her first appearance in an American publication.

Bruce Holland Rogers is an accomplished short story writer who also writes under the pseudonym Hanovi Braddock. His fiction has won a Pushcart Prize, a Bram Stoker Award, two Nebula Awards, and two World Fantasy Awards, among others. His stories have been published in eight collections and he has also published two novels. His dedication to helping other writers is evidenced through his teaching fiction writing seminars in Finland, Denmark, Portugal, and Greece. In 2010 he taught at Eötvös Loránd

University in Budapest on a Fulbright grant. He lives in Oregon.

Jacqueline Seewald has taught creative writing courses at both the high school and college level (Rutgers University), as well as expository and technical writing at the college level. She has also worked as an academic librarian and an educational media specialist. Her short stories have appeared in numerous anthologies, including *The Mystery Megapack* (Wildside Press), *The Call of Lovecraft, Dreamspell Nightmares, Passion-Ate Hearts*, and *Lost on Route 66*, among others. Her story that appeared in *Touched by Wonder* was nominated for a Nebula Award. Sixteen of her books of fiction have been published. Her short stories, poems, essays, reviews, and articles have appeared in hundreds of publications such as: *The Writer, The L.A. Times, Pedestal, Surreal, Library Journal, Reader's Digest, After Dark, The Christian Science Monitor*, and *Publishers Weekly*, and has won many awards. She lives is Fort Lee, New Jersey.
Email: jacquelinesw@nj.rr.com

Robbie Sheerin is a Scottish-born writer living in the United States. He is married with one daughter, a crazy dog, and a narcissistic cat. A fan of classic sci-fi, he is inspired by Isaac Asimov, Ray Bradbury, Robert Heinlein, Philip K. Dick, and Edmond Hamilton. Robbie writes "shorties" and essays. His book *Tales From Another Dimension; A sci-fi collection* was published in 2021.
Website: ww.talesfromanotherdimension.com

Marge Simon began writing and illustrating for the small press in the mid-1980s, and went on to become an award-winning writer. Simon's poems, short fiction, and illustrations have appeared in hundreds of publications, including *Amazing Stories, Nebula Awards 32, Strange Horizons, The Pedestal Magazine, Chizine, Niteblade, Vestal Review*, and *Daily Science Fiction*. She is a former president of the Small Press Writers and Artists Organization and of the Science Fiction & Fantasy Poetry Association (SFPA). She is also a former editor of *Star*Line*, the SFPA's bimonthly journal. In 2013, Simon began editing the column "Blood and Spades: Poets of the Dark Side" for the monthly newsletter of the Horror Writers Association (HWA). She serves as the Chair of the HWA Board of Trustees. Simon's poem "Variants of the Obsolete" won the 1996 Rhysling Award for speculative poetry in the Long category. Her poems "Shutdown" and "George Tecumseh Sherman's Ghosts" placed first in the Short category of the Rhyslings in 2015 and 2017, respectively. Simon lives in Ocala, Florida.

Matthew Spence was born in Cleveland, Ohio and currently lives in Bloomery, West Virginia.

Austin Spradlin lives in Flatgap, Kentucky. At age 25, he is newer to writing, and has recently started to see his work in print. He sold a story to *Serial Killer* magazine, and he recently made his screenwriting debut in a horror film that is under development. Mr. Spradlin dreams of earning his pilot's license (especially for helicopters), but in the meantime he soars with his imagination and writes it all down.

Email: austinspradline425@gmail.com

Katherine Tomlinson has published works in numerous anthologies including *Weird Noir, Pulp Ink 2, These Campfires Don't Sparkle, Blood and Roses, Alt-Zombie, Alt-Dead, Absolute Visions,* and *Drunk on the Moon.* Her short stories have also appeared on sites like *Do Some Damage, Shotgun Honey, A Twist of Noir, Eaten Alive,* and *Thuglit.* She is also a former reporter who prefers making things up, and thus her love of writing fiction. She lives in the Pacific Northwest within walking distance of a haunted cemetery. She does not drink coffee. A shorter version of her story in this anthology appeared in the now-defunct magazine *Dark Valentine* and that version also appears in the *L.A. Nocturne Collection.*

Email: katherine@storyauthority.com

Stephen Scott Whitaker is a member of National Book Critics Circle, and the literary review editor for *The Broadkill Review. All My Rowdy Friends* was published in 2016 by Punks Write Poems Press, LLC. His previous chapbooks include the steampunk inspired *The Black Narrows,* the award-winning *Field Recordings,* and *The Barleyhouse Letters.* His writing has won numerous awards, including the Pushcart Prize, and the National Press Award. He lives in Onley, Virginia.

Email: esteph20@hotmail.com

Dean H. Wild grew up in east central Wisconsin and has lived in the area, primarily in small towns surrounding the city of Fond du Lac, all his life. He wrote his first short story at the age of seven and continued to write while he pursued careers in retail, the newspaper industry, and real estate. His short stories have seen publication in various magazines and anthologies. And he's a long-time member of the Horror Writers Association. He and his wife, Julie, reside in the village of Brownsville, Wisconsin.

Email: scrybe@deanwild.com

The Editors

Jason J. Marchi has written over 800 articles, stories, essays, and poems that have appeared in *Amazing Stories, Weird Tales, The Sun, élan, Milford Living, Coast Magazine*, and several other magazines and newspapers. Jason's first book, *The Legend of Hobbomock: The Sleeping Giant*, a children's picture storybook, was a Revere Awards finalist and a Barnes & Noble recognized perennial bestseller in his native Connecticut. Jason's second children's picture book, *The Growing Sweater*, won a total of 13 awards after its publication in late 2014. He was also the founder and executive director of the former New Century Writer Awards, a not-for-profit writing contest and educational organization that worked in close association with the editors of Francis Ford Coppola's *Zoetrope: All-Story* magazine between 1998 and 2005. Jason writes (and edits books) for readers of all ages, from his childhood home in Guilford, Connecticut.

Email: jasonjmarchi@yahoo.com.

Website: www.jasonjmarchi.com

Jeffrey L. Buford, Jr. is a multi-talented artist who works with equal ease between fiction writing, painting, and songwriting. A son of the American Mid-West, Mr. Buford lives along the shores of the Mighty Mississippi, the childhood stomping grounds of America's greatest writer, Mark Twain. Buford's tell-all memoir about overcoming his personal struggle with addition, *Possible Side Effects*, was published by Fahrenheit Books in 2017. His second book, *Out of What Crypt They Crawl,* is a collection of short stories of a speculative nature, was published in 2018.

A note about the type style used in this book

Bookman or Bookman Old Style is a serif typeface derived from Old Style Antique designed by Alexander Phemister in 1858 for Miller and Richard foundry.

Several American foundries copied the design, including the Bruce Type Foundry, and issued it under various names. In 1901, Bruce refitted their design, made a few other improvements, and rechristened it Bartlett Oldstyle.

When Bruce was taken over by ATF shortly thereafter, they changed the name to Bookman Oldstyle.

Bookman was designed as an alternative to Caslon, with straighter serifs, making it more suitable for book and display applications. It maintains its legibility at small sizes, and can be used successfully for headlines and in advertising.

from Typedia.com